The Woman

Carrie Hughes lives in West Sussex, where she is a copywriter and guest lecturer in creative writing. She can often be found dreaming up stories, communing with dogs and visiting the dark side. She loves creating female characters who are stronger than they appear and forcing them into difficult situations.

THE WOMAN FROM BOOK CLUB

CARRIE HUGHES

hera

First published in the United Kingdom in 2025 by

Hera Books, an imprint of
Canelo Digital Publishing Limited,
20 Vauxhall Bridge Road,
London SW1V 2SA
United Kingdom

A Penguin Random House Company
The authorised representative in the EEA is Dorling Kindersley Verlag GmbH.
Arnulfstr. 124, 80636 Munich, Germany

A CIP catalogue record for this book is available from the British Library.

Print ISBN 978 1 83598 342 3
Ebook ISBN 978 1 83598 346 1

Cover design by Head Design Ltd

Cover images © Shutterstock.com

Printed and bound in Great Britain by Clays Ltd, Elcograf S.p.A.

Look for more great books at
www.herabooks.com | www.dk.com

1

To Dawn Warrington, my first reader,

and Milo Warrington, occasional furry muse.

'We lose ourselves in books. We find ourselves there too.'

Anonymous

Prologue

Emma

They arrested me at book club. It was shocking and predictable all at once. Predictable because of Lydia. Despite us banning her from book club, she kept upending my life. Shocking because, well, they arrested me at book club. This latest move in her twisted game proved it wasn't over.

The five of us clustered around the wooden table in Rosa's tiny cottage garden. A riot of late summer flowers surrounded us. 'Do you ever wonder if books choose us instead of the other way around?' I said.

'How so?' Jules sipped her wine, then jabbed at a slick olive with a cocktail stick.

'You know when you're drawn to a novel? Then you find a message wrapped in the story just for you.' Was it too weird, saying that aloud? I tried not to be weird, but the other four went along with it.

'We read books for what we need from them at the time,' Jules said.

'Sometimes,' Marianne said in her commanding American accent, 'I keep a book for when I'll appreciate it most, like a fine wine.'

Reading a book was like catching up with a friend. Lydia set out to take my real friends, along with everything of value in my life.

The August sun dipped behind the rooftops and Marianne talked about our chosen book, *The Women*. 'The tragedy can be traced back to that one choice—'

Lucy gasped and pulled back in her chair, eyes wide at a sudden commotion behind me. I whipped my head around. A burly police officer charged up the side path, his laser gaze focused on me. Two more followed in hot pursuit, wired and on a mission. Yet another raced up behind them as if propelled by a sudden release of pent-up energy. Panic flared in me. They ignored the gate and launched themselves over the low fence.

'Emma Morland?' The officer came towards me. 'I'm arresting you on suspicion of conspiracy to murder.'

'Woah.' Marianne shot up, warding them off with her outstretched palms. 'What's going on?'

Jules clung to me. Rosa and Lucy looked on in stunned silence. I flinched as the big officer loomed in to click handcuffs on my shaking wrists. Fear surged through me.

'You can't arrest her.' Marianne's voice boomed out. 'She's the victim.'

The officers tried in vain to lead her and Jules to the other end of the garden, but Marianne stood her ground, issuing legal threats, gesturing wildly. If Rosa's neighbours hadn't noticed the commotion, they would now.

'…totally insane,' Jules ranted. 'It's a complete stitch-up by that woman.'

My sister was always the gobby one. I willed her to shut up or she'd be arrested too. Then what would happen to the twins? I needed their Aunt Jules to swoop in and make it a little less bad for them. I tried to speak, but no words came out. The big-bodied officer reeled off my rights, telling me I did not have to say anything. I stayed frozen in place, my copy of *The Women* in my lap, about a character who prided herself on doing the right thing.

I'd intended to skip that book club night. I'd every reason to stay home. It was too soon after Elliot's death, which consumed my every waking moment. But the others convinced me to keep things normal for the twins and me. And despite the many shards of heartache digging into me, keeping things normal had a lot going for it. I needed 'normal', but it wasn't panning out. Of course not, with Lydia determined to ruin my life.

'I can't believe that woman is still calling the shots,' Marianne raged.

My heart jangled as if coming loose. I looked at Jules, who'd adopted a battle-ready stance. 'Look after the twins for me.'

A pounding inside my ears beat in time with my crazed heart. I went to clutch my arms around myself, but the handcuffs dug into my wrists. I slid my book on the table, in an awkward two-handed move.

'Bring it with you,' the officer said. 'You'll be there a while.'

His small act of kindness threw me. I held the book to my chest, as if it would save me, or at least take me somewhere other than the police station. I flushed with heat, my brain on fire. But I was chilled inside. As they led me away, Marianne called out, 'We'll get you the best lawyer.'

I nearly laughed. The best lawyer was how I'd landed in this mess, since my husband was considered the best divorce lawyer in London. Dubbed 'the boss of break-ups', Elliot worked exclusively on high-value cases, arguing over the Mayfair townhouse, the yacht in Monaco, the holiday villa with stunning Med views. His clients kept the most because he always came out on top. Until Lydia.

In the back of the police car, I suspected she lurked nearby, crouched behind a shrub, thrilled at her latest plan coming together. My eyes stayed downcast, not risking the sight of Lydia and her smug smile. My hands balled into fists. She thrived on whipping up drama, the world her stage.

Somehow she'd dragged me into this awful mess. My lifelong guilt complex gnawed at my edges. It came from growing up with a twin hell-bent on mischief. Whenever we landed in trouble, Jules did the talking, me red-faced while she told a colourful version of the truth. Now I was ready to confess that Elliot's death was all my fault for making a terrible hash of things. I checked myself. Best not to say that to the police.

Despite my fear and panic, a sudden clarity struck me. For the first time, I was ready to fight Lydia. It was my word against hers. You'd hear different versions of what happened, but Lydia was a liar.

She had breezed into Marianne's book club night with her swishy hair and dewy skin. Her radiant smile and curvy figure. She had played the newbie looking for friends, acting like my kindred spirit. A woman after my own heart. But she was after my husband's heart and my children's hearts and those of everyone close to me.

I tucked my unruly hair behind one ear. Okay, Lydia, I'd play along this time. I had no choice but to tell my side of the story. And when it came to Elliot's murder, it was her word against mine.

Emma was getting away with murder.

I was still holed up in the police station, talking to my lawyer in a grotty room. He wasn't even listening to me. He looked down as I yelled my case at him.

Emma had totally set me up, along with Jules and the rest of them. As for evil Rosa, she'd cursed me. And don't get me started on Marianne. Haters, all of them. You'd expect more kindness from women in a book club. They acted so ethical, sipping fair-trade wine and discussing characters' motivations. It was time they admitted their part in Elliot's death. I told the police this. Hopefully they were arresting Emma.

'I'm the victim of a conspiracy. Write that down.'

I had to set the record straight and fight this miscarriage of justice. If it came to a trial, I'd make the right impression, so the judge threw out the case. Emma stitched me up and now she was the blue-eyed innocent who everyone believed. Those stuck-up bitches closed ranks around her. It was a witch-hunt, like Vern's death, when his family blamed me. Couldn't anyone see that I was the victim?

When this horror show was over, I would claim compensation and sell my story. I'd do a deep dive into she-devils who went on about the sisterhood then trampled all over women like me just because I was competition. I would have my own podcast and a Netflix documentary to talk about my triumph over adversity. That would bring me to a wider audience and put me in the path of an attractive man who wanted to look after me. I could even get a book deal and show those book club bitches. They could choose it for their book of the month. Ha! Seriously though, no way was I going to prison. Emma was going down for this, not me.

Emma

Police interview transcript

DS Williams: We're investigating the murder of your estranged husband, Elliot Morland. His girlfriend, Lydia Steele, says you offered her £250,000 to kill him and make it look like an accident.

Emma Morland: That's ridiculous.

DS Williams: What was your relationship to Lydia Steele prior to your husband's death?

Emma Morland: She came to our book club and stirred up trouble. I only met her a handful of times. Then I found out she was having an affair with my husband, and I left him the same day. I've had no contact with her since.

DS Williams: Did you offer her a payment to kill him?

Emma Morland: The woman's a lunatic.

DS Williams: Please answer yes or no.

Emma Morland: No.

DS Williams: Did you ever discuss the killing of your husband with Lydia?

Emma Morland: No.

DS Williams: Elliot was a successful divorce lawyer who left you for a younger woman. That can't have been easy, Emma. I suggest his death is more convenient to you than doing battle in the divorce courts, given his reputation for ensuring the other side comes off worse.

Emma Morland: He's the father of my children. *Was*. They're devastated. There's no way I'd choose to put them through this.

DS Williams: So why is Lydia saying it?

Emma Morland: She's a fantasist.

DS Williams: You're set to inherit a large sum of money. You could easily pay Lydia £250,000.

Emma Morland: Did you see that video of her threatening me the night before he died?

DS Williams: You could have set that up.

Emma Morland: Oh, come on, she's unhinged. She's the last person I'd ask to kill Elliot.

DS Williams: So, you wanted him dead?

Emma Morland: I'd like to call a lawyer.

Lydia

Police interview transcript

DS Williams: For the record, Lydia, you've declined to have your solicitor present.

Lydia Steele: He kept telling me to say 'no comment'.

DS Williams: To clarify, you're now saying that Emma Morland offered you £250,000 to kill her estranged husband and make it look like an accident?

Lydia Steele: Yes.

DS Williams: Can you tell me exactly what she said?

Lydia Steele: She said, 'I'll give you £250,000 to kill him and make it look like an accident.' I said, 'How do you propose I do that?' She said, 'Poison his food? Push him off a cliff? You're resourceful. Work it out.'

DS Williams: You then proceeded to kill him and claim it was an accident.

Lydia Steele: It was self-defence. I told you. I thought he was going to kill me.

DS Williams: There's no evidence of threats or violence from Elliot. Everyone says he was charming and never raised his voice or laid a hand on anyone.

Lydia Steele: Well, he was nasty to me.

DS Williams: Did you kill Elliot in return for a payment?

Lydia Steele: No. But she knew he was volatile. She thought I'd snap and see it through.

DS Williams: Which you did.

Lydia Steele: I didn't. But when I turned her down, she said, 'The offer's there if you change your mind.'

DS Williams: And you changed your mind.

Lydia Steele: She set me up.

DS Williams: It sounds like you planned it.

Lydia Steele: If I'd planned it, I'd have done a better job.

DS Williams: Okay, Lydia—

Lydia Steele: This is a stitch-up.

DS Williams: If you keep changing your account of what happened, you're less likely to be believed.

Lydia Steele: It's a conspiracy. They planned the whole thing.

DS Williams: Who's 'they'?

Lydia Steele: Those women from book club.

Part One

Before the Murder

Welcome to Book Club

Chapter One

Lydia

Six weeks to the murder

I blamed Jules for bringing me to their book club. I first met her at the tennis club. She was on reception when I dropped in to ask about social events. Two players warmed up in the sultry June heat, the only sound coming from the rhythmical *thwack* of their tennis ball. Fragrant jasmine trailed up the clubhouse, scenting the heavy air. Inside the sleek, marbled clubhouse, the place was lemony fresh and cool from the air con.

We got chatting and she asked what level I played at. 'I'm improving my game.' I leaned my tanned arms on the walnut reception desk. My newly manicured nails shone blood red against the wood. Her lively face took me in. 'Are there any hot tennis players you can match me with?'

Jules laughed and gave me an appraising look. 'They're all hot,' she said. 'Hot and sweaty. And mostly old, if that's your thing.'

I grimaced. The club barman came over, giving me the eye. Mid-thirties, ripped body, shame about his stringy hair scraped into a topknot. Bet he lived in a dive. *No thanks*. I'd joined the club to find an attractive, high net-worth individual who would adore me. He'd have a track record of maturity in relationships and his income would provide us with a decent home in a prime location, along with exotic holidays, plus a car and credit card for me.

Of course, men of that calibre were always taken. Other women snapped them up in their twenties, while I was off having a good time. Now they had the house, the kids were growing up and their bored husbands would be craving fun again. That was where I came in. The right target had to be married, not divorced. I didn't want someone else's cast-off. When I looked at a divorced man, I wondered what was wrong with him for her to let him go. A man worth keeping was a man worth taking.

My quest to score a rich husband took me wine tasting in Soho, scouring fine art auctions and blagging every free trial going at upscale health clubs. I'd taken out social membership at the tennis club, which cost less than full membership.

'It's a friendly club,' Jules said. She hadn't acted upon any connections from this place, otherwise she wouldn't have been behind a reception desk in a drab polo shirt printed with her employer's logo. 'I'll find you some women to play.'

'Sounds great,' I said, even though I'd never owned a racket. 'But work's crazy busy over the summer. I can't commit to matches, so I'll come in for a drink and get to know people.'

Jules checked the watch on her pale wrist and picked up a shiny black bag that looked like some designer replica from Dagenham market, or the Surrey equivalent. I didn't know all the haunts round here yet.

'Going somewhere exciting?' I asked. Maybe she was meeting a bunch of people in a bar, and I could tag along.

'Home and then book club.'

Book club? It sounded as tantalising as the sweaty old tennis players. She had a spark about her though, so best not to write her off. Perhaps she knew a fun crowd at the rugby club or Sandown races.

'Are you into books then?' I asked.

'My other job's in a bookshop. Book club's interesting. It's like a look into a different world,' she said, her face animated.

'How so?'

'The other women in the group have fabulous houses. Not mine. I can barely fit us in my flat.' She laughed as if it didn't matter. No ambition. 'We're at Marianne's tonight. Her house is stunning.'

My 'aha' moment brought instant clarity. My heart sped. Did Marianne have a husband? 'Oh, what fun.' I dazzled her with my smile. 'I love books!'

'You should join us. We've been talking about finding someone new. It gets staid if we don't shake it up.'

'I'd love to.' I flashed her another winning smile.

'My sister's in book club too: Emma. She's hosting after Marianne. Another one with a gorgeous house.'

'Does she have a high-flying career to afford the house?'

'She doesn't work. She's married, with teenagers. Elliot's super successful. He earns more than enough for their charmed life,' Jules said.

'Lucky Emma.'

'I'll grab your number, if that's okay.' She tapped at her computer screen. 'Shall I check with the group and then WhatsApp you?'

I nodded my encouragement.

'I'll take your email too as Rosa uses a crappy out-of-date phone that won't take apps. Took us two years to get her on email.'

'Great.' I stepped towards the glass sliding doors, acting casual. 'Hope to see you later.'

'Hang on.' Jules pulled a hefty book from her bag and held it out. 'I finished it on my lunch break. If you make a start, you'll know what we're talking about tonight.'

She texted an hour later to say I had the seal of approval and then looped me into an email chain. I sat on the bed in my flatshare, all over the recipient list, the unopened book beside me. One of them was 'BookishLucy'. Beyond Tragic Lucy, more like. Emma's email was 'theMorland-Family', so not autonomous enough for her own email. I googled Elliot Morland and tracked down a London lawyer with sporty connections in Surrey. I zoomed in on his photo. Result! He was handsome and forty-ish with neatly styled thick dark hair. Even from the image, I sensed his confidence, his hidden depths. Hello, Elliot.

Emma's journal

This is my account of what happened from the day I met Lydia. Jules said I should do it now, to straighten it out in my frazzled mind. It's just for me, so I'm writing it as I remember.

I'd considered excusing myself from book club that night, not wanting to offend Marianne by saying I didn't like her book choice. What a dreary, long-winded novel, but Jules insisted. It was my turn to drive and her turn to drink Marianne's expensive wine. My sister was persuasive, so I let myself be convinced.

Even though she lived close by, I didn't see Jules as much as I'd have liked. She mixed tennis club shifts with part-time work in a bookshop, and she revelled in her hectic social life. My evenings had always been family time, although these days the girls were often out with friends, and Elliot worked late.

Now that the girls no longer needed me so much, I found myself on my own a lot. I had started to think about returning to work, having more of a purpose. Elliot was defined by his career, thriving on ambition and loving the status. When I gave up work for the twins, it felt like a luxury to have time for their activities and see their sweet personalities develop. But doing everything at home filled my time ever since, especially with Elliot so useless around the house and garden. He said I was good at it, and we could afford to live on his salary, as if that settled things.

On the way to pick up Jules, I drove the girls to Esher High Street. 'Have you thought any more about driving lessons?' I glanced at their bright faces in the rear-view mirror as restaurants and interior design showrooms flickered past.

'We won't have time till after the summer,' Isabella, my eldest by eleven minutes, said. 'Mum, drop us here.'

I pulled up sharp and the two of them spilled from the car, bursting with teen girl energy and the absolute joy of a night out with friends. Chloe waved a goofy thanks and goodbye through the windscreen, then rushed after her twin. As I pulled back into the traffic, I heard their excited squeals as they met their friends outside the cinema.

Be careful, stayed unsaid on my lips, as if merely thinking it would keep them safe. My heart clenched. How were they seventeen already? Life was simpler back when they ate what I gave them, wore what we picked out and in the evenings they snuggled up for a story. We loved *Matilda*, who was never alone because she had books. They barely read anything now, while I still craved the deep comfort of a good story.

Swinging the car around, I headed to Jules's flat. Despite the dreary book choice, going to Marianne's was a welcome change from running around after everyone else. Growing up, I was 'the quiet one, not like Jules'. I still got tongue-tied, but I could talk books with my friends.

I pulled up outside Jules's flat and lowered the window to the sound of birdsong, beautifully clear in the warm June air. It was so peaceful that I closed my eyes. Then Jules burst out of her communal front door in her usual rush, digging around in her bag and pulling out black sunglasses. A glance at the car clock confirmed that we'd be late.

'Phew, sorry I'm late. Thanks for the lift. Did you finish the book?' She climbed in and leaned over to kiss my cheek with a 'mwah' before fastening her seat belt.

'Slogged my way through.'

'Me too.'

I smiled.

'So,' Jules said. 'You ready to meet Lydia? She's quite something.'

Chapter Two

Lydia

I pulled into the sweeping drive and my heart soared at the magnificent house. The elegant Queen Anne mansion stood proudly with tall sash windows and a grand entrance of Italianate stone columns. Such a long way from where I grew up in Basildon and Southend, or *Saafend* as the locals might say, not that you'd catch me talking like that. Good diction was important when mixing with the social elite. I passed myself off as one of them.

I parked in the shade of a flowering tree, alongside a smart Audi, which might belong to one of the other book clubbers. I stepped from the car and walked with confidence to the door. My high-street – but catwalk-replica – wedge espadrilles crunched over the pale gravel with ease. I pressed the doorbell, fluffed up my hair and smoothed down my saffron-yellow silk dress that set off my highlights. The dress came from a West London charity shop. It sent the perfect message of a successful woman, totally at ease in the world.

'Who lives in a house like this,' I said to myself in a *Through the Keyhole* voice. A tall, older woman with arched eyebrows and spiky silver-grey hair opened the door wide. She wore an indigo shirt dress and strappy orange heels.

'Lydia? I'm Marianne. Come on in,' she said in a refined American accent, guiding me into an impressive entrance hall.

I clocked the huge diamond ring on her left hand and Chanel cuff bracelets on each wrist. She was the type to carry off big statement pieces. She was also a mugger's dream wearing all that bling. It was worth a fortune. I considered turning my hand to cat burglary and master-minding a jewellery heist.

'We're in the kitchen,' she said in her cultured drawl, sashaying through.

I sashayed along with her. We passed huge antique mirrors and framed photos of preppy boys who must be her sons.

'What a beautiful home,' I said. 'You have exquisite taste.'

'Thank you. We relocated from New York and chose this place for our sons to attend the American school a few blocks away. Crawford worked in the City. He's recently retired. That's him in the den.'

She motioned towards a doughy man slumped in front of golf on Sky. Not an attractive look. I ruled him out.

What a fabulous house though, with an interesting mix of antique and modern. Nice art, albeit showy. Marianne had her shit together and even if her husband had been younger and hotter, I'd never wrestle him away from her.

Inside the vast marble kitchen, two women faced the view of an azure swimming pool. *God, I'd kill to live here*, I thought. *Literally*. The women turned towards us. The old one had thin eyebrows and dyed black hair cut short. The other had limp blond hair and wore a bizarre patchwork skirt and gypsy top that didn't suit her. It wouldn't suit anyone. She must be Bookish Lucy.

'Lydia,' Marianne said. 'This is Lucy and Rosa.'

'Lovely to meet you.' I flashed my best smile.

'We've met before,' Rosa said.

'Have we?' I studied her haughty, lined face.

'At Luca's.'

'Who's Luca?' Marianne asked, pouring white wine into a glass.

'She's lodging with him,' Rosa replied. Her dark eyes inspected me, her hard stare moving purposefully up and down my face.

'I'm *staying* with him until I find the right place.' Had Luca mentioned a Rosa? I couldn't say, although I avoided him as much as possible. This was why I hated small communities. Paths didn't cross much in London, but I couldn't stay there after what happened. My living arrangements weren't my style, like my awful shabby Honda parked outside. This was my fresh start, but I didn't want them seeing me as some kind of loser.

'My good friend is Luca's mother.' Rosa folded her arms. 'We visited when he came home from working in Germany. He put antivirus on my tablet.'

It started coming back to me: two old women clucking around Luca, most likely his mum and aunt. They'd looked daggers at me, as if I had designs on becoming the daughter-in-law. *As if.* I doubted Luca had ever intimately touched another human.

'He is a very kind boy,' Rosa said. 'Good to his mother.'

I smiled and lifted up the bottle I'd bought on my way over. 'Champagne, anyone?'

'That's so kind, Lydia, but let's have this bottle first. It's Crawford's favourite.' Marianne handed me the glass she'd poured. 'He imports it from Chianti, along with some excellent cheese and olive oil.' She raised her glass to the group. 'New friends, old friends and *la dolce vita*.'

I sipped the velvety, rich wine. Apart from the old woman, this book club lark was better than I'd expected. The slam of car doors came through the open windows, and Marianne swooshed towards the hall.

Rosa and Lucy talked to each other about some boring old book, and I walked around the kitchen, running my fingers along the smooth granite countertops. So impressive. I took in the hi-tech oven, a giant fridge-freezer and a wine fridge in the kitchen island. Any moment now, a butler would appear and pour us more wine. It was that kind of place, although our formidable host had it covered.

I spotted a diary on the dresser and had a peek inside. If it showed any parties, I might wangle an invite. As I flicked through, the two murmuring voices behind me stopped. I cast a look over my shoulder. The drippy hippy stared at me, mouth agape. The old hag's dark eyes bored into me. I snapped the diary shut and went to say something, but Marianne reappeared with Jules and another woman behind her. Emma, I assumed. Jules and I waved hello.

'This, Lydia, is Emma,' Marianne said. 'Jules's twin.'

They looked similar, but Emma was slimmer, mousier, with wavy dark blond hair compared to Jules's layered, highlighted bob. Emma wore a Breton top and faded jeans, comfortable and mumsy. She said a shy hello and gazed lovingly at one of Marianne's books, drawn to it as if magnetised. She picked it up and held it like a cherished artefact. Then she came to the table, holding the book to her chest as if one of us might wrench it from her. She was clearly what you might call 'quirky' (if you were being kind), going gaga over a book.

They launched into talking about the book they'd read, discussing the characters and gossiping as if they knew them. I zoned out and imagined owning this place. Then I caught the salty one watching me, lips puckered, so I engaged with the conversation. Marianne and Jules disagreed on something trivial.

'But he was justified in saying that,' Jules insisted, waving her wine glass around.

'Even though he was proved wrong?' Marianne leaned forward.

Who cares, I nearly said. *They're not real people*. I looked at Emma instead, carefully thumbing through the book she'd brought to the table. Was she *stroking* its pages? Everything about her was muted, as if someone had taken a remote control and turned down her volume and brightness. She wouldn't stand a chance against me taking her husband. I would make sure he only had eyes for me.

'What's your favourite book?' I asked her in a quiet voice, and something strange happened.

Her face transformed before us, her eyes revealed as an incredible clear blue and her skin glowed with a luminous quality. She looked in the throes of a heavenly vision. The others saw it too. They stopped talking and gazed at her as if she were a piece of Marianne's art. In that moment I could see why a man would fall for her purity. A certain type of man who liked looking after his wife. I would enchant him into looking after me instead. Game on.

Emma's journal

The first time I went to Marianne's, I'd never expected to share common ground with the sort of person who lived in a house like that. Our mum used to clean one similar and she'd say, 'They're not our sort.' But Marianne welcomed me, and we bonded over books.

On that book club night, Rosa and Lucy were in Marianne's vast kitchen with a gorgeous younger woman. Her shining auburn hair tumbled around her shoulders. She leaned against the counter beside a bottle of champagne and stared right at me. Jules had already told me she was thirty, so younger than the rest of us. She wore a low-cut dress and watched me with rapt fascination.

When Marianne introduced us, I smiled a hello and veered off to a novel on the dresser, avoiding her intense gaze and brimming confidence. Lydia popped the cork on the champagne. Was she celebrating? When I looked up, her gaze still lingered on me, like a portrait with eyes that follow you around the room. I sat beside Lucy and leaned in to hug her. 'You look great,' I said in her ear, and she gave me a squeeze.

'Wasn't it a powerful novel?' Marianne poured champagne into crystal flutes. She was a wine buff and wouldn't approve of drinking fizz after Chianti, but Lydia was hell-bent on champagne. 'His prose works so hard.' She lifted her copy and quoted from it. I busied myself with a goat's cheese and cranberry tartlet. It tasted divine and melted in my mouth.

'Goodness,' Lydia said when Marianne finished reading aloud. 'It sounds dreadful! Thank God I was too late to read it.'

I couldn't help laughing. Did she really just stick a pin in Marianne's appraisal?

'Why'd you bring this philistine to our group?' Marianne joked to Jules.

This'll liven things up. Lydia tossed her hair and gave me a minxy smile, knocking back champagne as if she couldn't care less about offending our host. She reminded me of Becky Sharp, living on her wits in *Vanity Fair*, magnetising men with her good looks and vivacious ways.

'What literary sisters are you like?' Lydia asked Jules and me.

'That pair in *My Sister, the Serial Killer*,' Marianne said.

'I'd clean up your crime scene, sis,' Jules said darkly, before taking a long sip of fizz.

I rolled my eyes. 'You know I'd be clearing up your mess.'

'True. I'll spill the blood, and you disinfect.'

'Who will you kill?' Lydia asked.

'Good question,' Jules said. 'And what's your favourite?'

'*Gone Girl*,' Lydia said, quick as a flash. 'I love the mind games. So clever.'

'I loved it too,' I said.

'*Did* you?' She sized me up as a kindred spirit. It wasn't mutual, but she intrigued me. Jules must have invited her to shake things up. She always liked playing with fire.

'I felt sorry for Amy,' I said, 'stuck in that marriage. But the way it panned out was genius.'

'Absolutely. What's your favourite?' Lydia kept her gaze on me.

'*Rebecca*.'

They all murmured their approval. Marianne placed a theatrical hand on her heart and closed her eyes to recite the first line about dreaming of Manderley.

'Do you still fancy Maxim de Winter?' Jules asked me, her face full of mischief. Since childhood, we'd discussed 'book boyfriends' like other girls lusted over boy bands.

'Well?' Marianne asked me.

'He's quite compelling,' I said. 'The strong, silent type who's haunted by his past.'

Marianne snorted and raised her glass to me. 'Amen to that. I wouldn't kick him out of bed.'

'How does he measure up to your husband?' Lydia asked breezily. She leaned forward, elbows resting on the table.

'Let's not bring Elliot into this,' Jules said tartly.

Lydia wrinkled her nose. 'The second wife was a drip. She had no power.'

'She was an innocent.' I stuck up for the second Mrs de Winter. Quiet women needed defending. 'Eclipsed in her own home by another woman.'

'I love Rebecca,' Lydia said. 'Dead Rebecca, calling the shots from her watery grave. My kind of woman.'

'Psychopath,' Marianne said. 'Amy from *Gone Girl* and Rebecca are psychopaths.'

'Don't you just love a psychopath?' Lydia said in her honeyed voice. 'They stop at nothing to get what they want.'

Chapter Three

Lydia

The day after meeting everyone, Jules sent me Emma's address for the next book club. Jules had insisted they bring it forward two weeks because of people being away for the rest of the summer. It was a short book, so fortunately they'd all agreed. But I couldn't wait two whole weeks. Desperate to meet Elliot, I sought out the Morland house on Saturday morning.

It was more of a mansion, with a smart white-painted exterior. A beautifully landscaped front garden edged the circular drive. It lacked the grandeur of Marianne's place, but I preferred the location, overlooking a village green. I imagined standing at the big picture window, freshly brewed coffee in hand, keeping an eye on the hot young gardener who maintained the outdoor space.

A shiny red Ferrari looked amazing on the drive. The car of a successful, attractive London lawyer. A newish VW Golf lined up beside it. I pictured Elliot and me driving around town in the Ferrari. It would be our weekend car, and I'd also have a top-of-the-range SUV. Then a dog barked and punctured the dream. I hadn't seen Elliot as a dog person – or Emma, come to think of it.

I'd wanted a snoop around first, but not with a barking dog, so I rang the bell. The dog kept on until Emma answered the door, her hair pulled up in a ponytail.

'Oh, hello.' She wore another mumsy top and jeans that looked like they'd been washed a thousand times.

'Hi, Emma. How are you?' I smiled as a large black lump of a dog with a lolling pink tongue pushed past her legs to snuffle at my paper bag from the patisserie.

'Fine.' She touched her scrappy ponytail with her fingertips. 'I was doing some housework.'

'I thought I'd check where you live so I'm prepared for the next book club.' It sounded lame, and the dog didn't help by trying to push its big snout into the bag. 'And I'll take you up on your offer to borrow that book. Not the book club book. The other one.'

Emma paused and frowned. '*Fingersmith*?'

'Yes, *Fingersmith*.' Whatever. I'd no intention of reading it. I would find an online review and wing it. 'And I bought NYC cookies.' I tried to hold up the bag, but the dog clawed at my dress. Emma didn't seem to notice, and I wondered if I could nudge it away with the tip of my shoe.

'What are NYC cookies?' She stood back and I entered the pristine hall with its expanse of shiny white floor tiles.

I followed her through to the kitchen. 'They're big and deliciously soft in the middle. I got five in case your family are around. Since it's coffee time.'

'The girls are upstairs.'

The designer kitchen had bifold doors to the garden. Everything shone, from the glossy white ceramic countertops and top-end chrome appliances to the polished white floor. The house was spacious and contemporary with a pared-back style. Surprising, really. I'd expected a bohemian Home Counties vibe with twinkly lights and fair-trade pottery cluttering up the place.

'Beautiful house,' I cooed. 'Lived here long?'

'We bought it about ten years ago.'

We bought it. He had a few bob then. I would check the value back home, but it must be worth over two million quid.

I clocked the holiday photo on the wall of Elliot, Emma and their two gorgeous daughters, sunny smiles all round. The girls' flaxen hair shone in matching French plaits, friendship bands on their tanned wrists. Elliot looked effortlessly cool. It was all quite sickening, until I thought of him taking me on an exotic holiday. I looked fabulous in a sun hat and designer shades.

'Is this your husband? He looks nice.'

She smiled modestly. But Christ, he was killingly gorgeous. I'd seen his photo on the law firm's website, but he looked even hotter with the family in tow. Perhaps it was some primal allure of him as the provider. Poor guy, shackled to drab Emma. He deserved someone in a different league.

She'd never appreciate a red-blooded man. She was more interested in books than real life. Some effort wouldn't kill her. What did she do all day? She must have been pretty at one time, attractive enough to win Elliot in the first place, but she didn't seem to care about keeping her husband. I wanted to shake her until her brain rattled, then slap her dopey face for sleepwalking through her charmed life. She took all this for granted when it should be mine.

The dog nudged my hand for attention.

'He loves everyone, don't you, Barney?' Emma said.

When she looked away, I wiped the slobber from my hand. Why did people have dogs? She would have to take it with her when she went. 'What make is he?'

'A Labrador. They're a great breed for families. Easy-going.' She put the kettle on.

I wanted to ask why she didn't use the expensive-looking coffee machine, but I asked to use the loo instead. She pointed me to a closed door off the hall. I counted on her busying herself with the coffee so I could snoop in the room opposite, having glimpsed a bureau on the way past. I went and checked for paperwork. You never know what you might find.

'What are you doing?' Emma's voice came from behind me.

I spun around. 'Silly me,' I trilled, looking out of the large bay window. 'I went through the wrong door. You must love this view.'

'Coffee's ready.' She took a step back for me to follow her out, then closed the door behind me. Worth a try.

'Any plans for today?' I sat on one of the black stools lined up alongside the kitchen island.

'Elliot's out cycling. He's based in Kensington. He works long hours and likes a bike ride at the weekend. He won't be back till later.'

Shit. I'd missed him. 'Wow, cycling! He looks fit from the photo.'

'He's always had loads of energy.' She smiled. 'Right from when we met at uni. The other boys lolled around and drank a lot, but Elliot had this urgency to get on and make things happen. Still has.'

Perfect. So did I. 'Ah, so you've been together all that time?'

Her face took on a faraway look of enchantment. She must have still adored him, and why wouldn't she adore a gorgeous man who funded all this? She stared off into the distance, as if in her own private rapture.

'How long have you been together?' I asked with more emphasis.

She returned from memory lane, momentarily surprised to see me there. She shook her head as if shaking herself alert. Weirdo.

'Over twenty years.'

'Shame I didn't get to say hello to him.'

'You'll probably meet him at book club.'

I'm counting on it.

Emma's journal

After everything that's happened, it's weirdly satisfying to write the story of Lydia's exploits and the conversations as I remember them. Now back to the star of the show, who acted like she was dying to befriend me.

> Hi Emma, coffee was fun! Let's meet up again. Lydia xx

I frowned at her text message and tapped out a quick excuse. Her reply came through seconds later.

> Please let's meet up. I hardly know anyone here and you've been so welcoming. I'm loving Fingersmith! Can't wait to discuss it. xx

I'd always been an 'opposites attract' person, maybe from growing up with Jules, my strident twin. That's why I fell for Elliot and his confidence, compensating for my lack of it. People like Lydia fascinated me, the way she breezed in, firing off put-downs without bothering to read the room.

She was too intense for me alone, but Jules promised to join us. We agreed to meet after I'd been to the primary school, where I volunteered for Reading Hour every Tuesday. When I left the classroom, Jules texted to say she couldn't make it. Before I could suggest cancelling, Lydia jumped in.

Boo! But I'll have fun with Emma. Em, my phone's nearly out of juice, so I'll see you at 5 xx

I gritted my teeth, already regretting it. I nipped home first and stepped over the twins' bags and shoes dumped inside the door.

'Girls, move your stuff!' I called into the void.

They'd made tuna melts, leaving the open can on the kitchen worktop. Flies circled around discarded kiwi-fruit peelings that lay mouldering beside the Nutribullet. Their smoothies had turned the kitchen island into a sticky mess. I cornered them in the living room, hunched over their phones.

'You can't keep leaving the place in a mess.'

'Huh?' Isabella looked up.

'We've agreed that you clear up your mess.'

'What mess?'

'In the kitchen. Do I need to show you the state of it?'

They exchanged bored looks.

'We all live in this house, so we all do our bit to keep it nice.'

'Dad doesn't keep it nice,' Isabella said.

'Dad pays the bills. He works long hours to provide for us.'

'Not being funny, Mum, but most people don't clean like you. You should see Indigo's house. It's a right tip.'

'Her mum's like, an artist?' Chloe said.

'When you have your own homes, you can keep them how you want. Until then, you'll be considerate.'

'Yeah, but it literally doesn't matter in the scheme of things,' Isabella kept on.

'It's not like, super important?' Chloe said.

'We're a family. We pull together and show respect. I'm going to Grandma's when she has her operation, and you two will look after Barney and clear up after yourselves.'

'Why should the female do the cleaning anyway?' Isabella said.

A part of me liked them outspoken, or Isabella at least, who spoke up for them both. She'd always been the dominant one, racing ahead, the first down the slide. When she was five or six, I'd asked her to put her toys in the toy box. She threw her little arms in the air, gave me a pained expression and said, 'Seriously, you don't know the kind of pressure I'm under.' I laughed at the time, but I knew who she'd got it from. Chloe was like me, her voice soft and fluttering with uncertainty. A vivid red rash of anxiety spread over her throat and chest during stressful times.

'If you were boys, we'd have the same conversation. It's not about the female cleaning up after the man. It's the way we do it in this family because your dad earns enough that I stay home and look after everyone.'

It was tricky when I told them girls had the same opportunities as boys, yet they saw me clearing up after

Elliot, who avoided the dross. He turned up for school plays and parents' evenings looking for all the world like a hands-on dad. Jules called him a Disney dad, showing up on cue for the milestones and magic moments.

'Look, it's fine. Relax, okay?' Isabella said.

'If you want to be independent, you can look after yourselves. Starting now. I'm meeting a friend and you two are cleaning the kitchen and walking Barney.'

They stared at me, and I walked out.

Minutes later, I parked near Esher High Street. My phone buzzed with a text.

> I'm in the wine bar next to the coffee shop.
> L xx

I tutted at the venue change. I'd only wanted chai tea, not a drinking session. When I walked in she hugged me like an old friend. A bottle of wine chilled in an ice bucket, two long-stem glasses on the table.

'The house white is yummy. It's half price for happy hour.' She sat back at the little round table for two. 'We deserve a treat.'

I caved and she poured me a small glass. She reminded me again of Becky Sharp exploiting her aloneness to get ahead in *Vanity Fair*.

'To friendship.' She smiled and tapped her glass against mine. 'I'm so pleased I found you. It's good to meet such a great bunch of women at book club. Especially you.'

Did she know that the others didn't like her?

'And how are you *really*?' she cooed, touching my arm. 'You looked stressed when you came through the door. I thought, *Here's a woman in need of a drink*.'

I told her about the girls making a mess. 'Sometimes I fantasise about taking off and leaving them all to it. But I doubt the twins would manage, and they'd all forget to feed the dog. Chloe has anxiety, which Elliot just doesn't get.'

'Anxiety about what?'

'The environment, social inequality…'

'Is she political?'

'No. She's seventeen. She wants a kinder world.'

I didn't mention the knives, and how deep Chloe's anxiety went. She didn't trust herself around knives and scissors in case she stabbed someone on impulse. The experts called it an obsessive thought pattern that took hold in her anxious mind. We banished the knife block to a kitchen cupboard and then introduced the knives back slowly. She had it under control, not that we thought for a moment she would stab anyone. It was ridiculous to think our gentle, kind-hearted child could ever be capable of such a thing.

'She can't change the world, but she can focus on making a difference,' Lydia said. 'Like volunteering or a career to fit her caring ethos. Then she'll feel in control.'

I finished my wine. Maybe Lydia wasn't so frivolous after all.

'Don't mind me.' She topped up my glass. 'I'm reading *The 7 Habits of Highly Effective People*.'

'Oh. I never read business books.'

'If you're going to stick your nose in a book, it's worth choosing one that will help you in the real world.'

Growing up, people said I always had my nose stuck in a book. Not that I cared when I went to my second home in Narnia or ran off with orphaned Mary into *The Secret Garden*, unlocking the mystery—

'Emma?'

For a moment, I was in the garden, surrounded by cool Yorkshire air, led by a bird to unearth the tarnished key in the damp soil.

'Are you okay?'

I pulled myself back. I must stop taking my mind someplace else when other people were around. I slipped so easily into fictional worlds. They suited me better than the real one.

'I said it's a useful book. It helps in your personal life too. It's about taking responsibility for what you want instead of putting up with what doesn't suit you.'

'I'll look it up.' She made everything engaging, even a business book, not that I modelled myself on highly effective people. 'Where are you from?'

'Cheltenham. Great place, but I haven't lived there in a while.'

'And what brings you to Surrey?'

'Thought I'd try it when I came back from Dubai. My boss is based in Guildford, so we meet for strategy meetings every week.'

'You seem more of a London person to me.' I still tried to pinpoint who she actually was. *She's got more front than Blackpool*, my mum would say.

'I'll get more for my money here, property-wise. I've a contact who I'm staying with—'

'Luca.' Rosa had said she knew Lydia's flatmate, landlord, whatever.

'It's temporary until I decide where to live.'

A man and woman in business suits walked past us to the bar. Lydia's shrewd gaze took them in, judging them in some way. She'd assessed me in the same way at book club. They looked like colleagues stopping off for a quick drink after a meeting. I missed that, unwinding with a drink after work, defined by something other than being Elliot's wife, the twins' mum.

'Do you think they're shagging?' Lydia nodded to the couple.

'Um… they look like colleagues.'

'Good-looking guy. I wouldn't say no. What do you think?'

I laughed.

'I know you're married, but no harm in looking.' Her eyes twinkled. 'Are you and Marianne close friends?'

'We're friendly, yes.'

'I thought she was pushing it at book club.'

'In what way?'

'Going on about Jane Eyre's unethical wealth from colonial wrongdoing. Seriously? Wasn't Marianne's husband an investment banker?' She leaned closer, mischief playing on her face. 'Were his investments ethical? Are her diamonds conflict-free?'

I snickered into my nearly empty wine glass. She had a point. Not that I'd slag off Marianne. Lydia's playfulness was one thing, but her sly digs grated on me.

'And you, you dark horse! Having a thing for Max de Winter.' She smiled impishly over her wine glass.

It must be fun to speak your mind and live on your own terms, like Rebecca de Winter, whom Lydia admired. Rebecca didn't let any man dictate to her, least of all her husband. People who did what they liked fascinated me, as if I hoped their boldness would rub off onto me. Perhaps the second Mrs de Winter was the same, until she found out the truth.

'Jules was having a laugh,' I said.

'You're like Max's wife.'

'Mousey, you mean?'

'No! Bless you. You're good-natured and quiet.' She sounded so genuine, I could almost believe the compliment.

'She's the odd one out in her own home,' I said.

'What about you?' She leaned on the table, resting her chin on her clasped hands. 'Are you the odd one out?'

'It was a throwaway comment.'

'Did you work before you had kids?'

'I worked in London.'

'Oh, wonderful. You should totally get back into it, now your kids are older. What's stopping you?'

I toyed with the stem of my wine glass and something stirred inside me, an urge to do more with my life.

'A friend of mine took time out,' Lydia said, her voice creamy-smooth. 'She spent so long facilitating her family's life, she forgot how to have one of her own. I think she'd lost confidence.'

I thought of Elliot and all he'd achieved. I'd wanted to be there for the twins when they were little, but organising everyone's lives became my default role. Meanwhile, his career path soared. 'I've been out of the jobs market a while. Longer than I'd intended.'

'So, what's next for Emma?' she asked.

'I'd like a job again. Some independence.' I eyed the woman at the bar.

'You can totally do it. Have faith in yourself.' She beamed her encouragement. It was easy to be swept up by her breezy nature. 'It's good for us to have our own careers, not just for the money, but for respect.'

I sometimes scanned through job ads and imagined myself with a career. Elizabeth Zott from *Lessons in*

Chemistry sprang to mind, the way she stepped into a new career when tragedy struck.

'What are you guys doing at the weekend?'

I pulled away from fond thoughts of Elizabeth Zott, rowing against the tide of sexism. 'Elliot's cycling again on Saturday and he goes for a run on Sunday mornings, but we'll do something.'

'If he's off doing his own thing, why don't you take a minibreak at a spa? They can fend for themselves. When did you last take off without them?'

'Last year, when my mum had a hip operation.'

She laughed. 'For fun, you idiot.'

'Never.'

'What? You've never been on a girls' trip or a me-time break?'

'Not since having the twins.'

'Does Elliot have weekends away?'

'He has entire holidays without us.' I counted them off on my fingers. 'Snowboarding in February, yacht racing for Antigua Sailing Week, paragliding…'

'Sod that. It's your turn. Where will you go?' Lydia's face lit up with possibilities.

'My mum's. She's due to have knee surgery in two weeks. I'll help her when she comes out of hospital.'

'It'll do them good to manage without you. You can take the time to reassess what *you* want. Do the three of them take a turn at cooking?'

'Elliot can't cook. The girls can do spag bol and baked potatoes. They'll follow a recipe but make a huge mess, so I do it all.'

'Don't you mind?'

'I like cooking. The way to Elliot's heart is through home cooking. He tries to come home by seven and we eat together at the table. He's quite traditional.'

'Not many traditional marriages around these days.' She sipped her wine. 'Any plans for the summer?'

'The twins are going to France for six weeks.'

'Six weeks! Lucky twins.'

'It's the longest they've been away. My aunt and uncle moved to Normandy to renovate a château and some gîtes. We stayed at their B&B last year, and they invited the girls back for a working holiday. They're taking A Level French.'

'And you'll be a free agent. Are you and Elliot going away?'

'I'll drive the girls over on the ferry and stay two nights. I might have a holiday with Elliot, depending on his schedule.'

'Sounds like you'll need that spa break after caring for your mum.'

'Elliot's too active to lie around all day.'

'Do it for you, so they'll stop taking you for granted. Trust me.'

'I've never been on holiday without them.'

'Well, it's about time you did.' Her eyes lit up, same as when she turned up last Saturday and saw inside our house.

'I'll take a proper break when the twins move out next year.'

Lydia was certainly keen to encourage me to go away. She gave me a self-satisfied look. I'd had enough of this virtual stranger feasting on the details of my life. My interest in her ballsy ways had mutated into dislike. The wine didn't help, the sour aftertaste coating my tongue and making my mood a little darker.

I liked women, I really did. I liked our unspoken code of supporting each other. But not all women followed the code, like the cluster of school-run mums when the twins were small. Lydia would fit in with them, the way they looked me up and down.

Her intensity set me on edge. Prickles of heat travelled up my chest to my throat, heating my face. I needed some air and pushed my chair back. The metal scraped on the stone floor. I didn't even look at her before turning to leave. 'I have to go.'

Chapter Four

Lydia

Five weeks to the murder

Luca geeked away at his Mac on Sunday morning. Some awful reality TV for anoraks was showing on his massive telly on the wall, ugly black cables snaking down. He hunched over his screen to signal he didn't want me around. I couldn't bear that horrid flat with Luca and his bachelor-boy furnishings. A friend of his had put in a word and he'd let me flat-sit while he worked in Germany. Now he'd returned, consigning me to the boxy spare room. I tried some light flattery to keep him sweet, which only elicited strange looks. Enough of that loser. I said 'bye' to his back.

My urge to connect with Elliot had reached a fever pitch. Emma said I'd meet him at her book club night, but I had to get him alone. If I made an impact, I'd have a better chance of homing in when she went to stay with her mum. Her eyes shone when she told me the way to his heart. Epic fail, love. She must have led a charmed life to be so trusting. And the way to his heart was through my abundance of sex appeal. Obviously.

Emma said he went running on Sunday mornings, so I drove over to stake out the house. Parked in my car with a takeaway coffee, I trained my eyes on their drive. He eventually came out, just him and the dog. My heart raced. I sprang into action. By the time I'd grabbed my bag and leapt from the car, he was jogging across the green. *Bugger.* I couldn't run after him, since that would look weird. I slid back in the car and waited for nearly an hour before he returned at a brisk trot, the dog lolloping alongside.

I jumped from the car in a flash. He wouldn't elude me a second time. I reached the end of his drive as he clipped on the dog's lead to cross the road. He looked toned and tanned in a running top and shorts, the contours of his manly chest visible through a lightweight grey T-shirt. Thank God he wasn't one of those men who exercised in dayglo Lycra. He caught sight of me.

'Hi, Barney,' I called to the stupid dog.

Elliot narrowed his eyes, trying to place me.

'You must be Emma's husband,' I said with my most gorgeous smile.

'I am.' He came towards me, glowing from his run, his chest heaving.

'I'm Lydia, from her book club.'

'Elliot,' he said amiably.

'Did you have a good run?' I crouched down to pat the dog, who slobbered on my arm again. At least it gave Elliot a bird's-eye view of my boobs. I caught him fleetingly admiring my body. Good.

There was something sexy about a stolen look at an attractive physique. His gaze moved up and met mine. A spark of interest. Up close, I could see he hadn't shaved. The roguish stubble suited him.

'You look fit,' I said. 'Do you run marathons?'

'I've done London and New York. Running gets the blood pumping.'

So did sex. He liked my interest. He was my type: tall, fit, quite posh. His haircut was a bit schoolboy-ish. I resisted the urge to ruffle it, muss it up and kiss him full on the lips while squeezing his firm muscles.

'We ran along the river.' Deep voice, spark in his eye, already turning me on. *Oh Elliot, the fun we could have.*

'Wonderful. I was dropping a book off to Emma.'

'That's good of you. I'm not sure if she's in. Shall I pass it on to her?'

I didn't like to say that she hadn't left the house in the hour since he'd come out, so I pulled the unopened book from my bag and handed it over. I could invite myself in on some pretext, but why ruin the moment? Having created an initial impression, I'd reel him in with my 'less is more' approach.

'Nice to meet you, Elliot.' I dazzled him with my smile and walked away. He was the one and I would make him mine. We'd meet again on Thursday. The book club losers would be in my way, worst luck, so I had to keep his attention on me.

Back home, I planned my seduction of Elliot from the cramped back room. To escape this dump, I would hold my nerve and focus on the result, just like it says in *The 7 Habits of Highly Effective People*. Habit number one: be proactive. You design your life, so choose success or choose failure. I chose success.

Habit number two: begin with the end in mind. Visualise what you want, and reality will follow. I visualised an exotic trip to Maui with Elliot. I'd clawed my way out from my previous setback with Vern. Now I would apply the same drive to securing a new husband that someone might to a career change. It had taken longer than expected to find my target. I would zero in and make Elliot mine.

Emma's journal

I'd intended to write the facts of what happened as a memory jog in case I'm cross-examined in court, God forbid. But from the first page it flowed out word for word, conversations and all. Writing a journal is cathartic, so I'm going with it.

On that Sunday morning, I spotted my copy of *Fingersmith* on the hall table. My old favourite, with the betrayals and twists that snatched my breath away. I never imagined my own life would become a warped thriller, thanks to Lydia and her scheming.

Elliot half jogged downstairs after his post-run shower.

'Did this come through the letter box?' I picked up the book.

'Oh, that,' he said airily. 'One of your book club women dropped it off.'

'Lydia? You met her?'

'Briefly. She was heading here when I came back from my run.'

'Oh. She's not joining book club. We're keeping it to the five of us.'

Elliot walked away, distracted by a message on his phone.

'What did she say?'

He disappeared sharpish as if avoiding telling me. Had she come on to him? He went in the garden with a cold drink, and I called Jules from the bedroom.

'We have to uninvite Lydia. She sets me on edge.'

'She's looking forward to it. She messaged to say she's loving the book. Let her come this once, then we won't ask her back.'

'But—'

'Indulge me this one time.'

'I've indulged you my entire life.' A teacher once caught her bunking off, so she pretended to be me. Since I was the 'good twin' she got away with a verbal warning. We didn't look so alike now, otherwise she'd keep dropping me in it. But she still got her own way. Jules didn't know what she was unleashing.

My phone buzzed.

'I've another call.'

'Okay, bye.' She was probably relieved.

Marianne's name appeared on the screen, and I let it go to voicemail. When I listened to the message, she got straight down to business. 'Emma, it's about Lydia. I went to the bookstore and said to Jules, "We need to talk about that woman you invited. What are you thinking? She's not even interested in literature. We might as well invite Crawford." Then a customer commandeered her, so I left. If this is revenge for me wanting to keep the group to just us, she's proving my point. Lydia is trouble with a capital T. We need to uninvite her.'

Conflict *again*. The tone of book club had changed with Lydia joining us and bringing an undercurrent.

I messaged Marianne.

Let's go with it, then say we're having a long summer break. She'll get bored and latch on to someone else.

I just had to get through it on Thursday, then call time on Lydia.

Chapter Five

Lydia

Luca performed his usual 'Mac hunch' to stoke the hostile atmosphere. I wished he'd bugger off back to Germany. He put his earphones on in a pointed gesture. I retreated to my room, threw myself on the bed and screamed into the pillow.

Why was life so unfair? Drippy Emma got to breeze around, bankrolled by a rich, generous man. I deserved that, not her. I dug my nails into the pillow, my hands claw-like. Then I beat my fists against it. How could I get Emma out of the way? I grabbed the bottle of vodka I'd been eking out and took a swig. I smiled as I imagined pushing her under a bus on Esher High Street. How wonderful to live in a world of zero consequences and no CCTV.

The vodka calmed me, and I sat cross-legged on the bed to create a battle plan. It turned into a mind map of the people to win over: Elliot, his daughters, Marianne, even the poxy dog. A wall chart would help me keep tabs on the different elements, but I'd have to do it in code, so Rain Man didn't work it out. He might let that awful Rosa back in and I couldn't have her snooping.

Enough of this dump. I slicked on some lipstick and walked over to Jules's flat in Walton. She'd given me a list of everyone's addresses for book club. When I found her place, overlooking the river, she didn't respond to the buzzer. I sat on a bench in the mellow evening light.

Ages later, she came strolling towards me along the river.

'Lydia!' she said. 'Nice surprise. I went to see a film with a friend.'

'I met a friend too. Thought I'd stop off on my way home.'

'Coming in?'

We went up to her first-floor flat. Inside the cramped space, she flung open the balcony doors to let in some air. I surveyed the flat, stuffed with books and clutter, not a patch on Emma's place.

'Drink?' She picked up a bottle of gin from the counter in the tiny galley kitchen.

'Marvellous.' I smiled, sitting on the couch covered with a kilim throw. No awkwardness, unlike her sister, so I didn't resort to my book-borrowing excuse.

She poured the drinks. 'What do you think of book club?'

'It's fun. And lovely to take turns going around everyone's houses.'

'You've seen the best two.' She handed me a G&T, clinking with ice cubes. 'Not here – ha! – I mean Emma's. I hear you dropped in on her.'

'She has a lovely home.'

Jules sniffed, looked away and swigged her gin.

'No?'

'It's a lovely house, lovely kids, lovely dog.' Another nonchalant swig of gin.

'Lovely husband?' I ventured.

She paused. 'Don't tell anyone, but Em's not happy.'

'Not happy in her marriage?'

She sank low on the couch and swirled her gin. 'I know it looks like domestic bliss, but I think she wants more.'

I gave her a quizzical look.

'Don't get me wrong. She's a brilliant wife and mum, and Elliot likes her taking care of everything.'

'She's lucky to have a generous husband.'

Jules sat up straighter. 'Ignore me, I'm talking shit.'

'I like knowing what makes people tick. Couple watching is fascinating, isn't it? Whenever I see a married couple, I imagine them having sex.'

Jules nearly sprayed a mouthful of gin. She clamped one hand over her mouth and gulped. 'You're outrageous.'

'Do you like living alone?' I asked.

'Depends. I've lived with boyfriends, but it never works. I like my independence too much. What about you?'

I checked the time on my phone. 'God, it's late. I'd better go. Early start tomorrow.'

I walked home, bolstered by my progress. There was something sketchy about Jules. I was pretty sure her jealousy of Emma ran deep and she wanted to split them up. If she anticipated a spark between Elliot and me, would she fan the flames? How disloyal of the dominant twin, the loser in life, dragging her sister down to her level, living in a pokey flat.

When she talked about living with boyfriends, I could have told her about Danny, my first love. We could have bitched about men expecting you to be everything to them: lover, ego stroker, housekeeper. Jules would have loved that kind of talk.

Danny and I made a cool couple, way back. He ran his dad's car dealership and lived in a flat above the showroom.

His dad promised to buy him a house when he married the right girl. Danny told me early on, as if to say, *Stick with me, babe, and we'll have a nice house.*

I moved in. I always had my highlights done and kept my waxing appointments. I wore the perfume he liked best and made him my focus. I was the right girl. His dad always chatted to me. He fancied me, but his mum acted as if she had a bad smell under her nose.

Then Danny stopped noticing all the little things I did for him. He'd go out with his mates more than he would with me. He brushed off my plans for our next holiday. Undeterred, I walked around the flat in black lace underwear. I cheered him on when he played football, even when it pissed down. The more I gave, the less he noticed. A pressure built up inside me. One day, he watched rugby on TV and the four walls pressed in so much, I could've screamed. But I wanted that house.

I took a deep breath, tried to stay balanced. 'Shall we view the show homes at Minerva Meadows?'

He looked weirdly at me, as if I'd said, *Let's fly to Mars.*

'That new development near town?' I said. 'It looks lovely. Everything brand new. We could go into town in the evenings and walk home. We could have a hot tub on the patio.' I stroked his thigh to suggest raunchy fun in a hot tub.

He looked back at the TV screen.

'Shall we check out the show homes on Sunday?'

Nothing.

'It'll be fun.'

'I'm not keen on living there.' He scratched his neck.

'Where would you like to live?' I angled towards him, hope in my voice.

'It's okay here, innit?' He still didn't look at me.

'We could spread our wings. The show homes can inspire us.'

He turned up the volume and hunched forward, elbows on knees, as if I was spoiling the match.

'We've been together two years, Danny. Where do you see it going?'

'*Going*?' he snapped. 'I don't see it going to Minerva Meadows, that's for sure.'

I drew back. 'Do we have a future, you and me?'

'I don't want any more than this, to be honest.' He folded his arms.

I imagined grabbing his five-a-side football trophy on the windowsill, smashing it into his skull, knocking him to the ground. I went in the bedroom and punched his pillow, imagining it was him as I pummelled away. Then I grabbed my nail scissors and flung open his side of the wardrobe. How satisfying to slash his clothes. I laughed and imagined his face at seeing his favourite Hugo Boss suit ripped to shreds.

'What're you laughing at?' he said from behind me. I spun around, tucking the scissors in my pocket. He narrowed his eyes as if he didn't like what he saw.

After that, he froze me out. When I couldn't take any more, I moved in with a friend. Time apart would jolt the old Danny into wanting me back. Of course he'd want me back. My parting gift was laxatives mixed into the sugar canister, since he loved sweet tea. If the poor lamb felt unwell, he might beg me to come home and nurse him, since I was a caring person. But nothing. A few months later a so-called friend sought me out to say he'd got engaged.

Engaged? How could Danny do that? My Danny. Her family had money, apparently. Both sets of parents chipped in to reserve them a brand-new house. I fought the urge to trash his flat, then burn his lovely new-build to the ground. Serve the fucker right. I should have smashed his head in when I had the chance.

The next Sunday, I sneaked over late at night and opened the fuel cap of his Porsche 911. It only took super-unleaded, the premium stuff. I snickered as I poured diesel into the tank, along with syrup to clog up the pipes. He always got an early night on Sundays and went to the gym first thing Monday. The next morning, I followed him at a distance and saw the black smoke. Shame it didn't go up in flames with him in it, but he drove all the way to the gym, which must have damaged it. Bit careless, if you asked me. That's what happened when you didn't appreciate the good in your life. I met Vern not long after. He made me feel special.

Back at the flat, I drained my vodka and lay on the bed in a boozy haze, willing Elliot to have sweet thoughts of me. The smouldering heat of desire fired me up. The energy you sent into the world came back to you. I sent love to Elliot and channelled every ounce of my spirit into wanting him to want me. 'Elliot is mine,' I whispered. 'This one is going to be mine.'

Emma's journal

On that Thursday, I woke to dread thudding in my heart. Book club wasn't meant to be stressful, but I always hosted after Marianne and didn't reach her level of hospitality. She took pride in everything – her home, her cooking, her book choices – never any uncertainty with Marianne. Jules would say crack open the wine and get on with it, but book club wasn't just about the books. And Lydia was coming.

I texted Jules.

I'm telling Lydia it's cancelled. x

She'll know you're lying. Chill. I'll be there. x

You're making it worse. Don't encourage her. I mean it, Jules. x

Promise I won't encourage her. x

Elliot had rolled in at midnight last night after being out drinking. Sorry, *networking*, although God knows who'd do business with a drunk lawyer. He was so hungover in the morning that he couldn't pick up his wet towel from the bathroom floor.

My edgy state threatened to take over if I didn't keep moving. Staying busy would shake it off. I made coffee for Elliot.

'This coffee's too strong,' he said. 'It's making me feel ill.'

'Have some juice. I'll pour you a glass.'

'That'll irritate my stomach, not settle it.'

The girls shambled downstairs, subdued in the mornings apart from accusations of moving their charger or whatever else they'd lost. With Elliot running late, I walked Barney to escape his mood. At least Barney was always happy. His canine innocence reminded me of when the twins used to snuggle up. When I came home, Barney dozed while I cleaned downstairs.

It turned into one of those days. I couldn't find a parking space in town and walked half a mile in the rain for Elliot's dry cleaning, lugging back two shopping bags and his suits in slippery plastic covers. I managed an hour in the gym, since it was my set day. I could have skipped the workout, but the trick was to keep going, to stay busy. By late afternoon, nibbles were sorted and white wine chilled in the fridge. As an afterthought, I jotted down some notes on what to say about the book.

The girls came home when I was out on Barney's afternoon walk to tire him before book club. The rain wore off, leaving the sky the shade of a worsening bruise. I returned with a muddy dog to what should have been a clean kitchen, but Isabella and Chloe had left crumbs, globs of yogurt and pureed fruit over the worktops and floor again. Barney wouldn't let me clean his paws when he could snuffle up food scatterings, leaving paw prints and smears on the floor tiles. And they'd dumped sports kits in the hall, muddy trainers and everything, before going out for the evening. I cleared up again and saw they'd bloody well eaten my smoked salmon blinis. I'd do anything for them, but sweet Jesus, they wound me up. I caved and poured a splash of wine.

I ran my fingers through my damp hair from the drizzly dog walk. With just enough time to make myself presentable, I rushed upstairs and reached the bedroom as the doorbell rang. *Bugger.* I went down and opened the door to Lydia, looking stunningly overdone. Her glossy hair tumbled over her silky emerald-green dress, and she held up another patisserie bag. 'Macaroons!' She beamed. Who arrives twenty minutes early?

–

Half an hour later, I watched Lydia move around my kitchen filling crystal glasses with the white I'd chilled earlier. Rosa and Marianne eyed her with suspicion, while Lucy did a good poker face.

'What a good hostess you are,' Jules said to Lydia, accepting a glass of wine. 'Did you read tonight's book?'

'Yes, it's an *interesting* choice,' Lydia said.

'In what way?' Marianne asked.

'Well, it's about a marriage break-up.' Lydia's eyes flicked to me as she seamlessly topped up my glass.

Jules snorted and took a big gulp of wine. I ignored Lydia's snippiness. I hadn't had time to eat, and the wine was already going to my head.

'You know,' Lydia said, 'your home is beautiful. It makes me think, wow, here you are, perfect home and the perfect family.'

'Oh God, we're not perfect.' A smaller home would suit me once the girls left for uni. I hated the thought of rattling round without them. I directed my answer more at the others than Lydia. 'A lot of my favourite books have heroines who end up in a big house – Manderley, Thornfield Hall, Pemberley – but I prefer somewhere cosy.'

'Maybe you'll have a little place just for yourself one day.'

The room fell silent.

'Didn't you say you dreamt of that?' Lydia said, innocent-faced.

‘I think you’re twisting my words.’

‘Where does her husband figure in this?’ Marianne asked.

‘Big is beautiful.’ Lydia spread her arms wide. ‘It totally applies to this house.’

I reached for something positive. ‘Elliot’s done well in his career for us to afford it.’

‘You make his career possible,’ Marianne said. ‘He gets to have it all because you do everything around here.’

‘Even when he’s not working, he’s off cycling all day,’ Jules said.

‘Men didn’t have hobbies when I was your age,’ Rosa said. ‘They went to work and came home.’

‘Steve did go-carting,’ Lucy said.

‘*Go-carting*?’ Rosa struggled to comprehend. ‘With children?’

‘With men.’

She looked incredulous.

‘All that cycling’s given him a ripped body.’ Lydia nodded towards the family portrait on the wall.

‘Mmm,’ I picked up my book. ‘So, *Heartburn* by Nora Ephron, a fictional reworking of her marriage break-up. What does everyone think?’

‘I loved it,’ Marianne said. ‘Lots of anger but told with dark humour and recipes.’

Lucy had barely spoken. She might have been too raw for a marriage break-up book. Jules had chosen the book, and I kicked myself for not considering Lucy, who was still recovering from her divorce.

Marianne read a passage aloud about the character throwing a Key lime pie at her cheating husband, while wishing it was blueberry, which would have made a bigger mess. We all laughed, including Lucy. I relaxed a little.

'I could quote her all night,' Marianne said. 'What do you say, Lucy?'

'I'd never have thrown a Key lime pie at Steve. Waste of a pudding.'

'It sure is. It's Nora Ephron who said, "Be the heroine of your life, not the victim".'

'Always wear your invisible crown,' Lydia said.

We all looked at her.

'Coco Chanel,' she clarified.

'I can see you're wearing yours.' Marianne peered over the top of her reading glasses.

'I'd give this book to anyone going through a break-up,' Jules said.

'Who's going through a break-up?' Lydia perked up.

'Hypothetically. In the spirit of being a heroine, let's all choose a literary heroine.'

Lydia chose Cathy in *Wuthering Heights*. 'Because I'm passionate, like her.'

Marianne chose Scarlett O'Hara.

'Ooh, yes,' Lydia said. 'She's my second choice.'

Jules went for Lizzy Bennet in *Pride and Prejudice*. 'She didn't take any crap and she held out for what she wanted.'

'She didn't love Mr Darcy though,' Lydia said. 'She fell in love with his grounds at Pemberley.'

'That was tongue in cheek,' Jules said. 'She came to love him once she knew the real him.'

'Darcy wet from the lake would do it for me,' Lydia said.

'That didn't happen in the book, though, did it?' Jules hated it when adaptations eclipsed the book.

'I was named after Lydia in *Pride and Prejudice*.'

'Seriously?' Marianne arched an eyebrow.

'My mum thought Lydia had the most fun. Turns out that I'm ruled by my heart too.'

'Your mom was into literature?'

'She was into Colin Firth. I was born the year it came out.'

Rosa said her favourite was Esperanza from *The House on Mango Street*. 'My children loved her.' She smiled and her face lit up.

'Who's your heroine, Lucy?' I asked.

'Maggie Tulliver from *The Mill on the Floss* for preferring fictional characters to real people.' She glared at Lydia. 'I can relate.'

'Lydia,' Marianne said. 'What's your view on George Eliot?'

She swirled her wine in her glass and stood up to run her fingertips over the kitchen counter. 'His novels are dull.'

Marianne looked pleased with herself. Lucy opened her mouth to speak and thought better of it.

'What about you, Emma?' Lydia stood so close that her perfume enveloped me.

'Jane Eyre.' Obviously Jane Eyre.

'Interesting,' Lydia said with a head tilt, still standing over me. 'She walked out on her man.'

'She left when Rochester betrayed her, then returned on her terms.' The sharp edge to my reply surprised everyone, including me.

'It's no wonder his first wife went mad,' Marianne said. 'It's his fault she's clawing her way out of the attic. Why else would she set fire to his bed with him in it? I mean, wouldn't you?'

My body snarled up with tension. No way was Lydia coming back. Marianne looked at me as if assessing how offended I'd be if she spoke her mind. I raised my eyebrows sardonically, as if to say, go ahead and kick her out. That would be thrilling and mortifying all at once.

'You okay?' Jules asked. 'You look frazzled.'

'Oh,' I waved my hand dismissively, 'I've been rushing around, and the kids ate the nibbles I'd made specially.'

'My sons used to do that,' Marianne said. 'One time I took all morning to make a French pear tart with almond cream and amaretto poached pears. I walked in on them demolishing it like it were Oreo cookies. Thank God they've moved out. Saves a fortune in food bills.'

The girls came thumping in for a brief appearance, long enough to sniff out Lydia's macaroons before disappearing upstairs. She topped up my wine.

'You need a pick-me-up,' Jules said to me.

Lydia slapped her hands flat on the table. 'I know what…'

Everyone looked at her.

'You could be like…' She paused to think. 'Madame Bovary!' she said gleefully.

'Madame Bovary?' Marianne scrunched up her face.

'She had love affairs to spice things up. Emma needs an affair!'

Then the front door opened and Elliot walked in.

Chapter Six

Lydia

At last, Elliot breezed in, full of *joie de vivre*.

'Hello, my friends,' he said with genuine warmth, 'good to see you all.'

I loved his style. Great personality and proper sexy. His crisp white shirt set off his tan, and his rugged five o'clock shadow suited him. He hooked his jacket over the back of a chair and our brightened faces turned to him like flowers facing the sun. Even mean Rosa bloomed under the glow of his seductive charm.

Jules introduced him to me. He didn't give away that we'd met last weekend. How wonderful that we already shared a secret. Did he feel guilty for sneaking a look at my cleavage? He smiled, then said, 'Actually, we met on Sunday.'

He said it with nonchalance, clearly unwilling to give away our mutual attraction and wanting to throw the others off the scent. Wise move, Elliot.

'Yes. It's lovely to see you again,' I purred. There was something hypnotic about him. His unwavering gaze turned me as light-headed as Emma looked. But Elliot was the one intoxicating me, not the booze. I almost forgot to breathe. The others wittered on, but I conveyed a deeper meaning, returning his gaze.

Emma went even redder when he turned up. Talk of an affair must have hit a nerve. Jules gave her a look. *She'd love to split them up*, I thought. *She must be so jealous*. I returned my gaze to Elliot as he leaned on the kitchen island.

My heart raced. I could totally pull this off, kick Emma out and move into this glorious house with him. What fun we'd have. I imagined the master bedroom with a super-king bed, high thread count and luxurious en suite. Emma had decent taste in furnishings as well as men. It might be tasteful, but it was boring as fuck with no personality, like her. I'd introduce elements of me for colour and vibrancy.

We would christen my first night with champagne in bed. Cristal, ideally. I loved the glamour of money. Oh, to be wild and reckless without the threat of unauthorised overdrafts. I pictured living here with him, getting sloshed in the evenings, having sex on the worktop. We'd spend Sunday mornings lazing in bed, checking out exotic holiday destinations on his MacBook, only getting up for a gastropub lunch. I belonged here with him, once I'd dealt with Emma. I visualised Elliot giving me a flash car and a credit card so I could take off and treat myself. He'd also give me the keys to the house, of course. *Her* keys. We'd change the locks, since you couldn't be too careful.

I turned back to the women and took a sip from Emma's crystal cut glass. She had no idea what was coming. No idea at all.

Emma's journal

Elliot appeared and everyone lit up. 'Here's the handsome man of the house!' Marianne sing-songed and flung her arms wide.

'Hello, Marianne, you look fabulous.' He enclosed her in a hug. 'How's that husband of yours? Still winning on the golf course?'

Everyone forgot about book club. He made an impression, my husband, often just by walking into the room. People gravitated towards him at parties. He'd always had that *je ne sais quoi*, making whomever he talked to feel special. Even Jules made an effort and introduced Lydia.

He smiled his gorgeous smile and while he chatted, she greedily drank him in with her eyes, but he was used to adoring women. The others looked from her to me. I nearly clicked my fingers in front of her face and snapped, *I'm right here while you're eyeing up my husband.*

'You've made my favourite brownies! These are to die for.' He grinned at me and went to cram one in his mouth. 'What's the book? One about godforsaken orphans?'

Marianne chuckled. He was amusing, my husband.

'You're all so literary. You put me to shame with my techno-thrillers. Rosa.' He rubbed her shoulder. 'Your remedy for muscle strain works a treat. Thank you.'

He beamed his appreciation, and she beamed back. I saw him through their eyes, the way they responded to his engaging patter. He appealed more when I pretended to be someone who hadn't picked up his wet towels earlier.

Elliot coming home brought book club to an end. In the midst of everyone leaving, Isabella slunk in and reset the Wi-Fi router in the kitchen. She almost shot me a filthy look, since I sometimes turned it off by accident when dusting, but it was past their ten p.m. screen curfew so she stayed under the radar. I followed Marianne's loud voice to the hallway. Jules kissed me goodbye. The others did too, all except Lydia.

'I don't mind helping,' she said in the kitchen as I went back in.

'That's kind of you,' Elliot replied. 'But we'll manage. It's been lovely to see you again.' He kissed her on the cheek and guided her towards me.

'Thanks for coming.' I forced a smile and retraced my steps to the front door, opening it again.

'We'll do coffee soon.'

No chance. I never wanted to see her again. She air-kissed me and disappeared into the night. I cleared up while Elliot poured himself a brandy in the living room.

'Have you eaten?' I called through to him. 'I can do you something.'

'I had a late lunch and a panini on the train.'

I ran the water hot in the sink to wash the wine glasses. Elliot came and wrapped his arms around me. I turned my face to kiss him. He held me closer, his way of making up for his mood that morning. To meet Elliot, you'd think him blessed with natural charisma, but he had a vulnerable side. He cried when the twins were born. Neither of us could quite believe we had them. He promised to always look after us. Later that day, he went around our section of the maternity unit and chatted to the mums, admiring their babies in his endearing way. Then he came back and whispered that ours were the best. I looked around to check no one overheard.

'I'll take Barney for a quick walk,' he said. *Thinking time*, he called it, *for Barney*. They loved their walks together.

I was still gobsmacked by Lydia comparing me to Madame Bovary, who poisoned herself with arsenic.

Chapter Seven

Lydia

Four weeks to the murder

I'd invited Emma for coffee, suggesting we meet up today. She was busy, of course. She justified it by reeling off her movements, including driving her kids somewhere while Elliot went for a Saturday morning run. She mentioned his run as a stealth boast about her fit husband.

I lay in wait on the village green. Such an idyllic spot beside the duck pond and wooden cricket pavilion, circled by period properties. Little designer kids and au pairs fed the ducks and swans. I sat under a weeping willow with a view of the quaint village church, roses blooming beside it. It exuded calm and tranquillity. You wouldn't find shopping trolleys floating in this pond. Emma's charming house stood at the quiet end of the green, with the prestige properties.

I pulled out my mirror and checked that my Gucci sunglasses perched effortlessly on my head, sweeping my hair up with flattering tendrils tumbling around my face. *Look at me, Elliot, a casual girl about town who can't hide her hotness! And guess what? I'm ready to share my divine gifts with one lucky man.*

Two yummy mummies laid out a picnic blanket and shattered my peace. 'Milo loves the forest school, don't you, darling? Delilah, look at the swans. What colour are the swans? White! Yes. Aren't you clever?' God help those poor kids with that attention-seeker for a mother. 'No, don't throw teddy at the ducks. That's not kind.'

'Shut the fuck up,' I muttered, plucking a daisy and pulling off the petals.

The loud one wittered on about the extra value an extension would add to her house. The other one started up about the stress of getting into a school with the best Ofsted rating. They didn't know the meaning of stress. Stress was living hand to mouth. Some of us couldn't afford a rented bedsit in the grottiest part of Surrey. This middle-class enclave was way out of my reach.

I snarled, overcome with the urge to grab the louder one and drag her into the pond, kicking and screaming. My hands mimed ramming her neck underwater with enough force to keep her down until her last gurgling breath.

Then Emma came out with the teenagers trailing behind in jodhpurs and riding boots. Entitled brats. I would have loved to try horse riding. Leather boots suited me. She ushered them into her car and drove off. *Crash the car and die, bitches.*

Playing the waiting game, I admired my bronzed legs. I'd applied a careful layer of fake tan last night. I weighed up the differences between Emma and me. She was slim and nervy. Pretty once, but she'd let herself go. I was the right side of curvy and watched what I ate because, unlike some, I couldn't afford the gym. I took care of my figure and dressed to show it off. Men often gave me admiring glances. I was more than my cup size, but play to your assets. Determination was my best asset.

I pinged a message to Bookish Lucy, inviting her out for coffee. God knows what we'd talk about, since she'd no original thoughts, hung up on some dead author bloke called George. I could take her shopping maybe, be her personal stylist, then she'd owe me. I would tempt her away from Emma and have her as my loyal little lapdog. No swift response from dithering Lucy.

I'd also suggested coffee to Marianne, angling for an invite to her place. Another brush-off. I'd have to work harder to win her over. I didn't know her haunts, so couldn't accidentally bump into her unless I stalked her.

Talk of the devil, her name flashed up on my phone.

'Marianne, hi,' I answered. 'How are you?'

'Fine, fine. You still okay to meet up?'

'That would be fabulous.'

'How about a pub lunch on Monday, say one o'clock? I don't work Mondays and Crawford's on the golf course.'

'Wonderful,' I purred.

'Great. I'll make reservations and text you. We'll catch up then.'

'Looking forward to it,' I said warmly.

Marianne needed vibrant people like me in her life. I'd swallow the cost of a pub lunch to have her on my side.

Elliot appeared on the doorstep. I stood up, ready for action as he came my way in pristine running kit. Emma kept him too perfect, like her house. I bet she ironed his boxers. *Careful, Elliot, she's turning you into a bore.* But I'd fix that and turn him into a full-blooded metrosexual. He had the raw ingredients. I did love an athletic man: plenty of stamina, firm body. Boded well.

He started at a trot. I strolled towards him for our paths to cross. He spotted me and upped his pace. Good that he saw me as someone to impress. I gave him a dazzling smile from twenty paces.

'Hi, Barney.' I flung my arms wide for the stupid dog to come wagging up to me. 'Hi, Elliot. We meet again.'

'Oh yes, hi,' he said with a cautious smile.

'Out for a run?' I gave him my best grin, my wicked grin, the one that said I was up for anything. We'd be great together. He knew it too, but the luscious lawyer kept his cards close to his manly chest.

'Barney usually takes me for a run at the weekend. He likes you.'

Just as well, if he needed me to mind the dog on weekdays when Emma left. But he could kick out the dumb dog along with his dumb wife. 'I'd love a dog, but I'm single and working. Have you heard of BorrowMyDoggy.com? Dog lovers like me can sign up and look after dogs in the local area.'

'I bet you're popular. He's giving you the seal of approval.'

Why did dog people always think I would give a shit what their mutt thought of me? I tilted further forward to ruffle its ears and remind Elliot of my cleavage. I wanted to touch him – Elliot, not the dog – but couldn't be too forward. My skin tingled from seeing him again. I was like a thrill-seeking teenager hell bent on fun. 'What a lovely day! Thought I'd come out and have a speculative look for a flat.'

'Excellent,' he said. 'Property's a solid investment round here.'

As if I could afford to buy in prime Surrey commuter belt, or anywhere. But if he had me down as a buyer, he'd think me solvent and trust me more. I didn't say I'd already found my perfect house. His.

'We like living here,' he said. 'The schools are excellent.'

'I don't have children.' Wasn't I the perfect catch? Attractive, solvent, no kids. And I didn't want any, so no more whiny rug rats for him. Although I might get pregnant just by looking at him.

He cocked his head as if intrigued. His lips so kissable that I imagined them on my mouth, my body, hungry for me.

'My career's taken me abroad a lot, but I'm looking for a base now. Your twins are adorable.'

'Thank you. So, we might be seeing more of you.'

I fully intended for him to see more of me, given his interest in my boobs. But no need for innuendo when we already had a connection. A mutual admiration. I didn't give him my full-on vamp; he was married, after all. He signalled his interest with a smile and a gaze that said he was already into me. He swallowed my lies about flat hunting and the dog, accepting me as one of them. My refined accent helped me blend in.

He wasn't making any moves. I didn't take it personally, not out here where any nosy neighbours could spot him. But the gleam in his eye suggested the poor guy must be sex-starved to the point of forgetting what a decent shag felt like. *Fear not, Elliot, I shall awaken your libido.* He'd no idea how amazing it would be between us. And then he'd be mine for keeps.

'Why don't you take my number?' I said. 'In case you need help with Barney.'

'I'm sure Emma has it.'

'Useful for you to have it too, since I'm moving here.'

He wavered and scratched his head.

'You never know when you'll need someone to step in and help out,' I said sweetly. 'Emma said she's going to her mum's next week.'

'It's not necessary.'

Clearly he was too tempted to even take my number, knowing he wouldn't be able to resist calling me. *I get it, Elliot. I'll shine brighter than Emma until you're ready to sweep me off my feet.*

'Enjoy your run, marathon man.' I turned and walked away, flicking my hair and glancing back. He checked me out from behind. We caught each other's gaze. He gave me a boyish grin and jogged away. *Result.* I kicked off my shoes and did a barefoot cartwheel on the grass. To pull this off I needed the spark of attraction between us. How amazing that we had it. He was already magnetised by yours truly and my sexual prowess. You had to differentiate yourself from the competition. Be special to make an impact.

I did a happy dance to my car, imagining him naked. Naked and mine.

Emma's journal

I remember the day it turned weird, starting with Marianne in the farm shop. I'd dropped in for some fruit and veg to take to Mum's later that day. Marianne was loading up her trolley, so I went to say hi. She turned sharply and marched her trolley to the deli counter.

'Marianne?'

She looked over her shoulder and gave me a measured stare.

'What's wrong?' I asked.

Her lips tightened as if she'd resolved not to speak. She turned away and started ordering from the counter. What did I do? If I ever bumped into her, she launched into animated chat about food, books, family, whatever. When she finished ordering, I drew alongside and placed a hand on her arm.

'Are you okay?' I asked.

She looked down at my hand and sighed. 'I can't talk to you right now.'

I backed off and returned to selecting fresh peaches, hiding my upset at her snub. No time to speculate when I was going to stay at Mum's. Chloe and Isabella could go the whole stint on sandwiches, cereal and smoothies, but I prepped meals so they would eat with Elliot in the evenings. Marianne paid at the till, still pointedly ignoring me.

After unloading from the farm shop, I went to the gym. I did some weights and twenty minutes on the awful stepper thing. It killed my thighs, and I churned over Marianne's strange reaction. It still niggled at me when I walked Barney later, on the green under a dark, muggy sky. We were due a storm to clear the air. I weighed up whether to head home before it poured down, when a man I didn't know approached me.

'Hello.' He caught up and walked alongside me. 'That's a nice dog. I used to have a dog like that.'

I cast him a suspicious look. Dog walkers tended to chat, but he was alone.

'I've just moved to Esher. Are you from round here?' He studied me with a strange intensity.

'My husband and I live in the area.' I didn't like his weird energy.

'It's nice here, isn't it?'

I strode ahead, Barney pulling me along. The man kept pace.

'What's your dog's name?'

'I'm off now. My husband will be looking for me.' I doubled back towards home. 'Good luck with settling in.'

'Would you like a coffee?'

'No thanks.'

He kept stalking alongside me. 'It's been great talking to you. I'm Phillip.'

He held out his hand and I hesitated, not wanting to touch him. Without warning, he launched into an awkward hug, pressing his body against mine.

'No!' I pushed him away and backed off. My heart pounded at the shock of a man I didn't know pouncing on me. Barney barked to warn him off. 'Stay away from me.' I clenched my fists and marched off with Barney, who fired a filthy look at the man. My face flushed with heat.

'I'm sorry,' he called after me.

Bloody cheek. I held the lead and my mobile tighter to steady my shaking hands. Back at our front gate, Anne from next door deadheaded flowers in her garden. I tried to breathe normally, casting a look back to check he wasn't watching to see where I lived. I didn't want him turning up on the doorstep.

'Are you all right?' She peered at me. 'You look flustered.'

I scanned the green. He'd gone. 'I'm fine. Lots to sort out before going away. Thanks for saying you'll look in on Barney.'

'It's the least I can do. Looks like rain.' She squinted at the darkening clouds.

'It'll clear the air.' A bead of sweat trickled down the back of my neck.

No point in telling her about my strange encounter. A widow living alone might worry about a strange man on the green.

Chapter Eight

Lydia

On the Monday before Emma went away, I launched into phase two of my plan: turning her friends against her. They couldn't go sympathising with the wronged woman. I had to plant the seeds of doubt. Anyway, she wasn't that nice. She'd ghosted me since her book club night. The rest of them would see through her too. She'd brought it on herself.

Still no reply from dozy Lucy to my text about going for a coffee. Waste of space. She'd spent more time at Emma's fussing over the idiot dog than listening to me, like it was dog club not book club. She shared the mutt's level of intellect. It didn't matter, since I was meeting Marianne for lunch. I arrived to see her feeding ciabatta to the swans by the riverside pub. Even Surrey wildfowl had middle-class tastes.

Once inside, we started with her choice of Kir royale.

'Great place,' I said. We clinked glasses. From our window seat, I admired the river view and the pub's interior blend of vintage and contemporary styles.

'Crawford and I come here for Sunday lunch with the kids.'

I showed an interest in her sons and pictured Sunday lunches with Elliot. Vern and I used to have boozy Sunday lunches. Shame he couldn't stop once he'd started. I pushed my marriage from my mind. Couldn't have the past weighing me down.

'Tell me about you,' I said. 'Do you plan to stay in the UK?' She saw me as a kindred spirit in the personality wasteland of book club. My cut-glass accent appealed to Americans. They loved Brits with clear diction.

'Sure. I'm a fan of British culture.'

People loved talking about themselves. If I needed someone on my side, I took an interest in their dull life.

Marianne drawled on. 'Yesterday, I zipped down the A3 to Jane Austen's house in Hampshire.' She polished off her fizz. 'She's misunderstood from all the beautiful film adaptations, but life was tough back then.'

She ordered Chablis and seafood because 'they do fabulous seafood'. I chose a lower-cost halloumi salad and stuck to one glass of wine in case she ordered a second bottle and expected to split the bill.

'You're disciplined,' she said about the wine.

'I'm working this afternoon. Have to keep a clear head. Tell me about your fundraising.'

'I'm good at sales, but I don't like hawking stuff. I put my sales skills to use with a charity.'

Bugger that. I was good at sales too but lacked a banker husband to subsidise a do-gooder career. I once dated a City boy who liked to flash the cash in West End champagne bars but only when showing off to his insufferable mates.

I told people I worked in client relations, which was true when I temped in telemarketing. My skill set involved bringing people round to my way of thinking, gaining their trust, then closing the deal. The pickings were slim, the glory days over. Too many people hung up now society had become ruder.

'What about you?' she asked. 'What's your line of work?'

'High-level client relations.'

'What does that involve?'

'I head up a concierge service for wealthy clients.'

'Oh, fabulous.' She knocked back her wine.

'We arrange whatever they want – private jet hire, VIP access to money-can't-buy events, bookings in exclusive restaurants that mere mortals can't get into – you name it.'

In my official life story, I'd returned from working in Dubai and the US, although I didn't mention the US to Marianne in case she rumbled me. She swallowed it along with lots of wine.

'Rosa thinks you're unemployed.'

'What?' Fucking Rosa. I knew she was trouble.

'She says her friend's son lets you stay rent-free so long as you do the housework.'

'Ah well, his mother thinks I'm not suitable. He lets her think he's doing me a favour by letting me stay.'

'And is he?'

'Only until I find a decent place to live. He was abroad when I moved in, so I looked after the flat. It was an easy option when I returned from Dubai and had to hit the ground running. I won't stay longer than necessary.'

'Why does she think you're unemployed?'

'I mostly work from home. That's the thing with old people. They don't understand hybrid working.' I'd deal with Rosa one way or another.

'What's the company?' she asked.

'Sorry?'

'Who do you work for?'

'You won't have heard of them. It's a niche service, even the website is invitation only via a password.'

'What's it called?'

Shit. I'd have to wing it. 'Faulkner and Associates.'

She'd drunk enough to forget the details. Our food arrived, which distracted her.

'Hey, would ya look at those *moules-frites*!' She launched into them and talked about her first trip to Paris, where she loved the food and the Parisian lifestyle, and how she'd wanted to live in Europe ever since. When she began slurring, I returned us to the matter in hand.

'What do you think of the rest of book club?'

'They're a great bunch of gals. Jules is fun. I talked books with her in the bookstore where she works. That's how it started. Have you known her long?'

'A month or so.' Even less, in fact.

'Is that all? She was so keen to get you in. I thought you two went way back.'

'No. We met when I joined the tennis club. What about Emma? She seems reserved.'

'Most Brits are reserved compared to me, but yeah, she's quiet. Charming husband, isn't he? So handsome.'

No wonder she liked Elliot compared to her stuffed shirt of a husband. Literally stuffed with his elderly paunch. I pictured him reclined in front of Sky Sports, fiddling with his phone. All those women stuck in dull marriages, wedded to the lifestyle. Why shouldn't I take one for myself, although not Marianne's.

'Elliot seems nice. And Emma… well. It's always the quiet ones.' I gave a cheeky wink.

'Gorgeous kids. They look like Disney princesses. So well mannered. I wish mine had been like that. Blame the mother – ha!'

'I bet your kids have personality.' Not that I cared.

'Even the dog's adorable. You know the twins were conceived naturally? Not IVF. It's down to him. Superior sperm.' She sucked juice from her finger. 'Same with Roger Federer. If she'd had more kids it would've been a second set of twins.'

'She could be a dark horse,' I kept on.

'How so?'

'There's talk about her at the tennis club.'

'Emma? I didn't know she was a member.'

'People know her there, maybe through Jules. They say she's having an affair.'

'*An affair*?' She dropped her fork, aghast.

'That's why I joked about an affair at book club. To test her reaction. Then he walked in, and she went bright red.'

'Wait a minute.' She looked sharply at me. 'Who says she's having an affair?'

'Passing comments. Might be nothing. It's funny when she's quite possessive of him. She said you flirt with him.'

'Me? I was just talking to the guy. I'm a guest in their house, why shouldn't I?'

'I assumed you two aren't that close, from the way she talked about you.' I waved it away. 'I might've got it wrong.'

Her face clouded, but she kept eating with gusto.

After lunch, I walked along the river. With Emma going away, I could turn everyone against her, including her husband. It made sense to target the big mouth of book club first. If she blabbed to Emma, I'd say Marianne got drunk and took offence over nothing.

I'd done well to stay sober around that lot. I rewarded myself with a litre of voddy from the off-licence. Pat on the back for my incredible self-restraint while Marianne polished off the vino. At least she paid the bill.

Emma's journal

Nothing felt right and I didn't want to leave for my mum's. But I couldn't abandon her, so I stuck a list of Barney's routine on the fridge and called the twins to go through everything. Despite the weird guy on the green, I didn't tell them not to talk to strange men, since Isabella would huff about me treating them like children.

'Chloe, have you set a reminder for Barney's meal-times?'

She swiped at her phone and showed me the reminder. I pointed out the home-made lasagne and shepherd's pie in the freezer with written instructions for heating them up.

'Mum,' Isabella said. 'Will you stop fussing?'

'Phone me if you need anything.' I would stay two nights with Mum, after she was discharged. Her friends had arranged a rota for taking her to hospital and visiting until then.

I kissed the girls and Barney goodbye, loaded my holdall into the car and drove off. Leaving felt wrong. Dread seeped through me. Was it because of that strange man trying to hug me? Or the covetous way Lydia sized the place up and drank Elliot in, even as I watched her every move? Two hours later, when I'd parked at Mum's, Jules had messaged me.

I've got Rosa on the case.

Doing what?

You know the guy Lydia's staying with? Rosa's fact-finding. There must be some dirt on her. She's bound to have a past.

An image flashed in my mind of vampy Lydia clicking up the drive in her stripper heels, dangling a bag of macaroons and bad intentions, her face lighting up when Elliot opened the door.

Chapter Nine

Lydia

She's gone. From my vantage point on the village green, I watched her drive off. I went home and made myself beautiful, keeping my eye on the prize.

I returned to see Elliot's red Ferrari on the drive. Spurred on, I rang the bell. My stomach flipped with first-date excitement. The dog barked and one of the daughters came to the door. *Bugger.* Didn't teenagers go out in the evenings or shut themselves in their bedrooms? I always did.

'Hi, is your mum in?'

'No.'

'I'm Lydia from her book club. Do you know when she's back?'

Elliot appeared from the kitchen in a T-shirt and chinos, followed by the galloping mutt licking its manky chops from eating. I leaned forward to pet the dog and remind Elliot of my boobs. The girl shambled off.

'Hello again.' I looked up and smiled. 'Just dropping off Emma's cardie. She left it when I saw her for a coffee.' I handed him the pink cardigan from my bag, which I'd swiped during her book club evening.

'She's away at her mum's.'

'Ah, yes. I forgot. How are you managing?'

'All good. Emma left supper, and my daughters are clearing up. Thanks for bringing this over.'

I sank down on my heels. 'How are you, Barney? Still taking your dad for walks?'

'Full of beans, aren't you, Barney? We're off for a walk now. I like taking him out in the evening.'

'It's a lovely evening for fresh air and exercise. I've been stuck in the office all day. Shall I join you?'

He was too polite to refuse. He fastened the lead, and the dog pulled him outside. I expected us to saunter round the green in full view of the neighbours, but Muttley raced us towards the woodland alongside the village. The stupid thing wheezed ahead, straining on the lead. I half jogged to keep up in my wedge sandals.

'It's lovely round here.' I tried to sound breathy instead of out of breath.

'We like the village feel. It's a nice place to bring up children. Are you okay?'

'Sure.' Although it was a warm night and we were powering along. My words came out in gasps. 'I like a walk…' I gulped air. '…in the evening.'

'We used to live in London, then we came further out when the babies outgrew the flat.'

'They're lucky girls.' Another big breath. 'So well mannered.'

'Thank you. They're bright kids, especially Isabella. She takes after me. She has a legal brain.' He gave me a boyish grin and I forgave his boasting.

'You must be proud.'

'I am. Isabella's brilliant. Chloe takes after her mum. She's arty. They're both lovely.'

It amused me that he favoured one child yet pretended to love them equally. Isabella was the one to win over. If the arty one was like Emma she'd fall into line. We passed the last house and continued on the sleepy road alongside the woods. The encroaching dusk had an eerie feel, giving me a reason to walk closer to Elliot.

'Have you handled any big-name divorces?' I asked, getting my breath back.

'Yes, but I don't talk about them. They like their privacy the same as everyone else.'

'Do you enjoy it?'

'I enjoy helping people sort out their lives. Divorce is difficult, but it's often for the best. It's rare to see a client who hasn't thought things through and who didn't try to make it work.'

He was far less mercenary than I'd imagined.

'And if the parents are arguing or communication's broken down, divorce is better for the children in the long run.'

I focused on walking without stumbling. 'It's not all men trading their wives in for a younger woman?'

'You'd be surprised at how many women initiate divorce, but it might be prompted by the husband's infidelity. People change over time. They want different things from when they met. Sometimes they have to face the reality that they don't love each other. I take some of the burden off their shoulders.'

I liked his compassion, his hidden depths. 'I bet you do it very well.'

'I'm not sure about that.' His smile turned self-effacing. 'I do my best for the people involved.'

I stroked his ego. If he saw me as someone who appreciated him, it would bring us closer for when I moved in for the kill, any minute now.

‘What brings you to the area?’ He gave me a warm smile of encouragement.

I told him about my sparkling career in New York and Dubai. ‘I’m here to restructure the London office. I love what I do. It’s important to work hard for what you want to achieve.’

‘Where’s your office?’

‘Canary Wharf.’

We turned into the woodland. A man passed us on his way out with two panting dogs. He said ‘evening’ and left us to walk into the cool, earthy dusk of the woods. Elliot let his dog off to race along the path. The woodland secluded us from prying eyes as darkness began to fall. I revelled in my mounting excitement.

‘Do you mind Emma going away?’

‘We miss her.’ Another smile, rueful that time. ‘She does a fantastic job of keeping everything running smoothly.’

‘You’re trusting to let her go.’

‘She’s only visiting her mum.’

‘Yes, but…’

He looked sideways at me.

‘How long have you been together?’

‘Since university. It’s our twentieth anniversary next year.’

‘Wow. You’ve done well to stay together, considering you married young.’

He didn’t reply.

I grasped a wispy branch and yanked it, crushing the leaves in my hand. We’d gone deeper into the darkening woods. Time to deliver my bombshell. ‘Elliot?’ Nervous energy bubbled up. ‘I have a confession.’

Adrenaline coursed through me. He turned to face me, eyes narrowed, getting the measure of me.

'I knew Emma was away. It's you I came to see.'

He plunged his hands in his pockets and eyed me warily.

'There's something you should know. I couldn't say it with your daughters around.'

'What?'

'This isn't easy.' I bit my lip for effect. 'You're a nice guy. I bet you work hard for your family. My ex cheated on me, and I wish someone had told me before everyone else knew.'

'What are you saying?' He stepped back, his face appalled.

I pulled my phone from my pocket, called up a photo and tilted the screen towards him. He came close and cupped his hand behind mine holding the phone. It felt intimate, his face inches from mine, so close I could kiss him. I could reach forward and kiss his lips, but he leaned into the photo.

Emma was turned away from the camera, unmistakably her, the tip of her nose visible, hair a mess from walking the dog. She stood in a clinch with a lanky man. He embraced her, lips puckered as if kissing her hair.

'Who is he?'

'She confided that they're having an affair.'

Frozen to the spot, he stared at the photo, mouth fixed in a grim line. I touched the screen to stop it fading out.

'I hate doing this, but I have a thing about infidelity.'

'Where was this taken?' He looked at me, and then back at the phone, still not quite taking it in.

'On the green. She's getting reckless, as if she wants to be caught. You need to know in case people are gossiping.'

'Are you certain she said it's an affair?'

I nodded. 'I told her she had to stop or come clean to you. I said for her to think it through when she goes to her mum's – if that's really where she's gone – and then come home and deal with it.'

'And?'

'She just laughed and, well…' I bit my lip again.

'What?'

'Sure you want to hear this? I don't—'

'Tell me.'

'She says it's better with him… the, um, sex. She's bored apparently and can't give him up. I get the impression she's staying with you because of the girls. But it's not right, is it?'

He stepped back and clutched the top of his head with both hands. Poor Elliot. So much for him to take in. It wasn't even a great photo. That man could be any random bloke who hugged her too close before she pulled away.

'Who is he?' Elliot asked. 'How does she know him?'

'I don't know.' Anguish came through in my voice. 'I'm sorry for being the one to tell you. It's just that I believe in family values. If you're with someone, make it work or leave. Don't go creeping round behind his back. You deserve better.'

'I don't believe it,' he said plainly.

'I recorded her too.'

He gawped at me. 'What did you record?'

'Her telling me about it.'

He looked at me, incredulous.

'I know it's mean, but I knew you wouldn't believe it on the basis of one photo which she could explain away.'

He straightened up. 'Play it.'

I took out my phone and called up the voice memo app. My hands visibly shook. 'You sure?'

'Play it,' he repeated.

I tapped the screen.

'He's not a bad person.' Emma's voice played out amid background noise of conversations and a coffee machine grinding and frothing. 'But I need more. We only have the kids in common and they're leaving next year.'

'Is it wise to have an affair?' My voice sounded grave.

'I didn't plan it. We're being low-key until next year.'

'You're keeping it secret until then?' I asked.

'I'll get my ducks in a row and leave him.'

Elliot stood rigid, one hand covering his mouth.

The recording ended. Hands still shaking, I fumbled with the phone. 'Shit, I deleted it.' I dropped the phone. 'Sorry. I was so nervous about telling you, I'm all fingers and thumbs.' My voice wobbled.

He picked the phone up and handed it back. I grabbed his hand that held my phone.

'I'm so sorry, I shouldn't have told you.' I leaned in to hug him, the two of us united in our upset. Elliot let me hug him, one arm awkwardly on my back. *Mmm*, it felt good pressed against him. *He* felt good with his firm muscles and reassuring manliness. I nestled in, enjoying the chance to sample his manly physique.

As for Emma's affair, my waster friend, Phil, had done the honours. Everyone needed a mate with no money or morals to help them out. I wanted Phil to hit it off with her, but just setting up the kiss was a big ask. He could pass for a literary hermit, so Emma might have surprised me by warming to him.

I told him to cover his tattoos and had to buy him a long-sleeved top from the nearest charity shop. Then

I dragged his complaining arse to the village green and rehearsed his cover story. I promised him a pouch of Golden Virginia to feed his sorry nicotine habit. He was twitchy because I wouldn't let him smoke for the two hours we waited for Emma to come out with the dog. I made him chew fresh-mint gum to mask his stale ciggy breath. Fortunately, he wasn't stoned. He got ratty with me for insisting we role-play. I acted the part of Emma and put on a wimpy little-girl voice. When she finally appeared with Muttley, I sent him to befriend her.

Emma must have felt sorry for him. He managed an embrace of sorts, more of a grapple, which I filmed on my phone. She pulled away sharpish, but I got a suitable photo from the video of him kissing her hair. He even angled his kissing face towards the camera, earning his baccy.

Elliot stepped back from the embrace. 'You need to send me that photo, okay?'

I bit my lip to hold back the smile trying to spread over my face.

'Fuck.' He turned away and kicked at a rock. 'Everyone knows except me.' He looked on the verge of storming off.

'I don't think anyone knows yet.'

'Marianne was waiting outside when I got home.'

'Marianne?' I froze, held my breath.

'I play golf with her husband. She heard gossip about Emma having an affair and said I should talk to her.'

I breathed again. My lunch with Marianne had worked a treat. Thank God she wasn't still there when I arrived. 'What did you say?'

'I didn't believe her.'

'Thing is, Marianne knows her well. Women don't often go behind a friend's back like this. She must think you need to know.'

He kicked the rock again, deep in angry thoughts. He couldn't avoid the facts when two different people had told him. And the evidence was damning, thanks to the magic of AI.

Phil was a conspiracy theorist and keyboard warrior whom I'd met in the off-licence. He'd never tried voice cloning but, between the two of us, we made a decent fist of it. I'd recorded Emma at every opportunity. Then I chose short, common words for her script, which Phil then muffled and overlaid with background noise. I deleted the recording to avoid Elliot listening again and detecting the robotic cadence, even though it suited Emma, the robo-wife with zero personality.

'What can I do to help?' I asked.

Silence.

Fortune favoured the brave, so I manoeuvred to face him. He raised his hurt eyes to mine. I stepped closer and licked my lips. Kiss me. Kiss me. *Kiss me. I'll make it worth your while.* He didn't move, so I lowered my gaze, looked shyly at him and then I kissed his cheek. 'I'm sorry for what's happening, Elliot,' I murmured. 'You're so lovely.'

'I don't want an affair,' he said.

'Neither do I.'

He wanted stability, not a fling. With a look of near resignation, he leaned in and kissed me on the lips. Eyes shut, ego bruised, he took revenge on Emma. I handled his lack of affection for the sake of demonstrating my availability. My hands roamed up his strong abs. He relaxed into it and his lips became less tentative. His kiss was sublime, soft yet sexy. I revelled in the illicit thrill of drawing him in.

He pulled back. *Shit*. I was losing him. He whistled for the dog and headed back down the path in the subdued dark. The dog bounded ahead of him, and I followed. Was that it? Would he even speak to me again? We reached the woodland entrance beside the small parking area. He stopped and paced around, running one hand through his hair, too agitated to go home yet. I sat on a low fence made of logs. When he looked my way, I patted the space beside me. He perched next to me and stared straight ahead.

'I know it's a shock,' I said. 'But don't rush into a bust-up. Hold off until she's back. Then you'll have a clearer idea of how to deal with it.'

He leaned forward to rest his elbows on his knees, hands clasped in front of his mouth as if in prayer.

'Where's your phone? I'll pop my number in.'

He didn't move.

'So I can send you the photo.'

He tapped his phone and passed it over. I added my number to his contacts and pinged a message to myself, ensuring I'd captured his.

'The girls will wonder where I am.'

I touched his arm. 'Take it easy.'

He stuck out his lower lip in contemplation.

'If you'd like to talk, call me, even if it's the middle of the night.'

'But she's your friend.'

'Not now. Not after what she's done.'

'Will you tell her I know?' he said.

'I won't breathe a word to anyone.'

We walked back in silence. I broke away from him before we reached the green, so the neighbours didn't see us slinking back after dark.

'Goodbye, Elliot.'

Eyes full of hurt, he nodded in acknowledgement.

'Call if you need me.' I wanted him to need me.

Emma's journal

'Did you leave the gas on?' Mum had recovered enough from her surgery to fret. *Is the back door locked? Can you close the bathroom window?* She stayed tuned to a negative frequency, her life a minefield of dangers.

Elliot hadn't replied to my text.

'Is your car all right out there?' She was propped in front of the TV, her feet on a padded footstool.

'It'll have to be. I can't bring it in, can I?'

'Yes, but if I had a garage… Did I tell you about that woman who went on a cruise?'

'What woman?'

'A woman in the *Daily Mail*.'

I tried not to roll my eyes the way Isabella did with me.

'She got food poisoning on the boat and they put her off at the next harbour. Just left her there, being sick.'

The walls closed in. Mum watched the hourly weather forecast on the BBC News channel.

'Rain's spreading in from the east.'

'It doesn't matter.' I brought her a cup of tea. 'You're not going anywhere.'

'Oh, you've got the mug with the birds on. My birds are dead.'

I needed to stop checking the clock on the mantelpiece, since the time dragged even more. I opened my book but couldn't read more than a sentence without her speculating about blocked drains or telling me what shops had closed down. She'd always been an old mum, having us after years of trying to conceive. In photos from back then, she looked old before her time.

Dad left when we were nine. We saw him on Saturdays until we were teenagers and then he faded from our lives. Mum scraped by, working as a cleaner and at the local newsagent until a supermarket opened and she worked on the checkouts until retirement.

The doorbell rang, and I gave up on reading.

'That'll be Sandy,' Mum said.

Her friend bustled in with a pineapple and some Ferrero Rocher. 'Don't sit there all day,' she said to Mum. 'Move around or you won't get up again.'

'The hospital said to rest.'

'My kids gave me a tandem skydive for Christmas,' Sandy said. 'I told them I want another one for my birthday.'

'Good for you,' I said.

'Live life while you can.' She went through to put the kettle on.

'You're a long time dead,' Mum called through. 'Emma always has her nose stuck in a book.'

'I love Jack Reacher,' Sandy called through, 'but you gotta go out and have fun too.'

I went upstairs to text the girls. Still nothing from Elliot. An hour later, Sandy left, the door slamming behind her.

'Are you all right up there?' Mum called.

'I'll be down in a minute.'

'*Pointless* is starting.'

I came out of the bedroom. She stood at the foot of the stairs, holding the remote.

'It's *Pointless*.'

'I know.'

No wonder Elliot refused to visit. A text pinged through from Jules.

> You okay, lovely? x

At least someone back home was talking to me. I phoned and updated her on Mum. Then we moved on to Lydia.

'What if she's with him right now?' I said.

'She's not.'

'I saw how she acted towards him in front of me.'

'She'll try getting a foot in the door, but Elliot won't let her in with the kids there.' I heard laughter in the background, meaning Jules was out. She was always out. 'I have to go. Stop worrying. Love you.' She hung up.

Holed up in Mum's fusty spare room, my thoughts took on a darker tone. I couldn't help it, with Lydia on the prowl. When Mum went to bed, I read my novel until late. Before I turned off the light, Chloe texted a string of hearts.

Lucy had picked a courtroom drama for the next book club. A he said/she said. It struck a chord, working out who was telling the truth when it was the woman's word against the man's. Elliot said people rarely told the whole story if it involved wrongdoing, and they'd be mad to give away their power. He would say that.

Chapter Ten

Lydia

My heart soared the next morning when Elliot messaged me.

Please send me the photo of Emma.

I deflated, but pinged it over.

Here it is. How are you, Elliot?

Not great.

I had to raise my game, prove myself a viable alternative to Emma. An hour later, his number flashed up on my phone. My pulse raced. I answered with a kittenish, 'Hello.'

'Sorry to disturb you.' He sounded all business. 'But you said to call if I wanted to talk.'

'Of course,' I purred. 'How are you feeling?'

'I just got off the phone to Marianne Jennings.'

Fuck. Why couldn't I work on him without these distractions? 'What did she say?'

'I wanted her take on the situation with Emma. Since she knows what's going on.'

Typical lawyer, seeking out the evidence. Marianne gave credence to Emma's affair, but she'd play marriage counsellor and might alert Emma.

'And?'

'Marianne heard talk of an affair at the tennis club. She didn't want to believe it, but she noticed Emma drinking more and thought she was acting differently.'

That worked to my advantage.

'Emma's a dark horse,' I said carefully, not wanting to rile him. 'Shall I come over this evening?'

Silence.

'So we can chat.'

'My daughters will be home.'

'Are you walking Barney later?'

'We can meet at eight thirty in the woodland car park.'

'That suits me.' We'd had our first kiss there, albeit with him seething over the photo and not thinking straight. This time I'd make it meaningful. He'd handled the call with no attempt at sweet talk, but he'd taken me into his confidence. I'd help him recover from Emma's betrayal.

He had to fall for me. I'd fire up the pleasure centre of his brain with a heady mix of passion and desire. It didn't take long to work out a man's specific desires. *Et voila*. Alpha males were hardwired to fall for women like me. All that testosterone had them craving forbidden fruit, like those politicians caught with their trousers down.

I arrived early and parked in the darkest corner of the woodland car park, so Elliot wouldn't see my crappy car. I sat on the low wooden fence and aimed for my best 'girl next door' look. He turned up, his body tense, his dark eyes and clenched jaw signalling his hurt. The dog raced along the path, more interested in the woodland than me, thank Christ. I stood up and Elliot loomed in for a kiss on the lips. He pulled back to check I was game, since we'd both said last night that we didn't have affairs. I was worth more than a cheap fling. As for Elliot, his bruised ego urged him on.

We followed the woodland path, neither of us talking. He turned to me and I smiled demurely. He took my hand and led me off the path and through the undergrowth, drawing me into secluded darkness. We stopped at a clearing beside a huge oak tree, which Elliot manoeuvred me against. He cupped my face and kissed me. I enjoyed the kiss and the sensation of his other hand roaming from the neckline of my dress down to my thigh. He started unbuttoning me.

'Gosh,' I murmured, toying with the buttons on his shirt. 'I wasn't expecting this.' My modest smile showed it was a pleasant surprise.

'I shouldn't be doing this.' He breathed heavily. Urgency fired his lust. We both felt the palpable thrill out there in the secluded twilight clearing where anyone could steal up on us.

'Feels wonderful though,' I said.

He pressed against me, properly hard, and started pulling up my dress.

I cast a look around. 'Oh, Elliot, it's too risky. Anyone can see us.'

'No one's here.' He tilted my face to him and kissed me deeper, one hand roaming up my bare thigh.

'You're gorgeous. I'd love to get to know you better, but we don't want the police arresting us.'

'That won't happen.'

I bit my lip to convey the forbidden nature of my lust for him and ran my index finger over his strong biceps. A branch snapped underfoot. Elliot pulled back. He scanned around. It was probably the dog snuffling through the undergrowth.

I placed my fingertips on my lips as if savouring the memory of his kiss. 'We'd better go.'

He looked dejected, but an al-fresco quickie set the wrong tone. He wanted me and I had to keep him hooked.

'Can we meet again before Emma's back?' I asked.

'She's back tomorrow night.'

My voice lowered to a murmur. 'We can arrange something more private before then.'

He texted me after I came home.

> I'm dropping my daughters at college in the morning. I can come to you at 9 a.m. for a short while? X

> My flatmate works from home. Shall I drop in on you at nine? x

> Ok. X

An invitation to the house. My last chance to work on him before Emma returned. The next morning, I slipped on a figure-hugging dress and my prized Christian Louboutin stilettos. I looked expensively understated, so he wouldn't mistake me for a bargain-basement gold digger. I'd never had a date first thing in the morning, but with Emma back this evening, I had to pull rank on her. Emma was the type to allow a grudging fuck once a week. I intended to do it anytime, with pleasure, starting in the next half-hour.

At Elliot's, I rang the bell and stepped back to give him the best view of me. The dog went into a yelping frenzy. Elliot opened the door, one hand on the dog's collar. He smiled to say he liked what he saw.

'Hel-*lo*.' I smiled sweetly.

He freed Muttley, or whatever it was called, and the bloody thing launched onto me. I fended it off, trying to look sexy and keep up my dog-loving credentials while it bounced around me.

'Just as well you like dogs,' he said as I stepped inside, trying not to fall over the bloody thing.

Elliot looked hungrily at me and launched straight in for a kiss.

'I want you,' he murmured into my ear.

I thought he'd need warming up, but no. He shut the door and kissed me deep, palms on my hips, guiding me to him. He smelled of money: a heady mix of success, testosterone and rich man's aftershave. Blood rushed to my head and other parts of my body. His hand found my breast, circling around it, his breathing fast. I wanted to pull back and draw him in with some teasing moves, but we had a tight schedule.

'You're so sexy, Elliot.' My shallow breathing brought a seductive note to my voice.

His hand roamed up my dress to my thigh. It might be revenge sex for him, but we weren't having a quickie against the wall. I gave him my best *come hither* look.

'Why don't you show me the bedroom?'

He took my hand and led me upstairs. I kept on my Louboutins and smiled because I bet Emma banned shoes on the upstairs carpet. Carpet was the last thing on Elliot's mind and we went up two flights to a guest suite. It looked like a boutique hotel room in shades of dove grey and blond wood, understated yet expensive-looking.

'If the girls come home unexpectedly, they won't look up here.'

How tedious to work around them, but they'd know who the boss was soon enough. I unzipped my dress and stepped out of it in one graceful movement. He took in my figure, perfectly framed with silk and lace, my legs sexy in high heels. I watched his pupils dilate with lust. Anticipation rushed through me. God, the fun we could have together. He went to pull me onto the bed, but I resisted.

'Let's take your mind off what's been going on.' I unbuttoned his shirt. 'Oh my, what a gorgeous body you have.'

I admired his toned physique. What a total catch. Why had no one else snapped him up? He looked pleasantly surprised at my appreciation. His complacent suburban wife must have blinded him to his hotness. I bent forward to remove my shoes, burlesque-style. I left one upturned to show the trademark red of my classy footwear. He whipped off my sexy lingerie and sat on the bed to yank at his socks, not taking his greedy eyes from me.

'Let me give you some stress relief.' I eased him back onto the bed and climbed on top, in control, teasing, kissing, exploring with my mouth. At one point I turned my gaze to his face and he looked down at me with utter surprise that any of this was happening. My hands went to work with a light massage in the right places. He lay back and sighed. I had him exactly where I wanted, showing him the silver lining of Emma's affair. I loved claiming him and making him mine.

'I'll explode if we don't… soon.' His face determined, he eased himself inside me.

I stayed on top and kept up a steady rhythm. His breathing quickened, I tilted my upper body towards his. His hands tangled in my hair, a look of exquisite pain on his face as if he couldn't bear it, along with his wife's infidelity. He groaned, satisfied, and lay back with his eyes closed, breathing audibly. I lay alongside him and stroked his chest. I must have glowed from effort and sheer delight.

He'd settled a score with Emma, but this wasn't a one-off. I hadn't come this far for a charity fuck. I only had sex with a new man if it led somewhere beneficial. I would make him powerless to resist my charms.

'What about you?' he said.

I guided his hand and showed him how to make me come quickly. He needed to think of himself as a stud who could turn me on, although his approach was somewhat teenagery. Once we'd rid ourselves of Emma, I could mould him into a considerate lover. Until then, this would give him a taste of how his life could become better than he'd imagined.

'You're very handsome.' I gazed into his eyes.

He smiled dreamily, lay back and fell asleep. Not what I'd intended, but he felt at ease with me. I watched his sleeping face, angelic and untroubled. I resisted the temptation to run my fingertips through his thick dark hair and kiss his lips, slightly parted in sleep. Such kissable lips.

Careful not to wake him, I took a quick shower and put my sexy lingerie back on. We could fit in a second shag when he woke up, but I bet once a day satisfied him. His phone pinged with a message. He woke and checked the time.

'Hey, hot stuff.' I smiled down at him. 'Shall we have a coffee?' I said before he got rid of me. Such a poor show, inviting me over without offering me a drink.

'Sure.'

Sharing a coffee would normalise our fledgling relationship so he didn't mistake me for a sex worker. I slid my dress back on and followed him downstairs. I checked out the master bedroom on the way, admiring its tranquil simplicity. When I moved in, I would introduce some accent shades of red for a touch of passion.

'You have a beautiful home.'

'We chose everything together. I like a certain style.'

'You have superb taste.'

We went downstairs and the bastard dog jumped up and scratched at my dress.

'Careful, darling,' I said.

'He has a thing for you. He doesn't usually jump up. Emma has him well trained.'

She had Elliot well trained too. He made coffee from the shiny coffee machine.

'Working from home?' I nodded towards the notepad and files on the kitchen table.

'It was an excuse to see you. I'd better head in.'

I accepted the mug of coffee. 'Have you found out anything about Emma?'

'No. She's texted, but I haven't spoken to her. Yet.'

'Take your time,' I said soothingly. 'You're still coming to terms with it.'

'I'm too angry to speak to her.'

He was a passionate man, so he could channel it my way. He leaned against the kitchen island and knocked back his coffee.

'Will you wait till she's home?' I asked.

'She's home later. I'll have it out with her then.'

'Is it something you can forgive?'

'From what you and Marianne say, she's into this *person*, whoever he is. I need to know what's happening from her.'

'What if she denies it?'

'I have the evidence, thanks to you,' he said sourly, draining his coffee. 'But this is our home. I don't want to leave.'

'Why should you leave?' I asked, innocent-faced.

'We can't both live here. I know people do. They try living separate lives, but it's not ideal. I can tell you stories of clients going down that route.'

'I don't mean both of you live here. If a wife found her husband cheating on their doorstep, she'd send him packing. It should follow for a man whose wife is having an affair.'

'But the girls need looking after, the dog needs walking, the shopping… Emma does it all. If she takes the girls, I'm left rattling round here alone.'

'There is another way.' I tapped my top lip as if it had just pinged into my head. 'Let's say she leaves. When you tell the girls what she's done, they'll be devastated, but they'll take your side. This is their home. Why should they leave when they've done nothing wrong?'

'Yes, but I can't run the house.'

'I'm just thinking aloud.' I paused for effect. 'If the girls stay here with you, they'll have stability. Emma can go and sort her head out. Then what if I help you hire a housekeeper?' An old trout, obviously, who wasn't any competition. 'Meanwhile, I can fill in the gaps, like walking Barney. And I'll look after the man of the house.' I gave him a coquettish look.

His expression changed to one of interest.

'And you'll keep the girls, because I can see how much they adore you, and why should the three of you suffer?'

'I like your thinking.'

'Not just a pretty face!' I only needed a foot in the door. The daughters wouldn't want to live in reduced circumstances, not if I had anything to do with it. They'd have fun with me around. They'd appreciate me not giving them the third degree about where they were going. And once I'd moved in, I wouldn't care if they were out all night, meeting strangers off the internet, so long as they stayed out of my hair.

He checked his watch.

'And now, handsome, I'm going.' I reached in for another smooch, giving him something to remember. 'I'm meeting someone in Walton for a drink this evening, but let me know how you get on.'

His face dropped. 'Who are you meeting?'

'A friend. I promised him.'

'When will I see you again?'

'Text me.' I headed for the door, and he followed.

'I'd like to see more of you.'

'I'd like to see more of you too. What I've seen so far is lovely.' I turned and kissed him goodbye. His soft, warm lips tasted of coffee. 'We'll work something out.'

He looked crestfallen as I walked out. Good. I'd left him wanting more. He'd had his taster session. He could have amazing sex on tap, which had an allure for a red-blooded man. He messaged me after I left.

Thanks… for everything. X

I peeled off my dress in Luca's depressing back bedroom with its tired beige carpet and flat-pack furnishings. I suspected Emma's bathroom didn't have black mildew that refused to shift. The crappy bedroom reminded me of my room when we first came to England. Until then, I'd lived in a sun-drenched Spanish villa with its own pool. I virtually lived in that pool. We had barbecues and I ran around barefoot. Dad would drive us to the beach. Then one day, Mum dropped a bombshell.

'We're going home.'

I didn't understand. 'But we are home.'

'We're going back to England.'

I knew about England. I'd seen *EastEnders* and heard my parents talk about growing up there, but it didn't appeal. 'We live here.'

'Not any more. It's being sold.'

That's when she told me the villa wasn't ours. They'd been looking after it for a friend of my dad's. The friend was coming out of prison and wanted his villa back.

'We can get our own villa,' I'd said.

'We don't have the money. We have to go home.'

I boarded a plane for the first time in my eight years, with my parents and little brother. We flew back to a cold and rainy Luton. Christ, the shock of it. Ritchie cried the whole time from when we stepped off the plane.

We ended up in a grotty maisonette in Southend. It felt like my childhood ended. I couldn't believe how my life had been reduced. British weather, awful school, the dump of a home. I wanted to burn that block of flats to the ground. School too. I loathed the unfairness. My parents argued all the time and I hated them for ruining my life. I'd lie awake in bed, dreaming of having a villa with its own pool again.

I kept Elliot hanging on and didn't reply to his thank-you text until lunchtime, since I was girl-bossing at Canary Wharf.

Pleasure's all mine. Hope to see you soon.
xx

By creating a sexual high and then pulling back, the power balance moved towards me. Acting as forbidden fruit wasn't easy when I wanted to dive back into bed with him. Their sex life must have been vanilla, Emma sidelining him in her busy life. *I'm so busy*, these women boasted. But they had time to sit around at book club wanging on about being *so busy* that they didn't finish the bloody book.

Not long now and I'd claim to be as busy as them. I'd take over Emma's life. She would have a divorce payout, but not much, hopefully. A divorced man guarded against a new woman once his ex had stripped his assets, but if I got in first, she couldn't shaft him.

We would keep the daughters to keep him grounded. Give a divorced man his freedom and he regressed to selfish man-boy, buying a motorbike and going out drinking with his mates. If we did it my way, he would be the responsible provider, with me instead of Emma. I would take over so his ego and assets stayed intact. She'd have less of a claim on the family home if I moved in and we kept the girls. If she was difficult, I'd be the soothing voice of reason. *Get a quickie divorce and marry me, Elliot.*

That was a big ask, but I would convince him of our stronger position to keep the house if we married and gave the kids stability. Elliot was my ticket out of this dump. We'd be a golden couple, flying off on luxe holidays, throwing fun parties, him showing me off to his jealous mates. I couldn't bloody wait.

My solitary whisper of self-doubt had been a fear of losing my edge. But the past few days had confirmed I could still snag a hot guy. I smiled at the reversal of fortunes. Emma could bugger off and decompose in a mouldy bedsit, and I'd have the life I deserved.

Emma's journal

Elliot eventually replied to my message with a terse:

> Text me when you get back.

Trepidation thudded in my chest. He withheld his usual kiss. An ominous gloom descended as I drove back. I walked in the house to Barney's joyful welcome, which eased the tension. I messaged Elliot and took Barney out. Jules pulled up and waved through the open window.

'Why aren't you at work?' I asked.

'I swapped for a late shift yesterday.' She joined me on the walk. 'I didn't want you coming home alone. Lydia's been stirring.'

'Oh.' My grip on the lead tightened. 'I knew something was up.'

'Marianne says you're the village slut.'

'*What*?'

Barney hurtled round the green with one of his doggy mates, and Jules told me that Lydia claimed I was having an affair.

'Why would Elliot believe that?'

'Lydia's got her claws into him.'

'Christ almighty.' I felt sick.

'And he's a git who doesn't appreciate you.' With Jules on the warpath, it wouldn't go well if she was here when Elliot came home. They were bound to clash. 'I have a plan,' she said.

We went home when Barney was exhausted. I still didn't understand how Lydia had moved in on Elliot so quickly. She'd peddled some ridiculous story about an affair, but why would he believe it?

'Em? Did you hear what I said?' Jules shut the front door behind us.

It was bad. I got it on some level, but it hadn't hit home.

'I'm here,' she said. 'We'll deal with it.'

I didn't want to deal with it. It floored me that another woman had turned my husband against me.

'Pack some things. You're staying with me tonight.'

Was Jules overreacting? She made coffee, and I went upstairs. When you did your own cleaning, you knew every inch of your home. Our bedroom looked no different, so I checked the guest room and saw the ruffled bed sheets, the used towels in the shower room. A smudge of red lipstick marked the pure white pillowcase, a long auburn hair curling beside it. I pulled back, covering my mouth in shock. *What. The. Fuck.* They'd had sex in our home.

The front door opened, and Barney scampered to greet the girls. But it wasn't them. My stomach clenched, my heart beating in my throat, I came to the top of the stairs and saw Elliot in the hall, looking up at me with betrayal in his eyes.

'I know what you've been up to.' He faced me at the foot of the stairs. 'I've seen the evidence of you with your *lover.*'

My lover? I tried to speak but the words didn't come. Blood pulsated in my ears and I could hardly hear. I didn't need to when his expression said it all. Everything around him blurred, leaving a hyper-focus on his face.

'Well?' he demanded.

'What's been going on?' My voice choked. I held the banister for support. 'You've had Lydia here… in the guest bed.'

'You've got a nerve when I hear from two people that you're having an affair.' His gaze seared into me.

I swallowed, cleared my dry throat. 'But I… there isn't anyone… I haven't done anything.'

'Don't deny it,' he snarled. 'I have the evidence.'

'What evidence? This is ridiculous.' I felt light-headed. It was surreal, him accusing me of an affair.

'I work all hours for this family, and you make a mockery of me.'

'I've seen evidence of *your* affair in the guest room.' My voice wobbled with emotion.

'I didn't suspect a thing until your friends – *your friends* – told me my wife was leaving me for another man.'

'It's not true.' Nausea swelled in me, spreading to my throat.

'Don't act the innocent. I can't bear to look at you.' He turned his head away.

'I'm not having an affair, but Lydia's—'

'Shut up about Lydia,' he snapped.

'*Elliot*?' My voice breathless, tears stung my eyes. We'd never argued like this and I was half blind with upset, staring down a terrible tunnel vision that focused on him. I never could handle confrontation. My brain froze and my emotions took over. I tried to steady my swaying body, overcome with woozy vertigo from staring into an abyss. 'I promise you I'm not having an aff—'

'What are *you* doing here?' He looked daggers at Jules, who appeared from the kitchen, arms folded in defiance.

'Listen to yourself, Elliot. You're such a fucking *lawyer*.'

'I'm a *divorce* lawyer, which means your *fucking* sister will come out of this badly.'

Divorce? How had we jumped ahead to *divorce*? This was mad. I felt weirdly displaced, disconnected, as if the stairs beneath me would crumble away, the banister turning to dust in my fingers so I'd nothing to hold on to. All the while, Elliot looked like Rhett Butler, not giving a damn.

'Em,' Jules said. 'C'mon. Let's go.'

My legs wouldn't work.

'And don't come back,' he snarled.

She pushed past him, grabbed my wrist and tugged me away.

'The girls are staying with me,' he said. 'You won't get custody. They live here.'

We both stopped and gawped at him. A cold hand squeezed my heart and snatched my breath.

'Why are you talking about divorce and custody? I've only been at Mum's…'

Jules pulled me towards the front door. I should stay and fight, but this wasn't about hammering out differences. Elliot dared me to challenge him so he could come back harder. He had to win every fight no matter what.

There was no reasoning with him, especially with Jules inflaming him. I couldn't have the girls walk in on him spouting off about divorce and custody, me a sobbing wreck, which I would be if this carried on. In the face of his hostility, the urge to leave overwhelmed me.

He kept glaring, his face a snarl. I couldn't think straight, let alone have a rational conversation with Elliot, whose anger was absolute. It was the worst I'd ever seen him, pure hate in his face. Leaving was best, until I worked out what to do.

'I'll take Barney.' My voice shook.

'Barney's staying. I've got someone to look after him.'

'Come on.' Jules tried to usher me out. 'We'll sort it out,' she muttered to me.

'No, you won't. You'll stay out of it.'

'Yeah, right,' she scoffed. 'You play the big man. We won't darken your door again. Say hi to Lydia from us, Mr Holier-Than-Thou.'

'Get out.' His eyes glistened, mouth downturned in disgust.

'Where am I supposed to go?'

'You should have thought of that before you went breaking up our family.'

'But—'

'Leave,' he snapped. 'Now. Before the girls come home.'

He couldn't force me out, but it had spiralled out of control from Jules goading him. In Elliot's lawyerly world there were two sides – his side and the other side. Even in his personal life, you were either with him or against him and, therefore, out in the cold. I'd seen him cut people off over perceived slights, but I never expected this. I seized up from his anger and it took Jules to drag me away.

'Stay classy, Elliot.' Jules pulled me out the front and he slammed the door behind us.

The enormity hit home.

'The brute. The absolute fucking brute,' Jules raged, ushering me to her car. 'What a hypocrite. How did you stay with him this long?'

She drove us along the road. I reeled from the confrontation, the shock of him throwing me out of my own home. I was floored by Lydia's effect on him. I could have cut through his crap about 'evidence' and shown him her auburn hair and lipstick on the bed, but I was never a match for his argumentative streak.

Jules pulled up at the end of the road. 'You okay?' She wrenched up the handbrake and turned to face me.

'I couldn't… I just…' I shook my head and tears spilled down.

'Oh, Em, I'm sorry. It'll be okay. You'll be okay.'

'How?' I covered my face with my hands.

Chapter Eleven

Lydia

He did it. He kicked her out. I suspected he would only want me as his side piece. But he stood firm and I flew high. She would try to kiss and make up, of course, once it sank in.

'I reckon if I keep the girls,' he said when he phoned me with the news, 'she should be the one to move out. That's what I told her.'

'Good thinking.' Nice of him to take the credit, but if he saw it as his idea, he'd be more invested. The allure of sex on tap with me could increase his urgency. 'Did she deny the affair?'

'Of course. She's shocked I found out.'

She had herself to blame, the stupid doormat. But what if she really was having an affair? That could be why she'd left. How perfect if she had some bookish bloke hidden away, a librarian or English teacher. You had to watch the quiet ones.

'Jules was there, stirring it up. She dragged Emma out.'

Jules was instrumental. Surprise, surprise. The jealous twin wanted me breaking up his marriage all along. She hated him coming between her and Emma, so she betrayed her sister. I wondered which one found my lipstick mark and strand of hair? I chuckled at planting clues for them, like in one of their crime novels.

If Elliot had any sense, he'd arrange a quickie divorce. He'd better not be amicable about it, staying friendly for the sake of the children. I shuddered. Sod that. She would definitely use the kids to wangle her way back in.

'Can I come over?' he asked.

'It's not possible.'

'Why not? I'd love to see you.'

'I'm staying with a friend while I'm flat hunting. We agreed I wouldn't bring my social life home.'

'She'll make an exception for me. I'll be extra nice to her.'

No way was he coming anywhere near Luca and his grotty flat. It would only confuse Elliot to see a classy woman like me living in a dive. 'My flatmate's a pain. I need somewhere else to live. Prices have shot up since I've been in Dubai. Decent flats are just out of my price range. I won't live anywhere grotty.'

'Of course not.'

'I'm considering a transfer to the Birmingham office.' I upped my game.

'Birmingham? Stay put for now. I can't rush things with the girls. They're in all evening, but I'll nip out after supper for an hour with you. Your flatmate won't mind.'

'I'm meeting a friend this evening, remember?' Actually, I was microwaving a ready meal. Luca was home, so I'd eat it in my room. He thumped around the flat, wanting me to leave, but he lacked the balls to kick me out when I was always nice to him.

'Can you cancel? See me instead. Tell them something's come up and I'll drop round to yours.'

'We'll have to meet in a bar. I'm relying on this place in the short-term, although I do need somewhere else to live.'

He lowered his voice. 'I want to be alone with you.'

The urgency came through, the tension.

'The bust-up was awful,' he said. 'It got out of hand. Thank God the girls didn't walk in on us. I was too harsh. I didn't shout at her or anything, but I said some things…'

'Poor you. That sounds hard.'

'Clients sometimes come to me in tears. When it happens to you it hits home.'

Shit. I didn't want him to regret throwing her out. 'I'm sure you're handling it.'

'I have to see you. Shall I book us a hotel for the evening? There's a decent one near Richmond Park. Meet me there?'

'I'd love to.'

Minutes later, he pinged me a link to the hotel website. Excitement flared inside me. Everything was going my way.

Emma's journal

I pressed my hands to my burning face, but I was stone cold inside from Elliot telling me to go.

'You never could handle confrontation,' Jules said as we sat in her parked car.

I blew my nose. 'Why confront him when he's like that? Shouting and screaming won't help.'

'The bastard. He should know how you retreat inside yourself when you're upset. No point going head-to-head with him, although I bloody well would.'

'How can he expect me to leave? What about the girls?' They'd see it as me leaving them. But I couldn't stay, not with Elliot treating me as his courtroom adversary.

'They're going to France in two weeks. By the time they're back, you'll be sorted with a divorce lawyer.'

'And Barney. I should've brought him with me.'

'Barney's fine. Elliot cares more about the dog than you. He'll sweet-talk the neighbours into looking after Barney.'

'He'll calm down and realise it's crazy.'

'Don't count on it now Lydia's got her claws into him. I know it's a shitstorm, but I'll help you.'

'I think you made it worse.' It would have played out differently without Jules muscling in. He hadn't expected her to appear from the kitchen, inflaming him so it spiralled out of control.

'Stay at mine. He can't stop you seeing the girls and Barney.'

'He threw me out.' If I said it enough, it might sink in.

'You're better off without him. His shitty performance back there was to cover up his own guilt. He's humiliated by your supposed affair, then Lydia offers a revenge fuck. He's an adrenaline junkie. Revenge is another high. You'll get the twins back. He can't look after them. He can barely work the toaster.'

'I have to see them before they go home.'

'I'll drive you.'

'No, I'll do it. I'll call you when I'm done.' Thank God I had Jules, even though she wound Elliot up to the hilt.

'You're in shock. You shouldn't drive.'

'I'm fine.' We both knew I wasn't, but I could drive.

'Em?'

She waited until I looked at her.

'I know it's bad, but you'll get through this.'

'He'll want me back when he's calmed down.'

'Have a break and don't put up with his shit. Instruct a lawyer who's paid to put up with his shit.'

'Aren't we jumping ahead?'

'It's best to lawyer up.'

'How do I pay for it?'

'Elliot's money is family money. If he cuts you off, they'll help you access it. He can bloody well pay his legal costs *and* yours. Let him have the house for now. We'll see how he copes doing everything himself.'

I knew it would come to this if we ever split up. Elliot always had to come out on top. Not that we had split up. It was a row that had spooled out of hand. Jules said I should have fought back, but Lydia's impact on my life stayed just out of reach. The rawness stopped me going near the worst of it. I'd go mad with hurt and loss if I let it touch me.

Twenty minutes later, I tracked the twins down. We met in a cafe, where they each had a Frappuccino, while I knocked back a double espresso and disguised my upset.

'I'm going back to Grandma's,' I lied.

'Mu-*um*, you can't go back. We've missed you.'

'Give Aunt Jules a shout if you need anything.'

'Dad's grumpy with you away.'

'He keeps going out in the evening,' Chloe said.

I bet he did. I tried holding it together, hoping they didn't notice me shaking.

'Are you and Dad splitting up?'

'Oh, love, I just need to go back to Grandma's. You can text me. We'll do video calls. Can you keep looking after Barney?' What was I thinking, leaving them like this? Chloe's anxiety might escalate. She looked strained.

'Chloe.' I reached out my hand to cover hers. 'Remember your coping strategies.'

She nodded, eyes wide.

'Don't worry, Mum,' Isabella said. 'We're on it.'

Home was their best option. I couldn't uproot them in term time. Elliot might have thrown me out, but he doted on them, otherwise I'd never leave them. They were busy until the end of term and then away for six weeks, by which time I'd have worked out how to handle things.

'Mum?' Isabella put on her pleading face. 'Molly's having a party on Saturday. Please can we go?'

'Will her parents be there?'

'No, but her brother's back from uni,' her more honest twin said.

Isabella shot her a withering look. 'Relax, Mum. It's legit.'

If Chloe weren't a twin, she'd spend too long inside her head. They fitted together, Chloe keeping Isabella grounded, who in turn handled Chloe's anxieties.

'Ask Dad and tell him her parents won't be there.'

'Muuum.'

'And arrange a lift home.'

'Dad's never home.'

'Ask him for what you need. If he's grumpy, give him a wide berth. Remember he's got a stressful job.'

Chloe's phone buzzed.

I jumped. 'Who's that?' Was it Elliot?

'Alicia.' Chloe looked suspiciously at me. 'What's wrong?'

The espresso ramped up my nerviness. I drove them home and pulled up along the road to give them fierce hugs goodbye. I drove off with the terrible thought of Elliot turning them against me.

Jules had sprung into action and lined up a holiday home for a week. Lydia was right about one thing: I did need a break. I'd go away for some space. Jules met me outside her flat and gave me the address. She loaded up my boot with things I might need and clasped me to her as if we'd be wrenched apart for a long time. I drove out of town, eyes blurry from tears. I pulled into a lay-by, leaned on the steering wheel and sobbed into my sleeves.

The windows fogged. I texted Elliot through gritted teeth to say I'd gone away and that no one else knew where. I didn't expect a reply, I just didn't want him pumping the twins for information.

I tried taking strength from Jane Eyre fleeing from Mr Rochester and Thornfield for an uncertain future. She had it worse, adrift on the moors with no one and nothing to tether her. I had choices, not that I'd worked them out yet. I clutched the steering wheel to stop myself going into free fall.

Chapter Twelve

Lydia

Elliot had parked his sexy red Ferrari outside the hotel. I went through the reception, with its traditional styling, and up to the room. Who'd have guessed this staid place had rooms for drop-in sex? He greeted me with a warm hug. I breathed in his sandalwood aftershave and he hungrily undid my blouse.

'Let's order champagne.' I grabbed the room service menu. We deserved to celebrate him kicking Emma out, but he'd had enough revenge sex. Tonight was about us. I ran a finger down the bar list. 'How about Laurent-Perrier?'

He called room service while I took in the softly lit room in shades of taupe. We'd have regular trips away to nice hotels. I unbuttoned his shirt and slid it off him, ramping up his anticipation before the fizz arrived. Not many men his age looked hotter without clothes, but his baggy outfits were bought by Emma to keep him hidden. His hands roamed back to my demure white blouse.

'Let's take it slowly.' I stood back to sexily undress.

I wore a pencil skirt with a thigh split to peddle my career-woman myth. I undressed to my silky lingerie. He watched me as if the anticipation would kill him. I loved taking command.

Room service knocked and I wrapped myself in a hotel bathrobe to bring in the silver champagne bucket and crystal flute glasses. Alone again, I shook off the bathrobe and demonstrated my trick of transferring the tingle of champagne bubbles from my mouth to his erection. The fizzy sensation hastened his orgasm, the champagne masking the salty bitterness. Then he set to work on me.

'Oh,' I said breathily. 'Elliot. It's too much. You're so… sexy.'

All lies. He might be an alpha type at work, but he lacked mastery in bed. He kissed like a pro, but the lovemaking felt rushed. I put his initial attempt down to lack of preparation. Emma's fault for not setting higher standards. Thanks, Emma, for turning your husband beige. In the fullness of time, I'd slow him down so he savoured me. Right now, he only needed to lust after me.

'Christ,' he said after we'd finished. 'That was fantastic.'

'A man like you needs rampant sex.'

He looked curiously at me. 'I can't work you out. You're Emma's friend, but you've no qualms about this.'

'I just know her from book club. Do you still love her?'

He shook his head and sat up. 'I only love my daughters and my dog.'

But you'll love me soon. I'll be so good to you, Elliot, you won't be able to resist me.

It reminded me of a man I'd dated who said, 'The only person I'll ever love is my son.' The son was a snotty, incoherent three-year-old who ate with his mouth open and kept interrupting. I soon knocked his mean-spirited dad into touch. Elliot was in a different league.

His phone buzzed from the brats wanting to know when he'd be home. He fired off a reply and stood up.

'Can't you stay longer?' I watched him dress.

'I wish. Then I could ravish you all night.'

'Wouldn't that be amazing? A whole night together would be total bliss.' I stretched out, cat-like, on the bed.

He looked longingly at me.

'How will you handle it with the twins?'

'I'll speak to them. Explain how they can have the stability of home with me or be uprooted to God knows where with their mum. Home's the best option. I don't want to disrupt their studies.'

'You're a good dad. What about you? How will you cope?'

He sat on the edge of the bed and buttoned his shirt. 'It's hard.' He looked down at his buttons. 'I never expected Emma to be so… brazen.' He shook his head as if trying to throw off the thought.

I knelt behind him and massaged his shoulders. 'I know it's hard, but you have me to help you through it.'

He twisted round to kiss me. 'Did you mean what you said about walking Barney? I think I can get away with telling the girls you're the dog walker.'

Thanks a bunch. At least he'd worked out how to bring me into the home. 'Of course I meant it. And I'm happy to help you find the right housekeeper,' I reminded him, since we couldn't have the place go to shit.

He reached down to tie his shoelaces and didn't reply.

I sprawled on the bed in my best temptress pose. 'I'll stay here tonight, if that's okay. Take a break from my flatmate. You can settle up on your way out.' I kissed him to show my gratitude. 'I feel spoiled to be in a swish hotel with a gorgeous man.'

'It's even harder to leave now.'

Before he left, I offered to walk the dog tomorrow. 'Do you have a spare key?' I asked.

'What?'

'If I walk Barney when you're out.'

He mulled it over. 'I'll let you know.'

I could win his kids over, acting as a wayward, fun aunt who gave them more leeway than their neurotic mother. Once they were too old for Emma to demand maintenance, they could bugger off. If they dug in, I'd make it difficult. They would never win. I'd already left home by their age. With Emma gone, nothing stood in the way, not with my new life so tantalisingly close.

He gave me a slow, lingering kiss. 'All I'll think about is you in this bed.'

'I'll luxuriate in thoughts of you.'

He left and I finished the champagne in bed, pleased that I hadn't lost my powers of seduction. The hotel ignited my desire for luxury. We'd have a suite for our first trip away. We could leave his kids and take off for a luxurious minibreak to Barcelona. A hot Spanish trip with drinking, dancing and tapas would loosen him up.

I'd been a happy kid in Spain. Give me sunshine and some water to splash about in and I was content all day. When we left Estepona, I thought the council flat in Southend was bad, but at least we had the beach, a poor imitation of back home. Then we moved to a godawful dump in Basildon, too far from the sea. The flat was above a parade of takeaways and an off-licence. The stench of oily onions and garlic permeated the place, along with traffic fumes if we ever opened the windows.

My parents promised we'd have more money for beach holidays. I would fall asleep clutching my Thomson Holidays brochure for the Costa del Sol. If we went back on holiday, I planned to run away, sleep in a pool house in one of the uninhabited villas. I would find a kind person to take care of me. That was all I wanted. That and a life of luxury.

Emma's journal

I drove through the evening to Dorset. In my imagination, I went to Manderley and took the pathway to the secluded bay. When I returned from the world of *Rebecca*, I was still a mess and had to keep reminding myself to breathe. My need to escape overwhelmed me, but putting distance between Elliot and me wouldn't change anything.

The weather worked itself into a night-time storm, no doubt sent by Elliot. I drove with the wipers on full pelt, my whole body tense. When I turned onto an unlit road, the storm buffeted the car even more. Nearly there, I squinted through rain, searching for a cottage called Rosings. The satnav said I'd arrived, so where was it?

At the end of the village, I doubled back and saw the slate *Rosings* sign on a fence. I stopped the car and it rocked in the wind. My head swam. Cut adrift, the storm could sweep me away, like debris in the sea, discarded in the night.

I opened the car door and the wind ripped it from my fingers. Grabbing my overnight bag, I forced the door shut and ran through horizontal rain to the borrowed holiday home. Inside the frigid cottage, rainwater dripped from me onto the flagstone floor. I leaned against the door. Why had I come here? Me, who'd never stayed anywhere alone.

I shook myself off and went from room to room, turning on lights. It was sparse, with rustic buttermilk painted walls and Shaker-style furniture. Still breathless, I tried to squash down my brimming emotions.

Jules sent a text.

You okay? x

I'm here x

Hang tight, as the young people would say x

I was struck by the dizzying question of *what do I do now*? It had been years since my days weren't dictated by the family's schedule. Suiting myself was a long-forgotten luxury, except it didn't feel luxurious. My life had been snatched away, even though I was the one to leave. Rain lashed against the windows and I couldn't turn off the torrent of hurt. The gravity of abandoning the twins hit home and a wave of panic rushed through me.

I opened a bottle of red from the wine rack, reminding myself this was my breathing space. I would see it more clearly from a distance. At least Jules had arranged for me to stay rent-free. 'Good job we know a few rich people who care about you,' she'd said. With summer fast approaching, they would want it back. It must cost a fortune to rent in the school holidays. 'It's just for a week,' she'd said. 'Until we work out what to do.'

The wine took the edge off my panic. I drank more of it in the cold, tasteful cottage. I tried drinking enough for my terrible day to disintegrate. But it didn't change anything, so I curled up in the queen bed of the guest room. Being alone reminded me of my first time away from home. I'd struggled to hit my stride at university until I met Elliot.

Worn out, I lay awake, the storm raging around me. The wind howled and the rain hammered down overnight. By morning it eased, and I woke up remembering what I went to bed trying to forget: Elliot's face on the stairs when he threw me out. Did he regret his heat of the moment reaction? His pride would stop him asking me to come home, but he'd calm down.

The repercussions of leaving kept coming like aftershocks. It all felt wrong. What the hell was I doing? I hadn't been thinking straight when Jules suggested the plan, and now I went breathless at the danger of it backfiring.

Chapter Thirteen

Lydia

Three weeks to the murder

Over my hotel breakfast, I scrolled through the texts Elliot sent me from his bed last night. God, I'd really fired him up. I asked the cosmos to transform my intentions into reality. Manifesting helps you achieve results. A ring on my finger was the ultimate prize, transforming my status and spending power. I texted him a reminder about the spare key.

> We have it covered with Barney. X

What? But they needed me. Walking the dumb dog was my foot in Elliot's door. I left the hotel, fuming. I'd show the bastard, going back on our agreement. I tapped out a reply.

> Ok. I'll have a run with friends instead. Need my daily exercise! We usually go for a drink after. xx

As if. I could never keep up with serious runners, despite matching Elliot's energy level in the bedroom. But a shared interest brought couples closer, even if mine were stage-managed. I left for the flat, deflated after the hotel stay.

He texted back:

> I can meet you for a drink tonight. I'll bring Barney so they'll think I'm walking him. X

I held my nerve.

> Sounds lovely, but I'm running this evening. Another time? xx

> Lunch today in London? I'll buy you oysters and champagne. X

That was more like it. Back at the depressing flat, I slid a few overnight essentials in my tote bag for our London lunch. Good to be prepared in case Elliot booked us into a swish Mayfair hotel. If he had to leave, I'd take myself to Bond Street for window shopping in readiness for when he gave me a credit card. Oh, for spendy West End afternoons! I wanted to ask if he'd cancelled Emma's cards, but I couldn't be too forward.

On the way there, I detoured to Harrods Salon De Parfums for a spritz of my favourite daytime fragrance. Like me, it was fresh yet decadent, suiting the mood of our romance. Elliot met me outside the restaurant and kissed me on each cheek. I'd have preferred a passionate embrace, but he kept the PDAs under wraps.

The restaurant was one of those old-school places with oak panelling and overly attentive staff. Elderly people dotted around the dining room in upholstered chairs.

'They look after you here,' Elliot said as a waiter pushed in my chair and draped a white napkin over my lap.

'You need looking after,' I said, although I preferred a livelier atmosphere.

He was engaging company when not fixated on the animal and those kids. We talked about neither to start with, flirting and drinking champagne.

'To us.' I toasted him. 'And a fabulous summer.'

He sipped champagne, then cupped one hand under his chin and gazed into my eyes. 'Tell me about yourself.'

We chatted like a proper couple and talked about me while the champagne flowed.

'You smell divine.' He laid into the basket of warm bread.

'Why thank you.' *So I should, at £210 a bottle.* I nibbled delicately at freshly baked walnut bread. It was delicious, but I couldn't smudge my lipstick. Our oysters arrived on a silver platter. Would he book us a hotel room for this afternoon? It was almost the weekend and we needed to crack on and develop a meaningful relationship. I could always cancel my fictional running plans.

We talked about Elliot's work. I couldn't quite break through his guardedness to the real him.

'I love talking to you,' I said. 'High achievers are the best company.'

'Is that so?'

'I like ambition. I admire your success.'

He smiled and I felt a lightness, a flutter of something sweet in my chest. I wasn't falling for him, as such. I was falling for us: Elliot and me, a gorgeous couple living our best lives together. That was what made the endorphins flow.

Our steaks arrived, beautifully presented, and the waiter topped up my champagne. Elliot placed a hand over his nearly finished glass of fizz and gave the waiter a small shake of his head. Not a good sign.

'To us.' I lifted my glass again. 'To a happy life.'

He tapped his glass against mine. 'It'll take me a while to be happy again.'

I made a sympathetic face. 'How did the girls take it, about their mum moving out?'

He sighed and we both started eating. The steak melted in my mouth.

'They don't know yet. Emma told them their granny still needs looking after.'

'Is that wise? They need to know sometime.' Otherwise how could I move in with their dad?

'I'd rather keep it stable now Emma's smoothed it over with them.'

'But isn't it better if you take control? What if she sets up home with the mystery man and tempts them over to live with them?'

'I've told her that's not going to happen.'

'But if he has a decent home, the girls could live with them. They're old enough to choose.'

He looked troubled.

'You're handling it well. Taking charge of the situation.'

'Have you ever been married?' he asked.

My throat constricted as I swallowed a mouthful of champagne.

'There was someone.' I looked wistfully into the middle distance. 'The love of my life.' My voice cracked with emotion and my fingers smoothed over the starched white tablecloth. 'He passed away.'

'Oh God. Sorry.' He reached across and took my hand. 'What happened, if you don't mind me asking?'

'He was alcohol dependent. There were complications.' I shook my head and fought back tears. 'Sorry. I can't talk about him.'

He wished he hadn't asked. Men like him hated crying. I put on a brave face, cleared my throat and regained my composure.

'This is wonderful. Thank you for inviting me.' No need for Elliot to hear the low-down on Vernon's death, now or ever.

I was about to suggest we moved on to liqueurs when he slid his hand away and checked his watch.

'That time already?' He signalled for the bill, not asking if I wanted coffee.

'You work too hard.'

'Work hard, play hard.'

The bill swiftly appeared and he laid a gold Amex on the silver dish.

'Lovely to see you,' he said, as if wrapping up a client meeting.

'When shall I walk Barney?'

'We've got it covered. The girls will take him out.'

Fuck. That blew my plan to show them how useful I was, like a favourite aunt who gave them cigarettes and talked about her colourful exploits. Teenagers were fickle and easily bought. With Emma out in the cold, they would soon warm to me.

On the street outside, he gave me a quick peck on the cheek. 'Enjoy your run.'

'What? Oh, yes. Thanks.'

He strode off. What a let-down. But the lunch showed promise, and he didn't just see me as the dog walker. Once we were a proper couple, we would have leisurely dinners out. It still felt precarious though. I walked down the road to a Costa and dug around for my loyalty card.

I sat by the window and planned my next move. Champagne and oysters were a start, but I wanted the full works. Elliot needed to accept that moving me in was perfect revenge against Emma. If I could stop his kids getting in the way, he'd fall for me. A lesser woman might doubt her ability to pull it off, but self-doubt played no part in my grand plan. At least he hadn't probed about Vern. It was good to show my relationship history, but I had to deflect difficult questions by being too upset to talk about him.

-

Elliot phoned when I lay in bed the next morning. I held off a few moments before answering.

'Ooh, sorry,' I said, breathless. 'I was in the shower. I'm soaking wet!'

He groaned. 'Don't do that to me. I want to be with you.'

'Plenty of time for that,' I said in a low purr. Men were such simple creatures.

'How was your run?'

It took a moment to remember my fake run from last night. 'Great. It's fun, exercising in the fresh air. A bunch of us go along and have a drink after.'

I'd given myself a range of wholesome and cultural pastimes because high-status people went for that sort of thing. I exercised, loved theatre and visiting art galleries, creating the impression of a vivacious woman living a full life.

'Which running club is it?'

I faltered and told myself to wing it. 'It's not a proper club. Just a few friends.'

'Where do you run?'

'We took the Thames Path past Hampton Court.'

'I might come sometime. Do you go every week?'

'It's not a regular thing. I was at a loose end.'

'How far do you run?'

I grappled for a credible answer… 3K? 5K? *Keep it vague, Lydia.* 'It takes an hour or so. I just run along with the gang. I'm not a proper athlete, like you. For me, it's about enjoying the outdoors.' Enough of my pretend running. 'How are you getting on?'

'That's why I'm calling. Would you nip round and walk Barney?'

'Sure. I'm working from home, but I'd love to see Barney.'

He had to rush off but texted to say he'd hidden the key by the summer house. He said to hold off until after the girls had left the house. Bloody cheek to put them before me, but until we were married I'd use them as bargaining chips. I would also encourage them to be independent. They would love me for it. Or not. As long as they were out of my way I didn't much care.

I went to retrieve the key, dressed down because the idiot dog would slobber over me. One of the daughters had left a pair of decent trainers in the hall. They fitted, so I wore them to walk the mutt round the green.

'Is that Barney?' A woman trotted her pair of yappy fluffballs over.

I nodded and checked out her athleisure-wear. I'd already passed a younger woman in similar kit, pushing a sporty baby buggy. The pointy-faced dogs pranced around on their dainty legs.

'Are you a dog walker?'

As if. 'No. I'm a friend of the family. Helping out while Emma's away.'

'Oh, shame. Dog walkers are like pixie dust, apart from the ones that load the doggies in a van, and mine won't like that.'

I made a sympathetic face.

'Elliot's nice, isn't he?' She tossed her mane of chestnut hair and gave a biscuity morsel to each dog.

Hands off. He's mine. Barney crunched the dog biscuit with enthusiasm.

'They're so sweet, those two.' She patted Barney, who snuffled her pocket for more food.

Did she mean Emma and Elliot?

'Aren't you, Barney? You and your daddy, jogging off together.'

She could jog on too. I fake smiled and carried on walking. Dog owners could be precious about their mutts for some unknown reason. I needed some athleisure kit to fit in with the women walking their dogs. I'd hotfoot it to Sweaty Betty or Lululemon as soon as Elliot put me on the payroll.

Back at the house, I made myself useful where he'd notice. Emma had frozen some meals, so I took out a lasagne. After a cursory tidy-up, I went through all the drawers and cupboards. No bank statements, and the laptop needed a password. I'd wangle it from Elliot somehow. I opened a well-ordered linen cupboard and resisted the urge to mess it up.

I perused the dressing room in the master suite, confirming my fears about beige chinos. Elliot lacked sartorial elegance. I liked his old-school brogues, but he needed a sharper look. We could shop for slim-fit Italian cotton shirts and extra-fine cashmere sweaters to show his physique, paired with designer suits and jeans in a dark shade.

I flicked through a glossy business magazine on the table, since I still needed skin in the game. A bookmarked page opened to a photo of Elliot in a wood-panelled boardroom. Moodily lit, Elliot owned the space, undeniably handsome in a pale pink shirt and blue silk tie.

The headline on the opposite page shouted, *The Boss of Break-ups*. It boded well for his own break-up. I scanned through. Elliot was portrayed as a self-effacing people person guiding clients through the difficult process. *That's my Elliot*, I thought proudly. The family man had never been divorced and loved spending time with his wonderful wife and daughters. I tossed it back on the table and took the dog out again.

I walked Muttley to the farm shop and bought salad for the lasagne, and pricey cheese from the deli counter. Elliot and I could have the cheese with a little something from his drinks cabinet. I spotted a footballer's wife selecting booze from Surrey vineyards. Did her husband play for Chelsea? She wouldn't let me catch her eye, but I'd look out for her in the future. I would wear my slinky leather trousers and heels next time to come across as a kindred spirit. These were the sorts of people whom I would hang out with in my new life.

I came back and played my Ibiza Club Mix at high volume, throwing some shapes to loosen up and raise my energy. Then I slid the lasagne in the oven on a low setting. Home-cooked aromas would waft around when Elliot arrived back. He'd love my domestic goddess vibe. I changed into the AllSaints floral top that I'd brought with me, a casual and classy Vinted find. When the girls came crashing in, they dropped their school bags and hyped up the dog. I appeared from the kitchen holding a tea towel to look non-threatening.

'Who the hell are you?' one of them demanded. She wore earbuds, her voice too loud.

'Hi, I'm Lydia. From your mum's book club. I brought the macaroons, remember? Your dad asked me to walk Barney.'

They eyed me with suspicion. Nice-looking girls, but unnervingly like their mother. Their childhood photos dotted around the house, them dressed the same, creepily identical. In one photo, they held hands and stared solemnly into the camera like the spooky dead twins from *The Shining*. Enough to send anyone deranged.

They'd rung the changes since then. One was dippy and bohemian with a short fringe and messy blond hair. She had that kooky style I detested, trying too hard to look offbeat. The bolshie one had her hair in a loose bun and stared at me with a hint of swagger. She was the challenge, probably the one Elliot likened to himself.

'I'm helping out while your mum's away.' I smiled and flapped the tea towel.

'Nice to meet you,' the dippy one said, and they both trailed upstairs.

'What time's your dad home?'

'Dunno. Ask him,' the loud one said without looking back.

Charming. My phone rang a minute later. Elliot's name flashed up.

'Hello.' I didn't put on a sexy voice in case they heard me upstairs.

'What are you playing at?'

'Sorry?'

'I asked you to walk the dog, not take over the house.'

'There was nothing in the fridge for dinner, so I got it started for you. I just wanted to help. Barney's been out and I've cleared up downstairs.'

'Thanks. That's kind of you, but the girls had no idea who you were. I'm trying to keep it stable, and they text me to say some strange woman's in the house.'

Strange woman? They'd pay for that. 'Lasagne's in the oven. Turn it back on for forty minutes. I've left a salad in the fridge. You take care, okay?'

'Thanks. You're a diamond.'

No, I wasn't a diamond, but I wanted a well-cut one of at least two carats. I switched off the oven. Fine, we wouldn't eat *en famille*, but I could play the long game, keep my eye on the ultimate prize. I took the cheese with me.

His turn to make the next move. I'd allow some sexting, but no more proper sex until I stayed the night. That should focus him. If Elliot had any sense, he'd see me as a great catch and realise my worth in keeping his kids and the house.

'Bye, girls, nice to meet you,' I called cheerily up the stairs.

They didn't reply. Sod them. I left and went to have another door key cut as a spare, just in case. Now that the kids knew the nice lady who did the cooking and walked the mutt, I'd no reason to stay away. They could start getting used to their stepmother.

Emma's journal

Alone in the cottage, I missed Barney's clamouring welcome and the girls' voices. Those were the sounds of home. I regretted taking flight to this unfamiliar place, so I pulled on my wellies and strode towards the sea, ready to find my bearings and blow away the emotional hangover of leaving home.

I heard the roar of the sea before the hedgerows gave way to the pebble beach and waves crashing on the rocks. There was something atmospheric about the seaside on a rough day, remote and windswept. The rhythmic rushing in of the waves soothed me. A dog leapt about at the water's edge, barking with crazed joy. I envisaged heading out for bracing walks with Barney barking at waves and getting soaked. The dog shook off seawater and hared off, and the brisk wind urged me to get a move on.

Walking back, I stopped at the village store that belonged to the West Country of my childhood. A dated sign advertised clotted-cream ice cream. The bell tinkled when I stepped inside the pokey shop, empty of customers but crammed with basics and smelling of overripe fruit. A woman behind the counter stared at me.

'Good morning,' I said, pleased to speak to someone at last. She nodded, stony-faced.

I stood before the rows of jars and tins, hating the prospect of cooking for one. I filled my shopping basket and paused at the alcohol section. The woman behind the counter watched as I selected a bottle of white wine and approached her to pay. When I reached the till, she didn't speak except to tell me the price.

The dislocation gnawed at me. I returned to the cottage, steeling myself for its emptiness. With no one there would I turn into Mum, endlessly fretting about whether to bring in the washing in case it rained? I'd never lived alone, moving into Elliot's student digs in my second year at uni. I'd worked in London after graduating but not long enough to call it a career, since I became pregnant and everything changed. When they said it was two babies, I couldn't believe it, despite twins running in the family. We agreed to give them the opportunities we'd lacked growing up. I loved Elliot for already being a better dad than mine.

I grew so large during my hot summer of pregnancy that the commute into London felt oppressive. 'Take early maternity leave,' Elliot said after one sticky journey on the Tube when a man pushed past me to nab the last seat.

Then I had two beautiful girls. People said twins would be hard work, and if one woke up crying, the other would start too. But they always seemed like a miracle. Childcare for two babies would have outstripped my salary, and having it all was never an option. I'd have had sleep deprivation and the guilt of leaving them. Elliot forged ahead, more determined to do well so we could afford a proper home. He said he did it for us, but his unshakeable self-belief powered him.

Isabella texted me.

Mum, a woman from your book club was here when we got home! She was cooking supper?! xxxxx

My heart twisted. I stood in the kitchen and gripped the back of a chair. What was Elliot playing at, letting her in the house without telling the girls? I screwed my eyes shut and counted to ten. Then I called Isabella, who launched into telling me how Lydia had acted as if she belonged there.

'Is she being nice to you?' I hid my fury.

'S'pose. But why was she even here? When are you coming home?'

'Yeah, Mum,' Chloe chimed in on speakerphone. 'We want you home.'

'I expect she offered to help your dad out. Are you both okay?'

'Yeah, but we told Dad it's weird.'

'It is weird. Maybe he didn't think it through.'

'We miss you, Mum,' Chloe said.

'Miss you too. Are you still looking after Barney?'

'You keep asking that. He's having a blast,' Isabella said. 'We gotta go. There's a thing starting. Love you.'

They blew kisses down the phone. Chloe pinged me a selfie of them hugging Barney, who panted and looked smiley. I found myself cry-laughing. Tears streamed down my face. I paced around, filling the kitchen bin with damp, balled-up tissues. Then I sat at the table and sobbed into my hands: ugly, gulping sobs. My nose blocked, I took hiccupping breaths through my open mouth. I needed some air and went out in the grey blowy evening. My God, I hadn't expected to wade through all these messy emotions that spilled out of me.

I hiked up a wild, craggy cliff path and along the collapsing coastline. Why couldn't he move out to be with her? Or at least not bring her home until the kids left for uni. The speed of it snatched my breath away. Should I tell them? Better to keep things stable until I'd packed them off to France and worked out my options.

What if Lydia was okay with the twins? She brought them cookies and had a refreshing take on Chloe's mental health. A therapist once warned me not to 'exacerbate the cycle of anxiety'. She said it to me, not Elliot, who'd sat beside me in the therapy room exuding warm smiles and easy charm. She implied that I indulged Chloe's anxiety by providing reassurance. I learned how to handle it and Elliot refused to engage, as he did with all vulnerabilities. But Lydia might talk Chloe out of her anxiety, so long as her knife fixation didn't surface.

It dug into me, Lydia getting away with all this. Thinking of the twins liking her brought a wave of fresh horror. What if they preferred her? What if I hardly saw them again? I stared out to sea like *The French Lieutenant's Woman*. The wind buffeted me. I stood at the savage cliff edge till after sunset, and I was so cold it hurt. Jules phoned as if sensing I needed her. The wind whipped around me.

'Where are you?' she asked. 'Is there a hurricane?'

'I'm on a cliff,' I shouted. The signal faded in and out. I started walking back, but my legs had stiffened in the cold.

'Why are you on a cliff in the dark? Shall I come and get you?'

'I'm going back indoors.' I kept walking, the distant thunder of sea behind me, and I told her about Lydia fast-tracking her way in.

'Don't worry about the twins,' she said once the signal became clearer. 'They'll stick together. Just think of us at their age. We'd grown out of home by seventeen.'

'But kids are different now,' I said. 'Younger.'

'Lydia's cooking for them. She's going all out to impress the bastard, which includes sucking up to the kids. We'll keep an eye on it, and Isabella's a force to reckon with. She'll let you know if Lydia oversteps. She'll let Lydia know too.'

'I'll hear about it with an indignant text.'

Isabella made her feelings clear moment by moment. Chloe was quieter, but I could read her moods. It cut me deep to think of Lydia at home with them. They couldn't have sussed her motive, since Elliot would surely keep the affair secret until they went away for the summer.

'What do you know about her?' I asked. 'Does anyone know who she is?'

She sighed. 'I've googled and nothing comes up. Which is suspicious in itself.'

'Nothing would come up about me either.'

'That's different. She's supposedly a high-flyer, living it large. Oh, I nearly forgot, Rosa's going to her flat for a nose round.'

I laughed. 'Lydia'll love that.'

'Let's hope there's a stand-off.'

'I need to know who she is, now she's in the house with the kids. What if she's a serial killer?'

'Isabella would kill her first,' Jules said. 'What if Elliot wants you back?'

'He won't, not with Lydia homing in on him.'

'It won't last, but don't go back to him,' Jules said. 'He shagged her in *your* home while you looked after Mum, then he kicked you out. The git. Staking a claim to the moral high ground.'

'It's his ego. How did she take over so fast? She's not his type at all.' He'd lost his mind. Other men might do that, but not Elliot.

'He's using her to make you jealous. It's your chance to break free. Come on, Em, the kids have their own lives. Take some time for you.'

'It's not that easy.'

'I know, but work out what you want to do. The girls can crash here anytime.'

I was nearly back, glowing from the windswept walk.

'I've put *Feel the Fear and Do It Anyway* in your bag of books. Anyway, I'm at Cazzie's leaving do, so I'd better go.'

'Okay. Speak soon.'

'And remember your secret weapon,' she said darkly, and hung up.

I came inside and finished the bottle of red I'd started last night. *My secret weapon*. I'd forgotten about it in the shock of leaving home. My fingertip hesitated over my phone screen, then I tapped the icon for my secret app. Elliot would kill me if he knew.

Chapter Fourteen

Lydia

Saturday evening and still no plans for our weekend together. I walked through the park in the mellow sunshine, longing for a cool G&T or a chilled glass of rosé. But funds were low and I preferred it when someone else paid. A cluster of teenage boys kicked a football nearby, showing off to three girls on the grass who leaned back on their hands, pushing their chests forward in seductive poses.

That first miserable winter after we moved to Basildon, I'd asked my parents about booking our holiday. 'Let's get Christmas out of the way,' they'd said.

I'd longed to step on a plane and escape the dishcloth-grey sky, the eternal gloom of an English winter, dark when I got up, dark when I came back from school. On Boxing Day, the TV ads switched from Christmas scenes to elated kids swishing down water slides, families playing in aquamarine surf, everything vibrant.

'Can we go?' I'd pleaded.

'Christmas cost a lot. We'll look for a late deal nearer the time.'

There was always something: the car needing a new clutch, the electricity in arrears. When you had no money, it became everything. Money fixed everything. I bared my teeth and kicked at a tuft of grass. Kick, kick, kick, like the boys playing football, until it uprooted into a clod of brown dirt.

People around me enjoyed the weekend. I should have been one of them, but Elliot had turned silent. He didn't reply to my last message. He would think me desperate if I texted again. Such a waste of a beautiful evening, an evening for lovers. We could be walking hand in hand along the river to share a bottle of wine beside that pub I went to with Marianne. I arrived home as it got dark and resolved to raise my game.

Sunday morning and still nothing. We'd strayed into the danger zone. Had Emma come crawling back? Even if she hadn't, I couldn't let him gravitate towards Tinder, nor did I want his divorced mates leading him astray. When word spread about his newly available status, a gold digger could swoop in and take advantage.

I messaged him.

> A friend invited me to London for some Sunday fun. Shall we do something instead? x

I chuckled at not saying whether my friend was male or female. Let him think the worst. I had to keep pulling his strings since alpha types like him were hardwired to hunt. He had to win me over in order to appreciate me. An hour later, he called. Result.

'Hello, you,' I said.

'Lydia, hi. The girls have a sleepover tonight. Would you like to stay the night?'

We're back in the game! A whole night in my dream house.

'Won't be as exciting as London,' he said.

'I'm already excited.'

He softened a little. 'Can't wait to see you. I'm out cycling, so we'll chat this evening, yes?'

To celebrate our first night together, I bought Veuve Clicquot champagne on offer in Sainsbury's and some half-price strawberries and cream. Perfect seduction food, which fit my image of someone who splashed out on the finer things in life. I took them over with the cheese from yesterday. We could have a nibbly supper if he hadn't made plans to take me out or cook for us.

When I arrived, he kissed me passionately and went to pull me upstairs.

'Let's celebrate.' I lifted the champagne from my bag. 'We can take it to bed.'

He grabbed two flute glasses and led me to the bedroom. I popped the cork and we drank some fizz, like a civilised couple.

'Our challenge is to savour the feeling,' I said.

All my powers of seduction came into play as I slipped out of my clothes and undressed him. Delayed gratification worked its slow magic and I rewarded him with another fizz-infused blow job, since he'd liked it last time.

When he was about to come, he returned the favour. It felt lovely and tingly. He'd improved now we took it slowly. He just needed an expert steer after the wilderness years with Emma. We barely spoke. It was slow and powerful, desire burning strong in his eyes. I ran my hands up and down his firm muscles.

'I have some massage oil.' I motioned to the bottle of scented oil I'd placed beside the bed.

He clicked the flip-top lid and warmed the oil in his hands. The spicy scent drifted over me and I melted into his touch, his hands in possession of me. I lay still, soaking in the fragrance and the feeling. Then he lay beside me and we kissed. I revelled in our passion and the growing rush of sensations.

'I want you, Elliot.' And I did. I wanted more of him. All of him. We made a good couple. A good-looking couple. We could have a wonderful life, and it was all within my grasp. Lying in bed together, I luxuriated in the beautiful surroundings. I could live here as his wife. Emma had better not come back. He was mine now.

'Hungry?' He pulled on his jeans and sweatshirt to go downstairs.

I slipped on his bathrobe and hugged him close. 'Famished.'

'You look sexy in my bathrobe.'

We ate the cheese with olives and rustic bread. Then we dipped strawberries into the cream and fed them to each other.

I gazed admiringly round the kitchen. 'Do you have a cleaner?'

'Emma does it all, or she used to.'

'This is such a beautiful house, it would be a pleasure to keep clean.' *Lol.* As if I'd choose to clean anything. But it would be a pleasure to instruct the staff. 'Your daughters are adorable.' Were they fuck.

'Thank you.'

'Were they okay about me walking Barney?'

'They were surprised to find another woman in the house. But they're not that interested. They just think you're some woman from Emma's book club.'

Charming. I'd make them interested. They were my side project. I'd turn it around so they sang my praises to their dad and Emma. That'd wind her up and cement my position in his life. We finished our sensuous strawberries and carried gin and tonics upstairs for Netflix and chill. The sex had brought us closer, but did he like me enough to move me in?

Emma's journal

I collapsed into bed that night, wiped out and broken down. When I hauled myself up, seeing my puffy face and bloodshot eyes in the bathroom mirror nearly sent me back under the duvet. But I forced myself into the shower instead.

When I towelled my damp hair, doubts seeped in along with a draught from outside. How could I find a job when I hadn't worked in seventeen years? I needed to come at life with a clearer purpose. Jules's copy of *Feel the Fear and Do It Anyway* taunted me from the coffee table.

I pulled on my trainers and went out. Despite it being July, the air felt damp and cool. Jules phoned. 'Just checking you haven't gone loopy holed up there alone.'

'I'll be talking to myself soon.'

'I already do. You know Rosa's detective work? She checked with this Luca bloke who Lydia's staying with.'

'And?'

'Luca spoke to the guy who'd passed her number to him, but he'd only met her once, wine tasting. Sounds like she charmed him into helping her find a rent-free place.'

'Anything else?'

'Nope. It's like she didn't exist before turning up here.'

'Surely Elliot would have checked her out? Due diligence and all that.'

'He checked her out all right. Checked out the cleavage she thrust in his face. Now he's having sex on tap. Blinded by feel-good hormones, the dickhead.'

'For now.'

'Don't take him back.'

'Did she leave any documents lying around?' I asked.

'No. Looks like she keeps everything important in a locked suitcase. She came back when Rosa was there having a cup of tea.'

'I bet Lydia loved that.'

'She was fuming. Gave Rosa a death stare and shut herself in her room.'

'Talking of a rented room, with the kids going to France, I'm looking for temporary work, waitressing or something. Then I'll find a room to rent.' I'd stay in Dorset when the girls were away for the summer. Supporting myself would be a challenge, but I had to start somewhere.

'What about office work? You've got an English degree and your business studies diploma.'

'There won't be much temporary admin work. Hospitality's my best bet.'

'Go easy on yourself. Absorb what's happened first.'

'Who needs self-help books with you dispensing advice?'

'Be like Lucy Honeychurch in *A Room With a View*. She goes to Italy and learns how to be happy.'

'I love Lucy Honeychurch.'

'That awful Cecil didn't deserve her. Thank God she swooned into George's strong arms.'

'I don't need a man to rescue me.' I looked out on a pheasant ambling about the garden. The stream beyond gushed down the valley to the sea, just visible in the distance, merging in watercolour tones with the moody sky.

'George shows Lucy how to live and love. Has the bastard been in touch?'

'No.'

'Good. Don't talk to him. The bastard. He can text, but no direct contact.'

Elliot didn't care about me, not with Lydia massaging his ego and whatever else she got her hands on. I shuddered at the thought of them having sex where the twins could walk in on them.

Jules went back to work, and I shoved her self-help book back in the cloth bag, not wanting to feel the fear and do it anyway. My deepest fear was being alone. Being a twin did that. Jules was always out with friends and doing two sociable jobs. Who would I be if I started again? I could forge a new life, but not with the twins still at home.

That night, I jumped when the gate rattled in the wind, trying not to let the total blackness spook me. I'd no idea how all this would pan out, only that Lydia would keep playing dirty. I chewed my lip and engaged my secret weapon. The app that spied on them.

The audio file appeared on the phone screen. I held my breath and pressed play, ready to listen in to what was going on at home. The sound range covered most of the downstairs area where Barney lived and the girls came and went. The voice activation recorded whenever it picked up talking. I felt grubby for spying on them, but I wanted to check on Barney. The twins could text me but Barney couldn't. He wasn't allowed upstairs, so I kept the surveillance downstairs only.

I know it was mad. The whole situation was mad. I found the journal cathartic at first, letting it pour out, but I've had enough. This is my last journal entry.

Chapter Fifteen

Lydia

Elliot woke me in the morning with aromatic coffee and his big dick. After he'd ravished me, we basked in the afterglow.

'How about breakfast?' I suggested. 'Let's go to one of those hipster cafes on the High Street.'

'It's too soon for us to be seen out.'

I looked at him as if to say, *Don't be a bore, Elliot, it doesn't suit you.*

'Emma and I know too many people round here.'

'People will know soon enough.'

'The twins don't know, and if we go out together I won't be able to keep my hands off you.'

That's the point, you dummy, in my plan to fast-track us into the public domain.

'The girls are back later, since they're not in college today. I'll work from home and see if they want to go out for lunch. In the meantime…' He launched on top of me and I squealed with delight. Afterwards, when he took a shower, I checked messages on my phone. The front door clicked open. My heart leapt at the dog's scamper and the kids' chatter. What perfect timing.

A different type of person would have shut the bedroom door, warned Elliot and thrown on some clothes. A lesser type of person. I reclined on the bed and let my bathrobe fall open to expose my bare legs and boobs. The shower kept running, masking their noise. I held my breath. One of them padded upstairs. The top of her head came into view. The ditsy one. I grabbed my phone, pretending she'd caught me unaware.

'Dad-dee?' She saw me and shrieked, jumping backwards like a startled fawn.

'Oh no!' I scrambled to rearrange myself and my bathrobe. 'Your dad's in the shower.'

Eyes wide, she covered her mouth with both hands. The bolshie one rushed up the stairs as Elliot flung open the en-suite door, dripping wet, sweeping a towel around his torso.

'What's going on?' the pushier one demanded.

What does it look like? I'm fucking your dad.

'You're cheating on Mum,' she said to him.

Mission accomplished. I took my clothes in the bathroom and dressed behind the door, listening with glee.

'I'm telling Mum,' the bolshie one ranted. I punched the air. Served him right for not dealing with it sooner.

'She already knows. Listen, we need a chat—'

'I can't believe you're having an affair when Grandma's ill and Mum's looking after her.'

'She's not looking after Grandma. She's left me.'

'No, she hasn't. I'm calling Mum. I'm calling her *now*.'

'Isabella, shush.'

'You can't go around having sex—'

'Isabella, let me finish. Please.'

She shut up. I pictured her pouting at him.

'Listen, I didn't want to tell you yet, but your mum's left me for someone else.'

It was met with cries of 'it's not true' and 'no, no, no'. He kept on, in a measured, lawyerly voice. Good on him for blaming Emma.

'I know it's a shock,' he said. 'But you'll live here with me. We're still a family, and you'll carry on as normal. Your mum and I were planning how to tell you.'

'I want Mum,' the drippy one wailed. 'She can't leave us.'

'We need to work together on this, the three of us, okay? We're a team, right?'

More murmuring from the girls.

'I'd like you to step up and show your mum you're happy here, otherwise you'll have to move God knows where and I won't see you.'

'Dad! We can't move. We've got exams. I can't believe you and Mum are ruining our lives.'

'You're not going anywhere, sweetheart.'

'But who's that woman? She was in the kitchen the other day. This is mental.'

'We need help with Barney since your mum's not here.'

'You're literally having sex with her.'

I did a barefoot happy dance on the tiled bathroom floor, thrilled at the confrontation.

'I wish you hadn't seen it, but it's nothing serious.'

Nothing serious? I was deadly fucking serious, so no need to insult me.

'Let's not upset your mum. If you're both grown-up about this, and don't tell anyone yet, when you've passed your driving tests I'll buy you a brand new Mini to share.'

They fell silent, either considering the offer or staring him out for trying to buy them off. Lucky bitches. I wanted a new car too. But they could bugger off in it and not rely on us for lifts.

'Come on,' he said, 'let's have breakfast on the High Street, and talk it through.'

Bastard. But he could sort out the teen drama to our advantage, since I may have pushed it a tiny bit too far too soon. He had to pull it back so Emma didn't pounce back to rescue them from the den of iniquity. When they went out, I rifled through his suit pockets and briefcase, but didn't find anything of interest. I cast a glance over my future home and left.

Emma: the real story

Writing my journal helped focus my mind, but I couldn't write about the plan. The journal was my 'official' account of what happened, which I tucked away in a drawer for safekeeping. Now I could return to the real story, the one I'd covered up, including the spy app. Its sinister undertone buzzed through me, my life turning shades darker. I'd said in the journal that the app helped me check on Barney. It was half true, but Jules called it our secret weapon against Lydia. She was brazen, but she wasn't the only devious one.

I fortified myself with wine as Lydia schmoozed Elliot on the playback. I couldn't believe she was in my home making moves on my husband. They both shocked me beyond belief. The device picked up their latest kitchen conversation. I recoiled from the flirty small talk, Lydia trying to impress Elliot. But a grim fascination kept me listening, a fist over my mouth. The sound of his voice took me back to when he had accused me of having an affair.

'Fuck you,' I muttered under my breath. I swigged wine and said it louder. 'Fuck you. Fuck the pair of you.'

How dare they? I paced about, fingers pressed to my temples. The girls didn't reply to my text. Had he turned them against me? I self-medicated with the whole bottle of wine to blot out the pain.

The next morning, light filtered through the curtains, and my head thumped. I hauled myself up as the boozy after-effects reverberated around my head. I had to detach from Elliot's antics. He might be calling the shots, but this was my chance to make it on my terms. Today I'd do better. I would drink less and go out.

A call came through from Lucy. 'Are you okay?' she asked, warmth in her voice.

'Getting there. Thanks for sorting the spy apps. I've been listening in.'

'It must be hard going,' she said. 'In case Jules hasn't mentioned it, the listening devices aren't traceable back to us.'

'That's good.' I didn't want Lydia and Elliot finding them and accusing me.

Jules had swiftly added the spy devices to the TV remote and Wi-Fi box just as Elliot turned up in a rage to throw me out. Lucy might be quiet but she was tech-savvy. Her work on an IT help desk gave her the inside track. Jules had enlisted her help, since we knew Lucy had form with surveillance. When she'd suspected her own husband's affair, she confronted him and he denied it, calling her mad. So she became a dab hand at covertly tracking him. When certain of her facts, she sent him a compilation of the evidence and signed off as *Your mad soon-to-be ex-wife*.

After the phone call with Lucy, I remembered Jules had packed me a swimsuit, so I wriggled into it, pulled on some clothes and grabbed a towel. Closing the front door behind me, I breathed in salty fresh air. My fingertips brushed over the lavender bushes that lined the path to the cottage, releasing a soothing scent. I walked towards the sea with an all-consuming need to lose myself. By the time I reached the shore, the hangover had eased enough for me to wade into the turbulent sea. The waves were crashing and so was I.

A huge wave built, ready to knock me over. I dived under and came up gasping for air in the cold water. I needed to feel something other than heartache. The pull of the sea tugged me back, the waves knocking me over, pebbles and silt dragging under my toes. Saltwater stung my nose, my eyes. I kept diving under the waves again and again, fighting against the tide.

Breathless, I let the waves push me back to shore, where I sat on a rock and the wind dried my hair. My skin tingled bright red, my legs shook, but I felt more alive than I had in ages. I was only supposed to stay for a week, but with the kids going away, this was a good place to recover myself. It was far enough from Esher for some distance, close enough to drive back in a couple of hours. I'd tasted freedom and liked it, despite the sense of foreboding from what lay ahead.

Ours would be a bad divorce. I didn't need a big house and expensive holidays, but once you had that lifestyle for your kids, it locked you in. My priority was keeping things stable for them, but the boss of break-ups was already creating havoc, while Jules insisted we take back control.

The swim had energised me, along with the brisk sea breeze. I missed my walks with Barney and the way he dozed at my feet when I snatched some reading time before they all came home. He would love the beach, but he was looked after back home. Listening in, I'd heard the rattle of the lead, Barney's excited scamper and kind words directed at him.

I walked to the village store, where they'd optimistically hung inflatable beach toys, buckets and spades from the shopfront, blowing wildly in the wind. I stood at the notice board of advertising cards. I wanted to stay for the whole summer, find a cheap place to live. I could offer my services for dog walking, cooking, whatever, but jobs must be scarce in a sleepy place like this. One notice caught my eye: *Seasonal cleaner wanted. Flexible hours.* It could be a stopgap until the girls returned from France. When things settled, I'd find somewhere closer to them.

With no signal on my phone, I went in the shop and faced the unfriendly woman from before. She was reading *Chat* magazine behind the counter.

'Hi, there's a card outside for a cleaner at the caravan park. Can you tell me the way, please?'

'Cleaner? Are you living here then?' She peered at me.

'I'm staying up the hill.'

'You'll struggle to afford a place on a cleaner's wage.' She kept staring, as if trying to work me out.

I didn't tell her my plan to see about renting a small caravan in return for cleaning and maybe some extra pay. She gave me directions and I strode over there, hoping the job hadn't been filled. I hadn't seen the caravan park on my walks since it was tucked in on the other side of the bay.

At the entrance to the caravan park, I gathered my confidence at a Portakabin with *Manager's Office* on the door. I knocked. No answer, so I looked inside. Paperwork, keys and random junk piled up on the two desks. The landline rang but no one rushed to answer it. I surveyed the rows of caravans, looking for someone to ask. A man fed some goats in a field alongside the caravans. Two small children watched him.

'Excuse me,' I called over. 'I'm looking for Will.'

'Who wants him?'

'It's about the cleaning job.'

'For you, is it?' He looked at me, the wind blowing his curly hair in his eyes. It needed a cut.

'Yes.'

He finished feeding the goats. He was dressed like a farmer, with holes in his jumper, grubby jeans and mud-splattered wellies. I came closer, expecting him to elaborate.

'Watch it.' He nodded towards the bleating goats. 'They're buggers for escaping.'

He banged the gate shut behind him and trudged towards the Portakabin. Had the conversation ended? He stomped mud off his wellies and went into the scruffy office.

'Where do you live?' He held the door open for me.

'Over at Hillcombe.' I motioned back the way I'd come. 'I'm new to the area. Is Will around?'

'I'm Will.'

'Emma Morland.' I held my hand out to shake his.

'Are you already doing cleaning work?'

'Not yet. This is the first place I've tried. I'm a hard worker. Do you still need someone?'

'Just for the holiday season. Up to thirty hours a week, but I'll split it between two people so there's enough cover.'

'I can do thirty hours a week.'

'Seven days a week?'

'Except I'm away for four days next week with my daughters. Apart from that I'm available.' Once I'd dropped the girls in France, I would be a free agent.

'The shower and toilet blocks need doing every day. The rental caravans are cleaned on changeover days. It averages four or five hours a day, but it varies.'

'That's fine.' I'd never aspired to being a cleaner, but it was a job I could do. What would I say when he asked for references?

'When can you start?'

'Today?'

'I was hoping you'd say that. Do today as a trial. I'll pay you and we'll see how it goes.'

The phone started ringing again.

'Can you get that?' he asked, distracted by sifting through the pile of keys on the desk.

I picked up the phone and scrabbled for something to say. 'Caravan park. Can I help you?'

Someone wanted a summer booking, so Will grudgingly took the phone. I cast my gaze around the messy office until he finished the call.

'Do you need help in the office too?'

'I can't afford it.'

No matter. The cleaning job would keep me busy over the summer. When the autumn term began I would find a place to live with the girls. They still hadn't replied to my texts. I pushed through the hurt, nagged by a fear of Elliot and Lydia turning them against me.

Chapter Sixteen

Lydia

Now his daughters knew the score, we could move things forward. When Elliot phoned to update me on their teenage histrionics, I squashed the urge to laugh at their moral outrage. They posed a threat to my future happiness, so I made supportive noises.

'I should've locked the front door,' he said.

'It's done now. Shall I walk Barney later?'

'It's too soon.'

'It's already out there, Elliot. Let's deal with it. If they can't talk to you, they'll go running to their mum. Communication is important for girls.'

'They've got a dim view of you.'

It's mutual.

'They'll come round,' I said smoothly. 'Buying them a car is fine, but girls need emotional support.' He was clueless about teen girl hormones if he thought a car would solve everything.

'I just want it sorted.'

'We both want that. They know I help out with Barney, so if they see me doing that, they'll warm to me. Why don't I walk him when they're at college?' I said. 'When you're home, we can have an adult conversation with them.'

'I'd rather let it settle.'

'They're intelligent, like their dad. If you don't take control, they'll gravitate towards Emma.' I could make an effort with them for a week or so until they buggered off for the summer.

'I don't want to lose them.'

'Why don't you tell them you'll sit round the table like adults? If you say "like adults" they'll appreciate it. You'll validate their feelings, which helps them come to terms with it. Then you bring them around to your way of thinking.'

'I'll see. So you'll walk Barney tomorrow while they're out?'

The next day, I walked the stupid dog and then went to Marianne's for lunch. She must be keen for gossip. I was too, about Emma. I sifted through Isabella's wardrobe and picked out a loose pink top with *Wanted* emblazoned on it in diamanté studs.

Marianne opened the door in an orange batwing jumper and blue cropped trousers. 'Cute,' she said, looking at my top, hand on hip.

'I'll take off my shoes in case they're dirty. I've just walked Barney.'

She led me to the kitchen and poured us some wine. 'You don't hang around. Already taking over from Emma.' She gave me the side-eye. Her voice had an edge. She'd better not lecture me about husband-stealing.

'Elliot appreciates me stepping in. The twins need looking after.'

'I didn't have you down as the maternal type.'

'They're charming girls.' I accepted the wine and took a sip. 'The marriage has been shaky for a while.'

'Did you know I'm Crawford's second wife?'

'*Are* you?'

'He was married when we met. I was his PA.'

'And look how that turned out.'

'Sure, it can work, but you're the woman so you'll be blamed.'

'What about Emma?'

'Her too.' She swept around the kitchen taking food from the fridge and laying it out on the polished granite worktop. 'Dollar to a doughnut, if a wife cheats, it's her fault. If the husband cheats, it's the other woman's fault. But sometimes marriages don't work out. They gave it a decent go, raised two beautiful kids.'

'Are you in touch with her?'

'No. She must have gone off with the man in question, whoever he is. No one seems to know. She needs a new start. With the kids nearly grown, she realised she had zilch in common with her old man. It happens. But it's kinda worked out – she has a new man and you have Elliot.'

These women were ruthless, Marianne dropping Emma for leaving her husband, while my status increased. Emma leaving him meant she'd lost her social circle. Marianne was nowhere near as judgemental as I'd feared. I liked the thought of a female friend; someone on my level, shrewd and intelligent. We both spoke our minds. If I had my own girl squad they would be smart, successful and brilliant company, and they would prove their loyalty to me. I'd never fared well with female friendships before. Men adored me, but the women needed watching.

'Thank you for understanding.'

'I understand a lot, which is why I'm saying don't expect an easy ride. Elliot's charming, but he's a high achiever. He might earn a lot and be the life and soul of the party, but his type isn't the easiest to live with, not if you're the one keeping the home fires burning. You'll need to stroke his ego.'

'I'm already stroking it. I see his ego as big-dick energy, and the perks are wonderful. I get to sleep with him.' I took a congratulatory swig of wine.

She raised her glass to mine in a toast. 'Here's to wonderful perks.'

'He's a passionate man,' I said. 'There's something compelling about him. Successful people have that effect on me.'

'Elliot's a lucky man.'

'What about Jules?' I asked. 'What's her view?'

'You can bet your life she'll *have* a view. I haven't seen her since book club, so I'll let you know.'

I liked her dismissive tone. Even so, I was dying for Jules's take, since she'd introduced us, knowing the marriage had expired. Indiscreet, if you asked me. If Emma wanted to blame someone, her beloved twin was first in the firing line.

There was usually a dominant twin. I bet Isabella bossed her twin around, and their meek mum was controlled by her twin. Jules had basically handed me a loaded gun. Was that her dirty little secret? She was jealous of her twin's perfect family and home, the handsome man paying for everything, while Jules had to fend for herself in menial work and a pokey flat?

Marianne laid out a platter of smoked salmon and cold meats with salad and bread.

'I'm ditching book club.' I'd no use for it now. I was tempted to drop into Jules's bookshop though. She couldn't be vile to me at her workplace.

'Wise move. Are you still working?'

'I do flexitime. The hours fit around me.'

'It doesn't sound like a flexitime job,' she said. 'All those demanding VIPs.'

'I'm strategising. It's higher level.' *Total girl boss, that's me.*

'What does that involve?' She looked pointedly at me.

'I'm producing a five-year plan.'

'Which is?'

'It's an exit plan to build the business up and sell. I'm looking at the optimum income streams to target. We aim to maximise the return in the short- to medium-term.'

'What's it called again?'

I dredged up the name from my memory. 'Faulkner and Associates.'

'I bet you're excellent at strategising.' She arched an eyebrow. 'I suppose you plan to move in with Elliot? I'm sure he can't wait.' Surrey's answer to WikiLeaks kept digging for information.

'It's early days. We're considering his daughters.' Christ, I sounded like Elliot.

'Well, Emma's gone and there's a vacancy to fill.'

I bet Marianne moved in on her husband in a calculating way, which spurred me on. After lunch, I parked outside Luca's and texted Elliot, not mentioning that I'd seen Marianne.

> I'll meet some friends this evening if you're busy. x

His reply pinged back.

Come over. I've decided to speak to the girls. I'll explain that you're a temporary fix. X

A temporary fix? x

Bloody nerve.

You know what I mean. I'll smooth things over with them and see how they are with you. 8pm suit you? X

I didn't need their approval, for fuck's sake. I wanted to scream and rant and break things, but instead I bared my teeth and thumped the steering wheel. I just needed a rich man who saw my true worth and appreciated me. Why was that so hard when Marianne could steal herself a wealthy husband? *Newsflash, Elliot! I'm a catch, in case you haven't noticed.* I slammed the car door and stomped up to the flat.

Emma: the real story

Will gave me a brisk tour of the caravan park. He walked fast, tea slopping over the side of his mug. I nearly ran to keep up. A pink caravan with bunting in the windows caught my eye.

'Does anyone live in this one?' I asked about the caravan set apart from the rest.

'God, no. A pair of hippies abandoned it. It's a dumping ground for junk.'

It could see me through the summer, if I had the nerve to ask.

'How old are your children?' I said.

'My son's twenty-three. He lives in Bristol.'

'Oh, I thought those two little ones were yours. The ones watching you feed the goats.'

'Their parents have a caravan here. They like the goats. What about you? You said you had daughters?'

'They're seventeen. I'm separated from their dad, so this is a fresh start.'

'Here's as good a place as any.' He forged ahead, pointing things out, and then left me to clean the shower block.

At the end of my shift, he gave me three twenties and asked me to come back in the morning. He ran the place single-handedly and spread himself thin. If I lived in while the twins were away, I could help in peak season, then return to Surrey in September.

Back at the cottage, evening gloom settled around me, the weather still overcast. The lack of street lights or houses nearby unnerved me. Anyone might lurk in the shadows. I couldn't even focus on reading, not when I kept checking for non-existent messages from the twins.

With no word from home, I ventured into my secret app. A tingle travelled from the roots of my hair down the back of my neck when I heard murmurs from the girls preparing food and chatting with Barney, along with sounds of him being fed and taken for walks. They hadn't forgotten him even if they'd forgotten me.

Elliot would tell me stories of clients' infidelities and the awful ways that divorces played out. He wasn't much of a reader, but he'd read a novel about a man who set up surveillance cameras in his home. It gave me the creeps that a husband would spy on his family like that. Yet I had done the same. I curled up in bed and struggled to sleep in the murky, muggy night. Relief crept through me when dawn light filtered through the curtains.

I walked to the caravan park and arrived early for my shift.

'You're keen,' Will said. 'I'll put the kettle on.'

I followed him into the cluttered office. With some work, he could fit in a fridge and a wall of shelves to sell a few basics for caravanners, or a vending machine that dispensed useful stuff like toothbrushes and toiletries. The answerphone screen on his phone unit showed eight messages.

'Shall I check these messages?'

'I've been avoiding them but go on.'

I pressed play and grabbed a pen and scrap of paper. One man sounded annoyed at the lack of response to his phone message and email.

Will rolled his eyes. 'Pain in the arse. I'll do it dreckly.'

'Directly?'

'Dreckly. It's the West Country version of *mañana*, as in, whenever.'

'Can I?' I motioned to his email screen on the desktop, and he nodded for me to go ahead.

I found the man's email. Will dictated a reply and I fired it off. Then I crossed it off the message list and handed it to him.

'Wow. You get stuff done.'

'You know that caravan you're using for storage?' I asked.

'I'll sort it out sometime,' he said without conviction.

'Can we have a look before I clock on?'

We took our coffees over and he unlocked it. I peered inside the neglected space with random stuff piled on every surface. A TV aerial overhung the sink, a yellowing extension lead curled uselessly on the draining board and flimsy curtains were slung over the seating. The floor could hardly be seen under cardboard boxes and rags hardened with dried stains. It looked watertight though, with a dinky hob and microwave. I checked out the tiny shower room at one end, and I could use the caravan park facilities.

'Do you live on-site?' I asked.

'No, I'm doing up a place near here.'

'What if people need you out of hours?'

'I'm always driving over in the evenings when people lose their keys or if things don't work.'

I bit my lip and steeled myself, feeling the fear and doing it anyway. 'What if I lived in temporarily? I could clear this out and live in it.'

He looked incredulous.

'Could I have it rent-free in return for being on call?' I braced myself for rejection.

'This skanky thing? Why do you want to live here?'

'It'll scrub up okay. I can do it in my own time.'

'Take one of the better caravans until the season picks up.'

'Thanks, but I'd rather get settled here.' I liked its quirkiness and the pretty setting. A hedge covered in clusters of white buds ran alongside it, wildflowers grew all around and a neglected herb garden sprouted from a wooden barrel.

'You might regret it. I won't though, with you on call.'

He grinned and I glowed from his trust in me. If he saw my home in Esher, he'd doubt me starting again in a rickety caravan. But the nearby rush of the sea calmed me and I wouldn't be so alone here.

'You're not on the run from the law, are you?' He looked searchingly at me.

'No. It's a new start.'

I cleaned madly on my shift, then pressure washed the outside of my new home, blasting away dirt and green algae. The wind blew the spray in my face, soaking me, but it felt like progress. I arrived back at the cottage and phoned Jules with the news.

'I can't believe you've got a cleaning job,' she said in a pained voice. 'You're supposed to take a break from cleaning up other people's mess.'

'It's a stopgap for the summer.'

'It proves you don't need the bastard after all.'

'Have you heard from the girls? They've gone quiet on me.'

'Because that bastard's bribed them with the offer of a car. They caught Lydia in your bed. He made them promise not to tell you, so they told me instead. They don't care about the car, but they didn't want to upset you about Lydia.'

I stared blindly out of the window. 'Are they all right?'

'They're outraged in their usual way. Or Isabella is.'

It didn't play out through the listening devices, since the range didn't stretch upstairs.

'He tried to justify it by saying you're having an affair. They think you've buggered off to be with a mystery man.'

'What did you say?'

'I said you're not having an affair. They asked why he'd lie, so I said maybe he's upset and it's important for them to know it's not true. You'll be pleased I didn't call him a lying, cheating psycho.'

I fell silent at them feeling let down by both parents.

'They're okay,' Jules said. 'They're bright enough to see Lydia for what she is.'

I had to tell them I wasn't having an affair. When my marriage turned cold, I had poured all my love into them. No way would I have chosen to leave home before them. I tried phoning them in turn, but they kept up the silent treatment. Served me right for abandoning them, but Elliot infuriated me. The absolute bastard. It pushed me to do what I'd been psyching myself up for. I called a woman named Sally from Elliot's past.

Chapter Seventeen

Lydia

Isabella and Chloe faced us across the kitchen table. Chloe pursed her lips and petted the dog, avoiding eye contact. I bet her mother was a sulker too. Isabella thumbed her phone.

'Put the phone down,' Elliot said.

'It's okay. Start. I'm listening.' She kept on messaging with her father's efficient brand of confidence.

'Put the phone down.'

She clunked it onto the table and folded her arms. He commanded some respect now. 'What's this about, exactly?' Isabella looked down her nose.

'Well…' Elliot studied his clasped hands. 'I want to speak to you about what's going on.'

'We can discuss it like adults,' I said.

Isabella glared at me. The other one kept petting her emotional support dog. Stroke, stroke, stroke.

'Your mum was having an affair,' Elliot said. 'She decided to leave when I found out. I know that's hard for you because it's a side of her you haven't seen.'

The two of them exchanged a deadpan look. I expected Elliot to go on, but… nothing. Strange of him to find it uncomfortable, considering his line of work. A muscle pulsed in the side of his face. So that was why he wanted me here. He couldn't handle this alone. It worked in my favour. Without Emma to handle the girls' emotions, he could outsource that to me too.

'I offered to help out with Barney,' I said, 'because he's a sweetie and I know you don't want him left alone all day. Your dad was lonely on Saturday night with you two away, and we ended up spending the night together.'

'You were actually making out in my mum's bed.' Isabella looked at me in contempt. 'Are you married?'

When did teenagers become so judgemental? I couldn't have cared less at her age. Chloe stopped playing with the dog and pouted at me.

'No. I'm single.'

'Are you moving in?'

I should bloody hope so. 'Let's not get ahead of ourselves. I know it's a shock. Your dad wants you both to be okay. I'd like to carry on walking Barney to help out.'

Elliot sat back in his chair, letting me handle his dirty work.

'Does that sound okay?' I asked.

Isabella picked up her phone. Chloe looked away.

'Chloe?' I said, going for divide and rule, since she was the weakest.

She nodded.

'Good,' I said. 'And what about you, Isabella? Can I help with Barney?'

'S'pose.' She lifted herself from the table with both hands. 'Is that it?' She flashed a resentful look at Elliot.

'Yes, you can go.'

They both walked out. Elliot went to the fridge and took out the Chablis. He closed the kitchen door behind them. I awaited my praise for handling it so well. He slumped back down, pressing his fingers to his temples.

'That was awful.'

'They might not like it yet, but they'll be fine.'

He poured us a glass of wine each. He wasn't chucking me out yet, so I stood behind him and massaged his shoulders. He sighed and leaned forward, responding to my fingers working on his tense muscles.

'No wonder you're stressed, dealing with all this.' I kept kneading his shoulders. 'It was special in bed with you on Saturday night.' I wrapped my arms around him and murmured, 'You're so sexy.'

He groaned and stood up to face me. 'If you knew what you did to me.'

'Tell me.'

I pressed my body against his. He kissed me and ran his fingers through my hair.

'I'd like to take you to bed,' he murmured.

'Mmm.'

'But we have to hold off.'

'They're nearly grown up.'

'Let's see how they handled our chat. We can always take Barney to our favourite spot in the woods.'

'That was a one-off. Heat of the moment. We'll be arrested taking risks in a nice area like this. It'll ruin your reputation.'

'I want you *now*.' He buried his face in my hair and held me tight.

That'd focus him. I was worth more than a quick shag against a tree. I didn't like this weird limbo as unpaid dog walker for a man who preferred to pacify his sullen kids than spend time with me. My phone pinged and I fell back on what made him jealous.

'Someone wants to meet me for a drink.'

'Don't go.'

'You want me to stay?'

'I mean don't go out for a drink. I can't be stuck here when you're going out.'

'Oh, Elliot, if we're not together I can't say no to going out.'

'We are together. Just bear with me.'

What a nerve, expecting me to stay home alone. 'Let me know what you plan to do.' I gave him the briefest kiss on the lips and left.

When I walked in the flat, Luca turned to look at me. It threw me, since he usually hunched over his computer and ignored me.

I recovered myself and smiled. 'Hi, how are you?'

He turned back to his keyboard. 'You need to leave by the end of the month.'

I gasped. 'Why?'

'Um.' He bowed his head. 'A friend's coming to stay.'

'But you don't have any friends.'

He rubbed his thumb between his eyebrows, up and down.

'Can't this *friend* sleep on the couch?'

I waited for him to back down, but he kept rubbing with his thumb and staring at the keyboard.

'If you don't want me here,' I said in a sad voice, aiming for sympathy, 'I'll try to find somewhere else.' I bet that witchy Rosa put him up to this.

Emma: the real story

Lydia moved in on my territory and I swallowed it, along with mouthfuls of wine.

Your mum was having an affair.

You're so sexy.

Why was he letting her poison spread to the girls? My fury surged. The selfish idiot couldn't even wait for them to go away before indulging in his own lust. And he was flaunting her to the twins as revenge on me. I eventually got Chloe on the phone and my heart cracked open at her small, sad voice. I arranged to go back for a visit.

The next morning, I went in early and found Will playing football with the goats.

'I'm sorry to ask,' I called over the fence. 'But can I take this weekend off?'

He stopped running around. The goats bleated and butted him with their horns. 'Had a better offer?'

'No. I need to check on my daughters. I'll blitz the place on Friday morning. I know it's a big ask when I've already booked time off, but I've no plans for the rest of the summer.' Getting the job surprised me and I hadn't been thinking straight, but I couldn't abandon my children.

'My friend's teenage son does casual work. He's not a patch on you, but he can do the weekend cleaning. When the season hots up, I'll need you for more important things, since you're good with the punters.'

It helped that the place was nowhere near full. We were still in the doldrums of overcast weather before the school holidays. Rain had made the caravan fields sodden, but the temperature crept up and the hills and hedgerows looked lush.

Later in the day, Lucy called me on WhatsApp video to say she'd picked the combination lock on Lydia's suitcase.

'You did?' I scratched my head in confusion. 'Have you been in Lydia's flat?'

'We're there now, me and Rosa. Luca's just put the kettle on.'

The camera panned to Rosa waving. Behind her, a young man in a darkened kitchen sniffed dubiously at a milk carton. Then Lucy trained the camera on an open suitcase with a pile of handwritten notes on top.

I snorted. 'How did you pick the lock?'

'There's usually a way,' she said darkly.

'You're a marvel. What did you find?'

'No ID, she must carry it with her. There's some strange notes and a mind map with all our names on it and how to win us over.'

'Except me,' Rosa said in the background. 'She calls us The Witches of Esher. She says "ignore the witch" about me.'

'Send me a screenshot.'

'We can't send anything electronically,' Lucy said, aiming the camera at a page of handwritten notes. 'Don't want to leave a trace. This is a list of seven things. It's from a book about seven habits.'

'Success habits not bad habits,' Rosa chipped in. 'It's for people with no imagination and no soul.'

'We won't read it for book club,' I said.

'Also, she's cleansing her aura of negativity,' Lucy said. 'Because she's spiritual.'

'Pah!' Rosa said, and Luca handed out mugs of tea, his face serious.

'I guess walking all over people is spiritual.' Lucy turned the screen back to herself. 'Her seven things are, "Be proactive: convince Elliot to value the good in life (me)".' She did a perfect impression of Lydia's breathy voice, accompanied by hair flicking and eye fluttering. '"Dazzle him with my charm and gorgeousness while channelling millionaire energy like a queen".'

'What a treat,' Rosa said, deadpan. 'I wish she'd write a self-help book.'

Lucy dissolved into peals of infectious laughter. Then the three of us were laughing like it was the funniest thing ever, laughing at the absurdity of it. Lucy normally laughed easily, but she hadn't since Lydia had turned up and looked down on her. She and Rosa wiped away tears, shoulders shaking as they stifled a fresh wave of hilarity. Luca looked baffled, which made it even funnier.

Rosa took over reading. '"Think win-win: Elliot is thrilled to wake up beside a total babe like me".' It was bizarre to hear Lydia's words read aloud by Rosa. 'You want me to carry on?'

'I've got the picture, thank you.'

'I detest her, the con artist. Kick her out, Luca. You're not safe. We'll change the locks.'

I was lucky to have them as friends, even though our actions were warped from the Lydia effect.

I drove back on Friday to stay with Jules, still seething about Elliot. Lydia was nuts, but he should have known better. The girls told him they were going on a sleepover. He didn't ask who with, since he didn't know their friends' names. Jules and I sunned ourselves on her balcony. It lowered my stress levels before picking the twins up.

'Marianne had lunch with Lydia,' Jules said, 'her new bestie.'

'I expect Marianne's plying her with wine and wheedling out the details.'

'I'd need a sick bucket. Is your new boss okay about the time off?'

'Will? He's been great.'

'Is he single, this Will?'

‘I’m not thinking in those terms.’ I gazed out at the river view from her balcony.

‘Why not? Elliot hasn’t let the grass grow. It’s like *The Guernsey Literary and Potato Peel Pie Society*. I love Juliet, leaving her entitled man for Guernsey and a pig farmer.’

‘Will doesn’t have pigs.’

‘You said he has goats. Same ballpark.’ She went straight to her copy on the crowded bookshelves lining her flat. She called them insulation from the neighbours. ‘Here. I prescribe this for your mental health.’

I slid the book in my bag.

‘You know we thought Lydia must have a false name?’ Jules said. She’d been trying to verify Lydia’s background ever since she was in the house with the twins. Anything dodgy and I’d swoop in and take the girls away. ‘Lucy says she’ll do a reverse image search. We just need a photo, which she can upload somewhere. If her photo’s been online anywhere under a different name, we’ll find it.’

‘Can we get a photo?’

‘I can’t get close enough without her noticing. The twins could do it under some pretext.’

‘Let’s not involve them.’ I stood up. ‘I have to go, but I spoke to Sally Hill.’

‘Elliot’s old secretary? What did she say?’

‘I’ll be late for the kids.’

‘Tell me, quick.’

‘She gave me a whole pile of dirt on him. See you in the morning.’ I hugged Jules and left.

I drove to the end of the village just as the girls came bounding towards me, backpacks stuffed with sleepover kit, Barney tugging on the lead. He jumped up and I threw my arms wide to hug both girls at once. I buried my face in their hair, loving them squashed against me, breathing in the marzipan smell of their shampoo. Happiness surged through me at seeing them instead of covertly listening in. They'd hate me for it. I hated me for it.

Chapter Eighteen

Lydia

The kids left for a sleepover and took the stupid dog. I couldn't believe that my sex life was dependent on their social life. On the bright side, I had another night in the house, in his bed – soon to be *our* bed – without kids or dogs. I parked up the road until the three of them went shambling off for the night, then I took my overnight bag inside, as agreed with Elliot. The house felt exclusive and intimate without them. Our house, not theirs. I intended to put that on a permanent footing.

I decided to wow him with my gourmet skills by preparing salmon wellington and new potatoes with parsley and butter. It was 'Specially Selected' by Lidl, and yes, it did count as cooking when I'd bought it and put the bloody thing in the oven. Being a domestic goddess, I checked the ingredients so I could wing it if he asked how I'd made it. At least it was an opportunity to showcase the advantages of sex on tap and me helping out, since he hadn't yet hired a housekeeper. I turned on the oven and tipped the pre-prepared spuds into a dish for the microwave. Then I hid all the packaging at the bottom of the bin. Elliot came in around seven and I poured him a drink.

'We have the house to ourselves,' I said with a suggestive smile.

'I've told the girls to text me before they come home, so we won't have a repeat of last time. We won't lounge in bed in the morning, in case they catch us.'

'Fine.' I'd keep him up half the night instead, lead him on in the morning and leave him desperate for more. That'd teach him.

'If anyone asks, just say you're helping with dog walking until Emma comes home.'

'Is that what you think? I'm a stand-in until Emma comes home?'

'We can't rush this.'

'Let's not creep round as if we're having an affair.' I kept the indignant tone from my voice. 'Emma did the dirty on you, so you're free to be with me.'

'It's not that simple. If we're going to keep seeing each other, we need to do it right. Are you with me on this?'

'I'm with you.' I leaned in for a smooch to show how manly I found him, when the whole situation did my head in.

He was hard already and kissed me with urgency, his hands feeling their way around my body. Before I knew it, he was fucking me against the kitchen wall. He couldn't resist me. It was like a drug, but he needed a daily fix to become addicted so I could gain control.

Bloody cheek, calling me the home help. I would work on his mindset. By late evening, he'd downed a load of booze and fallen into a deep sleep before I could fire him up again in bed.

Fortunately, he was an early riser, in more ways than one, so I set the alarm on my phone and initiated a session first thing. It was less rushed in bed. He liked taking control, so I guided him to do it the way I liked. It was akin to dog training with praise and treats, so they did what you wanted.

'We should do that every day.' He lay back in bed. 'Wouldn't that be amazing?'

'I love sex in the morning. Gets me going for the day.'

'Me too. I meant to tell you though, my boss asked when I'm moving to the Birmingham office.'

His face dropped. 'Don't move to Birmingham.'

'I'm moving out of the flat at the end of the month, which means signing a six-month lease somewhere else. A decent place to live is pricey around here, so I might move a bit further out. It'll mean seeing less of you.'

I tested his generosity. If he wanted me, he could set me up in a pad or move me in.

'I want you here. It's just the girls…'

'If you give them some credit they'll surprise you. Young people are adaptable, and they're out a lot. If everything else stays stable, they'll accept me. I felt them thawing when we talked around the table.'

'Hmm.'

'They're off to France next week.' I was counting the days. 'And they're going to university in a year. It'll soon creep up and you'll be rattling round alone.' I stroked his chest with my forefinger. 'It's going well between us, isn't it? The sex is amazing. Be a shame to lose it.'

'Leave it with me. Don't go to Birmingham.'

He wanted me. The urgency would focus his mind. I didn't need tacit permission from his daughters. They'd find out soon who the real boss was. Then I'd make them pay.

The twins and I arrived at Jules's flat. She went to stay with a friend to give us some space.

'How's it going at home?' I turned the oven on for pizza.

'Why are you letting this happen?' Isabella said. 'It's crazy.'

'It is, sweetheart. I'm sorry you have to deal with it. Your dad's chosen to be with her—'

'Because you went off with another man. I can't believe you did that, Mum.'

'I didn't.' I held her gaze.

'But Dad said so.'

'There isn't anyone else. There was only ever your dad.'

'So he's lying?'

'People get angry over splitting up. Things get said that aren't always true.'

They stared intently, looking as if they believed me.

'So why should we stay in the house with Dad and *her*? You should be home.'

'Has she moved in?' Surely she hadn't moved in.

'We think Dad's holding off till we go to France,' Chloe said dolefully.

'If he asks us, we'll say no.'

'We have to text him before we come home tomorrow, in case they're *at it* again.'

They made disgusted faces. I tried not to mirror them. They talked to me in a way they never did with Elliot. He saw that as my job.

'Your dad's made up his mind. Can you handle it if Lydia's nice to you? Because that's best.' It wasn't best. It bloody well was *not* best. I said it for their sakes in a clipped tone to stop my raging emotions spilling out. 'You can call me anytime.'

'Why can't Dad move out?'

'We agreed to do it that way for now because he pays the bills—'

'Mum,' Isabella said. 'We're feminists. He can't kick you out.'

'I'm being a feminist by getting a job and my own place. He works in London, so it costs a lot to live within commuting distance. I've moved somewhere cheap until we sort it out.' I disguised the tug in my voice that nearly choked me.

'But we want you, not *her*.'

'I'm still your mum and things'll be more sorted by the time you're home from France. I'll find somewhere close to you.'

I slid the pizza from the oven. They laid into it and chatted about a friend's eighteenth birthday party in September. I took comfort in their changing tides of emotion, overcome with indignation before their faces lit up at the prospect of a party.

'Dad said he'd buy us a Mini,' Chloe said.

'If we don't tell you about Lydia shagging him,' Isabella said.

'You can tell me anything. It won't get back to your dad.' Let him buy them a car. Spending money on them would wind Lydia up.

'Why are you putting up with it?' Chloe asked.

'Sometimes you have to be the bigger person. You can't control other people, but you can rise above it.' And I was arming myself for the battleground of divorce. Elliot would accuse me of breaking up the family while he provided a loving home for the girls, so I had to play him at his own game. That was Jules's plan.

They looked solemnly at me.

'It doesn't stop me missing you like mad.'

'Can't you and Dad get back together?'

'I'm sorry, love, it's gone beyond that.'

They wanted me back, but the house might as well be radioactive. Elliot was making terrible choices and what if the twins' strong sense of right and wrong caused trouble? He made a living from warring couples but couldn't handle the emotional fallout of teenagers. And Lydia's mask would slip. She underestimated me at her cost. If she hurt them, I'd kill her. And I'd kill him too.

Part Two

'Half the truth is often a great lie.'

Benjamin Franklin

Chapter Nineteen

Emma: the real story

Two weeks to the murder

My *official* journal was filled with what happened from the day I met Lydia. It told the story of a woman in a tired marriage whose alpha husband had a fling with someone younger. It was a story for the police, for the law court. It wasn't the truth-truth, as the twins would say. The real story played out between the lines. The one I'd been covering up for years.

I set Lydia up. She thought she'd masterminded her seduction of Elliot, but I made it easy. Well, Jules made it easy. Anyone reading the journal would consider me another of Lydia's victims. I was downtrodden in places, a bit dopey here and there. But I'd rather the police thought me naïve and oblivious to Elliot's bad behaviour than see me for the conniving wife I became.

I didn't portray myself as a total saint. I included the bit about having my family under surveillance. Not quite the actions of a doting wife and mum but admitting some character flaws made me more credible. I claimed to have the spy app for Barney, which was half true. But I also monitored my lying, cheating husband.

It was Jules's idea to bug the house. She predicted Elliot would stray and then cover his tracks. She always sussed out people's motives, including characters in novels, and she guessed the twists. I didn't like the idea of surveillance, but audio wasn't as intrusive as filming them. Elliot and the kids might spot a hidden camera, but not a microphone inside the Wi-Fi router and TV remote.

The journal helped straighten out my cover story in case I was called upon in court. I was selective about what I wrote. It would do no harm if the police searched the house and found it; I would say writing it down helped me process the whole awful business. Journalling was therapeutic for a bookish introvert like me. But the best therapy was exacting revenge on my bastard husband.

Lydia was a good liar and so was I. In my darker moments, I wished Elliot dead. I wished for an avalanche to bury him on the ski slopes, or a racing-yacht drowning in Antigua. Or how about a parachute malfunction far away from the kids and me?

Elliot had people believe I led a charmed existence, and Lydia fell for it. But I lived in a gilded cage. Everyone thought me the tidy one, even the kids, but he wanted everything just so. Cleaning was my self-defence. I kept things perfect so he wouldn't hurt me.

At eighteen, I went to uni to find myself, but Elliot found me instead and made me his. How he changed from the man I had married! As his career progressed, he went from warm confidence to arrogance. 'It's me who pays for all this,' he liked to say once we'd had the twins, as if having an income excused him from showing consideration.

One time, I saw an interesting job advertised and wanted to apply. Elliot said the jobs market had become tougher and I would struggle.

'Don't set yourself up for a fall, not with your anxiety issues,' he said. 'It's better for you to look after everything at home. You're lucky. A lot of women would love to give up work.'

Then the school where I volunteered suggested I apply for a teaching assistant job. I could be home in time to sort out the house and dinner. Surely Elliot wouldn't be threatened by me working with children.

'Ungrateful bitch,' he snarled when I raised it with him. He grabbed my arms, his face inches from mine, eyes dark with anger. 'Caring for your family not good enough? Think you can pick up a school-run dad?'

'It's not—'

'If you so much as look at another man, you're in trouble,' he threatened in his nasty low voice.

I closed my eyes, willing him to lay off.

His grip tightened, his fingers digging in. 'Do you hear me, dirty slag?'

'Yes.' I screwed my eyes shut.

'Look at me.'

I stared him in the face, his eyes blazing and chin jutting.

'If you leave me,' he said with icy control, 'you won't get custody. I'll turn the girls against you. I know enough expert witnesses to discredit you.'

I shrank away. Reasoning or arguing brought out the lawyer in him and he had to win.

'If I pay for them, I keep them,' he kept on. 'You take them from me, I'll fight you in the courts, and we both know who'll win. Plus, you'll have no money until it's sorted. I know you can do without, but they can't.'

The girls were still little back then and I couldn't turn their lives upside down.

'Say sorry for being ungrateful.'

'Sorry,' I said, my voice shaking, every part of me shaking.

'What for?' He spat out the words.

'For being ungrateful.'

Then he came home with a puppy. The twins couldn't believe their luck and rolled around in ecstasy with the dog they named Barney. I didn't want a black Lab shedding hairs on the white tiles. He said the girls had always wanted a puppy, and my negative mood dragged him down.

A dog completed Elliot's image of a perfect family and it kept me busy walking Barney and cleaning the floor. He said it was cruel to leave him for more than a few hours. Homeworking wasn't an option, since he didn't want the house becoming a workplace. Never mind that it already was my workplace.

He chose family activities to suit his interests, teaching the girls to ski, cycle and sail. He played the doting father in public, often declaring that we were the three people he loved most, usually in front of someone he wanted to impress. The twins believed him, but he loved himself most.

He kept his reputation as a generous dad and rarely laid down the law in private. He didn't have to because I shielded the girls. I primed them not to clash, not to arouse his anger. They knew he wasn't perfect, but he was the proud dad and they believed in our traditional marriage. If he'd started on them, I would have found a way out somehow, even though he controlled the money and kept our passports locked in his London office.

Book club was the only outlet he allowed, because it was women only, and women he knew he could charm. Well, that and the women-only gym, the eternal birthday present from him, 'Because you don't want to let yourself go'.

He found ways to stay front and centre, accompanied by an edge of tension. He never hit me, although he sometimes threatened it. The lawyer in him ensured he left no evidence. I retreated into myself, giving him no reason to be angry.

As my life grew shades darker, I tried to keep it light and breezy for the girls. He dressed us up as the perfect family and I hid the truth from Isabella and Chloe. I hid the truth from everyone, including myself. If I'd faced how bad my marriage had become, my life would have unravelled.

The first time we went to his company summer ball, his colleague referred to me as 'Elliot's gorgeous wife'. A minute later, Elliot leaned in and murmured, 'If you ever leave me, I'll break you.' Anyone would think he whispered sweet nothings, his breath warm on my cheek. He was so charming, my husband. Everyone said so.

As the kids grew independent, the burden of marriage outweighed the benefit to them. To have my own life I had to break free, but I knew Elliot would never let me go. He would strip me of everything and turn the girls against me. I was stuck. Then along came lying, cheating Lydia.

In leaving Elliot, I didn't act alone. Jules knew I wouldn't go until the kids left home, but what if she found a replacement so he would let me go? She tried convincing me when the twins turned sixteen, but the idea of throwing an innocent woman in his path made my stomach roil. I wouldn't do it. No way. Until a year later when Jules met Lydia, scoping out rich men at the tennis club, and sussed out her motive. A flirty single woman who didn't play tennis stuck out. Jules told her about the swish houses at book club and Lydia became a heat-seeking missile.

Jules steered her into our lives, knowing it was not a done deal: Elliot might dislike her or avoid the risk of getting involved. Jules followed him one time after he left work and saw him meet a younger woman in a bar. They went to a hotel and up to a room. She told me later that the younger woman looked similar to Lydia. Jules kept the plan to herself, not expecting Lydia to go nuclear at the first opportunity. The rest of us refused to have her back after the first book club.

'There's a reason I want her there,' Jules said.

'Which is?'

'Read between the lines.'

'I don't know what that means and I don't want her back in my home.'

'She's on the lookout for a rich husband. You need to leave your rich husband.'

'*What*? Have you lost your fucking mind?' Every flaw in the plan screamed at me. Aside from anything, Elliot would never take the bait. He had too good a home life for Lydia to upset the balance, but I underestimated her. We all did. Jules predicted she would flirt with him when I was at Mum's and take it further when I took the girls to France. A covert affair might follow, which I would ignore until the kids left home next year. But it would take the heat off me, and put him in the wrong so I would be able to leave him.

When I recovered from the initial shock, Jules talked me round. 'She's ingratiating. Wants to be your bestie. Just go with it.'

I had a drink with Lydia at the wine bar. Conniving Lydia, so dazzled by her own brilliance, she'd no idea that I saw it all. The way she looked at me, my home, my husband, it sickened me. She would push me under a bus for Elliot, so I let her take him, not realising she'd take my children and our home too. I'd pictured him setting up a love nest until the divorce went through and the kids left home.

That's why I had the house under surveillance. I knew Elliot would look after Barney, but I had to check the twins were okay. I gripped my phone and listened intently, breathing out in relief when they sounded happy or stood their ground with Lydia.

Jules thought I existed in a permanent state of denial, but I'd managed the situation for years. He was out so much, his poisonous ways didn't permeate the house. Chloe and Isabella were brought up to have choices. They had Aunt Jules for a kick-ass role model. She stoked my urge to leave. I needed to look to the future, so it wouldn't just be him and me in the house. That would be a kind of death. The stumbling block was leaving the kids behind when Lydia's campaign escalated. I knew they would leave me for uni at eighteen. Me leave them? Crazy. Unthinkable.

'It's too soon,' I told Jules when we realised how far Lydia had pushed it.

'Now's your chance. No time to talk yourself out of it.'

'I can't just leave the girls.' My heart rate spiked.

'Em, they'll be off to uni next year.'

'A lot can happen between now and then.'

'They're out most of the time,' Jules said. 'They can text me if they need help.'

I clasped my hands tight. Jules covered them with hers.

'They'll understand. Not straightaway, but they'll get it. Go now while Lydia distracts him.'

Still, I had underestimated Lydia. The way she faked my supposed affair scared me. What if Elliot retaliated? But Jules stayed close and pulled me from the house, saying we should let it play out. Lydia stole my life, unaware of what lurked beneath the surface gloss.

She wouldn't go the distance, but the longer I had before they split up, the stronger I would be in standing up to him. Her plan to snag a rich husband dovetailed with my plan to escape mine. And Elliot had met his match.

Lydia

This was meant to be, the way everything had fallen into place from the moment I met Jules. The stars aligned, bestowing their cosmic gifts, calling me to step into this new life. I was destined to live with Elliot in our big, plush house.

I took the dog out on Monday afternoon and he launched onto every passing mutt. The girls walked up the road and I waved to them from the green. I would get those two airheads on my side if it killed me. The sharper one wore mirrored shades and a Panama hat. She fancied herself as a rebel. Pain in the arse, more like. The dippy one wore shorts and a baggy sweatshirt with *Peace & Love* on it. They ambled over and made a fuss of the dog.

'He's crazy about you two.' He was crazy about anyone who came near him.

'We love you, Barney Bear,' the soppy one said.

'Are you staying for supper?' Isabella asked.

'I'd love to. Is that okay with you?'

They petted the dog, glanced at each other and nodded in weird twin unison. They might as well be conjoined. It was a look I'd seen Jules and Emma exchange at book club. But I took it as a win and couldn't wait to tell Elliot.

'Shall we head back?'

Isabella took the dog lead and Barney pulled her towards the house.

'Do people call you Izzy?' I asked in my friendly voice.

'Never. I refuse to answer to it,' she said with a determined tilt of her chin.

Do you answer to 'stuck-up princess'?

'You both have lovely names. Have you seen your mum since she left?'

'Yeah.'

'How is she?'

'What do you care?'

'Your mum's a nice person. It just hasn't worked out between her and your dad.'

'Because of you.'

'She was having an affair.'

'She wasn't,' the gobby one snapped. 'Dad was lying. She's not with anyone else, unlike *him*.'

They'd better not repeat that around Elliot. They couldn't go creating doubt in his mind. But he didn't talk about anything that mattered, so hopefully they'd park that particular view.

'Where's she living?' I asked.

'None of your business.'

I hated rudeness but let it go, since they had to show allegiance to their mother. 'What did you do on your sleepover?'

They exchanged another look. 'We streamed the latest *Wonder Woman* film.'

'Oh, fun!' We arrived home. I thought of it as home. 'Shall we have a drink?' I could pour us some Prosecco to loosen them up. We could toast my amazing success and their new horizons, far, far away.

'We need to finish an end-of-term assignment.'

'What's for supper?' I asked as they clomped upstairs.

'Whatever.'

Charming. I messaged Elliot to say they'd invited me back, in case he came home and hit the roof. He could congratulate me on winning them over.

He replied:

> They want someone to cook. And I made them clear up the kitchen last night, which didn't go down well. Great that you're there. See you at 7. X

Emma would fall apart if she saw the state of the place. I knew why she ranted about them, but it was her full-time job, when I'd yet to benefit financially. I smarted at Isabella's gall, but it fired me up to succeed in my takeover bid.

The frozen meals had run out. I tried to get my head around menu planning for a family of four. What a bore. I surveyed the limited food stocks and decided on Thai red curry made from frozen chicken breasts, since I found rice and seasoning in the cupboard. I googled how to defrost chicken, because I couldn't kill them off with my cooking until I was married. But I couldn't be arsed to cook from scratch, so I drove to the farm shop for 'artisan' curry sauce in a pouch and frozen rice that could pass for home-made. While the chicken defrosted, I fried an onion for authenticity and left the curry seasoning beside the hob where everyone could see it. Elliot walked in just after seven. He handed me a bunch of shop-bought flowers wrapped in cellophane.

'Nice.' I put them in the sink. It was a gesture of sorts, but I preferred upmarket florist flowers with designer foliage you couldn't put a name to. Did he think I could be wooed via Tesco Express?

'Vases are up there.' He motioned to a kitchen cupboard. Were the flowers for me or the house? They weren't mine if he wanted them in a vase, seeing as I didn't yet live here. 'Supper smells great.' He reached for a bottle from the wine rack.

'It's one of my specialities. I've cleaned up too. The kitchen was a mess.'

'It's been neglected.'

We clinked wine glasses. 'So have you.' I lowered my voice. 'Now the girls have invited me in, perhaps I can help.'

'And I can have you in my bed.'

'The man of the house does need looking after.'

With a wicked look, he leaned forward to kiss me. The girls chose that moment to thump downstairs. He pulled back. I channelled my inner domestic goddess and pretended that cooking was minxy fun. They would warm to my sunny outlook. We sat at the table and loaded up our plates. The girls acted polite around their dad, and I kept the conversation flowing.

'What did you think of *Wonder Woman*?' I asked.

'It's awesome.'

'Isn't it? I saw it with my friend's daughter.' A lie, but I'd looked up a review before Elliot came home.

He looked stumped. 'I used to think Wonder Woman was stupid in her leotard.'

'She's empowering for girls,' I said to the twins, who looked interested, for a change. 'The film has a female director.' I warmed to the theme. 'If a woman is going to save the world, other women are perfectly capable of directing a film.'

The girls forgot themselves and looked approvingly at me.

'I think we need lots of female action heroes.' Did I fuck. Give me Idris Elba or Ryan Reynolds any day of the week. 'Because women can be superheroes too. In fact, a lot of women already are.'

The girls brimmed with interest at where this would lead with their dinosaur dad.

'That was delicious,' Elliot said, finishing his curry.

'It's refreshing, isn't it? Having a female lead to rescue the men?' I encouraged him to play along, but he thumbed out a message on his phone. Honestly, didn't today's parents encourage a feminist attitude? Not that anyone instilled one in me, but I believed in myself regardless. 'Obviously your dad's a feminist.'

They snickered.

'Only women are feminists,' he replied with a *touché* look.

'All intelligent people are feminists, so clearly you're one.' I leaned my elbows on the table, chin resting on my steepled fingers. I bet Emma didn't initiate conversations like this, not with Jane Eyre as her role model. 'By the way,' I said, 'you're running out of food.'

'Mum does the shopping... *Did* the shopping,' Chloe corrected herself. So much for female empowerment and encouraging their dad to pitch in.

'I'm tired,' he said. 'Girls, can you clear up and load the dishwasher, please?'

They rolled their eyes. Chloe stood up and took his plate.

'Thank you, sweetheart,' he said to her.

What about thanking *me* for cooking it?

'We've got an assignment to finish, Dad,' Isabella said.

He ignored them and checked messages. They brought the dishes to the sink.

'Ew.' Isabella recoiled from the frying pan. 'It's got oil all over it.'

'It won't take long.' With no conversation from Elliot, I wiped down the hob.

'Thanks, Lydia.'

'Yeah, thanks, Lydia. Can we go now?'

'Go on then,' I said indulgently, even though they'd only stacked plates and cutlery in the dishwasher. Whiny cry-babies. It was less hassle to do it myself.

Elliot went in the living room to watch Netflix, so I followed him through with my nearly empty wine glass and shut the door behind me.

'Hard day?' I massaged his shoulder with one hand, even though I was knackered.

'It's a lot to deal with work and the running of the house. I need all my focus for work. You handle the girls well. They need mothering.'

'You can't do everything.' Not that he was doing anything. I kissed his cheek and he turned to kiss me on the lips. 'I love the way you kiss me.' I'd started dropping the word 'love' into the conversation. *I love how you touch me. I love spending time with you. And soon you will love me.*

'You're a strange one,' he said. 'You cook for us and call me the man of the house, and then you go on about feminism.'

'I'm traditional at heart, but the Wonder Woman talk was about giving the girls confidence.' I *was* traditional. I had no problem with the man making money for me to spend.

'If you don't mind a late night,' he said, 'we can creep upstairs after the girls have settled.'

'That'll be heaven.'

He loved the sex, but not in an all-consuming way. I had to ramp up the sensual pleasure and get him hooked on a sex-induced dopamine rush. I would bypass his rational brain and create a heady cocktail of pleasure so he couldn't resist me. His passion and desire would trump parental responsibilities. I topped up my glass.

'Should you be drinking if you're driving home?'

What? I held the bottle mid-air. He couldn't expect me to drive home in the dead of night after I'd cooked, cleaned, and he'd railed me. Time to bite the bullet.

'Why don't I stay the night?' I said in a seductive low voice, my hand roaming up his thigh. 'The girls have accepted me, and we can spend some time in bed.'

He leaned back and sighed, already hard.

'Elliot, I need you to fuck me.'

He groaned.

'I need it badly,' I murmured. 'Shall we try it tonight? If it doesn't work out, I'll move to Birmingham.'

'Don't go to Birmingham.' He came in close for a smooch.

I would give him a night to remember so he'd never want to let me go.

Chapter Twenty

Emma

When I arrived back at the caravan park, Will waved from the goat enclosure. I started on the showers, troubled by the recording I'd listened to earlier, the hurt in Lydia's voice, when Elliot said she was a stand-in. Was he using her to spark jealousy in me? If his aim was to wind me up, it was working.

Will brought me a mug of coffee. 'Good weekend?'

'It was good to see the family.' I stood outside with him in the thin sunshine. 'Do you see your son much?'

'He comes back, but I don't kid myself it's to see me. He likes the surf.'

'Does he work?'

'He's a special needs teacher.'

'You and your wife must be proud.'

'I'm divorced. I've been on my own for a while.' He looked wistful, his face turned towards the sea.

'I'm surprised no one's snapped you up.'

He laughed. 'I'm no catch. I work all hours, then fall asleep by the fire. It's been a tough few years. My dad died, and then my mum got ill and passed away six months ago. I haven't had time for anything else.'

'Oh, I'm sorry.' Emotion fluttered in my chest. It must be sympathy. I had an urge to hug him, which I didn't, of course. There was something solid and reassuring about him, now he'd dropped the gruff exterior from when we'd met. The strange fluttery lightness inside me kept on and I realised it was hope. What was wrong with me? My emotions veered all over the place.

'What about you? Might you get back with your husband?'

'No chance. He's with a woman from my book club.'

He winced. 'That's awful. You must be livid.'

'It's hit my daughters hard. That's why I went back.'

'Will they be okay?'

I shrugged. 'They're off to France on Friday.'

'But why come here to live in a caravan? You should've kicked him out.'

I looked into my coffee. 'I needed to get away.'

'Tell me to shut up, but he's an idiot. I bet this book club woman isn't half the person you are.'

'That's kind of you.'

'It's not kindness. I can see the sort of person you are.'

Isabella and Chloe had been texting me, their messages peppered with emojis of love hearts, dogs and kisses. Elliot still hadn't contacted me, which was ominous, although Lydia kept him busy. I powered through the cleaning and then spruced up my new home-to-be, taking advantage of the first dry summer's day. Will set up a firepit outside, along with a pile of firewood under a tarpaulin in readiness for me moving in. His acts of kindness surprised me. Bad people did their worst, but the good people got you through.

Back at the cottage, I went over the notes I'd scribbled from speaking to Elliot's ex-secretary on the phone. Then I emailed her. Fury rose in me as I typed the email. So much that Elliot had kept from me over the years, but I pushed down my anger.

> Hi Sally,
>
> Thanks again for talking to me. I realise it was a bolt out of the blue. Please can I check the details below are correct? As discussed, I won't disclose your identity.
>
> During your employment, Elliot handled an eight-figure divorce settlement for a celebrity who's a household name. You overheard his first meeting with the client, in which he sought advice on how to leave his wife while minimising the financial payout. Elliot advised him to delay starting proceedings until he'd set up his accounts to conceal his earnings. The sooner the better so it didn't look like he was hiding assets.
>
> Elliot advised him to spend big if there was anything he wanted to splurge on, like a men-only trip of a lifetime. After the expected separation, he could carry on 'spending big' and, if so, he could hold off the divorce for around a year.
>
> Regarding custody of their children, the client only wanted access that fitted around his acting schedule. Elliot, however, advised him to issue a threat of fighting her for full custody. They had a nanny, so his working hours weren't such an issue, and the kids could be tutored when he was on location at a shoot.

To strengthen his custody case, he had private nude photos of his wife, which he could threaten to leak online.

All this should be told to her one-to-one before initiating the divorce, not in writing or over the phone, making it untraceable. Elliot advised him to butter her up first so she wouldn't be suspicious and attempt to record him.

If that threat didn't work, Elliot's private investigator could dig up any dirt. If none existed, the PI could set up a fake racy online dating profile for her on a trashy site, complete with lewd messages. He would take screenshots and delete the account before she discovered it.

Then the client remembered his wife had previous mental health issues that could also go against her in a custody battle. She'd had severe postnatal depression.

The above could be 'informally traded' for a lower financial settlement.

You were also aware of his unofficial policy of only representing men. If a woman sought a meeting, you were instructed to take the name of her husband, then politely tell her that Elliot was unavailable. You say it's standard practice to refuse to represent clients against those the firm already represents, so it's acceptable to say no without giving a

> reason. It is not, however, common practice to refuse to represent an entire gender.
>
> You were also aware that the PI had set up honeytraps and fabricated evidence against clients' wives, although you weren't aware of this happening during your time there.
>
> I appreciate you helping me.
>
> Emma

Elliot's legal secretary had overheard the conversation with his rich client, and when she tentatively questioned Elliot on his ethics, he had fired her. She agreed to go quietly in return for a good reference and 'no trouble'.

Elliot's earlier threat of discrediting me was why I tracked down Sally, to help me fight fire with fire. I hadn't known why she'd left, since the boss of break-ups never shared the details, but I had a hunch. Luckily, I found her on LinkedIn and now it was payback time for Elliot.

Lydia

Elliot's alarm woke me at stupid o'clock. I cuddled up to him. 'Hey, guess what?'

He buried his face in the pillow. 'What?'

'The four of us survived the whole night under the same roof.'

'I think they've accepted you.' He freed his body from mine and sat up to ruffle his hair.

'What happened about getting a housekeeper?'

'Haven't had time. Listen…' He took my hand and leaned into me. 'What you did last night was great. I don't suppose you could hold the fort until they go away on Friday? I'll make it up to you.'

'How will you make it up to me?' I said it saucily, but I'd want paying, one way or another.

He kissed me. 'When they go away, we'll do something special, just the two of us.' He stretched and headed for the en suite.

'Okay, I'll work remotely today and be here for Barney.'

'Great.'

'Any requests for supper?' Pot Noodles, ideally.

'You choose or ask the girls.'

'Is there a card I can use for the shopping?'

'What?' He looked over his shoulder.

'How did Emma pay for the family shop?'

'Oh. She had a debit and credit card.'

'Did she leave them behind?'

'No.'

He took his wallet out and put a wad of twenties on the bedside table. So insensitive. Asking him for money was demeaning enough, without him treating me like a prostitute. But he was proving a tough nut to crack, so I would keep house for one week and he'd realise his world was rocked for having me in it.

I worked my arse off with shopping, dog walking and watching YouTube videos on how to cook. We definitely needed home help. The girls came back after college.

'Can you give us a lift to Kingston in an hour?' Isabella asked with her usual attitude.

'Are you back for supper?'

'No. We'll make a snack now.'

'What time are you back?'

'About nine. Dad knows.'

They made sandwiches, smoothies and an almighty mess. Barney slobbered over them while they arsed around, talking shit and laughing like loons. They took a selfie pouting with the dog. Such narcissists, but I seized my chance to win them over.

'Shall we leave earlier? I'll treat you to cocktails en route.'

They brightened, and I was ready for a cocktail on such a gorgeous evening. We'd celebrate them buggering off for the summer. 'If you let me know when you're going out for the evening, I'll do you pizza.'

They beamed their approval. They took their food upstairs and moments later I heard Olivia Rodrigo blaring out. I would have liked them to send me the selfie, so I could upload it to my socials with the caption, *So proud of my girls!* Emma would foam at the mouth. She'd be easy to wind up.

Shame I had to delete my online presence after last time. It was tough for someone with my photogenic looks. I could picture my aspirational persona – a million Instagram followers and a load of free stuff, men saying I was sizzling hot – but that avenue had closed. I couldn't be geotagged, couldn't have anyone recognise me. Still, I dreamed of my fantasy Insta posts. *#LouisVuitton #PrivateJet #LosCabos #Blessed.*

The kids clattered back down. I grabbed my car keys.

'*Seriously*?' Isabella said when I tilted the driver's seat forward for her to squeeze in the back. 'I hate two-door cars. It's rubbish if you sit in the back.'

'It's not practical, especially with your dad's sporty two-seater,' I said. 'We need a four-wheel drive.' A new SUV would cheer me up no end, so I ignored her rudeness. 'Why don't you ask him?'

'This'll do,' she sighed. They shoehorned into the back and shared an earbud each.

'What are you listening to?'

'Just music.'

They bopped along and giggled. 'Did you hear when Laurel said Ethan said that thing about Molly and it was like, really funny, yeah?'

'Yeah?'

'So then, right? You know annoying Amy?'

'Not nice Aimee that's spelled differently?'

'No, annoying Amy. Well she said that thing to Indigo who told Reuben who told Molly and now everyone says she's stirring.'

'I know, right?'

'So yeah, I'm like, *what*?'

Quite. I nipped into a parking spot. We stepped onto the street, Isabella messaging.

'Let's go.' I wedged between them and linked arms, sweeping us towards the bar. 'We'll ignore our phones and be sophisticated, fabulous women out for cocktails. If anyone asks, say you're eighteen and knock a year off your date of birth.'

Isabella slid her phone in her pocket, keeping her hand on it. 'Can we have real cocktails?'

'Have mocktails if you prefer, but I won't tell your dad if you have the real thing.'

'He likes us to be safe when we go out,' the drippy one said.

'You are totally safe with me. One drink won't hurt, my darlings. It's an illicit pleasure.'

We walked in and I fixed the barman with a dazzling smile.

'Hello, you're a sight for sore eyes.'

'Been a long day?'

I read his name badge. 'It certainly has, Haris. I've promised cocktails to my team.'

'You've come to the right place.'

'Make mine a mojito, please.' I handed the twins a cocktail menu from the bar. 'You look like a man who does a mean mojito.'

He gave me a lingering smile and mixed my drink. The twins both chose some lurid sweet concoction made with cream. They always had a bag of Skittles or Haribo on the go, so their taste buds must have been shot to pieces.

'What line of work are you in?' Haris asked.

'Talent agency,' I said with a sparkle of personality to back it up. 'We've had an amazing week, landed some great deals. Isabella and Chloe are my talent spotters.' I placed a hand on each of their shoulders. 'They anticipate trends in the market.'

'Is that so?' he said genially, setting my drink on the bar.

The twins stood in rapt silence. They wanted cocktails and to pass as adults so kept their rosebud lips shut. It increased my credibility no end to procure alcohol through outrageous lies.

'Thank you, Haris. But enough of work, us ladies are ready to let our hair down.'

'Enjoy your cocktails,' he said, all smiles.

The girls took their drinks, and I ushered them to a table beside the window for us to bond over alcohol.

'He didn't ask for ID,' Chloe whispered, wide-eyed.

'He wanted the pleasure of our company. Feminine allure goes a long way, my darlings.'

'I can't believe you said that about the talent agency,' Isabella said.

'Why not? I know talent when I see it. You two are sensational. I bet you can do anything you set your minds to.'

Chloe glowed and even Isabella looked pleased with herself.

'A toast.' I raised my glass. 'To three fabulous women who are smart, gorgeous and fun. Here's to the best summer ever. I bet all the French boys will fall for you.'

We clinked glasses.

'You girls have the world at your feet – university, careers, finding love. How exciting is that? You can do whatever you like.' Preferably miles away. 'What are your dream jobs?'

'I'd like to be a human rights lawyer like Amal Clooney,' Isabella said.

'Oh yes. Amal Clooney is an example to us all.' Mainly for copping off with George.

'I think, basically,' Chloe said in her stupid voice, 'I'd like to be a dress designer to the stars, you know? Like actually, I'll dress them for the red carpet? That's my dream job and I'm going to study fashion.'

This from a girl who dressed like a daft hippy. It was two for one on cocktails, so I swiftly downed my mojito and gestured for another. That made their two cocktails free, because why should I pick up the tab? I feigned deep interest and let them witter on about their immature social lives. They were easy to win over.

On the way out, I waved to Haris and stumbled on my heel. I clutched Chloe for support.

'You shouldn't be driving,' Isabella said.

'Nonsense. I'm perfectly sober. But you can walk if you want.'

Back in the car, I made a point of demonstrating my exemplary driving skills. With them out of my hair, I went home planning sexy lingerie and Prosecco for Elliot's return. I prepared to further my seduction of him. The clock was ticking, and I had to move in before Luca kicked me out. *Time to commit, Elliot.*

Chapter Twenty-One

Emma

The caravan was nearly ready to move into. As I admired my handiwork in bringing it up to scratch, Will came over and said he was making other plans for the cleaning.

'You don't want me?' Panic flooded through me.

'Of course I want you, but you're wasted doing cleaning. You're better suited to operational stuff.'

A surge of pride welled up at his faith in me. Will helped me shove the remaining caravan junk into bin liners.

'I'll sort through it later,' he said. 'Are you done? I've something to show you.'

I'd intended to listen in on Lydia and Elliot, but I needed a break. Will walked me to his beaten-up Land Rover and cleared the heap of paperwork from the passenger seat. He jumped behind the wheel.

'Do you live in here?' I looked over my shoulder at the piles of receipts, chocolate wrappers and wet-weather gear in the back.

'What a cheek. I know where everything is. Sort of.'

I pushed aside a scattering of parking receipts with my foot so I didn't tread on them. 'Is that a bank card in the footwell?'

He reached over. 'My debit card! I meant to report it missing.'

He drove us over bumpy tracks to a tiny cove. We bought takeaway fish and chips and sat on the sea wall to eat it, seagulls circling overheard.

'Delicious.' I bit into a fat chip that tasted amazing. 'There's something life-affirming about fish and chips at the seaside.'

He nodded. 'They taste better by the sea. The salt air adds to the flavour.'

When we finished, Will led me along the shore to a rocky section at the edge of the cove. He offered me a steadying hand and we climbed over rocks to shallow pools of clear water.

'Feel how warm it is.' He crouched down for his fingers to play in the water. We watched tiny crabs and critters burying themselves or darting about in the clear water. He looked up at me with smiling eyes. I smiled too at his boyishness.

It reminded me of childhood holidays to the West Country. And when the girls were younger, I took them for caravan holidays with my mum, back when Elliot focused on building his career. All this had a simplicity I didn't know I'd been craving.

'Is this what you wanted to show me?'

'No. That's coming up.'

We climbed a hill near the bay and he talked about people at the caravan park who were either mad or 'characters' or who made him want to move to a remote farm with the goats. I'd already gathered that customer service wasn't his thing. People complained that he was hard to find and unresponsive. I told him how I missed walking Barney.

‘I’d like a dog. I’ve had sheepdogs in the past. I’ve been too busy for one lately.’

We sat at the top with two bottles of beer that he’d brought from a cooler in the car. As the sun set, we looked out on the pink-tinged sky, the breeze cool on my skin.

‘That’s what I wanted to show you.’

I could almost make out a silver lining on the clouds.

Will reached out to me. ‘Look.’ He leaned in close and pointed out to sea. I didn’t see it at first. Then I caught sight of graceful movements in the water and the sleek curve of a dolphin cutting through the waves.

‘There’s a pod of them.’

My gaze widened to take them in, diving down and arching up in harmony. A sense of peace enveloped me. We exchanged a smile, sharing the moment. I liked the easy way he put his arm around me, ducking his head level with mine to point out the dolphins. There it was again, the fluttering sensation, a sweet longing for something better. Not that I deserved it, with all my scheming. When the dolphins moved on, Will drove me home.

‘Wow. Nice place,’ he said, when we pulled up outside the cottage. ‘Why do you want a mouldy caravan when you’ve got this?’

‘It’s not mine. I can’t stay in it for long.’

‘You must have good friends to help you escape your marriage.’

‘Who says I’m escaping?’

‘Your husband can’t be that nice if he gets off with someone else and doesn’t even let you stay in the house.’

I stepped from the car, not wanting to go into my marriage. ‘Thank you for everything, including the sunset.’

I waved and he drove off. Was it obvious that I'd escaped Elliot? I braced myself for the war zone of divorce. Despite his line of work, I knew little about the process. When he talked about his work, it was office politics and outrageous stories of break-ups. Like the couple who argued more over access to their dog than custody of the children. Or the pair who wouldn't back down over who kept the Peloton Bike. They could have bought a second one for less than they spent arguing over it. He could spin a yarn, my husband. Cautionary tales perhaps.

This sweet taste of freedom showed me a different life. Buoyed by the unexpected evening of escapism, I felt freer, even though I missed my family so much it took on a form of its own. I'd needed a break from the rising panic of how precarious my life had become.

Lydia

Elliot still mourned the end of his marriage, but he had me to lift his mood. When he didn't turn up at seven. I texted him.

> The girls are out till nine. Where's my gorgeous boy? xx

> Working. Back soon. X

Prick. Ruining my plans. He walked in after eight.

'Hi, handsome,' I greeted him, smouldering and sexy in stilettos and a wrap-around dress to enhance my curves.

He barely glanced at me, kicking off his shoes, leaving them on the doormat.

'Bad day?'

'Hm.'

I went in the kitchen, expecting him to follow. He disappeared into the lounge instead and clinked around in the drinks cabinet. He must be one of those men who blew hot and cold. I gave him some space, or tried to, but we were wasting time.

'Hungry?' I said from the doorway.

'Sure.' He finished playing with his phone.

The sexy texts had dried up, but he was messaging someone. He had fingerprint security on his iPhone, so I needed the passcode to override it. If I sussed it out, I would upload Find My to track his whereabouts. If he noticed, I'd deny all knowledge and blame Emma. She was the needy type. I also wanted the passcode for the way to his heart. Emma was deluded if she thought it was through cooking.

He picked up his brandy glass and sauntered through. I eyed his shoes on the mat, ready for the girls to fall over.

'I'll move these, shall I?'

'They go on the rack under the stairs.' He ambled through to the kitchen.

Fuck's sake. But he'd had a bad day. I channelled my best self and put the shoes away, although I couldn't help a droll 'you're welcome'. He might be a hunk of manhood, but I expected better. Once we were married, I'd train it out of him. Until then, I would tidy his fucking shoes. I'd bought a stir-fry meal deal, since I could bung the lot in a big pan. I'd tipped all the ingredients into glass bowls that I'd lined up, the way they do on cookery shows. He talked about his session in the gym earlier.

'And how was your day?' he asked when we sat down to eat.

'Barney's had two walks. I've done a grocery shop and made sure the girls were fed before I dropped them off. And I've cleaned.' I spread my arms wide and looked around the kitchen, surveying my gold-star effort.

'Thanks. You're a gem.'

'I took the day off work to do all that. It's a full-time job.'

'Yeah, thanks.'

He didn't take the hint about money, and I couldn't lay it on any thicker. I wanted a joint account, or my account topped up by him. Getting through to him was hard work without coming across as grabby. Why hadn't he offered a remuneration package? I deserved more than Emma.

'I like having you here.' He covered my hand with his when we'd finished dinner.

'I love being with you. I'd like to make life easier for you, so we can be happy.'

'Let's go to bed before the twins come back.'

'Now you're talking,' I said in my sexy voice.

We took G&Ts to the bedroom and I undressed him, which always turned him on. Emma was wrong. The way to his heart wasn't through food. We indulged in leisurely foreplay, focused on him. I made it slow and sensual, tantalising him.

'What do you like?' I asked, gyrating on top of him.

'This.' He closed his eyes, revelling in it. He fast-tracked foreplay to get down to the business of a straight shag. I'd tried every trick to draw him in, but he just wanted no-frills sex. After he came, he lay back, breathing deeply while I stroked his chest. I wanted him to tell me it was the best sex he'd ever had, but he fell asleep.

I pulled on a bathrobe to let the dog out, so it didn't wake me up barking in the night. On my way down, the girls crept in an hour late, shamefaced when they saw me.

'It's okay,' I whispered. 'Your dad fell asleep before ten. I'll say you were back on time. Did you have fun?' I gave them a friendly wink.

They looked grateful and followed me into the kitchen. I'd keep giving them reasons not to dislike me.

'Do you have boyfriends?'

'Dad won't let us have boyfriends till we're eighteen.'

'Eighteen? Wow. Aren't there any boys you like?'

They laughed sweetly.

'I bet you hang out with boys on the sly.' Of course they had boyfriends. 'Are you on Tinder and Bumble?'

Their laughs turned nervous and uncertain. I said it to give them tacit permission to date online. Anything to keep them out of the house. How old-fashioned of Elliot to enforce a no dating rule, not that he'd have any idea what they were up to. If I wanted rid of them, I'd stir things up in the boyfriend department to force them out, but they'd better stay until the all-important ring glinted on my finger.

The next morning, Elliot woke early and spooned against me. Making love would give him sweet thoughts of me through the day, so I turned in his arms. He kissed me, softly at first and then deeper, in perfect silence. Light spilled through the curtains, highlighting his muscular arms. I melted into his touch. He'd mastered the near-silent orgasm. Being a parent must do that, so I muted my volume, not wanting to break the spell of my attentive lover returning.

When he went in the shower, I made coffee and then did up his tie for him. He liked the small touches. I would out-Emma Emma so he didn't miss her.

'You're too gorgeous to sit in an office all day.' I patted his tie and admired my handiwork. 'Stay in bed with me instead.'

He grappled me to the bed, and I gave a tiny ladylike squeal until he kissed me. Why wasn't he like that all the time? I loved him doing sexy things to help us build a connection that nobody could break.

'What are your plans for today?' he asked.

'I'm going out to earn some money. Much as I love it here, I can't afford to stay home all day.'

'Me neither.'

He was useless at taking the hint. Did he expect me to do everything without reward? But he was used to Emma the pushover.

'I'll show my face at home.' God help me. I'd stayed away from Luca since he'd told me to move out. 'Can you lot fend for yourselves tonight?'

'No. I want you back here.'

'I can't keep two homes on.'

He paused. 'You might as well stay here for a bit. Do you have much stuff? I can't believe I haven't seen where you're living.'

'I've been travelling light since I worked overseas. So just clothes and a few things.'

'Great. I'm back at seven. Can you move yourself in?'

'Sure.'

I'd done it. I'd actually done it.

Chapter Twenty-Two

Emma

I baked chocolate brownies to thank Will for yesterday evening. The chocolatey baking aromas reminded me of when the girls loved stirring the brownie mixture. At least the fog of upset had started to clear. My phone pinged with a text from Isabella.

> L has moved in! We are being nice to her!

She'd moved in already? I nearly threw the phone across the kitchen. What was wrong with Elliot, moving her in before the girls went to France? Jesus Christ. I shook my head in disbelief. You were supposed to date for a while before introducing a new love interest to your kids. How dare he tell them not to have sex before marriage when he'd shagged Lydia with indecent haste?

We are being nice to her stabbed at my heart, but the speed of it took my breath away. Thank God the girls were going to France on Friday. After my evening with Will yesterday, I forgot to check the listening device, relieved to enjoy myself instead of spying like some creep and withering from Lydia's poisonous words. I'd better stay vigilant.

I bashed about washing the baking tin, repeating my mantra, 'If they're okay, I'm okay.'

I cast around for something else to distract me. The limestone floor was clean. Alone here, there were just a few crumbs and expired insects to sweep away, a far cry from cleaning the shiny white tiles at home.

I walked to work and placed the plastic tub of brownies on Will's desk. He came in as I left to start the cleaning. 'There you are. I wanted a meeting with you.'

'A meeting? That's ominous.'

'It's about the expansion plans. What's this?' He lifted the airtight lid and exclaimed at the brownies. 'They look amazing.' He made coffee in the corner of the office and told me his plans to have a row of lodges, each on a landscaped plot. 'I'd like Airstreams, but they're too pricey. If I can swing it with the council, I'll do the same in the camping field.'

'How about some en-suite tents or yurts with solar showers? It'll appeal to the glamping crowd and it's cheaper to set up. We can do them up with camp beds and bedding. Then parents can take the kids camping without roughing it. What about communal barbecues and firepits to hire?' His enthusiasm rubbed off on me.

'Fantastic. That's exactly why I'm promoting you.'

'Promoting me?'

'I need someone to make things happen. You can help plan it and keep us on track. You're wasted doing the cleaning when you're a people person.'

I leaned back in the chair. 'I'm not a people person.'

'Rubbish. I've seen you with the punters. I've heard you on the phone. Everyone likes you. You're not grumpy like me.'

'You're not grumpy.' I thought him gruff at first but not once I'd warmed to him. 'You said you can't afford help in the office.'

'If we push ahead we'll get faster results. And we qualify for a council grant, so you can do the online application.'

'All right.' I smiled, not sure what I'd done to deserve a promotion, but I could kick-start his plans for six weeks. I'd move closer to the girls when they returned from France, even if I'd like to stay here forever.

'You're in charge of bookings and enquiries, and you can set up a temporary shop in here. I'll get you a card for the wholesaler. Any extra business can cover your wages. It's spurred me on, having you around.'

'That's great, except I'm back in Surrey from September.'

'Cross that bridge when we come to it.' He plonked my coffee down and launched into the brownies, making appreciative noises. He offered the box to me, with his mouth full.

'No, thanks.' After the news from back home, I might stress-eat the lot.

'These are sublime. You should sell them. Not here, or I'd eat them all.'

'Why didn't you get help sooner?' I asked.

His hair fell in his face, and he brushed brownie crumbs from his chin. 'I'm useless with people. I prefer animals.'

'The goats won't help you run the place.'

'I hate interviewing. I always end up with someone who says impressive things but doesn't live up to the hype. Better to get to know someone like you who under-promises and over-delivers.'

'Thanks.'

'You're a grafter. Your daughters are learning to look after themselves. It's time for you to live on your terms.'

'The promotion I can handle. Living on my terms might take longer.'

'Takes as long as it takes. Just give yourself credit.'

He sounded like Jules. She would like him. Elliot hated my bond with Jules, who was non-negotiable in my life, so I kept them apart. Nor did he like me having friends. He tolerated book club. Thanks to Crawford, he thought Marianne had set it up, not Jules. Talking about books with Crawford's wife was acceptable within the confines of my life. He would have banned me from it had any men joined.

Lately I'd been drawn to edgier fiction, engrossing morality tales with sweet revenge. I was rereading a novel about a marriage break-up that turned deadly. Jules chose it for book club a while back. Marianne said the main character let her husband get away with too much until it boiled over. The narrator said at the outset that her husband's affair made a killer of her. The story echoed my disquiet. How much provocation would I need? I'd kill to protect my kids.

Lydia

I arrived at my new home in a blaze of triumph. My worldly belongings amounted to one carload. Thank God I'd moved on from Luca's awful flat. It turned unpleasant when I walked in on vile Rosa, looking pleased with herself after a nose around. Well, ha fucking ha because I'd won, Emma had lost. It was my turn at the top. Game over.

I shunted armfuls of Emma's clothes to the spare room to give me hanging space. I needed new clothes. With luck, Elliot was arranging a credit card for me. One look at the messy kitchen dampened my jubilation. I couldn't wait for the kids to bugger off to France tomorrow. About bloody time. By late afternoon, I'd begun getting on top of everything when they barged in and made smoothies.

'Aren't you here for supper?' I asked.

'Yes,' Bolshie Boots said. 'This is a snack. What are we having?'

McDonald's? 'Do you two want to cook?'

'Um, no. Mum cooks.'

'*Cooked*,' the quieter one said.

'Do you ever get Deliveroo, or eat out as a family?'

'We never have takeaways,' Isabella said, impatience ringing out. 'Mum cooks – *cooked* – and we sometimes go out, but Dad likes restaurants for old people.'

I ignored the subtle underlining of *Mum does the cooking*. 'What's your favourite place to eat?'

'Giggling Squid.'

Elliot might take us out to mark my arrival, albeit to a 'restaurant for old people'. He came home just after seven and left his shoes on the doormat. I ignored them this time, but despite the domestic comedown, my celebratory mood spurred me on.

'Hey, Beefcake.' I smiled, ready for him to take me in his arms and express his happiness for our new lives together.

He smirked.

'How was your day?' I asked, when he should be asking about my day, since I was the one who'd moved.

'Quite tricky. Had a difficult case to resolve before it comes to court. The other party isn't playing fair, so we'll crack down.'

He sat on a stool at the kitchen island and wanged on about work. Why couldn't he ask about my day?

'I'm sure you'll sort it out. Have you started proceedings against Emma?'

'Not yet.' He swiped a finger over his phone screen.

'What's the timescale for that?'

He used his phone as a shield and didn't answer. I came up behind him to wrap my arms around his waist. I glimpsed a WhatsApp message with a kiss at the end. He swiped a finger over the screen before I could focus.

'Who are you messaging?'

'Just a sports thing.'

It had better be. Kisses from women were emotional infidelity. I'd assumed his cycling buddies were a pack of blokes, but there could be women in the mix. I stuck with the matter in hand.

'I've no idea how long a divorce takes.'

'At least a year, if it's no contest.'

A year? 'You'll be in a strong position to keep the house and the kids if we can give them a stable home,' I mused.

'Leave it with me.'

Get a move on then, I refrained from saying. He arranged divorces for a living and should crack on since Emma had checked out of the marriage, disappearing without a murmur. Had Elliot killed her? That would explain his caginess and lack of urgency to divorce her. But no, it would be too perfect.

'How was your day?' he finally asked.

'I moved in,' I said, flinging my joyful arms wide. 'Let's celebrate.'

He went back to his phone and smiled at something.

Are you listening to me, jerk? 'I said I moved in.'

'Right. What's for supper?'

'Seafood pasta in a spicy sauce, with focaccia bread. It's my signature dish.' And it just needed heating up, apart from the penne, which I knew how to cook. Even so, it was still a massive faff. I turned on the oven to warm the bread. His offhand attitude grated on me. After all the effort of getting a foot in the door, I expected a romantic celebration. But having achieved phase one, we needed to tackle the prickly matter of his divorce, so I trod carefully.

'I'm starved,' he said. 'Have we any nuts or olives?'

'I haven't bought any. Tell me your favourite things and I'll try to oblige,' I said saucily.

He smiled in response and made eye contact.

Emma, you dope, the way to his heart is through his dick. It was also the way to me moving up in the world.

Chapter Twenty-Three

Emma

I strode along the shore after work. Lydia moving in clawed at me and I tried to walk it off. When we set her up, there was a strong chance she'd repel Elliot. He was in charm mode that night at book club, an illusionist directing his audience to only see what he presented. Lydia looked bewitched.

'It's a book club, not a knocking shop,' Jules scoffed afterwards. 'Have you noticed the way she stares?'

'Yeah. She does it to me. Unnerving,' I said.

'She stared at you with a smug face, then Elliot turned up and she's gazing at him like he's the Messiah.'

Lydia finagled her way in with questions about my marriage wrapped up as friendly interest. I said the way to Elliot's heart was through his stomach, when his heart dried out years ago. I only wanted her to cook for the kids in case she ended up in their lives.

It threw me when he banished me from the house so fast. My defence mechanism kicked in on the stairs, numbing me. When I tried to speak, my voice sounded tight as if his hands gripped my throat.

Jules called, so I gave up trying to shake off my fury and sat on the sea wall while we dissected Lydia's fast work.

The speed of her moving in stung me, and his silence brought an ominous sense of him plotting against me.

After the call, I turned towards home and saw a familiar figure standing along the shore, hands in pockets, staring out to sea. Will. I didn't want to disturb him, but he looked towards me, squinted and waved. I waved back and he strode over, grinning broadly.

'Don't tell me,' he called out when he was close enough. 'My favourite beach is now your favourite beach.'

'I didn't expect to see you. I'm off home now.'

'Me too. Walk this way and I'll show you where I live.' He walked me back along the beach and down a sleepy lane. I noticed his shorter hair.

'You've had your hair cut. It suits you.'

He looked bashful and ruffled his neatly trimmed hair that gave him a younger look.

'Here we are. Home sweet home.' We reached a small stone cottage on a big, scrubby patch of land, set back from the shore.

'It's lovely.' It really was. Reclaimed stones and tiles were stacked at the side of the quaint cottage, alongside foundations laid for an extension.

'I'd like to get stuck in, but I haven't had time.'

'Are you doing it yourself?'

'I'm a builder by trade. Then I inherited the caravan park from my dad. I've been bogged down ever since. Literally, from all the rain. It's got potential now you're on board.'

We went inside. 'Oh, how lovely.' I marvelled at the stunning fireplace. 'Did you do this as well?'

'Yes. The hearth is from slate round here.'

I followed him into a small, light-filled kitchen. If houses had souls, this had a good one.

'Would you like a drink?' he asked. 'And I can cook us something?'

'Thanks, but I have to go and make some phone calls.' I stepped back and went to leave.

'Another time,' he said, as I left the cottage, waving goodbye.

Night-time brought out the darkness of my situation. I'd taken to snooping while glugging wine, and didn't want to inflict my brooding ways on Will. I reached the cottage as dusk fell, glowing warm from the walk and from knowing I could stay another six weeks. My phone pinged with a text from Isabella.

We're not going to France!

Lydia

'Is there an account for housekeeping?' I asked Elliot in the kitchen.

'What?' He looked up from his phone.

'So, um, how shall we play it? Because there are household costs.'

'Give me your account details and I'll set it up.'

Set what up, exactly?

'Emma did a monthly expenditure spreadsheet. I'll email you one as a template.'

What? She accounted for her spending? No, just no. She must have OCD, what with that and the cleaning. I poured boiling water into the pan. He expected me to emulate her when menial tasks and household budgeting weren't my style. But I couldn't rock the boat while I was cosplaying the doting wife-to-be. Since the brats were buggering off for the summer, I decided to go all in, minus the spreadsheet. He could pay me the housekeeper's salary plus benefits in nice jewellery and nights out. I'd carry on Emma's dull duties, plus my USP of amazing sex. I would be Emma 2.0.

'I've taken time off work to be here.'

'Mm-hm.' He fiddled with his phone.

'I can see Emma put in lots of work, since she didn't have a job. I can't reach that level of effort without giving up work. I'm happy to keep things running smoothly. I'm freelance, so I needn't give notice.'

He looked perplexed. 'You didn't say you were freelance.'

'Or you can employ a housekeeper and dog walker.' I turned and stirred the pans of pasta and shop-bought sauce. *Please don't tell me to carry on working.*

'You said you'd look after everything if you moved in.'

'Yes, if I took over from Emma, who didn't have a job.' I hid my irritation.

'You said you loved your work.'

'I do, but I've nearly finished my London project. Then I'll move on to Birmingham if you don't want me here.'

'Stay and we'll see how it goes. It's useful to have you around now the girls aren't going to France.'

'What?' I spun back to face him.

'France was Emma's idea. They're not keen.'

'But…' My face flushed from the simmering pans. They'd ruin my summer. I didn't want those annoying morons under my feet. Why hadn't he consulted me? I nearly hurled the pan across the room, but I wrestled my anger under control. 'But… it'll help their language skills.'

'They're not bothered. I'll take them to La Rochelle for a week in August to practise their French. My friend has a private plane. I'll see if he'll fly us.'

'How fabulous. I hope I'm invited.'

He checked his phone without replying, but of course he'd include me. I'd love to fly in a private plane and feel like a proper jet-setter. On the bright side, he needed me even more with the kids hanging around, not that they would hang around. I'd kick them out during the day. Seriously though, how could he expect me to do all this for free? I bit down my frustration.

'Did you have a cleaner when the kids were small?'

'Emma did the cleaning.'

I hated cleaning, especially when those brats kept messing it up again. They kept me occupied in some pointless merry-go-round of housework. It was Emma's fault for depriving someone of a job. But the money he saved on her gym membership alone could go on a cleaner, since I'd no use of a women-only gym. Why join a women-only *anything*?

'You all need looking after, so if Emma's household funds are transferred to me, running the home can be my job, now the girls aren't going to France.'

He swiped his screen indolently, as if the conversation was beneath him. Him and me both. I fought the urge to drop his bloody phone in the pan of boiling water and tell him to stop behaving like a prick.

'Or I'll renew my contract and you can employ a housekeeper for about forty thousand.'

He put the phone down and looked at me. 'You can do everything.'

He still hadn't revealed the payment for picking up after him and his kids. My mention of forty thousand was a pretty big hint.

'My car finance is two hundred and ninety-five pounds a month. I've been giving lifts to the girls.'

'Two-nine-five for that cheap thing?' He gave me a lawyerly stare. 'Do you have a bad credit rating?'

Yes, but I won't admit it to you.

'No. Is that a lot then? Isabella's complaining that it's a two-door. If you want a better deal, we could trade it for a four-wheel drive… for the girls.'

'We'll stick with yours.'

For a career go-getter, he lacked urgency. Pushing for everything made me look grabby. If I somehow wrote off the car, though, he could replace it with a Range Rover Sport. I could suffer whiplash and score a lump sum from the insurance just for me, and they could pamper me for a change. The girls walked in, having smelled the cooking or the conflict, but we needed to get it straight.

'Okay. I'll run the house, sort out the girls, the dog, everything. I'll give up my income and email you my account details, since I need money for myself as well.'

He pursed his lips and gave a slight tilt of his chin in acknowledgement. Given that I didn't need to pay household bills, a couple of grand a month in my account would suffice in the short term. He might do the decent thing and stump up the entire £40k in return for housekeeping *and* sexual services.

Isabella gave us a sly look. Her twin hung back, chewing on a fingernail. We'd had enough hard talk for now. I'd give him an extra-special blow job later to remind him of my true worth.

'Dad-*dee*?' Isabella said.

'Hello, my darlings, how are you?'

I smarted at his immediate interest in them when it took him ages to ask about my day.

'Can we have some money, please? We're horse riding tomorrow. We need lunch money too.'

Fakers. So transparent, the way they played him for money. Those sociopaths had him twisted round their entitled fingers. They'd never have meaningful connections with men.

He slid some twenties from his wallet. 'Have a lovely time.'

They kissed him and said thank you. He puffed up with pride. Isabella flashed me a look as if to say, *See how he gives us money? He loves us more.*

You're not that special, I wanted to say. *And he's fucking me, so I'm his favourite.*

She had a point though. He treated them like spoilt princesses while I worked myself into the ground. I dished up the food, indulging a fantasy in which we married and then he died. So tragic, but black suited me, paired with vampy red lipstick. I'd cast the little shits out with nothing, inspired by Emma's dusty old novels.

I told myself that he bought them off because Emma couldn't maintain their lifestyle without him. He bribed them with hard cash to fund their gilded social lives, otherwise they'd favour her. Money mattered to high-maintenance teenagers, but not as much as it did to me.

They expected me to look after their needs, but I mustn't neglect mine. I expected better. After the twins disappeared upstairs for the evening, we relaxed on the couch. He went back to WhatsApp. I tried to see the screen, but he held it close to his chest.

'Who are you messaging?'

'It's for my sports.'

'Shall I book a restaurant at the weekend? You can take me for a spin in your Ferrari.'

'Love to, but I'm not going public on it yet.'

'It?'

'Us. As far as everyone's concerned, Emma's looking after her sick mum.'

'And I'm looking after you.' I stroked his hair despite his ungenerous attitude. 'I just want us to be happy.'

Later that night, I sneaked two twenties from his wallet. Served him right. My salon conditioner had run out, and I needed to look gorgeous for him. If he noticed, I'd blame Isabella, because she looked light-fingered. I wouldn't put it past her.

Unlike Marianne, I wasn't a Jane Austen fan, but I'd seen a quote of hers that said a large income was the best recipe for happiness. Not much had changed between the sexes, not for me anyway. I was as dependent on Elliot as a lady in a bonnet from the parish of Jane Austen. I could've had a sparkling career, but the rat race didn't appeal. In Jane Austen's day, marriage was the smart move for a woman of a certain class. Me too. Having come this far, I had to remove every obstacle in my way.

Chapter Twenty-Four

Emma

I phoned Isabella, my blood boiling.

'Dad called Uncle Trev to cancel the trip,' she said, unbothered. Elliot had obviously done it to spite me, when the bright spot on the horizon was taking them away from his fling with Lydia.

'Why don't I tell him you're still coming?' I said. 'We've got the ferry tickets, and it's better than hanging round all summer.'

'Mum, it's cancelled, okay? We're chill.' My plan for a Dorset summer slipped through my fingers, replaced with tears and meltdowns back home, me mopping up the mess. That's what he wanted, of course, forcing me to change my plans because the girls would need me. I logged on to the app and listened agog to that woman and her flirtations. I covered my mouth at the audacity of her trying to extract an income from him.

I arrived at work just as a caravan owner marched up to Will outside the office.

'What are you doing about those goats? Bloody hooligans! They ate my wife's lavender.'

'Yeah, I've had a word with them.'

'What?'

'They asked if she'd plant lettuce instead. Lavender gives them indigestion.'

I went in the office for our meeting about the business plan, and he burst in moments later. I raised my eyebrows.

'What?' he said. 'It's their home too. They need to cut loose now and then.'

'Bloody hooligans,' I said, and we both snickered.

In the last few days, he'd swapped his ragged T-shirts for brighter ones suited to his new mood. 'Tell me again why we're doing this?' he asked. 'Business plans are for the bank, and I hate banks.'

'It helps us work out how best to do it.' I pushed the bad news about France from my mind, but I couldn't shift the tight knot of dread in my chest. If Elliot cancelled the trip to spite me, along with moving Lydia in, what would he do next?

'Or we could just get on with it,' he said.

'The plan shows the scope and projected outcome with costings.' And a plan would focus his scatty mind.

'How do you know all this?'

'I did business studies a few years ago.' I'd kept the course secret from everyone except Jules, taking classes on Tuesday afternoons. I'd rushed through the coursework in a covert frenzy when the family were out, hiding all trace. I'd also squirrelled away small amounts of cash that Elliot wouldn't notice, and jewellery I could sell. I'd packed some things he wouldn't miss and kept them at Jules's.

My phone buzzed and I jolted, my stomach clenching.

He looked strangely at me. 'You sure you're not on the run?'

I held my breath and checked the text. A reminder about a dental appointment back home, which I'd have to cancel. I breathed out.

'I'm assuming it's your ex by the look on your face.'

'No, he hasn't contacted me since I left.'

'Did you say he's a divorce lawyer?'

'Yup.' I grimaced.

'He'll know how to play dirty. If he's not in contact, are you wary of what he might be up to?'

'Like?'

He shrugged. 'Like tracking you remotely.'

'How would he do that?'

'Through your mobile.'

My face burned because I was the one monitoring Elliot. Dismay that he might be tracking my movements sat uneasily when I was the spy.

'I've got a spare mobile you can have.' He opened a drawer to rummage through. 'God knows where I put it.'

'How did we make the jump from him being a divorce lawyer to tracking my movements?' Although he was right about Elliot's unethical practices.

'Bad associations. My divorce was a bloodbath once it went legal.'

I braced myself for my own bloodbath of a divorce. It would come down to what I relinquished for an easy life. An easy life had a lot going for it, like climbing a hill to watch dolphins beneath a setting sun. But I needed enough for a new home with the girls before he turned them against me.

'You made it through,' I said to Will. 'How else could he keep tabs on me?'

'A tracker on your car.'

I looked at him in dismay. 'So he'll know I'm here?'

'I'm not an expert, but I used to get spam emails flogging some gizmo to track my car. Not that I'm saying he's tracking you.'

'I've kept the same mobile number, so he can call if he wants. Anyway, let's do the business plan.'

'You're flustered.'

'I didn't think of him tracking my car.'

'Why would you? And what do I know?'

But Elliot could make me pay, like cancelling the French trip. I came away for some space and perspective, but he would fixate on me having an affair. Jules had asked around and texted me the name of a Surrey divorce solicitor. I had to phone her.

'I won't need those four days off now. My husband cancelled the trip to France without telling me.'

'Silly bugger. Rise above it. He's trying to get back at you.'

'Do you mind if I take next weekend off instead?'

'If they're not going away, you can take alternate weekends off, since you'll be working on the expansion during the week.'

'Thanks. The shower rooms for the yurts could be the first thing to tackle.'

'Or the swimming pool. We'll convert the barn into an indoor pool.'

'Let's start with the glamping site. It'll give the fastest return on investment.'

'Spoilsport.' He grinned. 'I've always wanted an indoor pool. I'm looking forward to getting the digger in there.'

'Don't you need permission from the council?'

'Minor point.' He shrugged. 'You'll love it here in spring. The bluebells are gorgeous. Shall we get some alpacas?'

His mind bounced all over the place. I didn't have the heart to remind him I couldn't stay beyond September. He left to fix something and I had a quick google to see how to find a hidden tracker in a car. But Elliot could have tucked one in anywhere, and it was too late anyway.

After work, I strode along the cliff edge. It was easier to think on a walk, spurred on by a sea view. It cleared my head better than any gym. I grimaced at the memory of my gym membership.

When I returned, I saw a man in dark overalls trying to open the door of my caravan. Panic rose in my chest.

'Who are you?' I steadied my voice.

The man turned to me.

Will appeared from behind the caravan with an extension lead. 'Emma, this is Matt, my electrician.'

I breathed out.

'He's testing your security light,' Will said. 'I thought you'd feel safer with an outside light.'

When the electrician left, Will brought over two deckchairs and we sat back with bottles of beer and looked up at the moon in the evening sky.

'You can stargaze once it's dark,' he said. 'If you stay still long enough, you'll see a shooting star.'

If it weren't for the complications back home, I could begin to see a future here. Each time I listened in at home, my chest tightened, but I had to make sure the twins and Barney stayed safe. I felt devious for listening in and for contacting Sally to get the dirt on Elliot, but this was about survival. A text came through from Marianne, a message I'd been waiting for. I took a breath and opened it.

Lydia

My anger powered me through the housework. I clonked the hoover around the kitchen. Emma looked down on me from the big family photo, her judgy eyes following me. I'd have liked to smash the bloody thing to pieces. If Elliot had any tact, he would have removed it.

'It's your fault,' I snapped at her.

It was time people recognised my status. I liked a challenge, but Elliot's lack of response was beyond me. I could pull him in sexually, but the feel-good vibe never lasted. He switched his rational brain back on and, *Hello, drudgery*. Everything grated on me, from the way he swiped at his phone to the lack of compliments on my lovingly prepared meals.

I stopped and checked my emails. He'd sent Emma's spending spreadsheet. That woman was a total stranger to fun and passion. He'd dropped £500 into my account but didn't say it was a regular weekly payment. Even then, it didn't leave much for personal spending. He shelled out for his kids, so I would encourage him to do the same for me. As well as hard cash, I craved romantic gestures like him sweeping me off to exclusive resorts and draping Cartier jewellery over me.

Just put a ring on it, Elliot, for fuck's sake. I took my dark mood out on the hoover by attacking the upstairs carpet. The twins could clean their own rooms in return for their generous handouts. Elliot was still licking his wounds from Emma's affair, his eyes glazed with pessimism. Alpha males needed to be top dog, but Emma had done the dirty and guys like him hated losing. He lacked trust because of her. Habit number one: be proactive. I would keep showing him the affection of a real woman, and when the divorce came through, we'd marry. Habit number two: begin with the end in mind. I googled wedding venues.

It didn't need to be a large affair since I'd nobody to invite. We'd go for an intimate yet lavish do at the Dorchester. I'd check into our suite the day before for pamper sessions. Or we would jet off to New York and tie the knot in the Ritz-Carlton at Central Park. I'd a mountain to climb before then, but I visualised our wonderful honeymoon in the Seychelles, just us, tanned and gorgeous, the perfect couple. Then the kids could bugger off and I'd be *numero uno*.

When I took the dog for a walk, the old woman next door trundled her bin along the path. I said a smiley 'good morning' over the privet hedge. She scowled at me.

'Where's Emma?'

I've got rid of her.

'She's gone away.'

'Where?' she said sharply. 'She was going to her mother's for a few days.'

'I'm not supposed to say anything.' I hesitated for effect. 'So don't breathe a word.'

She leaned forward expectantly. Women like her lived for gossip. Muttley strained at the lead, trying to pull me towards the green.

I lowered my voice. 'Elliot caught her having an affair. She's left. Elliot thinks she's gone off with the man in question.'

She looked horrified. 'Emma wouldn't do *that*.'

I shrugged to say, *What can you do?*

'What about the children?'

'I'm helping out. We're managing. I'm Lydia.' I stretched my arm over the fence to shake her hand.

She reciprocated grudgingly. 'Anne.'

That was enough for starters. I'd planted the seed of Emma being in the wrong, unlike me: the nice lady who'd stepped in to look after the family. The mutt pulled me away and she watched through narrowed eyes. I'd been on the receiving end of small-town mentality, women making nasty judgements. It would need managing. I looked around for anyone else who might know Emma. Now I'd tested my script, I was ready for a wider audience.

Marianne phoned while I trailed after the dog.

'How goes it?' she asked.

'Elliot asked me to live with him.'

She whistled. 'You've moved in already?'

'It suits everyone.'

'How are the girls taking it?'

'We're all getting along.'

'Wow. I'm amazed. You visited their house last month for the first time. You met Elliot, for what… a few minutes? Now you're living with him. That takes some doing.'

'Some things are meant to be.'

'Absolutely. Would you two like to come for dinner? We can do next Thursday.'

'We'd love to.'

Elliot preferred a low profile, but Marianne knew about us, so it didn't count. If they accepted us as a couple, he would loosen up and I could showcase my social assets. He had the perfect partner in me, especially as I admired and supported his ambition. Elliot and Lydia Morland, the power couple.

Chapter Twenty-Five

Emma

> Hello, my beautiful friend, how goes it in Thomas Hardy country? Got yourself a lawyer yet? I have that photo you wanted. xx

Good old Marianne. Her spell of blanking me didn't even last a day. I replied, asking her to send the photo. It arrived on my walk across the bay that morning, the 'evidence' of me with the mystery man. It all fell into place, me on the green, grappling with the strange man who'd lunged at me. How did Elliot believe me unfaithful based on that? He'd really fallen for Lydia's persuasive powers.

When Marianne first visited me at home, several years ago, she'd marvelled at the house. 'You have a maid, right?'

'No. I do it all.'

'What? You don't employ someone? How the heck do you keep this floor clean?'

'I'm home all day. Elliot likes it tidy.'

'That's fine if he does the tidying.'

I looked away.

'I'm guessing he does nothing.'

Marianne often invited me for lunch or coffee and to enthuse about books, food, everything. Then Lydia began her campaign to turn everyone against me. After Marianne froze me out at the farm shop, she changed tack and came to see me, unable to hide her opinions any longer.

'Emma, we need to talk,' she'd said. 'Whatever you say I won't tell Elliot or Crawford.'

'Okay.' I steeled myself.

'Are you having an affair?'

'Did Lydia tell you that?'

'That gal's trouble. She's bad-mouthing you. I think she's trying to break up your marriage.'

'Barney needs a walk.' We couldn't discuss it in the house. Not when Elliot had it bugged.

The night I hosted book club, before Lydia arrived, I'd dusted noisily beforehand and 'accidentally' turned off the Wi-Fi. He used it as a listening device, spying on my conversations while monitoring our internet activity. I'd suspected for a while and Jules confirmed it. Our IT guru, Lucy, showed her how to check, although Jules didn't tell her that we'd suspected Elliot.

I didn't want him to hear any raucous conversation at Lydia's final book club, so I turned off the router. And then we turned the tables. The spied upon became the spy. We put our rival device in the router and the TV remote control.

Jules had clumsily added it to the Wi-Fi box just as Elliot turned up in a rage to throw me out. We'd been unaware of the looming murder and hadn't considered that the police might do a thorough search. She feared they would find both devices plus her fingerprints, so we decided to mention the spy app in the 'official' journal. It was screwed up for a married couple to spy on each other, but Lydia wasn't a dog lover, so Barney provided my cover story.

'Let's take a walk,' Marianne had said. 'I've only done two thousand steps today.'

I left my phone at home and told Marianne about Lydia's plan to bag a rich man.

'I knew it! Soon as I set eyes on her. She waltzed into my house like some real estate agent working out the price. It's all there on her face. She checked out Crawford and dismissed him.'

'I thought she'd turned you against me.'

'She's sly. She almost had me believe you were bad-mouthing me. If you don't fight back she'll take Elliot. It's us against her and she ain't winning. Have you told Elliot?'

'No.'

'We need to put a stop to this.'

'We can't tell him.'

'Why the hell not?'

I took her into my confidence, testing her out. I said I wanted to leave my marriage once the twins left home, and he would let me go more easily with Lydia paying him attention.

'It's starting to make sense,' she said, 'what Jules was doing by bringing that woman into our group. I should've read between the lines, like she said.'

I swore Marianne to secrecy.

'I won't breathe a word. Not even to Crawford. He's no gossip, but he forgets and says the wrong thing, the idiot. Elliot won't believe Lydia when she tells him you're having an affair, but I'll back her up. Give credence to her story.' Marianne revelled in it. 'I did wonder if your marriage was as sterile as your house. I assumed the fire went out of it. You could've told me sooner.'

'I thought you liked Elliot.'

'Pur-leese. I'm a woman of the world. You seem a cute family, but you never know what goes on behind closed doors. I saw the way you looked at him when Lydia ogled him at book club.'

'How did I look at him?'

'Like he was an alien species when he charmed his way around the room. You never criticised him. You always stopped short. I thought you were depressed, but I guess you were scared.'

I'd looked a wreck that night, which helped Lydia stand out beside me. Jules had overruled my Maggie O'Farrell book choice for one on marital disharmony to further set the scene.

'Why are you helping me?' I'd asked Marianne.

'Because she's ruthless. It's a crime against the sisterhood. And it goes against the spirit of book club.'

'Which is?'

'We open our homes to talk about books that move us. Books about love and loss. There's intimacy in that. It makes the betrayal worse.'

After reading Marianne's message a second time, I realised she'd left me a voicemail. 'I'm telling Lucy to take the project live.'

My heart thudded at 'the project' gaining momentum. The morning grew oppressively hot. I cranked the office windows open and pulled the blinds down. Will's voice carried through the open window as he talked to a man outside. I made him a coffee and reminded myself to feel good about moving out of the cottage. I couldn't control Elliot, but I had a room of my own, in the spirit of Virginia

Woolf, or at least a caravan of my own. I promised myself a sea breeze after work.

'…her name's Emma Morland,' the man outside said to Will.

My whole body tensed. My mind whirled.

'But she might go by her maiden name of Gardiner or a different one altogether.'

I gasped and gripped the jar of instant coffee. Will had been right. Elliot was tracking me down.

'Who is she?' Will asked. 'Is she in some kind of trouble?'

'She had an argument with her husband and ran off. He's worried about her.'

I backed into the shadowy corner of the room. My stomach twisted in knots. What if Will brought the man in here?

'Who are you, then?' Will demanded.

'Mr Morland asked me to find her.'

'Bit suspicious, if you ask me. If my wife disappeared, I'd call the police.'

'She left the marriage of her own accord. He asked me to make discreet enquiries, for the sake of their children.'

The cluttered space closed in. What was Elliot playing at, hounding me out, then sending someone after me.

'I don't know her, so you're in the wrong place,' Will said, his voice firm.

'In that case I'll ask around.'

'Not here you won't. People are on holiday. I don't want them thinking there's a criminal in their midst.'

'She's not a criminal.'

'With the tone you're taking, people might assume. You're leaving. Understand?'

'Why so touchy?'

'I'm allowed to be touchy on my land. I don't like the sound of this. Shall I phone my mates at the police station?'

'No need for that.'

Their voices faded out, as if Will escorted him off the site. My hands shook as I finished making coffee, my breathing shallow in the muggy heat. Will barged in, making me jump. He slammed the door shut. At least he was alone.

'I heard.' I handed him his coffee, my fingers trembling, and I retreated to the far side of the office.

'Why are you hiding here?'

'I'm not hiding.'

'Are you in some kind of trouble?' He looked intently at me, his brow furrowed.

'No. I came here for some space.'

'So you'll leave now your cover's blown?'

'What cover? I like it here, if you'll still have me.'

'Why is your husband paying good money for a private investigator to track you down?'

'He has my number.' I shrugged. 'He could just call me, but it's like you said, he's a lawyer. He must be gathering evidence.'

Will kept staring at me. 'What aren't you telling me?'

The PI was Elliot's ominous calling card. He was gearing up for something. Fear gripped me by the throat. I thought of Sally's account of Elliot offering clients the services of a private investigator. But this wasn't business. This was personal, since I'd betrayed him. He liked pushing my buttons. Over the years, I had learned not to react, not wanting to give him the satisfaction, so I'd focused on the kids and retreated inside my books. But now I was reacting with the project. Playing him at his own twisted game. If he found out, he'd kill me.

Lydia

I cleaned furiously and worked out how to handle Elliot. Two could play at being distant, but we'd never get anywhere. *Demonstrate commitment, Elliot, or else.* It took three hours to clean the floor downstairs. Three hours! What a ridiculous waste of time. There was too much of it for a start. The expanse of shiny white tiles looked amazing at book club, but they showed every crumb and dog hair. Why combine a hair-shedding black Lab with a glossy white floor? I hoovered and mopped, which left it covered in smears, so I buffed the whole bloody lot. *Exhausting*. I was too gorgeous for this. Girlfriends of rich men weren't supposed to clean floors. A considerate man would appreciate my charms without expecting me to skivvy for him.

The twins came home as I finished and had a love fest on the patio with the dog. 'Can you take him for a walk?' I asked.

'Sorry,' Isabella said, not sounding remotely sorry. 'Downtime.' She grabbed two bags of crisps from the cupboard and threw one to Chloe. 'These are the last of the crisps.'

'Well, I haven't eaten them.'

'Can you buy some?'

They trooped upstairs, belting out a song followed by shrieks of laughter. I gave them the finger, not that they could see. Then I did the same to Emma's photo on the wall, presiding over me. The fucking dog raced in, leaving a trail of grubby paw prints and clods of mud with mangled leaves and twigs. He must have had a mudbath at the end of the garden.

'Fucking dog,' I shouted, as he shook himself. 'I'll fucking kill you.'

'Don't say that.'

I spun round. The dopey one stood by the fridge.

'He's not a fucking dog,' she screeched. In a flash she pulled a knife from the knife block. She held it like a dagger, pointing the blade right at me.

I drew back, instinctively clutching my throat. 'Calm down.' What had got into her?

'You won't fucking kill him. I'll fucking kill you!' she screamed in a frenzy.

Jesus Christ, she was a raving maniac. I backed into the kitchen unit, the worktop edge digging into me.

The other one burst in, eyes wild. Had they gone completely off the rails? I always felt they were a bit unhinged. Isabella clasped Chloe's face, muttering to her. 'It's okay. We've got this.'

Tell her to drop the knife, I wanted to shout, but Isabella cast a strange spell on her, talking in a low voice, their faces almost touching. Chloe came out of her demonic possession and Isabella took the knife from her. She dropped it on the counter, shot me a warning look and walked Chloe back upstairs.

I took a huge breath, only then aware of my tortured breathing. I frantically called Elliot before they got in first and made me the bad guy.

'Hi, is everything okay?' he asked in his lawyerly voice.

'No.' My voice shook. I didn't even put it on. 'Chloe just had some kind of meltdown. She pulled a knife on me.'

'What happened?' Urgency came through in his voice.

‘I’d polished the floor and Barney came in muddy from the garden. I swore. Next thing I knew, she pulled a blade and nearly held it to my throat—’

‘Hang on,’ he snapped. ‘Isabella’s calling.’ The bastard cut me off. I paced around. That bitch would make me the evil one for swearing at the dog, but his kid needed professional help, threatening me with a knife. She ought to be locked up. That would at least be one irritating brat out of the way. I listened in the hallway to check if Isabella was off the phone. I heard the murmur of a voice, which might be her soothing the psycho twin.

I tried Elliot’s number again. It went to voicemail. ‘Hi, Elliot, how’s Chloe? I’m shaken up. Are you coming home? She needs to know it’s not okay to threaten to kill people. See you soon.’

I poured a stiff vodka and sat in the garden. Elliot didn’t return my call, so I escaped the madhouse and took the *fucking dog* out. It showed my dedication to the bloody thing, even though it had caused this to happen. Elliot’s Ferrari finally glided down the road. I waved and rushed back to him, Barney tugging me forward. The car swept into the drive.

Before I reached him, Isabella opened the door. Unlike her twin, she didn’t need a knife to look threatening. She gave me an evil glare and muttered darkly to her dad. The dog went ballistic, so I let him off the lead to dash in. Elliot went straight in without a glance in my direction.

He pacified his psycho spawn upstairs.

But I’m the injured party, I wanted to say. Why was no one pacifying me?

He drove them to a friend’s house. It wasn’t wise to let a knife-wielding youth into the community, but rather that than let her near me. I drank another vodka to steady my fractured nerves. At this rate I'd need danger money.

He came back and kicked off his shoes. I poured him a drink and went to kiss him, but he avoided eye contact, took the glass and sprawled back at the kitchen table. I looked expectantly at him.

'She's fine.' Authority came through in his voice, as if warning me not to challenge him. 'She has issues, but we'll deal with it.'

'She pulled a knife on me. Doesn't that bother you?'

'She wouldn't hurt you. It's a strange impulse. It flared up with Emma leaving. We'll have it back under control.'

'It was scary, Elliot. Terrifying. She was…' I was tempted to say demonic but went for 'possessed'.

'That's my child you're talking about,' he said in a hard voice.

'But—'

'I'm on top of it.'

I didn't push for an apology because they'd bleat about me swearing at the fucking dog. But she could have killed me.

Chapter Twenty-Six

Emma

'It's not my business,' Will said about the mystery man, 'but if you need help, I'm here.'

'Thanks.'

'Wouldn't you rather be back with your kids?'

'It's tricky now they're not going away, but I like it here.' I couldn't help seeing a future in Dorset, if only it were that simple.

'And you're right about the business plan. I read it last night.' His face lit up with enthusiasm.

I went to the wholesalers, then looked in on Will at the end of my shift.

'Will you be okay in the caravan?' he asked.

Would I be okay? I questioned my haste in leaving the cottage keys behind, now a strange man was prowling around trying to track me down.

'You can come and stay at mine.'

'Thanks, but I'll be fine.' I had to look after myself.

'Have the spare room. It's full of junk, but I'll clear you a path to the bed.'

'I can't believe it's full of junk.' We both surveyed the four obsolete computer towers gathering dust on a crowded shelf and an ancient printer beside a huge sack of goat food.

'I know,' he said cheerfully. 'Not when I'm so organised at work.'

'That's not a fax machine back there?'

'It's full of spiders.'

'Do you ever throw anything out?'

He shrugged. 'Not if it might come in useful.'

I didn't walk on the beach after work in case I came face to face with the man paid to track me down. I'd seen too many films where the PI kept going until he faced down his target. The caravan seemed flimsy now. Will knocked on the door before leaving for home in the muggy grey daylight.

'I'm off now. Are you all right here?'

'Yes, I like the lighter nights.'

He looked up at a break in the cloud. 'The moon's nearly full. Battles were often fought on full moons, to take advantage of the light.'

'I don't want to fight any battles.'

After he left, dark clouds covered the moon. My spine prickled at the eerie shadows cast by trees. The night pulsed with the noise of wildlife scuffling. Hypervigilance kept me awake along with movement and sounds around the caravan site. It was harmless, I told myself. Until it wasn't.

At some point, I fell asleep in the airless night, then I woke with a start. Where was I? My confusion cleared as the caravan bedroom came into focus. A pitiful wail sounded outside my door. All my muscles tightened in fear. Was it a child? I heard it again and sat up, grabbing my phone. I stood at the door and heard the cry, further away. It must be a cat or a wild animal. Sleep mostly eluded me after that, and I got up at dawn, bleary-eyed and unsettled.

Why did Elliot hire an investigator when he could contact me direct? He hadn't shared his reasons in the kitchen with Lydia. He didn't share much, sounding detached and offhand when I listened in, as if he'd tired of her already. I hadn't monitored them since moving to the caravan, but I steeled myself now and checked the app.

The commotion with Chloe and the knife played back loud and clear. I held my breath in appalled shock, fighting my instinct to run to the car and drive straight back. At least Elliot got them out of the house. I phoned Chloe.

Isabella answered in a sleepy voice. 'Hey, Mum.'

'Hey.' I tried to sound normal. 'Sorry it's early, but I was thinking about you both.'

'We're staying the night at Indigo's. We had to get away from that bitch.'

'It's best you don't call anyone a bitch.' Even though I liked her calling Lydia a bitch.

'We hate her. Legit hate her.' She was more awake now, her voice indignant.

'You can still go to France.'

'Why should we move out? We're at Indigo's because of her, but she's the one who should go. So anyway, me and Chloe, right? We're not standing for it. We went through all her stuff when she was out but there's nothing, no dirt. She doesn't go anywhere without her phone so we can't get into that.'

'Isabella—'

'We need to get rid of her. We told Dad we don't want her here and he said we'll have to do stuff round the house. But why should we? We've done our exams and now it's the summer. We've got our own lives.'

I sighed and let her burn out.

'So, Mum, don't freak out, okay? We did something bad.'

'What did you do?' I hid my note of panic.

Lydia

Before Chloe's meltdown, I was stalking a stunning red dress online. A dress with attitude. I called up the web page to soothe my poor emotions. I couldn't add it to the household budget so soon, worst luck. A lesser woman would squirrel away the housekeeping, but that wasn't my style. If Elliot wanted me, he could buy the dress and appreciate me in it. I would look fabulous on his arm, schmoozing his business contacts.

As soon as he invited me to a posh do, I'd make a case for the dress. I opened the spreadsheet that he'd sent before everything went to pot. The one for May covered grocery shopping, petrol, cash for the girls, sports kit for the sodding girls and something called mulch, from the garden centre. No personal spending for Emma apart from a few books, unless she hid her luxuries under spending for the little shits. That's what I'd do.

No wonder Emma was dowdy. She didn't fight it. My polished looks needed cash to maintain. I'd factor in visits to the hair salon along with facials and manicures. I needed to splurge on self-care in order to look after myself. I couldn't let his lack of consideration create a division, so when he came home, I pasted on a smile and poured him a drink. He sat at the kitchen table, and I tried to kiss him, but he busied himself brushing crumbs into a pile.

'I cleaned it earlier,' I said. 'Then the girls made snacks, but look at the floor.' I stood on the shiny white tiles and made a sweeping gesture, presenting them to him. 'It's been washed, mopped and buffed.'

'Nice.' He sipped from his glass, barely glancing at my handiwork.

I'd cleaned the floor again since the knife debacle because I wanted to keep him on my side.

'Thank God it's the weekend.' He sprawled listless in his chair. 'Tough week.'

'Our first weekend of living together. What shall we do?' I brightened at the prospect of two whole days of bringing him round to my way of thinking.

'I'm cycling. A bunch of us are going up Box Hill. It's a killer climb.'

'Mountain biking?'

'Racing bikes.'

I lifted the pasta bake from the oven to the table. 'Marianne's invited us for dinner.'

'I hope you said no.' He took the serving spoon and helped himself.

'She already knows about us. I'm finding this difficult, Elliot. It's quite isolating if I can't talk to anyone.'

'Tell her no. I don't like dinner parties.'

'But if we—'

'Tell her no.'

'Okay, but I'd like us to spend some time together.'

He was back fiddling with his phone while I ladled pasta onto my plate.

'…As a couple.'

He kept swiping.

'…Getting to know each other.'

'But you're already living here.'

'I mean quality time—'

He cringed. 'I hate Americanisms.'

'Call it what you want. We need time together without distractions.'

'I'm busy at work and I'm already committed to my sports.'

What a liberty, expecting me to cook every night and not set foot in a restaurant or go to Marianne's. Worst of all, he kept shutting me down. I masked my fury, thinking of all the ways I'd make him pay.

The next morning, he got ready to leave. At least he was dropping the twins off somewhere en route, so I'd have the place to myself. The girls lumbered downstairs. I came face to face with Chloe for the first time since she pulled the knife on me. She turned her head away.

'Okay now?' I asked in a concerned voice. It was her prompt to apologise, but she only gave the smallest nod. The other one stared darkly.

'Grass needs cutting.' Elliot filled his water bottle from the tap.

'Will you get out there tomorrow?' I'd sit back with a Pimm's and watch him.

'Emma does it. There's a Flymo in the shed.'

He ushered the kids out. *Emma does it.* The dog stared at me. Why was I always stuck with him? I had a leisurely coffee and left Muttley to snuffle round the garden. Today was my day off from walking, and no way was I cutting the grass. If anyone could kill that lawn, I could. Then we would replace it with a swimming pool.

I expected Elliot home sometime in the afternoon since he wouldn't have the energy to cycle up hills all day. The floor was grotty again, so I pushed the hoover around and the big hairy lump chased after me, barking at it. What was the point of dogs? When I returned the hoover to the cupboard under the stairs, he barged in and dragged Elliot's squash racket out to chew. I wrestled it away, and he started growling and nipping at my feet. I ended up taking him for a walk just for some peace.

I revisited my wedding options. A tasteful little do somewhere iconic would be perfect, but drastic action might be called for. If he took me to Vegas, we could get shit-faced and I'd manoeuvre him into the Elvis Wedding Chapel to get hitched.

Evening came and still no sign of Elliot. I couldn't settle. After all the household dross, I longed for retail therapy, cocktails and a massage. Emma should never have let him get away with cycling for half the weekend. She gave away her power. I held off from eating because he would be hungry after all that exercise. We'd eat together, he could tell me about his day, and I'd pretend to give a fuck. He rolled in at almost nine o'clock.

'I'm shattered.' He grabbed a beer from the fridge. 'Off for a soak in the bath.'

'Have you eaten?'

'We had a steak in the pub. Best thing I've had all week.'

Bastard. He went upstairs and I fumed. What had happened to Elliot, the charming people person? He only gave me attention during sex. Even then, he slipped into his private world of ecstasy, then fell asleep. I said a silent affirmation and followed him to the bathroom. He lounged in steamy herb-scented water, eyes closed.

'Feeling better?'

'Loads.'

'I'd like us to do something together tomorrow.'

He considered it as if it were a trick question. 'What do you have in mind?'

I kneeled beside the roll-top bath and dipped my hand in to seductively stroke his thigh. 'You, me,' I lowered my voice, turning it husky, 'bottle of fizz in bed.'

His phone rang. He lurched for it, splashing bathwater. 'Excuse me,' he said, meaning for me to go. Was it Emma? I walked out, leaving the door open. 'Hi, what do you have?' he said in a low voice, pausing for the reply. 'Did you check the most likely candidate?'

I craned to hear from the bedroom door.

'It must be her. It's a professional job from someone who's not demanding a payment. She has the money from her settlement and an axe to grind.'

The bathroom door slammed shut. I stepped closer to listen through the door.

'My wife?' he snarled. 'She knows nothing about it.'

Another pause. Tension radiated from behind the door.

'We need to silence her.' His voice turned menacing.

Chapter Twenty-Seven

Emma

One week to the murder

'What did you do?' I asked Isabella, not disguising the upset in my voice. The return of Chloe's knife fixation was terrible enough without their confession of doing 'something bad'.

'Chloe's been really affected by you leaving, Mum.'

Here we go. I needed to find out about her threatening Lydia without giving away what I'd heard through the app.

'She's got her anxiety, right? So things like this don't help. Anyway, you know her impulse thing with knives? Don't freak, but Lydia swore at Barney, and Chloe grabbed a knife to make her stop. It was hilarious.'

I rubbed my forehead. '*Hilarious?* Oh my God. How's Chloe now?'

'I'm fine, Mum.' Chloe's sweet voice chimed through. I pictured their heads pressed together on the call.

'What made you grab the knife?'

'That's the thing, Mum,' Isabella jumped back in. 'You're never gonna believe this. I'm the daring one, right? But Chloe goes and pulls a stunt like this.'

'Sorry?'

'Tell her,' Isabella said.

'It wasn't the knife impulse,' Chloe said. 'I did it to warn her off.'

'Warn her off?'

'We want you, not her. So if I pull a knife on her, I can say it's my anxiety and we won't get in trouble with Dad.'

Isabella snickered in the background.

'*Chloe*!' I covered my shocked mouth. 'You faked it?'

They broke into uncontrollable laughter. I took a few calming breaths.

'I literally thought I'd die when she told me,' Isabella laughed.

'Chloe, you did it to scare Lydia?' I said.

'You should've seen her face. She really thought I'd stab her.'

'Love her,' Isabella chimed in through her laughter. 'I truly do.'

'Seriously, Chloe. You can't threaten people with knives.'

'Mum! She doesn't threaten *people*. She threatened Lydia, who's basically off her head.'

I was shocked and relieved all at once. 'Chloe, promise you won't do it again.'

'Yeah, but we want rid of the bitch,' Isabella said. 'We've had enough. If she goes and the house turns to shit, you'll have to come back. You love cleaning.'

I sighed, then I called Jules, who listened in glee.

'Just shows how awful Lydia is, making our placid Chloe murderous.'

'And how awful Elliot is to bring out the worst in Lydia.'

'What do you think of Operation Prince Charming?' Jules asked.

'Operation what?'

'We needed a name for the project. Lucy came up with it.'

I snorted.

'Team Emma is fighting back against that freaking lunatic. Gotta run. Watch the video.'

Lucy had sent the link to the finished project, aimed to take Elliot down, but I'd been terrified of watching the video. What if he found out I was behind it? I took a deep breath and pressed play.

Lydia

The family organiser hung in the utility room alongside the kids' crappy artwork. Emma had marked up their commitments in her neat handwriting. I belatedly checked on whatever entitled teen activities greeted me for the rest of the summer.

My heart somersaulted at the entry for this Friday: *Summer Ball*. What summer ball? He hadn't mentioned it. I bet he expected me to drop everything for him, which I would, of course. At last, I could go all out to look fabulous.

A quick google brought up a Facebook mention by a lawyer at Elliot's practice. A few rapid clicks confirmed that my stunning ruby-red dress was available. Joy of joys. I envisaged walking into a swanky ballroom on Elliot's arm, people turning to admire us, Elliot so handsome and proud beside me as we mingled with the elite. I clicked with his colleagues, and he appreciated the boost to his social standing. You go mighty, girl!

Abuzz with pleasure, I couldn't wait to collar him about the ball. He did his man-cave thing after work. *Patience, Lydia*. With supper nearly ready, I went through and asked about his day. He sat with a drink, moaning about office politics and a difficult client. When he finished, I went in for the kill.

'What about the summer ball on Friday?'

He rubbed his five o'clock stubble. 'It goes on till late, so I won't be here Friday night.'

'Am I invited?'

'I've only got one ticket.'

'Emma wrote it on the family organiser. Can I go on her ticket?'

'I gave it back. Numbers are limited and someone else wanted it. It's just a work thing. You won't know anyone.'

'Of course I won't know anyone if you don't take me anywhere.'

'It's too soon. We have to let things settle.'

'Elliot, we never go out. I've put my career on hold to do everything here. I want to go to the ball with you.' My voice quavered. Just because I projected self-assurance, didn't mean I could brush off snubs.

'We can go out together, but not to this. Why don't you scope out an overnight trip to the Cotswolds or something? Just the two of us on a Saturday night. Nice boutique hotel, lovely big bed, the works.'

'Okay, but they can squeeze me in to the summer ball as well. I'll be sad for you to go when I'm home alone.'

'You won't be alone. You'll have Barney. Won't she, Barney?'

'Elliot—'

'Look, I'm under a huge amount of pressure right now.'

'What pressure?' From Emma? Or the woman he wanted silenced, from that snarly phone call I'd overheard.

The doorbell rang. He shot up to answer it, unusual for him. The dog raced him to the door. I fumed.

'Marianne,' he said jovially. 'How are you?'

I went through and saw them kissy-kissy on the doorstep. Pathetic, the way she came on to him.

'Coming in?' He waved her in.

'Just checking that you kids can make it for dinner Thursday. We'd love to have you.'

'That's so kind, but it's not the best time.'

'Why on earth not?' she boomed.

Ha. For once I appreciated her direct approach.

'It's too soon. We have to be discreet out of respect to Emma, and because of the twins. We're asking the few people who know about it to respect our privacy while the girls are coming to terms with it.'

Respect our privacy? You'd think someone had died. What about respecting my right to a social life?

'Of course. It's a difficult time for the girls. They need looking after.' Her gaze flicked to me.

It was a difficult time for me when they should've fucked off to France. He kissed up to Marianne but didn't come near me. He stood the other side of her, putting distance between us to avoid any PDA. Sneaky git. Marianne kept looking from him to me. I pulled a sad face at talk of the girls' welfare. I imagined the story she'd take back to book club for those vultures to pick over.

'We'd love to do something with you and Crawford once the dust has settled,' he said.

'We'd love that too.'

'You're an absolute gem. Now, Lydia is cooking us something amazing. We can stretch supper to an extra one if Crawford isn't expecting you.'

Nice of him to offer when I was the one doing the stretching.

'That's so kind, Elliot. But we're going to the Thai restaurant in town.'

'Lucky you,' I chipped in. 'We haven't been there, have we, Elliot? Well, not together.'

We paused while Elliot rubbed his evening stubble and chose not to answer.

'Okay, good buddies,' Marianne said. 'Buh-bye.'

She accepted another kiss from him and left with a wave.

He closed the door and walked towards the kitchen. 'Thank God she didn't stay. Is supper ready? I'm starved.'

'Why do you pretend to like her?'

'I'm keeping in with them. Crawford's worth a mint. Just retired from investment banking. I don't think they like each other enough to spend their retirement together. He admires me professionally, so I'll be the one he calls for a divorce.'

'You'd represent him against Marianne?'

'Why not? It'll be a big-money divorce.'

'What if Marianne gets in first?' She'd definitely get in first.

He shrugged. 'I'll round up the girls.'

They sloped down for supper.

'What's this?' Chloe looked dubiously at her plate.

'Grilled chicken with salsa verde.' I passed her the dish of new potatoes. The chicken was ready-marinated, so I only had to bung it under the grill.

'Did you make the salsa?' Isabella asked.

'I prepared it all, yes.'

'But the salsa's out of a tub, right?'

How rude. Instead of intervening, her father shovelled potatoes onto his plate.

'It's from the farm shop, but I prepared supper.'

'Thought so. Mum makes her own salsa.'

And I give better blow jobs.

'The way Mum makes it, it's like, literally a superfood.'

'Mmm,' Chloe mused with a faraway look, as if nostalgic for a fucking sauce.

If Elliot agreed with them, I'd torch the whole kitchen, but he ate in silence, his thoughts impenetrable. I could poison them all, tip antifreeze into the salsa verde. That would stop their undermining behaviour. I'd lost my appetite after cooking for that ungrateful lot.

The girls chatted about themselves and horses. Self-absorbed irritants. Shame they didn't choke on their food. Elliot's attitude to them was almost Victorian, doting on them at arm's length, peeling off twenties. I bet their sterile mother liked it that way. He kept me at an emotional distance too. Where'd the charming Elliot gone? Send out a search party.

'I love my girls,' he'd said to me a couple of times, chest puffed up in tedious male pride. I'd returned his indulgent smile, speculating on what he'd do if one got pregnant at seventeen or was caught shoplifting while high on drugs. He could love his girls so long as he loved me more.

Once we'd finished eating, I checked my watch. 'That time already. I'm meeting a friend.'

The three of them looked at me in total amazement, as if my only function was skivvying for them.

'I'll leave the clearing up in your capable hands. Don't forget that frying pan on the stove. Don't just leave it to soak. It needs boiling water, elbow grease and washing-up liquid.' I applied lipstick and kissed Elliot, leaving a vivid red imprint. 'Bye, darlings.'

The vile witch next door watched me from her window. She'd cold-shouldered me earlier when I said hello. I drove off to meet my imaginary friend, and parked up to listen to music and play on my phone. That would show Elliot. Horrible how he turned on the charm for Marianne but not me. I should have been flattered that she got the fakery and I saw the real him. But I preferred fake Elliot.

When did men become so ungallant? They didn't even wine and dine you now. In normal circumstances, if a man didn't work hard to win me, I would pull back. But we'd skipped the courtship and got straight down to business. If I had somewhere else to go, I could let him come running, except I'd no faith that he would.

He was still down about Emma and feigned indifference because he struggled to express his emotions. He avoided intimacy through long hours of sport and staring at his phone. Emma had hardened his heart, but the twins could melt it and I must too. We'd never been drunk together to the point of silliness, so I could try that. It had worked every time with Vern, my happy drunk. A bottle of Jacob's Creek always made his day. Vern liked me getting plastered and doing the splits, but Elliot was a trickier customer.

They were all in bed when I returned just after ten. He hadn't texted me a goodnight or asked when I'd be home. The next morning, he was up at five thirty sharp and left without a word. I didn't surface until the girls left.

I went down for coffee, and my heart lifted when I saw he'd left me a note. But then I read it:

Need some milk. Pls clean en suite and iron shirts.

He had added a kiss at the end, scored deeply into the notepad. I snatched a carving knife from the block and stabbed the note on the wooden chopping board.

Chapter Twenty-Eight

Emma

Lucy had flexed her creative muscles in producing the video. It started with an authoritative male voiceover warning us about the divorce solicitor, Elliot Morland. A photo showed him from the feature that a business magazine had run, calling him *The Boss of Break-ups*. The narrator said Elliot's professional image hid the dark truth behind his business practices, promising to blow the lid.

The photo changed to one of Elliot on the phone, an old image I recognised from his law firm's website. Then a series of recordings played out of women phoning his office to request appointments regarding their impending divorces. Each time, Elliot's secretary took the caller's name and her husband's name, put her on hold, then returned to say, 'I'm afraid Mr Morland is unable to represent you at this time.'

An on-screen call log showed that all three phone calls had been made on the same morning in July. Each caller was rebuffed. Then a man phoned and was immediately given an appointment. The on-screen call data showed he phoned just minutes after the last call from a woman. The screen changed to a highlighted section of Sally's anonymous witness statement saying Elliot only represented men. Not a crime in itself and the recordings could have been staged. None of this would hold up in court, but still, it didn't look good for Elliot that someone had gone to all this trouble to discredit him. It would infuriate him.

A different man's photo appeared on-screen. It was the PI who had come looking for me at the caravan park. Audio of a dialling tone signalled another call, from the same male caller who'd scored an appointment with Elliot. The man said Elliot had recommended he call the PI to discuss how to discredit his estranged wife. I recognised the PI's voice from his visit to the caravan park. After some matey back and forth, the PI offered to 'capture' online evidence to show his wife's infidelity.

'There isn't any online evidence,' the caller said.

'There will be once I've done my job.'

This was followed by another highlighted section of Sally's witness statement, detailing the investigator's services to Elliot. Then the narrator read aloud from the magazine feature about his devotion to his wife and daughters, before showing us how the family man spent his spare time. Jules's video evidence played out. The exterior of a swanky London bar zoomed in to a view of Elliot through the window. He only had eyes for the younger woman beside him as they cosied up in a corner booth. They emerged from the bar, his arm on her back, and went to a nearby hotel, where he handed over his credit card, then disappeared into the lift with her.

The camera returned to the magazine feature, gushing about Elliot approaching his twentieth wedding anniversary and proclaiming his love for his wife. A close-up showed the magazine had come out the same month as Elliot's hotel liaison, evidenced by a screenshot of the timed and dated video. The voiceover told us that he had kicked out his loyal wife and moved a younger replacement in, although a different younger woman to the one in the footage.

The video ended and left me reeling. I knew it all but had palpitations from seeing it laid bare. I'd hate to be near Elliot when he saw it.

I messaged Jules.

Where did Lucy get those call recordings?

The three women are Lucy, Rosa and me. She disguised our voices for the recording so Elliot wouldn't recognise us. The man is Crawford.

I gasped.

Crawford???

We enlisted him to the sisterhood on a need-to-know basis.

All their support strengthened my resolve, but the plan fortified and terrified me in equal measures. Elliot would have received our letter along with a link to the incriminating video. He hated criticism and couldn't bear anyone else having the upper hand. And he would explode from our threat to go nuclear over his actions. Surely he would know I was behind it. I felt sick with fear that he would hunt me down.

At least the caravan park was blissfully uneventful. I worked full out as I was having the weekend off to see Jules and the girls. That Thursday, I dropped into the office for some keys and Will told me about his heated run-in with the local planning officer. He laughed as if there were no hard feelings. I laughed too since his problems were easier than mine. Still laughing, I opened the office door and walked into Elliot.

I jumped back like I'd had an electric shock. A bolt of fear ran through me. I felt as defenceless as I had the last time I saw him, back home on the stairs. 'What are you doing here?' I gasped, the breath knocked from me.

His intense stare burned into me. I backed away and bumped into Will, right behind me. His placed his hands protectively on my arms. Elliot glared at him.

'What's going on?' Will stood firm.

Elliot sized him up. 'Who are you?'

Lydia

The day started well, going into London for a splurge. The dress was to die for. Heady with excitement, I bought it on my credit card and pretended Elliot had treated me. Screw it all. I went for broke and had a salon wash and style. My goal was to crush at the ball. It wasn't until tomorrow, but I would win Elliot over tonight with my polished party look. He'd never seen me properly dolled up, and I'd render him powerless in the face of my allure.

I was on a high until the pouty twin vampires turned up to suck the lifeblood from me. They demolished the kitchen with their snack making.

'Where's my phone charger?' Isabella demanded.

'Where you left it.'

She huffed and they took the food upstairs.

'Can you walk Barney?' I called after them.

'We're going out.'

Bitches, but at least they'd be out at *who-the-fuck-cares* tonight. I sifted through the mail, not that any of it was for me. A slim white envelope addressed to Elliot caught my eye. The address was printed but looked more bespoke than his usual mail. *Personal, addressee only* was printed at the top and it was only sealed at the tip. I took out the sharpest, thinnest knife, slit through the sealed tip and removed the single sheet of typed paper.

Elliot,

I'm following up on the email sent this week, to which you have yet to respond. I know you've clicked through to the video link. Compelling viewing, yes? Professional misconduct, fraudulent behaviour and an unsavoury personal scandal… not looking good for the Boss of Break-ups, is it?

You have 48 hours to respond before the video goes live on YouTube. I will send links to your entire professional circle. Everyone will see you for the power-hungry bully and cheat that you are.

As for kicking your wife out and moving in a younger replacement, this won't do. To stop the video going live, inform your wife in writing that she will keep the house in the divorce settlement. If you then dare to break your promise, the video will be posted online. You must also respond to the email I sent you with a genuine, heartfelt apology to all the women you have crushed professionally and personally, and a pledge to never treat women badly again.

Yours sincerely,
An avenging angel

What the fuck was this? It must be connected to his bathtub call last Saturday. He wanted evidence of a woman's identity, the avenging angel. I needed to see the video, but I didn't have access to the email link. A YouTube search didn't throw up anything in his name. The blackmailer couldn't get away with it. The house was ours, not Emma's.

My mind churned it over as I assembled some nibbly bits for supper – smoked salmon, cheese, olives. *An avenging angel*. Elliot didn't need this when he had to focus on me. I hid the letter and left the food in the fridge to eat with warm flatbread after he'd ravished me. I would keep up my summer ball campaign and take his mind off the blackmailer, since I was the main attraction.

Chapter Twenty-Nine

Emma

I tried to recover from the shock of Elliot turning up. He must have known I was behind the plan to play him at his own game. I clasped my shaking hands together. He looked ragged round the edges, his usually neat hair reaching the top of his shirt collar. And he looked pissed off.

Will stood up to him. 'I own this place, and I don't want any trouble.'

Elliot ignored him and stared hard at me. 'We need to talk. It's about the girls.'

In that case, he'd come to talk me round. The knife incident had pushed him to seek me out, and he'd be sick of the drama back home. So long as he didn't suspect me, I was safe. I walked away from the office, to avoid a showdown between him and Will.

'I'll drive us somewhere for a coffee,' he said.

'I have to work.'

'You *don't* have to work.'

We walked to the edge of the caravan park, to the point overlooking the bay. I looked at the sea, arms wrapped around myself to stop my hands shaking.

'How did you find me?' I asked.

'It was easy.'

Easy when he'd hired a PI.

'Let's walk along the beach,' he said.

'I don't have time. Why are you here?'

'The girls aren't coping. You need to come home. We can pack up your stuff and be home in time for dinner.'

In time to *cook* dinner.

'Emma?'

'I've a six-week contract here. It was arranged before I knew you'd cancelled the French trip. I don't let people down.'

'Don't your children come first?'

I turned to face him, searching for any trace of an apology. He looked at me, perplexed.

'You threw me out. You wanted custody. You cancelled their trip to France.' *You, you, you. It all comes back to you.* I wanted to shove him off the cliff. Instead, I spun on my heel and marched towards the office, fists clenched.

'Wait.' He caught up, grabbing my arm.

'Don't.' I jerked my arm away.

'Look, we all do stupid things.'

Was that how he justified his terrible behaviour?

He ran his hands through his hair. 'I'm willing to forgive and forget. Come home and we'll say no more about it.'

'Ha! That's big of you.'

'Have you lost your mind?' His voice was low and urgent. 'Not that you had much of one in the first place.'

I gasped and pulled back. He grabbed my shoulder in his steely grip, facing me down, eyes blazing.

'What the fuck is this? My children deserve a decent mother, not trailer-park trash. You should be ashamed.'

'*I* should be ashamed?'

'If you make this difficult for me, you'll regret it.' He issued the warning quietly enough so no one could overhear.

Will stacked pallets nearby, keeping a covert eye out for me. Elliot saw him too, so he didn't pull me back when I twisted from his grasp. Without Will's reassuring presence, I'd have struggled to hold my own with Elliot. After everything he'd done, I had a rush of satisfaction from standing up to him. Served the bastard right. Jules would be proud.

'Let me ask you one thing,' he snarled. 'Who is he? That man over there. Are the two of you—?'

'Don't be ridiculous. Unlike some people, I don't sleep around.'

'You'd be a fool to trust him. He's hostile, possibly aggressive.'

I spluttered out a mirthless laugh, then strode off.

He followed.

'You need to leave,' I said, reaching the office and slamming the door behind me. I grabbed my car keys and stood by the window, ready to drive off if he refused to go. Will kept watch, as if standing guard.

Elliot walked back to his car, not waiting for my shift to end, since he couldn't risk leaving the twins alone with Lydia all evening. I'd listen in later to check on them, and I was seeing them tomorrow, thank God. He drove away and I let out the long breath I'd been holding.

His visit prompted me to call Stella Musgrove, the divorce lawyer in Kingston that Jules had scoped out. We had an initial chat on the phone and I warmed to her friendly, down-to-earth approach. It might not be so bad with her representing me.

'Can I make a note of your husband's name?' she asked.

'Elliot Morland.'

'*Elliot Morland*?'

My heart plunged at the alarm in her voice.

'From Rooke Hamilton?'

'Yes.'

'I'm sorry,' she said gravely. 'I can't represent you.'

'But why?' I was ready to plead.

'I have to go. Very best of luck, Mrs Morland.' She hung up.

Lydia

Before Elliot came home, I carefully removed the dress labels and made myself gorgeous. The finishing touch was a spritz of Mitsouko, my go-to sexy fragrance to convey my goddess credentials. Elliot remained out of reach except during sex, so I would work my magic on him. When I heard Muttley rushing to greet him at the front door, I texted him.

> Meet you in the bedroom, Hot Stuff. I've something to show you… xx

He came upstairs, his feet heavy on the carpet. *Don't worry, Elliot, I'll revive you.* The anticipation of sex always fired him up. He walked in as I popped the cork from a bottle of pink fizz. I stood resplendent in the gorgeous dress and high heels, my hair artfully tousled. The dress matched the red soles of my Louboutin stilettos. Not to brag, but I was smoking hot.

'Hello, tiger,' I said in my minxy voice.

'Look at you, all dressed up.' He tilted his head, working out why I looked that way on a Thursday evening when we had no plans.

I came close and kissed him. Then I turned away, giving him a slinky look over my shoulder. 'Undo me, darling.' I presented myself to him, a gift to be unwrapped.

He unzipped me, revealing my vampy black lingerie. I stepped out of the dress, still in my heels, and turned to face him.

'You like?'

'I like.' He gave me a sly grin and kissed me with renewed passion.

I lay the dress over a chair, and we took the fizz to bed. Sex improved his mood, so I employed all the techniques he found irresistible. After his usual shuddering climax, he lay back, recovering his breath.

'You're sexy as fuck,' he said.

'Why, thank you. You're sexy as fuck too.'

Our fingers entwined as I lay beside him. I counted on the feel-good rush to last while I kept him engaged so he didn't fall asleep.

'What do you think of my dress?'

'You look amazing in it.'

'I'd like to wear it to the summer ball tomorrow.'

He exhaled with a loud sigh.

'I promise to be charming and show everyone how worthy I am to be on the arm of a luscious lawyer.'

He blinked at the ceiling.

'What do you say?' *Say yes, obviously.*

'I'm under a lot of pressure.'

'What pressure, darling?'

Another long sigh.

'I did notice that you haven't been yourself. Is something going on?'

'I'll check tomorrow and see if anyone's dropped out.'

'People always drop out. And you're a man of considerable charm. I bet you can pull a string or two.' I gave him an appreciative smile. 'They'll squeeze in a plus-one for you.'

'It's a popular night.'

'And we're popular people.' *And I'm not some mug doing everything on your terms.* I hated male power play. Mind games were a waste of time.

'I'll see what I can do.'

'I'm finding it quite hurtful, Elliot, after everything I do for you and the kids—'

'All right,' he said, his voice clipped. 'You made your point. Now drop it.'

Not the best response, but he could sleep on it and wake up convinced that we should be together tomorrow night. I kissed him to show my faith in him, but the fucker had better deliver. The ball was make or break.

'By the way,' he said, 'can you do something about the dog hairs downstairs?'

I can get rid of the dog. That'll fix it.

'The place isn't as clean as it used to be,' he added.

In other words, I didn't match up to Emma. 'I'll do a deep clean in return for the ball.' I resented it, of course. The prick had me exactly where he wanted. I'd nuke the dog hairs in return for a night out, but he should know that it cheapened our relationship and hurt my pride. My stress levels were off the scale. He'd better start appreciating me, fast.

Chapter Thirty

Emma

Jules and I sunned ourselves on her balcony, catching up before I went to collect the girls.

'…then after he sent the private investigator,' I said, 'he turned up unannounced when I was with Will.'

'Elliot?'

'He wanted to talk about the girls.'

'Elliot walked in on you in bed with Will?'

'*What*? No! I'm not sleeping with Will.'

'Yet.'

'Stop it.' I batted her arm.

'Book boyfriend?'

She meant which literary crush did he resemble. 'Darcy.'

'Ooh!'

'Except Pemberley is a caravan park.'

'Oh.'

That wasn't entirely true. Pemberley was a dream of a cottage near the sea, but she didn't need encouragement.

'Anyway, I was at work, and I walked slap bang into Elliot.'

'What happened?'

I told her everything.

'Bloody cheek,' she scoffed. 'Fetching you back to clear up his mess. Sod that.'

'I have to look out for the girls.'

'It's a proper love triangle with Will in the mix.'

'I told Elliot there's nothing going on.'

'Em, you don't owe him an explanation.'

'He wanted me to come home and I told him the score.'

'Of course he wants you home. When you have a lawyer, he can contact you through them.'

'He won't like that.'

'Bollocks to him. Stand up for your rights. After that law firm in Kingston refused to take you on, I spoke to a shit-hot divorce lawyer in London. I told her he'll play dirty, but she specialises in *complex cases*. That's code for dickheads who think they're above the law. She isn't fazed by a psychopath like Elliot. You can call her assistant and set up a meeting.'

Jules tapped on her phone and showed me a photo of the lawyer in a sharp jacket and silk shirt, looking like nobody would put her off her game.

'And if he won't play nice, we'll launch into phase two and go public on him setting up honeytraps and telling clients to hide money from their wives.' Elliot only had until Monday morning before the video went live and Lucy sent a link to his professional contacts. I had no idea how he would handle it.

'Have you heard anything?' I asked.

She gulped her tea and flapped her hand as if she couldn't wait to tell me. 'Oh, yes. Marianne dropped in on them. She didn't want to tell you in case it upset you. Apparently, he won't be seen out with her.'

'Ha, really? That's brilliant. Or did he say that to get out of socialising with Marianne? It's his annual company ball tonight.'

'We'll find out more when we see the girls.'

Jules was a pick-me-up after my nights alone in the caravan and Elliot turning up. She snickered into her tea, but it sounded like the situation was breaking down. We drove to the woodland car park at the edge of the village, our rendezvous for the girls. I kept my head down in case Elliot drove past towards his summer ball, but he usually went straight from work to the Ritz.

The girls turned up, rushing towards us with their overnight backpacks, faces flushed and animated. They laughed and ran to keep up with Barney straining on the lead. I stepped out of the car and flung my arms wide. Barney went loopy and the girls hugged me.

'We brought the clothes you wanted,' Chloe said, throwing her bag in the boot with Isabella's.

They piled in the back, squealing and creating a commotion over settling Barney, hyping him up even more. They boosted my spirits. A whole evening with my favourite people, and I would wake up with them in the morning.

Just then, a car sped around the bend and swerved into the car park. We all stopped and stared. It jerked to a halt, blocking us in. Lydia was behind the wheel, her face in a murderous snarl.

Lydia

In the early hours of the night before the ball, Elliot slept, and I poured another G&T. *Face facts, Lydia, he's not the man you took him for.* I hated to admit it after coming this far. I weighed up my limited options, which consisted of finding someone more open and generous if he failed to make the grade. I would consider downsizing for the right man, since the last few weeks had taught me that big homes were overrated. I could live somewhere small and chic, in Kensington perhaps. But I hated all this wasted effort.

I brainstormed how to infiltrate a book club in London. I needed contacts for a way in and would have to throw a fortune at Gyrotonic, or SoulCycle, or whatever the bored, brittle wives did around there. The gym membership alone would wipe out any conventional income from whatever crummy job I'd be forced to take. Wine-tasting evenings in Central London were a faster pick-up option. But last time they had turned into an expensive waste of time.

I would stay with Elliot for now and use his contacts and money as a way into London society. As his partner, I fitted somewhere in the pecking order of movers and shakers even if we weren't seen out together. By spending my days with the London elite, I could mirror their lives in art galleries and beauty salons, cruising the Notting Hill boutiques until I became one of them. I would use Elliot as a stepping stone, then bin him off.

In the morning, he stirred beside me. I picked up my campaign.

'How's my gorgeous boy?'

He groaned into the pillow. 'It's too early.'

'Want me to wake you up?' I said suggestively.

'Can you make me a coffee? I'll hit the shower.'

When I came back, he was shaving.

'Will you let me know by lunchtime about the ball? Then I'll make myself beautiful for you.'

'Hmm.' He pulled an overnight holdall from the back of the wardrobe and threw in some things. He slid a dinner suit into a suit carrier.

'Have you booked a hotel?'

'Yup. Gotta go. Speak later.'

At what point did he intend to mention staying overnight in a hotel? The front door shut behind him. I lay all my party things out in readiness. I hadn't given up. Far from it. I might meet someone better at the ball. When he hadn't been in touch by lunchtime, I texted him.

Will Cinderella go to the ball with her Prince Charming? xx

Nothing.

An hour later, I phoned his mobile, which went to voicemail. I tapped my foot and left a message. 'Hi, it's me. Let me know about tonight. The girls have a sleepover with Barney, so I'm all yours.' I considered phoning his office reception, but he might not like it.

By the time the girls returned, my foul mood needed an outlet.

'If you go in the kitchen, clear up after yourselves.'

They looked at me, slack-jawed, not that I cared. How dare he ignore me? I should've asked which hotel he'd booked and gone there all dolled up, leaving him no choice. But now he could avoid me until tomorrow. Ungrateful prick.

I went back to the Facebook post about the ball from his colleague to check her updates. *It's at the fucking Ritz!*

They were having a five-course dinner in the Michelin-starred restaurant, then dancing the night away to live music. Enough of this dicking around. I would turn up and surprise him, then they would have to fit me in. I threw myself in the shower. When I turned it off, someone rapped on the door. Was it Elliot, come to escort me to the ball? I slid on my silk robe and opened the door in a *ta-da!* gesture.

'Where's Mum's clothes?' Isabella stood before me, pulled up tall, fists on hips.

Anger surged in me. 'In the spare room.' I slammed the en-suite door in her face.

I heard the murmur of their bratty voices, then a thunderbolt of realisation hit me. He was taking *her* to the ball. She was staying in the hotel and had tasked them with finding her a party dress. What kind of mug did he take me for? I fought the impulse to charge in and confront them.

No, Lydia. Stop. I would follow them and have it out with her. That superbitch had gone swanning off for a break from her dumbass family, and they were taking advantage of my generous nature until she swooped back. What a liberty. They'd done a number on me, the bloody lot of them.

They came thumping back through to our bedroom. 'We need to take food for Barney. Can you help us?'

'Do it yourselves,' I snapped. 'He's your dog.'

They gawped at me in disbelief. Served them right. I wasn't their doormat. I strode to the bedroom window to check if Emma had pulled up outside. Minutes later, they went crashing out, scrambling after the dog, their overnight backpacks stuffed full and slung over their shoulders. *Don't tell me they're going to the ball too?* I rushed out for my shoes and car keys. This couldn't be happening.

Chapter Thirty-One

Emma

Lydia took us completely by surprise. If she hadn't blocked us in, I'd have ignored her. She'd muscled in enough, but she looked in no mood to be ignored.

'Where are you going?' She jumped out of her car, wearing a pink bathrobe, and squared up to me with wild eyes and clenched fists.

Her transformation shocked me. What had got into her?

'Are you going to the ball?' she said, her voice shrill and loud.

Jules leapt from the driver's seat. 'None of your bloody business.'

Isabella flung open her passenger door.

'Stay in the car.' I signalled for them to stay away from Lydia. 'Back off,' I told her. 'Move your car.'

'If you try taking Elliot from me, there'll be trouble,' she screeched. 'I'm telling him this isn't on. You want him back, but you can't have him. You hear me? Stay away from him—'

Jules cut across us and nipped behind the wheel of Lydia's car. Lightning quick, she drove it to the far corner of the woodland car park. Lydia launched towards her, screaming threats. Jules scooted back to us, triumphant.

'Get in,' she yelled to me. We both jumped in.

'Oh my God, she's fucking nuts,' Isabella cackled.

I should've told her not to swear, but no words came out. Jules and I exchanged dark glances. 'She's deranged,' she mouthed to me, starting the engine.

'This is sick!' Isabella squealed.

Jules sped us out of the car park.

'Stop!' Lydia screamed after us. 'Give me my keys or I'll call the police.'

Jules braked hard. We jerked forward in our seats. 'You okay, hun?' she called sweetly to Lydia, and tossed the keys through the window.

The girls thought it hilarious, but they couldn't return home with Lydia so crazed. Elliot clearly brought out the worst in her. He liked doing his own thing without confrontation, and Lydia wasn't the type to put up and shut up. The other three marvelled at her performance, but I had to call time on it.

We parked at Jules's and walked Barney along the river for everyone to calm down. Then we piled into Jules's flat and I cooked. I missed feeding them and chatting around the table. At home, I would lose myself in cooking, the same as I lost myself in a book. But not here, with Barney's excitement and the twins bringing us up to speed, words spilling out, finishing each other's sentences.

'She's awful. She sucks up to Dad—'

'And she's jealous of us—'

'She tries to join in—'

'And she thinks she's cool for talking about Tinder and Bumble.'

'It's so cringe,' they said in unison, laughing.

'She pretends to be our BFF.'

'Delulu or what?' They rolled their eyes.

'If she acts like your bestie,' I said, 'she's being nice to you, yes?'

'Yeah, but it's fake and she was like, *psycho-bitch* when we came home—'

'Like totally off the scale.'

'She's shown her true colours,' Jules said. 'As if we didn't already know.'

'If she has to actually do anything at home she gets in a huff,' Isabella said.

'Does she cook?' I stirred the risotto.

'Like this.' Isabella pulled a sour face and banged around the kitchen, tossing her hair. 'Are you girls out tonight?' she said in a haughty Lydia voice, hands on hips. 'Tomorrow night? You two could do some cooking, you know.'

We laughed. I missed them, but they hadn't changed. From what they said, Elliot had gone into a slump while he kept Lydia dangling on a piece of string. No wonder she was livid. Isabella had filmed her meltdown on her phone. We watched the playback open-mouthed. Seeing it again was somehow more shocking.

'Mum,' Chloe said, 'don't make us go back.'

'You're not going back with her there.'

It surprised me they'd stuck it out this long with Elliot turning Lydia into a raving lunatic, stirring up her raw ingredients.

'I'll phone Dad and tell him,' Isabella said.

We agreed that she could message him and send the video clip of Lydia. Jules and I helped her word it into less of a teenage rant.

Dad, Lydia went mental at us and we don't want to come home with her there. She's really scary. Watch the clip. Aunt Jules says we can stay with her. Love you xxxxxxx

His reply pinged back two minutes later.

Lydia is leaving. I'll let you know tomorrow when it's ok to come home. We'll get a takeaway in the evening. I want us all back here, how we used to be. I love my girls. Xxxxxx

They whooped and jumped about singing 'Ding dong, the witch is dead', hyping Barney up again. Then they collapsed on the sofa, giggling.

I love my girls. He used to say that about the three of us when the twins were younger.

'Have you ever heard Dad say, "We'll get a takeaway"?' Isabella exclaimed.

'Never!' Chloe said.

After everyone went to sleep, I lay awake. Much as I loved Dorset, the twins needed me. If Lydia went, other women would seduce Elliot and clash with the girls. And what if she refused to go? Our anonymous threat to go public on Elliot's wrongdoing piled more pressure on him. I'd wanted to call him out, but it felt reckless now. I knew what he was capable of, and our actions threatened to unleash the worst of him. God knows what we'd return to if I dropped them back tomorrow. I had to protect them, which meant walking away from a better life. A solitary tear trickled down my face and mingled with my hair on the pillow.

Lydia

Trust her to turn up at the worst time. It was my night to outshine her. Elliot must have been keeping their reconciliation secret. The spineless bastard never came back to me about the ball. Emma looked worse than ever, with a tatty ponytail and no make-up. Like a farmer's wife put out to pasture. I'd have laughed if the situation weren't critical.

I arrived home, still fuming. Shouting in the car park did me no favours, but I needed to vent. I forgot to tell her about the radical feminist blackmailing him. I'd show her the letter, since it hinted at him having affairs. Then she'd know he made a habit of behaving badly. As for the stupid ball, I didn't care. I'd make free with his booze and have a lie-in until it blew over. I turned off my phone and hit the vodka.

'Fuck you, Emma,' I said between sips of voddy. 'And fuck your fucking husband. He's not worth it. Have him back. I hate you and your pathetic book club losers who think you're better than me.' I lunged at the family organiser and scrawled *FUCK THE LOT OF YOU* across July. I ripped the page from the organiser and scrunched it into a ball. *Deep breaths, Lydia*.

I woke up feverishly hot at eleven a.m. My head pounded like I'd been on the lash all weekend. No sign of Elliot. I picked my way delicately downstairs and made strong coffee. I slid my sunglasses on to shield me from the dazzling white floor. Today was a scorcher. I opened all the upstairs windows in an attempt to breathe more easily. When I climbed back into bed, I turned on my phone to a text from Elliot. My gut wrenched.

> It's not working. You're upsetting my daughters. Please leave by morning.

Upsetting his daughters? Fucking kids were out to get me. What about *my* upset at him not taking me to the ball, and how dare he dismiss me by text? He'd forgotten my trump card: he needed me. He couldn't even cook. And given the choice of an empty fridge or me, even his vile daughters would choose me. I couldn't become homeless. I'd taken a gamble on this man, this house. I was committed.

I would stay and talk it over because that's what adults did. They weren't swayed by stupid emotional girls. My mind was already formulating a cover story in which his dipshit daughters had misinterpreted me. I could pull this off. The rush of adrenaline cleared the worst of my hangover. I took a shower and found a respectable black shift dress of Emma's.

He walked in around noon. My heart lurched. I checked my hair and make-up in the bedroom mirror. He'd mistaken me for a doormat. Time to assert myself.

He clunked his keys down on the hall table and glanced up at me, standing on the landing. His body tensed, his mouth set in a grim line. I was on a knife-edge, the atmosphere charged with negative energy.

'How are you?' I asked.

'It's over, Lydia. You need to leave before my daughters come home.'

I'm not leaving. I'm not. I've nowhere to go. I took a tortured breath. 'C'mon, baby,' I said in a hurt voice. 'We can deal with this. I'm still finding my way with the girls. It's a misunderstanding, that's all. They overreacted. We'll work it out.'

He stood at the bottom of the stairs, looking amped up.

'How was your night out? Did you have fun?' I asked in my innocent voice.

'Time to go.'

'Don't, please.' A sob built up. 'Don't do this to me. To us.'

'There is no *us*.' He was softer now – well, not soft as such but wearily resigned.

'I'm sorry, darling. I blitzed the house for you yesterday and skipped lunch, then my blood sugar crashed. I'll be careful in future.'

He checked his watch. Bastard.

'Can't you see how you're hurting me?' I pressed one palm to my heart. If I could just get him into bed I'd turn it around. I'd give him a special time. 'Remember how hurt you were when Emma rejected you, and then we made love?'

'We're not doing that again.'

'Once more for old time's sake?' I ventured.

He walked up the stairs, one arm outstretched to escort me out. 'Come on.'

He went to take my arm and I stepped back. How dare he?

'Give me one reason why I should go.'

'Because.' He pursed his lips. A vein pulsated on the side of his neck. 'I've had enough of your drama.'

'Drama?' I screeched. 'What drama?'

'I don't need your histrionics.'

'You used me.' I laid into him, not caring how I sounded.

'You forced yourself on me. You're a cheap slut.'

'How dare you insult me?' I yelled at the top of my voice.

'Your performance was filmed yesterday. You abused my family.'

'What? Who filmed me? It's an abuse of my rights. It's—'

'I want Emma, not you. Being with you was a mistake. A knee-jerk thing. You made yourself available.'

I couldn't believe it. Why would he choose *her* over me? His firm tone got to me. He saw me as a situation to manage.

'I gave up work for you. I'll need money to rent somewhere.'

'You've had enough from me.'

The more controlled he was, the more my blood boiled. Everyone had their breaking point and mine came on those stairs.

'Enough? Enough?' I yelled. 'You're the one taking advantage, considering I'm so *beneath* you. You don't know how lucky you are to have me. You walk all over me, never considering my feelings. I'm wasted on you.'

My anger got a reaction. He bared his teeth in a snarl. It thrilled me to have his full attention after all his apathy.

'I don't want to be with someone like you.' He said 'like you' with disgust, yet his voice stayed low, measured.

'Someone like me? What's that supposed to mean?'

'You're a bargain-basement stripper.'

'How fucking dare you?' I was on the verge of lashing out, wanting him to retaliate and slap me. I'd keep on until he bruised me.

'Get your stuff. You can stay with a friend.'

What friend? I had no friends. 'Don't do this, Elliot, I'm warning you.'

'You're warning me, are you?' His eyes narrowed on me, his words laced with menace. He grabbed my arm, gripped me tight.

I yanked it away and pointed in his face. 'You lay a finger on me, I'll call the police, and they'll throw *you* out for violence. I know what you're like beneath it all, you monster. I know what that radical feminist's been accusing you of.'

Anger flashed across his face. 'Radical feminist? You mean the anonymous threat? She's not a feminist. She's a bitter old hag whose ex-husband didn't roll over and give her half of everything he'd worked hard for.' Menace dripped from his words, his eyes burning into me. 'Nasty business, blackmail.'

I shoved him and he nearly lost his footing. He could handle it, a fit guy like him. The push was my opening gambit, so he would slap me. If he gave me a black eye, I'd threaten to call the police. I wouldn't move from the stairs without a pay-off. When it came to fight or flight, I chose fight every time.

His face contorted into a snarl. 'If you threaten me, you'll come off worse.' His voice stayed low, his words precise.

'Don't do this.' I tried appealing to his better nature, not that he had one.

'Go ahead and call the police. I'll be believed because I'm the one in control. Otherwise, go now before it turns ugly.'

'What's that supposed to mean?'

He brought his face close to mine. 'Women like you want shooting.'

The brute. How dare he? Volcanic anger erupted from me. I shoved him hard. He lost his footing and toppled backwards. Arms flailing, he thumped and crashed down the stairs, stopping at the tiled floor in a lifeless slump.

Was he dead? Frozen in shock, I couldn't take my eyes from him.

His leg twitched. He was alive, but in a bad way. He groaned, semi-conscious. My panicked mind screamed. *What do I do?* He'd threatened me. It was self-defence. But what if he recovered and gave evidence? Him so smooth and used to courtrooms, he would charm the pants off any jury.

I clutched the sides of my head. What if the girls walked in? *Do something, Lydia. Get a grip.* No time for half-measures. I stumbled downstairs and hauled him up by the shoulders. His head lolled backwards like an unconscious drunk. I slammed it hard onto the shiny white floor. I heard a sharp crack.

Silence. It did the trick. His eyes were closed, mouth agape. I grabbed his shoulders again, hauled him up and slammed him down once more. The back of his skull bounced on the hard floor. Blood spilled onto the tiles. It looked like injuries sustained from a bad fall.

I crouched beside him, checking for a pulse that I couldn't find. I placed a finger under his nostrils to detect breathing. Nothing. Thick dark blood trickled from his nose. Pinpricks of sweat broke out on my skin and my hands shook like crazy. I watched his life drain away on those cold white tiles. That blood would be a bugger to clean off.

Minutes passed and his face turned waxy. Like Vern when he died. I called 999, my sobs so pitiful the operator struggled to understand me. I was devastated. We could have been the perfect couple and led a charmed life, but Elliot ruined it.

When the paramedics arrived, I crouched at the foot of the stairs. 'Please help him,' I said over and over in a choked voice. All that mattered was putting on the performance of my life.

'What happened?' one of them asked.

'He fell downstairs,' I managed to choke out. I needed sympathy after everything I'd been through, but they looked stony-faced at each other and didn't speak to me. I stroked his bloodied face and tried to hold his hand.

'Stay back. Don't touch anything.'

Then the police turned up.

Chapter Thirty-Two

Emma

Heat shimmered from the road as I drove the twins home. It was the hottest day of the year. Elliot had texted them first thing, saying again that Lydia would be gone by lunchtime. He'd certainly become practised at throwing women out of the house. I made it clear to the girls that if Lydia was still there, they must walk straight out. Jules said we could stay with her. We turned the corner towards the house, where a cluster of police cars and an ambulance filled the road.

'What's going on?' Chloe strained forward, her voice panicked.

A police officer stood at the roadside.

'Stay in the car. I'll ask what's happened.'

Our front door gaped open, a hive of activity inside.

'It's Dad,' Isabella yelled.

'Daddy,' Chloe screamed.

They launched from the car and hurtled towards the house. Barney raced with them. The officer tried to stop them, but they pelted past. I abandoned the car and ran after them. We came to an abrupt halt inside. Bloodied medical supplies littered the floor and Elliot lay at the foot of the stairs in a puddle of dark blood. In the confusion, everything slowed into a surreal out-of-body experience.

'Daddy!'

Chloe jolted me back to reality, like when they were babies and woke me with their crying. Barney barked at Elliot.

'Get that dog out,' a man shouted.

I reached for Chloe. She clung to me.

A policeman stood on the edge of the devastation with a tear-stained Lydia. She wore my black dress. My hyper-awareness took in her brazen play for sympathy. She looked ready to fly at me.

'Get these people out,' the same male voice shouted.

'Oh my God, he's dead. He's dead. He's dead,' Isabella shrieked.

I reached out to pull her into a huddle with Chloe and me. But Isabella launched herself at Lydia.

'You've done this, you demented bitch. I'll fucking kill you. You went mental at Mum and now you've done this to my dad.'

An officer restrained Isabella before she attacked her target. With his help, I went to hustle the girls out the front, but Chloe had gone. She must have fled already. Then she darted from the kitchen, pure anguish on her face, brandishing a carving knife above her head.

'Chloe, no!' I shouted.

A burly officer lunged at her.

'Don't hurt her.'

My words were drowned out by three different men yelling, 'Drop the knife.'

The officer gripped her in an armlock, restraining her from behind, one hand grabbing her wrist.

'Drop the knife, Chloe,' I said.

She let it clatter to the floor and sobbed as the hulking officer carried her out. She put up no resistance, her feet dangling off the ground because he was so large. What if he arrested her?

'Please,' I said. 'It's their dad. It's a shock.'

The lanky young policeman posted at the door held Barney by the collar. It had only been seconds from when we ran in but felt like an age. Anne watched anxiously over the garden hedge. She reached out to me.

'Emma, bring the girls in. It's quiet in here.'

The police officer ushered us next door, a firm grip on Chloe's arm. She lurched into Anne's cloakroom and threw up in the loo, hands gripping her thighs. I crouched beside her, holding back her hair that had come loose in the confrontation. Isabella stood rigid in the kitchen, tears sliding down her face. Anne made tea and the officer coaxed Isabella to sit down.

'Sit down, sweetheart,' I called through, leaning back on my heels to see her. She sat.

'Is that your house, next door?' the officer asked.

Chloe slumped on the cloakroom floor, ashen-faced and shaky. 'Mum, did you see the…' A sob snatched her words away.

'It's okay, Chloe.'

She leaned against me, both of us on the floor. I positioned myself so I could see Isabella, who nodded in response to the officer.

'But Mum, did you see…' More gasping sobs.

'It's okay, baby. Breathe.'

'But did…?'

'Don't talk. Let's breathe together.'

'Did you see the blood? What did she do?' Her voice rose into a wail. 'What did she do?'

'She fucking killed him.' Isabella's voice rang through from the kitchen. 'The fucking bitch.'

'Isabella, love.'

'Who lives in your house?' the officer kept on in a steady, reasonable tone.

'Me and my sister, and our dad. And his girlfriend. *That bitch.* She did it, didn't she?' Her voice rose high. 'She's fucking mental. She went deranged at Mum yesterday.'

'Is he dead?' Chloe asked in a small voice. She listed to one side on the floor. I held her.

The officer took a breath, his face grimly resigned. 'I'm sorry to say that your dad has died of his injuries.'

Everything came crashing down.

'It's our fault. It's our fault,' Chloe wailed, her anxiety made real. Her greatest fear was her family dying and it somehow being her fault. 'All that blood. She stabbed him.'

'He wasn't stabbed,' the officer said.

'He wasn't stabbed,' I repeated, to stop her tipping further into the abyss, as if his cause of death changed anything.

'If we hadn't told Dad we didn't want to come back—'

'It's not your fault,' I said. 'Your dad let her move in. Whatever she did was not your fault.'

The day went in a blur of calming the girls and answering police questions. Anne offered comfort in the form of sweet tea, tissues and buttered toast. Chloe sat still, blinking. I tried to remember her coping strategies, but my head was wrecked. It took all my effort to hold it together.

Jules arrived and told the police about Lydia's screeching fit yesterday. She took Isabella's phone and played the video of Lydia's threats in the car park, then sent it to them. My heart raced at seeing it again in light of what she'd done to Elliot. Lydia was a murderer, but I'd no doubt the two of them made an explosive mix, Lydia fanning the flames until his infuriating ways sparked the final detonation.

Jules drove us back to her flat. The girls had withdrawn into silence. A different police officer turned up, even though it was cramped enough with the four of us and Barney. The officer wore a grey trouser suit and had a calm way about her. She talked and I struggled to breathe, as if my ribs and chest weren't strong enough to contain what went on inside me.

The officer coaxed information from the girls. Their answers veered towards slagging off Lydia and crying at the injustice. By evening, Chloe and Isabella were hoarse and shattered. I told the officer they had to rest.

'Mum, don't leave us,' Chloe said.

'Of course I won't leave you.'

That would be impossible. They climbed into the sofa bed that filled the tiny second bedroom. They looked adrift on a life raft. To my surprise they fell fast asleep. I walked Barney along the river and phoned Will to say I couldn't come back. It crushed me and I ended up sobbing out the facts.

'I'm so sorry to let you down.'

'Shush. Don't worry about anything here. Shall I drive straight over? I can help you deal with it.'

'No, I'm fine with Jules.'

'Let your sister look after you.' He sounded as if he really cared. When I went inside, Jules and I shared her double bed. We talked in tired, whispery voices until the early hours.

'You'll have to get your ducks in a row,' she said. 'Lydia will be spouting off, blaming Elliot.'

'It's awful. We set her up.'

'She set herself up. We didn't know she'd kill him. You need to get your story straight before the police ask difficult questions.'

Part Three

After the Murder

Chapter Thirty-Three

Lydia

Anyone could see that Elliot had fallen to his death, the way his body lay awkwardly at the bottom of the stairs. It was a tragic accident, but no one gave me an ounce of sympathy.

The twins came steaming in with the idiot dog to mess up the crime scene. The lairy one screeched that I'd killed her dad. I might've killed her too if it weren't for the copper by my side.

Your dad wasn't so perfect. I didn't say it aloud because I was in shock. True to form, the stabby one tried to knife me. They dragged her out. Those two belong on a sink estate with electronic tags as fashion statements.

'We need you to come to the police station and tell us what happened,' an officer said.

In the police interview room, I expected a cup of tea since I was bereaved, but the officer got straight down to business. 'We'll have to take the clothes you're wearing for forensics.'

'Is that usual?'

'A man has died of what appears to be serious head injuries. We need to investigate for the sake of his family.'

I clutched my heart. 'I am his family. I'm his partner.'

'Then you'll want to help us.'

A female officer gave me some awful police-issue grey tracksuit and plimsolls.

'I want my clothes. Can someone get me a change of clothes from home?'

'No.'

She didn't care, not when she wore navy polyester for a living. But it mattered to me.

'When can I have my things?'

'It's a crime scene,' she said. 'No one's allowed entry until the murder squad have finished.'

'Murder? He fell downstairs.'

She looked away. They took fingernail scrapings and swabs from my hands. Then they left me alone in an interview room with a plastic cup of bitter coffee from a vending machine. It hit home that I'd played this wrong. I should have faked a burglary and pretended to walk in on the crime scene.

A man and woman in business suits came to question me, a detective sergeant and detective constable.

'I've already told your colleague everything, back at the house.'

'And now you can tell us. Let's go over what happened.'

I talked them through the whole awful scenario to the point where he fell. 'It was self-defence,' I said, my voice wobbling. 'I pushed him away and he fell backwards down the stairs.'

'His injuries are terrible,' the woman said. 'He didn't get them from falling downstairs. We're looking at multiple impacts from a violent attack.'

'But he fell.'

She stared hard at me. 'What I'm saying is this: you argued with him and pushed him downstairs in anger. Then you inflicted further head injuries, as indicated by blood spatter at the foot of the stairs and repeated focused trauma to the back of his skull.'

'I *didn't*. Why are you treating me like this? I need help for *my* trauma. I want to go home.'

'Let's take a break,' the man said. 'Give you a breather. Shall we get you another coffee?'

The woman escorted me to the ladies'. I caught sight of myself in the mirror. Jesus, I looked a fright, like Alice Cooper with mascara streaked down my cheeks. Tap water and cheap toilet paper only removed some of it. I came out and asked the female detective if she had any eye make-up remover.

'It's a police station, not Superdrug.'

I gave her a scathing look. 'I'm leaving now.'

'We'd like you to see a doctor.'

That was more like it. The police had it in for me, but a doctor could verify I'd acted in self-defence. They left me in a different room with another cup of terrible coffee. After a long wait, a woman in her fifties turned up and looked me over. I said my face was tender where he'd slapped me.

'And here.' I showed her a bruise forming on my arm.

'It's barely visible.' She peered at it. 'Anything else?'

'I've got a headache and feel dizzy from him knocking me around.'

'Did he hurt you anywhere else?' She checked my eyes, pulse and blood pressure, then took a stethoscope to my heart.

'The emotional abuse was worse than anything.'

She didn't respond.

'Can you treat me for PTSD?'

Silence. Professionals tended to harden themselves and not get involved. Her face was pale with puffy dark bags under her eyes. If necessary, I would use her tiredness as a factor for missing the signs. She prescribed paracetamol and said to drink lots of water. Pathetic. She could at least have given me some decent drugs.

They left me in the nasty box of a room. By the time the two detectives returned, I'd had enough.

'I'm going home. Can someone give me a lift?'

'You can't go back there. It's a crime scene.' She was totally up herself, drunk on power.

'Can you find me a place in a women's refuge, since I'm an abuse victim?'

'A refuge? You won't be needing that tonight.'

'Come with us, please.' The man led me out.

They marched me out the back to a grim reception, set apart from the public area. Then I realised it led to the police cells.

'What is this?' I asked.

'The custody suite.'

Not the kind of suite I aspired to. The officers flanked me at a heavy-duty desk where a bald man stood behind a glass screen at a computer. The woman arrested me on suspicion of murder. I couldn't speak. She asked if I had any reply to the charge. I shook my head.

'No reply,' she said to the man behind the desk.

Two men in suits stood and watched, grim-faced, hands in pockets. They looked as if they'd turned out to see me charged. Didn't they need evidence before jumping to conclusions? Otherwise it was wrongful arrest, surely. I bet I could sue, and push for a compensation payout.

The man at the desk asked personal questions and tapped my responses into the computer. Then they took my photo. I bet I looked like a criminal in the mugshot, mascara smudges darkening my eyes. They said I was spending the night in a police cell.

'If you don't have a solicitor, one will be appointed.'

A decent solicitor would sort it out. 'I need top-notch representation. My partner's estate can pay for it.'

'If you can't afford a solicitor, one will be appointed for you.'

All I'd ever wanted was a better life and someone to love me. Now look what had happened. It was Emma's fault. The cell door clanked shut. I stared in disgust at the worn blue plastic mattress, the air heavy with a stench of disinfectant and microwaved ready meals. Emma would pay for this, along with her nasty kids. They would wish they'd never met me.

Emma

The night of Elliot's death, Jules and I lay awake talking in her bed.

'You have to shake off the guilt complex,' she whispered. 'It's not your fault he died.'

'It is.'

'Be clear about the state of your marriage and why you left.'

'I can't tell the police what he was really like. The girls can't deal with that on top of his murder.'

'If you stick to the facts, you needn't lie.'

'The fact that we banked on Elliot having a fling with her? So I could use it as justification to leave once the twins went?' Jules's plan had seemed hare-brained. I hadn't expected Lydia to take the reins and race ahead.

'Tell them you and Elliot drifted apart. Lydia convinced Elliot you were having an affair, and you left because you didn't want the kids caught up in the drama. You went away for some space. Then Elliot asked you to come back.'

I sighed at the enormity of it all.

'Say as little as possible and they'll put it down to shock. Write it down, from the day you met Lydia. Don't show anyone. It's just to work through your side of the story.'

'What if anyone finds it?'

'Say it helped you process what happened. Tell them you'd had enough. He was selfish enough to test anyone's patience. Enough to end your marriage, especially when you'd have nothing in common once the kids left home. You told Lydia you fantasised about having a little place of your own—'

'I can't tell the police that.'

'Why not? She will. And what married woman with teenagers doesn't sometimes dream of that? Don't say he was controlling, or Lydia will use it in her defence.'

In the morning, I woke to a gathering storm of trouble. I crept from the bedroom and checked on the two sleeping heads poking out from the sofa-bed duvet. If they played up when they were younger, I hid it from him, but it only took a stern word and one of his looks for them to toe the line. I was the buffer, not that he terrorised us, exactly. It was more covert. But I could be covert too.

I faced Jules's books crammed on the shelves. Her book club choices were for me. *Fingersmith* about the woman trapped in a patriarchal world, *Life After Life* about the woman living her life until she took the bravest action. They all came with a message from Jules. The message was *leave him*.

I would read for escapism, and for ways to navigate my life. Books made me bolder. Jane Eyre taught me how to leave. Vianne in *Chocolat* taught me to start afresh somewhere new. I rehearsed my escape through them.

Urged on by Jules, I'd been putting cash away, 'in case one day you have to walk out with only what you're wearing'.

I pulsed with fear when she said that.

'You can stay with me. You'll have money from the divorce. And there's your degree and business studies diploma. You'll find work,' Jules said. 'And that'll lead to something else.'

She made it sound easy, as if the biggest problem was in my head, but there was the very real problem of my husband. *If you leave, I'll break you.* Fear kept me in that marriage. Fear that my children would suffer. Fear of him not letting go. I nearly hyperventilated when he turned up in Dorset. I knew he would make me pay. Thanks to Lydia, he didn't get the chance.

Chapter Thirty-Four

Lydia

George, my rumpled solicitor, looked more at his notepad than at me. I wanted to shake him, grab him by the lapels and yell, *This is my life, you stupid fuckwit*. After a night in a cell, I wasted no time in telling him about the shoddy police treatment.

'When this living nightmare is over, I'll be pushing for damages. It's definitely wrongful arrest.'

'We'll worry about that later.' He sniffed and rubbed his nose distractedly, this person employed to be on my side.

'I'm led by my emotions. I'm a strong woman. That's not a crime.'

'Killing someone is.'

'Elliot was a six-foot athlete. He could easily overpower me. I'm the victim. What can you do to rein this in?'

'Rein it in?' He plucked a tissue from a packet and blew his nose.

'Make it go away.'

'I can't make a murder charge go away. The best option at this stage is a lesser charge of manslaughter.'

The same dour double act returned. They'd wedged me in a tight corner of the interview room, the table pushed against the wall. George squashed beside me with his laptop and writing pad. I would catch his germs cooped up in this scuffed room with no windows and no escape.

'Can you tell us about Vernon?' the woman asked.

Vern.

'He was my husband. He died.' My voice choked up. 'It's still traumatic for me.'

'How did he die?' she asked, without sympathy. Considering they worked with the public, they lacked people skills.

'Accidental death. He was a heavy drinker, an alcoholic actually. You can read the coroner's report.'

'We have.'

They both stared at me. *Come on, focus. You can do this.*

'That's quite a coincidence, isn't it?' hatchet-woman said. 'Two men you're in a relationship with both die.'

'I tried to help him. Do you know what it's like living with an alcoholic?'

They looked at me, poker-faced. 'You were the last person to see both Vernon and Elliot alive. How do you explain that?'

'What are you suggesting? What happened to Elliot was completely different. If you're suggesting—'

George interrupted to ask for some time alone with his client. They took us to another room without CCTV and I protested my innocence. He closed his eyes and raised a hand to shut me up. Charming.

'Tell me about Vernon, how he died.'

'It was a tragic accident.' I stuck with that as if my life depended on it, which it did. 'He drank himself to death.' They were treating me like some kind of serial killer with a penchant for murdering men. So insulting. It was only two deaths, which was pure bad luck on my part.

'The police are likely to reopen the case.' He wiped his nose. 'The situation's worse than it appeared. You need to say, "no comment" to every further question.'

'George, I'll do as you say, but you have to help me. They're making a massive mistake. I'm an abused woman who's under attack from the police.'

His shoulders sagged even more. We returned to the interview room and the officer kept on asking questions.

'Were you angry when Elliot told you to leave the house?'

'No comment.'

'A witness stated that they heard you shouting abuse at Elliot at around noon yesterday, but they could hardly hear his voice at all.'

'No comment.'

'His injuries came from a violent attack. What do you say to that?'

'No comment.'

'Why do you keep saying no comment? Is it because you don't want us to know the truth?'

'No comment.'

'It's not helping you, Lydia.'

I had to defend myself. Why shouldn't I tell my side of the story? They'd robbed me of my opinion, stripped back, no voice, no make-up or decent clothes.

'I thought you wanted to help us with our inquiries, Lydia, since Elliot was your partner.'

'I did want to help, until you blamed me for everything.'

'No comment,' George muttered to me.

I bit on the inside of my cheek. This was what happened when you put your trust in others. Everyone needed someone, but I had no one. It all came down to money, or lack of it. I'd been abandoned to the biased and unfair legal system in my vulnerable state. How could they use Vern against me? It caused a little stab to my heart. Vern would never have wanted me treated like this.

Emma

Jules shuffled from the bedroom, raking her fingers through her hair. 'I'll phone work. Say I won't be in.'

'No, we'll manage,' I said. 'Go and get ready.'

She squinted at me in the bright morning sunlight. 'You're not dealing with this alone.'

'I'm not alone.' I nodded towards the sleeping girls, who looked like children. Barney yawned and stretched, gearing up for a walk.

'Callie's coming back,' she said.

'Who?'

'Callie. She was here yesterday. The family liaison officer.'

After Jules left for her shift, Callie turned up. It was a strange job, babysitting the bereaved, but she gave Isabella and Chloe informed answers. They nibbled at toast and asked questions. *What's happening at home? Have they locked up the bitch? You won't let her out? The bitch.*

'Isabella,' I said, 'don't call her that.' She usually objected to misogynistic insults but was making an exception for Lydia.

'Arsehole then.'

Chloe kept on about her dad dying on the cold, hard tiles. 'Someone should've put a pillow under his head.'

Elliot chose those white tiles. I'd wanted a wooden floor.

‘Your dad was almost certainly unconscious. He passed away quickly,’ Callie said. ‘There was nothing anyone could do.’

I liked her no-nonsense way, but what if I put my foot in it? And what if they found out we sent Elliot the threatening letter? I was sick with guilt. Did it push him to the edge in the midst of Lydia turning unhinged?

Jules came back early, saying the shop was quiet. The flat felt hot and airless, even with the balcony doors propped open. The twins sat on fold-up chairs at the tiny bistro table on the narrow balcony. Just when I thought we couldn’t squeeze anyone else in, Anne arrived with flowers.

‘I live next door to them in Esher,’ she told Callie. Anne sat beside me, shaking her head in incomprehension. ‘He was a wonderful man. It should never have happened. I told the police he adored you all. The girls are so polite, which came from you and Elliot.’

Callie nodded.

‘He was so charming. I told them about that time he stepped in when the man doing my roof turned nasty. Do you remember, Emma? He demanded five thousand more than I’d agreed.’

Jules looked towards me from the kitchenette and pulled a goofy face. Callie was busy taking in every word.

‘He wrote that legal letter for me. I don’t know what I’d have done otherwise. He came over after he’d finished work to reassure me. I was scared the roofing man would come back, but Elliot said, “Send him to me if he does.” Such a considerate man. Never raised his voice. Not once.’ She placed her hand over mine. ‘He was taken too soon, my love.’

I bit my lip. So hot in here, I was burning up. I ignored the urge to go on the balcony and gulp air. The buzzer went and Jules let in another visitor. Marianne. I stiffened. What if she said the wrong thing in front of Callie? Helping me leave a controlling husband was one thing, but now he was dead, it became fraught with danger.

'My poor darlings.' She hugged me, her big personality filling the small space. 'What can I do?'

I was in deep trouble if Marianne or Crawford let anything slip. He might tell the police that I schemed against his golf buddy. Marianne talked of the sisterhood, but it wouldn't stretch to them lying to the police. I hoped she would keep quiet until I'd worked out what to do.

Anne stood up to leave. 'I'll see you at the funeral.'

I thanked her for coming and then introduced Marianne to Callie. 'The police liaison officer,' I said, pointedly, emphasising the word 'police'.

'What's the latest on the investigation?' Marianne asked Callie, who deflected her with talk of 'ongoing inquiries' and 'keeping the family informed of progress'.

'Didn't take long for the real Lydia to show up,' Marianne said. 'I hope you're charging her with homicide. Because if she didn't kill him, I'm the empress of China.'

'We're doing everything we can to ensure justice for Elliot and his family.'

'I started out thinking her worst crime was opportunism, but she's your basic bitch nightmare. She waltzes into this beautiful family, trouble written all over her, creating a trail of destruction.'

Callie silently filed her words away in her mind.

'She's a fantasist and a liar. The company she claims to work for doesn't even exist. Faulkner and Associates. Check it out.'

I could do without Marianne whipping up Isabella into another hate-fuelled frenzy.

'Girls, can you take Barney out?'

They went without a murmur, giving us breathing space.

'You need to know Lydia is a conniving piece of work,' Marianne said once they'd left. 'She moved in on Elliot the moment Emma went to stay with her sick mom. I bet she was blowing him before Emma arrived at her mom's.' She squeezed my hand. 'It needs saying.'

I stared at my feet.

'Elliot should never have gotten involved with that *femme fatale*. Real nice guy but led by his penis.'

'Have you made a statement to the police?' Callie asked.

'You bet I have. I'm telling you there was zero love between those two. I went over and saw the two of them together the other night. Their fling had already run its course. He was looking to manoeuvre her out the door.'

Once Marianne figured out Jules's 'read between the lines', it became her pet project to help me escape.

'Can you get away safely?' she'd asked. 'Lydia might be the decoy, but you can't take risks with a controlling man. Jules says you'll need a place to stay.'

'Somewhere cheap and away from here,' I'd said.

'You're having our holiday cottage in Dorset, rent-free. Crawford uses it for golf trips. If he wants to stay at short notice, I'll find you somewhere else, but he avoids it when it's wet.'

'I don't know how I'll repay you.'

'No repayment necessary. I know the trouble caused by women like her. She thinks the rest of us are idiots. Did you catch her dig about *The Stepford Wives*?'

'I caught all her digs. And the smirking,' I said.

'God, the smirk. That superior look, like she's won some victory. And Crawford says Elliot's a jerk. They went on that golf trip to Portugal and he talked about shafting the wives of his clients. When I told him about Elliot's fling with Lydia, he said he won't play golf with him again. He'd wanted an excuse to back off, anyway.'

I fled to Rosings, Marianne's holiday cottage, named after a house in *Pride and Prejudice*. Given my freedom, I held on to it, thanks to the book club schemers, who all played a part.

I used Lydia to escape Elliot. He used her while he planned what to do. I didn't expect them to make it beyond the first flush. Her brisk resolve and bright eyes didn't mask the psychotic quality ready to burst forth if she didn't get her way. Sparks would fly, since Elliot would never feed Lydia's attention-seeking ways. I had expected it to career off the rails, but I thought she'd leave in a dramatic huff, not smash his head in.

Chapter Thirty-Five

Lydia

The police charged me with manslaughter. I was too shocked to speak. George told me not to speak anyway. He said he could build a self-defence case to reduce the sentence. He said it in between coughing fits as if I should be pleased. I hated his low aspirations, wanting to make a bad situation slightly less bad. Sod that. I wanted to get off. Soon as they released me from this hellhole I would put things right. In the grubby interview room, George said I would appear in court and then they'd release me.

'They'll let me go?'

'They'll release you while inquiries continue,' he said. 'And they'll decide if there's a strong enough case to bring it to court.'

'Can I go home?'

'Not to the house where you lived with the deceased. You'll be told to stay away from the family.'

'But that's my home.'

'Do you have family or friends you can stay with?'

'I'll be homeless if I can't go back there.'

'Contact the local council and say you're homeless.'

I should have been playing the grieving widow, not Emma. The only funeral I cared about was the one for my lost opportunities. If only Elliot had put his trust in me instead of ruining it for us both.

I should have come of age in simpler times when a well-brought-up girl married a man who supported her. Men like Elliot took advantage of vulnerable women like me. That would form part of my defence. I told Useless George, who just sniffed. No way was I going to prison. No fucking way. Not without bringing that bitch down with me.

Emma

I called Will, braced for the reality of leaving Dorset behind.

'How are you getting on?' he asked.

'I'll stay here until the twins finish A Levels next June.'

'I'd like it if you come back for visits.'

'I'd like that too.' It gave me a thread of hope. We chatted about the site renovation. It was a relief to talk about something other than the awfulness here.

'What happens after your girls leave school?'

'They want a gap year, not that we can think that far ahead. Elliot would never have let them go. He kept them reliant on him, so now they can explore the world. I'll still help with your planning, even if I'm not there to see it take shape.'

'I'd like that,' he said, and I felt the warmth in his words.

The police had finished at the crime scene. None of us wanted to go back. We could find somewhere smaller, but the house might not be ours to sell. Elliot might have cut me out of his will and tied the house up in a trust for the twins, or some other control freakery. Jules went over and loaded up her car with the girls' things, stuffing her small flat to the rafters.

'Mum,' Chloe asked, 'what'll we do for money?'

'Don't worry. I'm looking into it,' I lied.

What if he hadn't left them provided for? I went outside and phoned Charles, the senior partner at Elliot's law practice. The police contacted him, and he'd left me a message of condolence, calling it 'an awful business'. He might throw some light on the money situation. Late in the day, I set off to Sunningdale, to meet with Elliot's boss who was giving me a copy of the will. Then I would get my life in order – or not, depending on who the police believed and whether Elliot cut me out of his will. The wind ruffled my hair through the open window, and I tried to remember what normal felt like.

I pulled up in front of Charles's imposing Tudor manor. He was lucky Lydia never came here, or he might be the one lying in a funeral home. He guided me into his study. It was comfortingly fusty, with ancient leather-bound books and dark furniture.

'Would you like some tea, or something stronger?' he asked.

'No, thank you. I can't leave the twins too long.' Now I was here, the need to know whether we had money to live on was overpowering.

'We're all shocked. He was so calm, and excellent with clients. Never once lost his temper. One time, a man pinned him against the reception wall. I expect he told you. Elliot's client was divorcing his wife, who'd taken up with this aggrieved man. Elliot handled it remarkably well. He spoke calmly to the man and referred him to the estranged wife's solicitor. I told all this to the police, of course, to illustrate his outstanding character.'

I nodded. Elliot kept his emotions in check. He occupied the moral high ground, superior to everyone. *A man might pin me to a wall, but I stay unruffled. You might cry, but I rise above it.*

'I know money won't be uppermost in your mind,' Charles said. 'But I believe Elliot had life insurance to cover your entire mortgage, which I'm sure you already know. We will buy back his partnership. And there's his company pension. It's all detailed in here, along with a copy of the will, which he kept with us.'

He handed me a fat envelope.

'Is it the last version of the will? With his recent life changes, I need to know if he provided for the girls.'

'This is the only one that's been registered.'

I stood to leave. 'Thank you. You've been so kind.'

He saw me out. 'I daresay there'll be a trial for manslaughter.'

I didn't want to think about a trial and whatever spin Lydia would put on it.

'We will verify Elliot's character if called upon.'

'I appreciate everything.'

I drove off and pulled up further along the road to read the will. Half of Elliot's estate would pass to me and half to the twins. Relief washed through me. He'd made a will when I became pregnant, to ensure everything came to me and the children. It was an act of defiance against his estranged family. He'd cut off contact with them before we met and didn't invite them to our wedding. My mum asked the guests to spread out over both sides of the church, so it didn't look uneven.

You were either completely in with Elliot or nothing to him. I would see the switch when someone crossed him, and he acted as if they'd never existed. He did it to friends over the years, often over a perceived slight. His family were dead to him, but we soon had our family of four. I married for love, but when it became about control, my feelings for Elliot died.

'I have a responsible, demanding career,' he said one time when the twins were young. 'I can change the path of a client's life by achieving the best outcome for them. I need a clear head. I can't be distracted by stinking kids and insignificant crap around the house. That's your job.'

Much as I loved Barney, I hated Elliot's chiding remarks about dog hairs and muddy paws from the dog he'd never consulted me on. I'd had enough of his shoes kicked off inside the door where anyone could trip over them. I'd never wanted the expanse of shiny white floor tiles to clean. Clearly Lydia felt the same. That floor was his downfall.

Chapter Thirty-Six

Lydia

They released me on bail, not that I'd anywhere to go. I went for my emergency appointment at the council offices, so they could find me a hostel place. The dough-faced woman tapped at her computer keyboard.

'Places are limited,' she said. 'They're under extreme pressure. Do you have any friends or family you can stay with?'

'No. What about a women's refuge?'

'You don't qualify.' She gave me a piercing stare.

'Why ever not?'

'The person you're seeking refuge from is dead.'

'Can I contact the refuges direct? If they hear my story—'

'Refuge details are confidential.'

You'd think they were the bloody Secret Service.

'The emergency shelters are full tonight.'

I waited for her to suggest another option. She looked at me in silence.

'Can you put me in a B&B?'

'It doesn't work like that. We don't have the funds for bed and breakfast accommodation.'

'Are you seriously expecting a woman on her own to sleep rough on the streets?'

She checked her notes. 'I see you're a car owner. If you can't stay with a friend, your safest option is to sleep in your car.'

'It's about to be repossessed.'

'Come back tomorrow and we'll check again. Here's some helpful numbers.' She handed me a wonkily photocopied A4 list and reached forward to underline a number with her biro. 'This is a local homeless charity.'

'Will they find me somewhere?'

'No, but they do sleeping bags.' She gave a listless promise of a phone call if a hostel place opened up for tonight.

I went for a coffee, charged my phone and called Marianne. She didn't answer so I left a message, then called a domestic abuse charity to explain my predicament. They promised to call back.

I was going stir-crazy in the quiet of waiting for the phone to ring, so I drove to Marianne's. A gossip like her would be gagging for the inside track, and she could put me up in one of her several guest bedrooms.

I rang her doorbell and arranged a humble yet warm expression on my face. I saw her through the frosted glass of the front door, bustling towards me. She peered through, slid the security chain on and opened the door a crack.

'*Marianne*,' I said warmly, 'how are you?'

She arched her judgemental eyebrows. 'I'm pissed with you. Those kids are devastated about their dad.'

'I'm so sorry for the girls. It was self-defence—'

'Like hell it was.'

'He threatened me on the stairs. I was terrified. That's when I pushed him away.'

'Bullshit.'

'It's true. Can I come in?'

'Crawford says you're not welcome.'

'I thought with your charity work you might help me.'

'What are your options?' She tilted her head.

If I kept her talking I could draw her back in. 'A domestic violence charity has offered to support me. They think the police overstepped the line. You won't believe how heavy-handed—'

'You'll have a tough time convincing a jury that Elliot was violent. There's no history of violence. Selfishness, yes, but it comes with the territory. He just wasn't the meal ticket you took him for.'

'Marianne, please. You're my friend.'

'Forget it, Lydia. We're not friends, but I know who you can call.'

'Who?'

'The police. Admit you killed him. Spare his daughters a trial.'

'But if you knew what really happened—'

She shut the door in my face.

'Thanks for nothing,' I shouted through the door. 'Rude bitch. Must be nice to have zero self-awareness.'

She stood firm in the hall. I could see her behind the glass.

'Showing your true colours now,' I kept on. 'I thought you'd have more intelligence than to take the side of Emma and her bitch daughters. You'll all be sorry when I've finished. I'm in this till the end, *bitches*. Elliot pretended to like you so he could handle your divorce. You only married for money. Crawford would leave you for me in a fucking heartbeat, but I have too much integrity.

I stomped back to my car. It was all Jules's fault for luring me in with talk of stunning homes and shaky marriages. With no one looking out for me, my one lifeline was to go full-out victim to the domestic abuse charity. These people were destroying my life. It was killing me. I could've had it all if it weren't for fucking Emma and her selfish wank stain of a husband. Fuck those book bitches. I'd make them sorry.

Emma

Callie asked to see me in private, so I sent the girls out with cash for Frappuccinos. I reminded myself she was a police officer and to watch what I said, since she was the sort of kindred spirit who might belong to a book club like ours.

'How are Isabella and Chloe?' she asked.

'Chloe's having nightmares. She blames herself that Elliot made Lydia leave.'

She was writing poetry, which she didn't let me read. Isabella said it was for the best. 'It's really dark, Mum,' she told me.

'Isabella vents a lot.' I didn't fancy Lydia's chances if she met her in a dark alley. 'The new term will distract them. What do you want to talk about?'

She sat slightly forward, hands clasped in her lap. 'It's about the spending spreadsheets for your family accounts.'

My heart dived.

'Did Elliot make you account for your spending?'

I shook my head because he didn't make me, technically. I went along with it. 'I didn't want us living beyond our means. When you have a sporty husband and teenagers with expensive tastes, the money soon goes.'

'It does,' she agreed. 'Not many of the items on the spreadsheet were for you.'

'If you've seen the house, you'll know we lived a pared-back life. I'm not bothered about designer clothes.' I smiled and looked down at my flowered top that was several years old.

Callie smiled too. She didn't look as if she coveted designer labels either.

'I love reading,' I said. 'Bookshops have their own force field. I can't resist them. I do buy books for myself.'

'You're a couple of bookworms.' She glanced at Jules's heaving bookshelves.

'If I'm not reading, I like to cook or walk the dog.'

'What about Elliot? Did he cook?'

'God, no. He was useless. The kitchen's my domain. It's the hub of the house.'

'I'm the same.' She paused and looked gravely at me. 'If Elliot kept money back from you, it might be financial abuse.'

'I've never heard of financial abuse.' I stared at Jules's copy of *The Women* on the coffee table, ready for Rosa's book club night. I hadn't read it, but God knows, I needed a book to help me escape this.

'It's a type of domestic abuse. Say if someone keeps their partner controlled by making them account for their spending or by keeping money from them.'

Financial abuse. So many terms for things we never had in the past. Like Chloe's anxiety, which I had as a child, but people just called me a worrier.

'Domestic abuse isn't just physical violence. It's about control. Sometimes women are conditioned to not recognise it's happening.'

I nodded slowly. When my marriage turned bad, I blanked out the worst, disconnected from my husband. I carefully managed my life to avoid his anger. It took Jules to drag me out of the marriage. Then I sought out the one job I felt equipped to do. No way was I admitting that to Callie.

'Everyone says you kept the house spotless.'

'The house had this simplicity when we moved in. We didn't want to fill it with stuff. It was easier to clean.'

Isabella already told her I liked cleaning. I couldn't admit the truth. I couldn't have it made official, so I'd be questioned in court. Lydia smashed Elliot's skull open, and nothing I said would change that. If she admitted manslaughter, we might not have a trial.

Most people wouldn't believe Elliot was controlling, including me since I didn't admit it for the longest time, even to myself. Elliot and his shrunken heart deadened my ability to feel things. Although I felt things enough to resent cleaning the white floor tiles.

Jules thought he had me where he wanted, disempowered. I escaped into novels, otherwise I'd have been as angry as Jules, as violent as Lydia became. She and Elliot both needed external trappings of success. He couldn't just do well in life, he had to prove it with a Ferrari and a nice house. He further proved his worth by running – never jogging, I made that mistake once – and scaling hills on his racing bike.

I changed tack with Callie. 'What if Lydia comes after us?'

'Call nine-nine-nine if she comes near any of you. She's been told to stay away. She has her freedom to lose.'

'She's not rational.'

Callie hadn't seen Lydia in full flow, including her violent mood the night before she killed him. I put up with him all those years and she turned murderous within weeks. If she was capable of that, what could she do to us?

'We expect her defence will come in strongly on Elliot being abusive. Your evidence is important.'

'I wasn't there.'

'You'll be asked what sort of husband he was, and whether he was controlling or abusive. There's something else you need to be aware of,' she said gravely.

I steadied myself for bad news.

'We have evidence that Elliot had at least one other affair before Lydia.'

I inhaled sharply, fixing my gaze on a pile of novels.

'I'm sorry to bring it up, Emma, but it's best that you're prepared. It might be used in court to show he wasn't a stable family man.'

'Can we stop now?' I bit my lip.

'The thing is, Emma, your story doesn't hold up.'

I stared at her, stricken.

'What devoted mum would move out and leave her daughters with a woman like Lydia who was having an affair with her husband?'

We locked eyes.

'You said yourself that Elliot wasn't much of a caregiver. He couldn't even cook. Why would a mum like you who's dedicated seventeen years to her family suddenly leave them because her unfaithful husband says so?'

'Because I thought it best.' My voice wobbled and I willed myself not to fall apart. 'For the girls' sake, so they wouldn't be exposed to an awful atmosphere. It was upsetting to go.' I looked down at my fidgeting hands, not trusting myself to elaborate.

She stood up. 'We'll talk again when the Crown Prosecution Service decides on criminal charges.' She hadn't mentioned the video. They took Elliot's devices to search for a motive, so they would have found Lucy's email that linked to the video. Did they suspect I was behind it?

Callie left. No one knew the truth of someone else's marriage. Now that Lydia had put mine under the spotlight, I needed to protect my daughters. If I spoke up, there would be another round of salacious headlines to upset Isabella and Chloe. I never exposed the darker side of Elliot to them, and if they didn't know, I couldn't say it in court.

Chapter Thirty-Seven

Lydia

The police summoned me back. A uniformed officer walked me to an interview room with George, still coughing. The dour double act strode in and pulled up chairs.

'If you break the terms of your bail,' the woman said, 'you'll be remanded in custody until your trial.'

'What's this about?'

'You've made a threat towards Emma Morland's family.'

I pulled myself up straight. 'What threat?'

'You went to the home of Marianne Jennings and made a threat about Mrs Morland and her children. Mrs Jennings could be called as a witness in your trial. You can't have any further contact with her.'

'How can she be a witness?'

'She's helping with our inquiries. You can't threaten her.'

'That's a lie. I didn't threaten anyone. Marianne has it in for me.'

'Her Ring doorbell recorded audio and visual of you saying these words.' She plucked a typed sheet from her folder and read in her flat voice. 'Thanks for nothing. Rude bitch. Must be nice to have zero self-awareness. Showing your true colours now. I thought you'd have more intelligence than to take the side of Emma and her bitch daughters. You'll all be sorry when I've finished.' She paused and looked at me for effect. 'I'm in this till the end. Bitches.'

Marianne set me up, the poisonous viper. 'You can't accuse me of threatening a witness when I didn't know she'd be one.'

'What do you mean by "I'm in this till the end"?'

'I meant they'll be sorry when they're exposed as liars who set me up.'

'There's a good chance you'll be locked up for this.'

'You can't lock me up. I'm the victim. I swear I won't go near any of them again. You have my word.' I placed my hand over my heart.

'Have you seen this before?' She slid a photocopy of the threatening letter that Elliot received across the table towards me.

I shrugged.

'For the recording, can you reply with a yes or a no?'

'Someone sent it to Elliot before he died.'

'Why was it found in the house with your belongings?'

'He was stressed about it so I put it out of the way.'

'Did you send it to him?'

'No! It came in the post. It's someone with an axe to grind. George…' I looked sharply at him to make sure he was keeping up. 'You need that as evidence. It shows I'm not the only woman he had a problem with.' I turned my attention back to the female officer. 'Can you find out who sent it?'

'You say Elliot read the letter?'

'Of course. It was sent to him.'

'His fingerprints aren't on it. The only fingerprints are yours, Lydia.'

Fuck.

'Why are yours the only fingerprints on the letter?'

'Because you want to stitch me up?'

'No comment,' George muttered. 'I need some time alone with my client.'

They let me go in the end, ordering me to stay away from everyone who knew Elliot, or they'd lock me up. I'd make them sorry. I channelled my anger and closed my eyes to picture a night-time ambush. In my mind's eye, I crept up on the evil spawn twin, stood over her sleeping form, held the knife above her with both hands and plunged it in her heart. She woke, our eyes locked and she realised her mistake in crossing me.

Served her right, the way she came at me – twice – with a fucking knife. She could wave a blade about, but I had the balls to plunge it in. In my imagination, I pulled the knife out, dripping with her blood. I did it again and again. Stab, stab, stab.

I really could kill her in cold blood. It would ease the hate consuming me. They'd pushed me to it. My body thrummed with adrenaline, my fist clenched around the imaginary murder weapon. I wanted revenge on her, on the lot of them.

Or I could sue the bitch for her knife threats. She was bound to inherit from her vile father, so they could pay me off or I'd have my day in court. I wanted £250,000 for my suffering. Emma would pay up to avoid me going public. I had witnesses, since all those police officers saw that psycho twin lunge at me with a carving knife.

Chloe should be hauled into court. I'd instructed George to update me on the criminal case against her. If they said she was traumatised, I'd say 'me too'. Such double standards. You could go to prison for knife crime, so either they prosecuted us both or neither. If not, I would make her pay. The psycho. I would follow her home from college, hunt her down.

Emma

I scrolled through online tributes.

> He was a kind and respectful man. We're so shocked. You're a lovely family.

Charles from his law firm was quoted in the press.

> Elliot was committed to fairness. He didn't deserve this. It's a tragedy for his family, and our thoughts are with his wife and daughters.

I drove the girls to view a rental house near their college, since none of us wanted to go home.

'Dad loved us, didn't he?' Chloe asked. 'He died because he wanted rid of Lydia, so we could come home. He wanted you back too. He was miserable without you.'

'He did, Mum. He wanted you, not her. We said that to the police.'

'We showed them his text. The one that said he wanted us home, how we used to be.'

That text sent chills through me. Had I returned, he'd have made me pay.

'We have to speak out for Dad,' Isabella said. 'People need to know what she was like. And that Dad wanted you back.'

They each kept one of Elliot's sweatshirts, several sizes too big, which they wore now. He would have liked that, having a hold on them still. Lydia had done them a favour. There was no such thing as unconditional love in Elliot's world. If he'd hated their boyfriends or they'd started coming home drunk in the early hours, there would've been hell to pay. I kept reminding myself to relax my hypervigilance. I didn't need it now he was gone.

We drove into the cul-de-sac, where one of the semis had a *To Let* board outside. It was boxy and dated but had three bedrooms and a scrubby garden for Barney. 'That's it over there. If you hate it, we'll find somewhere else.'

'It could be worse,' Chloe said. 'We could be displaced people from Ukraine or Gaza.'

'Or we could be evil like *that person* who'll burn in hell.'

Since I'd stopped Isabella calling Lydia an arsehole, she was 'that person'.

'She's got a shitload of karma coming her way. What are the police doing with her?'

'They've charged her with manslaughter,' I said. 'Callie told us.'

'Will she come to the funeral?'

'Yeah, Mum,' Chloe said. 'What if she turns up?'

'I'll smash her face in,' Isabella said.

'No, you won't. She won't come to the funeral.' At least I hoped not.

'We can walk to sixth form,' Isabella said, as the letting agent pulled up.

'If we like it, we can move in before the funeral.' Paying the rent in advance would speed things up. It was part-furnished, so we could leave most of the furniture in the house until it was sold. The girls didn't mind that it was shabby. None of it mattered, just that we were together.

'Mum, it's only ours for six months so you don't have to clean it loads.'

'Okay.'

At least I'd booked professional cleaners for the family house to clear up Elliot's blood and brain matter. After years of avoiding the truth, I could face it now, but I wouldn't expose the girls to the fact that their dad controlled me. Elliot's violent row with Lydia brought home how much danger I was in. All those years of staying closed off to avoid his wrath. Books took me somewhere else. They kept me safe in my head. Book club gave me the support of friends. When the time came to leave, my literary heroines emboldened me and helped me escape.

Now Lydia's crimes had caught up with her, she would be desperate. I didn't like what I saw in her face when she confronted us before Elliot's death. The pure hate, the unhinged glint in her eyes. She wouldn't harm the girls. She'd have to get past me first.

Chapter Thirty-Eight

Lydia

The sun beat down on the police station car park. George and I talked in his stifling car that reeked of hot plastic.

'Why am I blamed for everything?' I said. 'That threatening letter sent to Elliot came from a bunch of feminist killjoys. Those book club bitches are behind it.'

'Why did they only find your fingerprints on it?'

'They set me up. And then the Ring doorbell recording. Surely that's not legal,' I said about Marianne's antics. 'You can't record someone without their consent.'

'It may or may not be admissible in court, but you can't go making threats.'

'What are you going to do?' I demanded. 'Because this is victimisation.'

'It's a warning for you to stay away from everyone connected with the Morland family or they'll lock you up on remand until the trial.'

'And my warning for you is to fix this mess,' I snapped, getting out and slamming the door. I marched to my car and sped off with no idea where to go. I pulled up along the road, because the tank of petrol needed to last. I called the domestic abuse charity to update them on the latest injustice. They could fight on my behalf. After a short wait, a woman came on the line.

‘We’ve reviewed your case,’ she said. ‘I’m afraid we aren’t the best agency to help.’

‘I’m alone. I need your help.’

‘We have limited resources. We focus on giving a careful spread of support.’

‘Please. Whatever support you can give me—’

‘I’m sorry we can’t help.’

‘Wow. Thanks for nothing.’ I cut off the call.

I buried my face in a sweater on the passenger seat and screamed. A man cycling past wobbled in surprise and paused with one foot on the ground. He peered back at me through the windscreen. I gave him the finger and he cycled off.

Had Marianne used her contacts to stitch me up? I told her I’d spoken to a domestic abuse charity, so I bet she put the boot in. So much for the sisterhood. I wished I’d walked away from the evil prick. If I’d brushed past him on the stairs, head held high, I wouldn’t have been criminalised now.

I would have liked to post an inspiring daily update to online fans with a GoFundMe campaign for donations. A crowdfunder would help fight the miscarriage of justice. But I’d stayed offline since Vern’s death to stop his family trolling me. They never liked me. This would give them ammo to go back to the police. I’d landed in a nightmare of epic proportions. No way was I going to prison. No fucking way.

I went to a Polish shop and bought the cheapest vodka they had. I sat in the park and took small sips straight from the bottle. Christ, it was rough, but I needed to escape for a bit, and I didn’t have enough petrol to go anywhere.

The voddy worked its magic. It loosened up my brain which had been floored by the brick wall of challenges.

Now it eased into creative problem-solving mode. Emma had set me up, I was sure of it. She had a motive. She all but coerced me into murdering Elliot. My whole body buzzed with adrenaline.

I needed a strong enough case for the police to believe. The evidence was sketchy at best but I'd wing it. Emma could afford a decent defence lawyer and, if she got off, the manslaughter case against me would fall apart too. My vision blurred a little as I fumbled with my phone. I called the police station to share my crucial piece of intel: Emma had offered me £250k to kill Elliot.

An hour later, I was back in the police interview room giving them a heads-up. Served Emma right. It was her turn for police scrutiny. Not letting on that I was still half cut, I told the annoying female officer about Emma's proposition.

She cocked her head. 'That's a big accusation. You didn't mention it when we spent two days questioning you.'

'My solicitor advised me to say "no comment".'

'You told us what happened when we first brought you here. You know if you change your story, it doesn't look good in court?'

'I'm not changing it.'

'You never said the deceased's wife asked you to kill him.'

'I was traumatised.'

They regarded me with scepticism, her and the mute sidekick. I was sure they'd had training to make you dig a hole for yourself. So unfair. As the questioning intensified, I became more sober by the minute.

'I've post-traumatic stress. I'll refer you to the Police Complaints… whatever.'

'You don't have the power to refer us to the Police Complaints Commission.'

Smug cow.

'Lydia, if what you say is true, we're looking at charges of murder and conspiracy to murder, which are more serious than manslaughter.'

'What? How can it be more serious?' That couldn't be right if Emma started it and led me on.

'Because it shows intent.'

Fuck. How was I supposed to know? It was George's fault for being so useless I had to fire him. 'Look, I didn't kill him. I take it all back. It was an accident. I'm at the end of my tether, with the trauma of Elliot's death. I haven't slept and I can't think straight. That's why I was muddled. Please can you let me go?'

I slumped with my head in my hands. It wasn't my fault, not when I was desperate. That lot had driven me to it. 'You're penalising a marginalised person. If I had money for a decent lawyer, I'd have known that.'

'Wasting police time is also a criminal offence.'

The male officer intervened. 'I'll remind you that you can stop the interview at any time and request a legal representative.'

Emma

My copy of *The Women* sat on the table ready for book club tonight. We were supposed to read a courtroom drama, but the others made a tactful switch. The girls came home to our new rental house and asked if there was any news about the trial.

'Not yet,' I said.

They couldn't get over the violence of his death, and a conviction would give them closure. Elliot would curl his lip at *closure* and say he hated Americanisms. Never mind that he had his own wanky jargon, like saying, 'I don't have the bandwidth for this,' to avoid me troubling him with domestic issues.

But they were worth protecting with a lie. The same lie that saw me through my marriage. The lie of our charmed life that everyone believed, even Lydia at first. Even I believed it some of the time. But how far should I go to preserve the lie?

'If she gets off, she'll sell her story. What if the judge gives her our house?'

'They don't have the power to do that.'

Isabella was doing media studies and complained about liberties taken by the media. 'But if she gets away with it, and the house is sold, what if she asks the new owners for a photo shoot in *our house*? They might let her be photographed on the stairs.'

This wasn't beyond the bounds of possibility. I could picture Lydia playing the wronged woman to the hilt. I wished the house would burn down like Thornfield Manor or Manderley. 'It's unlikely to happen, so let's not worry about it.' I needed to keep them stable and stop Chloe spiralling into negative thoughts. 'I'm going to book club, so is it okay if we talk about this later?'

They didn't mind me going out, so Marianne picked me up on the way to Rosa's. I was uneasy, since Lydia derailed our last two book club nights. But they'd all insisted. Marianne hadn't stopped talking since I got in the car and then she asked whether I would give evidence in court.

'If you don't testify, Lydia could win on self-defence,' she said. 'If she gets off, she'll play dirty.'

'I can't lie under oath.' I clasped our latest book in both hands.

'You can bet your life she will. Remember your truth now is that you had a solid marriage and Elliot was a reliable provider. Everyone gets that. And when in doubt, put your kids first. Period.'

'What if I don't testify?'

'She might get off. If you testify, the jury will compare you to that crazed maniac and they'll believe you. You know the police interviewed me after the murder?'

'Yes.'

'I said he was a charming man and a wonderful father to those poor girls. Which is *true*.' She looked beadily at me. 'And how your marriage seemed fine until *she* came along. Which it did.'

I gazed out of the window.

'A court case is about winning,' she kept on. 'The legal teams manipulate the facts in their favour. If it goes in her favour, she'll make your life hell.'

'What about doing the right thing?'

'What about doing this for the right reason? AKA your kids.'

I needed a drink. At least the alcohol flowed at book club and I would have a lift home.

'It's too late to change your story from saying you had a solid marriage. You won't be a credible witness. Her defence team will crucify you. And the girls will see it all. Telling the unvarnished truth is a no-win situation.'

When we arrived at Rosa's and the others turned up, Marianne filled everyone's glasses and held hers high to toast me.

'To our dear friend, returned.'

They joined the toast and I reddened.

'This evening is dedicated to Emma and to fortify her in achieving justice,' Marianne said.

They all agreed.

'On that note, ladies, my book choice was by the indomitable Ms Agatha Christie. One of her shorter works, *The Witness for the Prosecution*. But you outnumbered me.'

We indulged her. She loaned me her cottage when I needed it most, which led me to the possibility of a new life. The wisdom of books and friends can help you through tough times. I readied myself to do battle with Lydia and took a big gulp of Chenin Blanc.

That's when the police steamed in and arrested me for conspiracy to murder. I never saw that coming. How far would she go to destroy me? I was prepared to guard my secret that I'd set Lydia up. But I couldn't expect the other four to lie for me.

When the police questioned me, I was consumed with fear. What if they charged me and kept me in a police cell? The funeral was on Friday. I had to be there for the girls. If I was charged, it would be all over the news and they'd be forced to cope without me. I had to tell my version of the truth, even though it brought on palpitations.

Chapter Thirty-Nine

Lydia

I curled awkwardly on the back seat of my car. I couldn't return it to the finance company when it was my independence, my place to sleep. Not that I could sleep. It beat another night in a police cell, which showed how low I'd been forced to go. The police had eventually released me from the shitshow. With any luck, they'd arrested Emma.

The traffic noise kept me awake, so I drove to the woodland car park near the village green where I'd seduced Elliot. It was secluded enough to shield me from traffic and street lights. Sleep still evaded me, so I crept off in the dark to see if they were home, in the house that should have been mine.

Emma's car wasn't on the drive, but if she had any sense she'd have changed the locks. Was she still in a police cell? I pulled up my jacket hood and sneaked round the back like a criminal. My pulse quickened at the thought of her and the brats catching me in the act. She hadn't even left a light on, as if she didn't care about burglary. Such a waste.

In the darkness, I slid the utility room key from my jeans pocket. I used to bring the dog in that way after wet walks. The door opened. Heart in mouth, I crept in, scared of a barking frenzy. Silence reigned. The dog basket was gone.

The full moon saved me from turning on my phone torch, since I didn't want the nosy bat next door rumbling me. My eyes became used to the dark. Satisfied I had the place to myself, I popped the ring pull on an ice-cold Diet Coke from the fridge and checked the house by moonlight. Emma had cleaned up the mess from Elliot's fall.

I filled the washing machine with dirty clothes, mixed a slug of decent vodka with my Coke, put my phone on charge and took a shower. I risked using my torch here and there to rifle through the twins' clothes and shoes, pulling on a grey hoodie with *Namaste* in big letters on the front. Screw mindfulness, I wasn't in the mood.

As dawn broke, I sifted through the kids' rooms and found £85 that they'd been saving. I also found some unused book tokens. I couldn't name any retail gift card less useful than book tokens. No sign of Elliot's wallet. The police must have passed it on to Emma, worst luck. When exhaustion crept up, the bed in the master suite called to me, but I'd better not risk it. It was still early when I sneaked back to my car and fell asleep.

Bright sunlight woke me along with a fucking bird choir in the trees. I drank the black coffee that I'd poured into a flask earlier and remembered that the police claimed someone had heard me through the open windows shouting threats at Elliot. His calm and reasoned tones had barely been audible. I hated people twisting the facts. He might have sounded calm, but his words had been incendiary. I bloody knew that old bag next door would be trouble. It took all my self-control not to go and wring her scrawny neck.

The police released me the day before the funeral. I came home and the girls clung to me like they were little again.

'I told the police everything,' I said. Not quite everything, I wasn't stupid enough to say we'd set Lydia up. I told them enough to paint the picture of a tired marriage. A wife hanging on for the sake of her kids. A husband sapping her spirit.

Callie's 'good cop' approach hadn't worked. They knew I'd been holding back. I doubt anyone believed Lydia's ridiculous accusation against me, but it gave them grounds to arrest me and pile on the pressure.

Before my arrest, Isabella had confronted me. 'There's a load of stuff you're not telling us. You and Aunt Jules do your secret squirrel club with Marianne. We heard you talking about bad things Dad did at work. Plus Callie's been asking us what he was like.'

I didn't know how to respond after protecting them from the truth about Elliot for so long.

'You know Dad said I had a legal brain?' Isabella kept on. 'This is me using it, but not as a divorce lawyer. I want to work in human rights. Me and Chloe are all about social justice, yeah? I know he was our dad, but if he treated people badly, they need closure.'

Elliot would curl his lip at 'closure'.

'If Dad was mean to you,' Chloe said, her soulful eyes wide, 'I get why you left us.'

'I didn't leave you. He didn't like me having a life. I'd have waited until you'd left home, but Lydia came along. It's hard for you to understand.'

'I think I get it,' she said. 'You always tried to make him happy.'

'I'm sorry.'

'Mum, you've said sorry a hundred times already,' Isabella said.

'Like, literally.'

This was true. 'I am sorry though.'

'We know, Mum,' Isabella said. 'It sucks badly, but we don't blame you.'

'I just want you to be okay.'

'We know,' they both chimed in together.

We talked for ages, then the police closed in. Under questioning, I denied offering Lydia money to kill Elliot. Then they questioned me on the video and showed me the threatening letter sent to Elliot. I seized up.

'The blackmailer tells him to give you the house in the divorce settlement. Did you send the letter?'

My heart rate spiked. 'No.'

'What do you know about a woman threatening him?'

'What woman?'

'He believed the ex-wife of a client was threatening him. She blamed him for the way her estranged husband treated her during their divorce. Elliot thought she'd used a private investigator to dig up dirt, then she had the video professionally produced.'

'What client?' I couldn't let another woman take the blame.

'We can't disclose that. Did he tell you she'd been threatening him?'

I stifled a smile at Elliot suspecting a disgruntled wife, unaware it was *his* disgruntled wife. He didn't even suspect Jules, assuming she lacked the means to orchestrate a hate campaign. He underestimated the women from book club. I'd heard him through the spy app, on the phone to his PI about a super-rich divorcee who had it in for him. But it was a fishing expedition by the police. They couldn't pin the blame on anyone else without evidence.

God knows how it'd pan out, but I had to focus on the funeral. The day of the service dawned bright and sunny, which seemed wrong. My appalled mum arrived at our rental house, and we were careful not to mention my arrest.

'Those poor children losing their father,' she said. 'Why did it have to happen? It's in the papers, and then there'll be the trial. It'll hang over our heads. Why should the girls suffer when it's not their fault? How will the three of you manage?'

At the crematorium, we waited in polite huddles in the manicured garden. Chloe chewed on her thumbnail, and Isabella kept up a defiant pout to stop herself from crying. The urge to pull them close overwhelmed me when I saw their pinched faces. My eyes scanned the gardens for Lydia.

A lone man pointed a long-lens camera at us from the nearby shrubbery. The girls knew to keep a dignified silence, or the media wouldn't leave us alone. They'd presented it as a cautionary tale of a family man lured to the wild side. Mourners were taking the tabloid line that the *femme fatale* snared him during his short midlife crisis. I didn't care what people thought, so long as the twins made it through.

Charles from the law practice stooped before me and took my hand in both of his. 'Let him not be defined by his ending.'

I nodded, but Elliot got what he deserved.

'I'm sorry for your loss,' people said as we stood in the shade of the building. They treated me as the grieving widow and skirted around the fact of him kicking me out and moving Lydia in.

'The twins have been hit hardest.' I couldn't say anything insincere.

In the chapel, the girls and I were flanked by my uncomprehending mum and Jules, who comprehended everything. The vicar said kind words, and I harboured inappropriate thoughts about my husband. I used to fantasise about him dying in a freak accident on one of his trips, never expecting another woman to finish him off. The messy conflict of emotions swirled around me: fury towards Elliot, relief that he was gone and the pain of it devastating the girls. And I was scared of what Lydia would do next.

At the wake, people were delicate and slightly awkward around me. It must be hard paying your respects to the grieving widow when Elliot's new conquest delivered the fatal blow. Then we returned to the rented house with my mum.

'Chloe's just like you at that age,' Mum said when the twins had gone upstairs.

'And Isabella's like Elliot,' I said.

'No. Isabella's like Jules.'

I found it comforting, after years of Elliot insisting Isabella took after him with her strident ways. It surprised me that no one tempted Elliot away sooner, an attractive man who kept his flaws under wraps. And he was charming, so people said. They said it with more emphasis since his death. *Such a charming man. Taken too soon.* People still clung to this view of him, despite what happened with Lydia. His deception went deep.

Chapter Forty

Lydia

Why should I live in a car when the house I had worked so hard for had Wi-Fi, booze and electricity? I kept an eye on the house, but figured they'd moved out, so I bought provisions to last a few days and sneaked back in at midnight. I slept in Isabella's room, since hers was the messiest and no one would notice if I roughed it up a bit more. I'd hide in the wardrobe if Emma turned up. What if the bastard dog sniffed me out? I should've poisoned it when I had the chance.

I'd spent the cash I swiped from the twins. They owed me. In daylight, I went over the whole house and found an additional £44, which would do until my benefits came through. I made beans on toast and wrote copious notes in my defence to help my legal team. No one understood what it was like to be me, caught in this situation. I would rid myself of Useless George and land a shit-hot barrister. My defence team must build a case around Elliot as a controlling abuser. Emma was central to my defence. I'd sussed the bitch out. She left without a backward glance to escape him.

We needed an expert witness to say that abused spouses cover up, collude and minimise. I couldn't wait to see mousey Emma crack under cross-examination. The haters would line up to discredit me, but I was coming out on top.

I stayed undercover in the house, steering clear of the windows. It was less risky than coming and going. I furiously researched cases of self-defence against domestic abusers, punctuated by moments of sheer panic. When footsteps crunched over gravel outside, I froze or hid, then when the letter box rattled with unwanted post, I stopped holding my breath.

Mid-afternoon, I went downstairs for a drink. I'd finished the gin and vodka, leaving the dark spirits, which drew out my anger. I poured an expensive brandy and added a splash of Fanta, smiling at Elliot turning in his grave. 'Burn in hell, you fucker,' I said by way of a toast.

I killed Elliot, which was justified, but I hated the police bringing Vern into it. Vern adored me and I never harmed him. He did it all on his own. We'd met on an all-inclusive holiday in Jamaica. His idea of heaven was a free bar. We drank rum punch on the beach and got stoned. I was twenty-seven to his thirty-seven and he looked even older.

I went into debt for that holiday, but I moved in with him after we came home. We talked about getting enough money together to move to Jamaica. Our dream. But that's all he was, a dreamer and a drunk. I didn't kill Vern. Yes, I thought about it. Who wouldn't? But the silly sod drank himself to death.

I sank back in Elliot's leather armchair in the living room, wanting more than squatter's rights. My idiot lawyer wouldn't be drawn on what stake in the house I could claim. I topped up my brandy, sipped it and winced. This one tasted stronger. Vern's alcohol tolerance had drastically lowered from his liver damage. He'd been warned about the risk of overdosing on booze. I called him a cheap date. The night it happened, I'd fallen asleep and woken up to his cold body beside me.

His family tried to say I'd suffocated him. But a doctor called it an alcohol-related sudden death. His parents called me a deadly influence and said I'd forced alcohol on him. As if he needed encouragement. All I did was bring a little joy to his short life. We always had a laugh together.

Footsteps on the gravel shook me alert. I slammed the laptop shut and froze in the semi-darkness, ready for the doorbell to ring or the letter box to flap open. A key turned in the lock. *Fuck.* I hid behind the armchair, clasping the laptop to my hammering heart.

The front door opened. My heart pumped like crazy. The armchair was angled in the corner, beside the window. I was vulnerable crouching there if they came near the window. Beads of sweat formed on my skin. Someone picked up the post scattered on the mat.

Was it a cleaner? They'd vacuum around the window and discover me. The rubber clacking of flip-flops on the tiled floor went from room to room. They came in the living room. I shrank back. They flung open the curtains and I caught sight of a slender leg, a floaty sundress. *Emma.* I held my breath.

She tutted and picked up my brandy glass. Maybe she thought Elliot had left it. Did she suspect? She went back into the hall. I breathed again. She resumed her brisk march around the house, opening windows. Her footsteps were overhead. Had I left anything in the bedroom? The bathroom?

Now was my chance to escape. But she might see me from an upstairs window. Worse, I'd left my keys in my bag upstairs. *God. Think, Lydia, think.* My only option was to dive into the cupboard under the stairs. I stole through to the hall. The gravel crunched a second time. I froze. The doorbell rang and Emma came to the top of the stairs.

Emma

Lydia's claim that I'd conspired to kill Elliot didn't stick. Like the twins, the police knew I was hiding something because I'd been nervy and evasive. My arrest provided an excuse to search my devices, but they found nothing. None of my messages to the rest of book club had incriminated me. We hadn't put anything in writing and Lucy was the one who had sent the encrypted email to Elliot, assuring me it couldn't be traced. My solicitor confirmed there was no case to answer.

At our old house, I went around flinging open curtains and windows. The cleaners missed Elliot's brandy glass beside his chair. Still some dregs in it as if he'd return to finish it. I shuddered and held it between finger and thumb as I marched it to the dishwasher. The place gave off bad vibes, as if a presence lingered here.

I was opening windows upstairs when the doorbell rang. He was early. I pattered downstairs in my flip-flops, focused on answering the door as a way of pushing through what happened on the stairs.

'Mrs Morland?' The large, dapper man on the doorstep shook my hand, a glossy information pack tucked under his arm. 'Roger Hillgrove. Pleased to meet you.' He wiped his feet profusely on the mat, and I welcomed him in.

'Call me Emma.'

'*Emma*. Thank you. Oh, this is very nice. Gosh, it's immaculate.' He looked in appreciation around the entrance hall.

'Thank you.'

I alerted his colleague on the phone to my reason for selling the house. We both ignored the elephant at the foot of the stairs, but it trumpeted round my mind instead.

'Shall I show you around?' *This is where my husband was killed. His bloodied corpse lay right there. His deranged lover smashed his head in.*

'Wonderful.' He beamed.

I guided him around downstairs, and then left him to look upstairs. It had been a hideous few days since the shock of my arrest and the funeral, but I was determined to get rid of the house so we could move on.

I was making coffee when he came down and asked to look in the garden. Then he returned through the back door with more lavish feet wiping. He marvelled at the 'beautifully presented' house and garden, then took a keen interest in Elliot's flash coffee machine. I was tempted to give it to him, but expensive touches could help sell a house and that was why we were here.

We took our coffees to the living room, so he could admire the view of the village green. We sat at opposite ends of the Chesterfield couch. The smell of brandy lingered in the air. He probably thought I was a daytime drinker.

'I must say, Mrs Morland, *Emma*, this is a marvellous house, and I would love to sell it on your behalf.'

'Thank you.'

'Depending on the level of interest, you may have to drop the price because of the, er, *incident*.' His voice lowered and took on a grave tone. 'We do have to disclose these things now. We will of course be discreet. Taking everything into account, we would invite offers in the region of three million pounds.'

Chapter Forty-One

Lydia

Three million pounds?

As if it wasn't bad enough, hiding in my own home. When he rang the bell, I raced back behind the armchair before Emma came down. I already felt punchy and now my fury built, hearing that smarmy git talk about the immaculate house. It was immaculate because I had bloody cleaned it. I wanted to confront them, but I clenched my fists hard instead.

He skirted around saying that Elliot's death devalued the house. She deserved to take a hit on the price. Even so, *three mil.* The estate agent could piss off and take his ingratiating patter with him. Then I'd have it out with her because she wasn't getting three mil at my expense.

She showed him out. I burned with rage. As soon as she closed the windows, I would confront her, so that witch next door couldn't listen in. Emma wouldn't know what had hit her. She came back into the living room and snapped the window shut.

'Oh.' She looked down at me in horror.

I shrank back. Too late. She stood there, stunned. Then she turned to flee. I scrabbled up, giving chase, my legs stiff from crouching. She slipped on her flip-flop, bashed into the coffee table and tripped. She lurched forward, stumbling out of the room. *You're not getting away. You're not.*

Emma

The estate agent shook my hand on the doorstep, then I started shutting up the house. I snapped the living room window shut. The hairs on the back of my neck prickled. The tang of Elliot's brandy hung in the air. I was aware of something feral that was breathing, watching. I spun around and caught a movement behind Elliot's armchair.

It was Lydia. I froze. She lunged, knocking me off balance. I stumbled against the furniture, then ran. She launched onto me, grabbing my arm, spitting venom. I tried to break free, tried to make it to the hall. If I could just reach the front door… Her nails dug into my skin. She hauled me back into the living room with devastating force, kicking the door shut. Blood pumped in my ears. Was this how it was for Elliot?

I sucked in an overdue breath, went to scream. Too late. She punched me in the face and I reeled backwards to the floor. I landed badly. A crack in my shoulder sent pain searing down my arm. She was on top of me. Her hands latched on to my throat, squeezing out the air, her face demonic. She pinned down my wrists with her knees. I struggled. *Oh God, oh God, oh God.*

I should've screamed when I had the chance, but I caught my breath and ran instead. Pain flared in my shoulder as I tried wrenching my arms free. Anne was next door. She waved from her window. She'd be looking out. *Anne. Ring the bell. Peer through the window.*

'Bitches… your evil bitch twins… it's your fault… you did this.' Eyes blazing, she snarled abuse.

I couldn't fight her off. Her grip was tight around my throat, her face blazing red. *Have to get her off me... can't breathe... I must... I can't... close eyes...*

'Die, bitch.'

Jolted back to consciousness, for a bizarre moment, it seemed Chloe was on top of me. But it was Lydia wearing her *Namaste* top. Dark spots blotched my vision. *Do something, quick.* I freed my good arm, but she shifted her knee to dig in my ribs. I wrestled my good arm away and blindly felt for the edge of the bookcase. It was too heavy to topple. Pain radiated from my shoulder. The intense pressure on my neck was excruciating. Her nails dug in, squeezing the breath from me.

My fingertips found something hard and cold – my pewter bookend from Jules, shaped as a pile of books, heavy as a dumb-bell. I was used to those. *Grab it. Finish this.* I heard my twin's thoughts with my own. I mustered my strength, grabbed it firm, swung my arm and smashed it on her head. She fell sideways and cracked her head on the hard corner of the granite fireplace. The bookend dropped from my grip, crashing to the floor. My heart rattled in my chest. Lydia lay motionless, blood trickling from a head wound.

Epilogue

Emma

That blow to Lydia's head ricocheted through me whenever I thought of her, then I was queasy and broken all over again. She left behind pages of notes for her lawyer – rambling justifications, mangled half-truths and vitriol about me and the 'evil spawn twins'. While my shoulder healed and the bruises faded, I read her scattergun accusations.

The girls sprinkled half of Elliot's ashes in the garden, which I later encouraged Barney to pee on. The rest went to Box Hill. We didn't know Elliot's favourite spot because he never invited us along, so we found a view from a hill. In the afternoon sunlight, there was a freshness in the air and the trees mellowed into autumnal shades. I expected the pink-faced twins to solemnly scatter his ashes on the ground, but they took palmfuls from the urn and held their hands high to let the breeze carry it away. The plumes of ash swirled from their fingertips, their arms wide, making something beautiful from their sadness.

When I asked where they wanted to go for lunch, I expected them to choose his favourite stuffy restaurant where we always went for his birthday and mine, but they said Nando's, which he hated.

'Great choice,' I said.

They're booked on a camping weekend tomorrow for young people who've lost a parent through murder.

After waving them off on their trip, I loaded Barney in the car and drove towards Dorset. To a future I never thought possible. As Dorset approached, a calm descended. When I pulled up at Will's cottage, he was there with a wide smile, and happiness washed over me. He lifted me off the ground and hugged me tight, then made a fuss of Barney, who cavorted around us.

It was like coming home. The sea air and the surf relaxed me. He'd found new cleaners, not that I needed to clean, but I was determined to work. He said there was a place for me, coordinating the site upgrade, which he'd put on hold while he finished the cottage. He showed me his progress, his enthusiasm spilling over. He'd nearly finished the extension, the reclaimed stones and roof tiles blending in with the original cottage.

'It spurred me on, you coming to stay.'

'You've done a brilliant job.'

'Does that mean you like it?'

'I love it.'

We stood side by side, and he hugged me with one arm. My body loosened and I felt normal. Better than normal. I felt like myself for the first time in ages.

'How are your daughters?' he asked.

'They seem younger since it all happened. Vulnerable.'

'What will they do after their gap year?'

'They both want to study in London. We'll buy a flat with money from the house sale.' Chloe's panic attacks might worsen away from home, or the gap year might be exactly what she needed.

'They'll be fine,' he said. 'Give it time.'

We walked a thrilled Barney along the beach, and then came back to grill fish and warm ourselves beside the firepit. The September nights were drawing in, but Will gave me one of his chunky sweaters to keep me warm. If I visited Dorset for short breaks, the girls could spread their wings. I'd wrapped my life around theirs and they would always be mine, but it was nearly time to wave them off into the world. I would spend more time here once they'd finished their exams, since nothing else made sense. Revamping the caravan park didn't feel like work. It felt like freedom. My heart pulled me back, to windswept walks and possibilities that I couldn't yet speculate on.

Even if I ended up living here, I would keep going to book club and I'd see the twins when they were at uni in London. Jules said I could stay with her. I'd buy a bigger place in our joint names that we could share. She always said she needed more room for her books.

Jules saved me. She told me I saved myself. 'I just nudged you in the right direction,' she said. She gave me good books to shake me from my bad marriage. Small parcels of love when I needed them most. Those books rescued me, as did book club. I found my escape one story at a time.

Will showed me the bookcase he'd built into his home extension. He said I might like to keep some books here. I brushed my palm over the nearest shelf and saw words carved into it. 'Oh, it's a quote.' I peered closely.

'Do you recognise it?'

'It's Jane Eyre.'

> I am no bird; and no net ensnares me; I am a
> free human being with an independent will.

While he made tea, I pinged a photo of the quote to Jules.

Moments later, she messaged me.

> I hope he's left space for the next instalment…

I tapped out a reply.

> Which is?

> Reader, I married him.

She ended it with a bunch of cry-laughing emojis.

Lydia

Dubai! I'm actually here in my new life as a blond bombshell. I love the energy of Dubai. It shines brightly, night and day, like yours truly. I'm magnetised to success and I can be my authentic self here, where people celebrate the pursuit of money. This is my spiritual home.

I sell real estate, commission only, so I've made fuck all. But Emma's cash injection is helping me project a monied image. My big break will come any day now when I sell my first luxe apartment. Meanwhile, I mix with the social elite who've already made it, including my latest target.

I arrive at Selina's penthouse, oozing confidence. The others are gathered on a plush corner sofa. Three couples, plus me. Selena's the only one I've met before, my new bestie. I size them all up in the flesh, having done my online homework.

Selina is the one. She provides for her girlfriend, who gave up her career to move here. Men are overrated and now I've come out, I'm Selina's type. First time for everything! It was a coup to slide into her inner circle, this powerhouse influencer, sponsored by a top Dubai aesthetics clinic. I'm pretty sure she's had everything done: Botox, fillers, the lot. Once we're a power couple, the clinic can extend its contract to me. I only need a few 'tweakments' to be an inspiration to others who aspire to radiate gorgeousness like me.

Her apartment's like something from an interiors magazine. It's the done thing for expats to employ housekeepers, thank Christ. Won't make that mistake again. A woman of my status shouldn't have to clean. Selina's a wonderful host. I maintain eye contact and give her my most dazzling smile, drawing her in with my infectious personality.

I should have come here after Vern died, started afresh. But it worked out in the end, thanks to £250,000 from Emma. I nearly sent my bank statement to Surrey Police with a note saying, *See! See! You useless bastards. I'm not a fantasist after all.* But she made me sign a gagging order. Okay, Emma, have it your own way. Pretend I ruined your life, but you and I know the truth.

We both know that she knocked me out. Attempted murder, actually. When I came round, she offered me the money in return for leaving her and the evil twins alone. She bought me off for trying to kill me with a fucking metal bookend. But it was also a thank you. *Thank you, Lydia, for killing my brute of a husband.* Genius of me to plant the seed of her giving me the money.

Unlike me, the idiot cops encouraged her to change her story, and people called her brave. Two-tier policing. She admitted covering up Elliot's abuse. In turn, they accepted that I'd acted in self-defence in the heat of the moment, despite using undue force. But I didn't know my own strength. Now I'm starting afresh as a free woman. By the time we're seated for dinner at the big glass table, I pick up a few hostile vibes. Women can be so jealous.

Emma

When Lydia lay unconscious on my floor, I needed a few moments to recover from her attack. Then I checked her pulse. Still alive. Her head wound wasn't pouring blood, so I delayed calling 999. I bound and gagged her with packaging tape and Barney's old extending lead.

She came round and launched into a furious struggle, thrashing and trying to yell through the masking tape over her mouth.

'I have a proposition for you,' I said, poised to hit her with the pewter bookend if she worked free of her restraints.

She switched from animalistic anger to interest.

'Cause more trouble and I'll call the police. They'll lock you up this time, so I suggest you listen.'

She nodded, eyes wide.

'Jules and Marianne are on their way, so don't try anything.' That was a lie. She hadn't been out long enough for me to call for backup. 'I'm prepared to buy your silence if you go now and stay away from us. I'll pay you that quarter of a million you've been banging on about to the police.'

She blinked at me.

'I told them Elliot was a shit husband, and they know another woman was threatening him, so they might swallow your claim of self-defence. I don't, but that's a different story.' I ripped the tape from her mouth. 'Deal?'

She gasped. 'Deal. Scout's honour. Up the sisterhood. Whatever.'

I untied her. 'I'll have my lawyer call you.'

Why did I pay her off? To get rid of her. And to spite my husband beyond the grave, Elliot the profligate spender who cut my budget if I didn't complete his spreadsheet. Afterlife Elliot would also hate my big donation to the domestic abuse charity that Marianne recommended. He didn't pay during his lifetime, so he can pay now. But mostly, the payout was to shut Lydia down. With a decent roof over her head, she can direct her talents at real work instead of stealing husbands. If she chooses to be an eternal Becky Sharp, targeting rich people, the other women will see through her.

Book club this Thursday, girls? It's Emma's pick. Kate Atkinson's Normal Rules Don't Apply', isn't it, Em? Remember to read between the lines. Jules x

A Letter from Carrie

Dear reader,

Are you Team Emma or Team Lydia? Emma has a terrible time, but Lydia's so wildly determined, you might be tempted to root for her. Whoever you prefer, thank you for reading this novel. I'm so glad you did.

Writers are often given the advice to write what they know, but I believe in writing what you love. Stories have always been a big part of my life, so it was an absolute joy to write this book as a love letter to some of my favourite novels. Beyond the devious goings on, I was in my element writing about a book club and the power of friendship.

If you enjoyed *The Woman from Book Club*, please leave an online review. If you're a book lover, you're in my tribe. If you know a book lover, show them you care with a novel about a murderous woman from book club! And for the Lydias out there, you underestimate us at your peril!

Carrie x

Acknowledgements

I'm wildly lucky that Camilla Bolton at Darley Anderson loved the pitch for this book from the first time we met, and she kept her faith in it ever since. She's been a driving force, along with the fabulous Jade Kavanagh, who worked her editorial magic and threw herself into finding it a home with Hera.

Also at Darley Anderson, thank you to Sarah Brooks, Ilaria Albani and Francesca Edwards. Thanks also to Katy Loftus for helping propel it to the next level.

My brilliant editor at Hera is Jennie Ayres, a creative genius with eagle eyes and a tactful way of keeping the story on track. She egged me on to make Lydia even more mad, plus she has a dog called Barney, so we're obviously kindred spirits.

Thank you to Head Design for coming up with such a fun cover. And thanks to the Hera team of Keshini Naidoo, Kate Shepherd, Hannah Cowie, Dan O'Brien, Rebecca McInerney and Kim Yudelowitz. Thank you to Ross Dickinson for the copyedit and Vicki Vrint for proofreading.

Thank you to Chris Moore for being an early reader and reality checker. And to Becky Edwards and Claudia Cavanagh, who never tire of asking if I have any book news.

Thanks also to David Blunden for that time we were meant to be playing tennis when I mentioned the gist of this novel, and we stood beside the court bouncing ideas around instead. You're an epic plotter.

Thanks, as ever, to my family for putting up with me.

Lastly, thank you to my very own book club friends. None of the characters are based on you! Special mention to Emma Hughes, who didn't mind me having an Emma in my fictional book club by the time we'd met.